SILK *and* STEEL

Also by Stephen Alter

Non-fiction

Wild Himalaya: A Natural History of the Greatest Mountain Range on Earth

Becoming a Mountain: Himalayan Journeys in Search of the Sacred and the Sublime

All the Way to Heaven: An American Boyhood in the Himalayas

Amritsar to Lahore: Crossing the Border Between India and Pakistan

Sacred Waters: A Pilgrimage to the Many Sources of the Ganga

Elephas Maximus: A Portrait of the Indian Elephant

Going For Take: The Making of Omkara and Other Encounters in Bollywood

Fiction

Birdwatching: A Novel

Feral Dreams: Mowgli and His Mothers

In the Jungles of the Night: A Novel About Jim Corbett

The Cloudfarers

The Secret Sanctuary

Aripan and Other Stories

Aranyani

The Phantom Isles

Ghost Letters

The Rataban Betrayal

Guldaar

Renuka

The Godchild

Neglected Lives

SILK *and* STEEL

a novel

STEPHEN ALTER

ALEPH

ALEPH BOOK COMPANY
An independent publishing firm
promoted by ***Rupa Publications India***

First published by Andre Deutsch, 1980
Published by Penguin Books in 1983

Published by Aleph Book Company, 2024
7/16 Ansari Road, Daryaganj
New Delhi 110 002

ISBN: 978-81-19635-04-7

1 3 5 7 9 10 8 6 4 2

Printed in India

For Ameeta

PART ONE

I

The torches were splinters of pine dipped in resin. They burned with a rich orange flame. The darkness seemed to overwhelm their light so that they illuminated the path only a few feet ahead of the men that carried them. Occasionally the flames reflected off the steel lance-heads and metal accoutrements of the soldiers riding behind. There were ten men on horseback. Five rode directly behind the torches. After them followed a palanquin which bobbed carelessly up and down in rhythm with the footsteps of the bearers. The rest of the escort rode at the rear with a few extra horses and pack animals.

Darkness provided anonymity. The miniature procession might have been riding at that moment through any part of the world, through English farmland along neatly laid-out roads, between precise hedges, or over the gently rolling hills of southern France, between manicured vineyards, or perhaps across the steppes of Russia, where the undulating grasslands spread away into vast distances. The tiny band could have been travelling from the castle of one Chinese warlord to another, through mountains whose terrain was as haphazard as spilled ink. The torches betrayed nothing, even when they spurted and crackled. It could have been any year or century in time. Genghis Khan or Sikandar could have been sweeping Asia. The ten soldiers and the palanquin they guarded moved through a void.

In the palanquin Colonel Augustine slept soundly. He had one good eye, which was squinted shut. The other was glass and stayed awake forever. Once in a while the torchlight shone in his blind eye with a ghostly blueness. His jacket was folded under his head as a cushion. His mouth hung open. One of his hands dangled from the edge of the palanquin like a tassel He was dressed with some care but his uniform was dirty. He has been wearing it for the past week and a half. His trousers were a light colour of moleskin and hugged his legs. His shirt was silk and his waistcoat woollen, each a different shade. Though he was curled up in the palanquin, one could tell he stood over six feet: the palanquin bearers were breathing heavily, from the way he slept, deeply and without nightmares, it was easy to tell that he was a casual man. Augustine was the sort of man who took long strides and did not look where he stepped, regardless of whether it was on a pile of manure or the hem of a lady's skirt.

The night was sinister, though, and those that moved through it seemed to be escaping something. A layer of clouds was spread over the sky. The ground was damp and muted their steps. Were they criminals or soldiers? Was Augustine an officer or a bandit? The road was only broad enough for the horsemen to ride two abreast. They rode calmly—no fear of ambush. None of them spoke. Each seemed alone in his own thoughts, as if the darkness obliterated relationships. The soldiers did not even seem to know each other. They shared no emotions, no fear, no hatred, no love. The smells of the forest were rich and stagnant, old moss, decomposing leaves, rotting branches. The odours did not mix with the darkness but oozed through it like oil in water.

Kirpan Singh's camp was on the western bank of the Jumna River, about a mile south of the village of Paonta Sahib. At that place the Bata Naddi, a small tributary, joined the Jumna. Augustine had spent the last week there trying to make an alliance with the Sikhs. But they had sensed his desperation and changed their minds over and over, increasing their demands, showing suspicion, and asking for assurances

Augustine was at their mercy. They had full control of the Punjab and were threatened only from Afghanistan to the north. What need had they for an alliance with Webley's army? Augustine made no secret of the fact that Webley was in a dangerous position. His army was trapped in an old fort at the foot of the Himalayas. He was there only because the Gurkhas had not bothered to chase him out. The Gurkhas tolerated him but they would certainly not leave the mountains to defend him against the British.

'If the Gurkhas refuse to leave the mountains to defend him, why should I cross the Jumna?' asked Kirpan Singh, twirling a long grey strand of his beard.

'Because it is in your interests that the British be defeated,' said Augustine.

'Why? The British are our friends. Ochterlony has drunk lassi with me in this tent. That is more than I have offered you, Colonel.'

Augustine ignored this. 'You are safe now,' he said. 'You have your borders. You have the Jumna just as the Gurkhas have their mountains. Ochterlony may not cross the Jumna for some years. You will smile back and forth across the river. But you aren't safe forever. Wait until he has conquered the Doab. He will cross the Jumna and chase you north. The Gurkhas squat on their mountains like a line of monkeys on a wall. They think that the British will never climb their mountains and knock them down. They also are mistaken.'

'No, Colonel Augustine. You are mistaken. You do not understand the English. They respect legitimate borders, legitimate armies, and legitimate colonels. But, you see, Webley has none of these. He is a bandit. He and his men roam the country looting and murdering. The English want to put an end to terror and chaos. That is what Ochterlony told me after he finished his lassi.'

'But what about Mysore? You must have heard what the

English did in Mysore?' said Augustine.

'Mysore is very far away. I do not trust news from that distance.' Kirpan Singh thrust a finger under his turban and scratched his scalp.

'And what about this last war with the Mahrattas? Wasn't that close enough for you to believe?'

'I do not like the Mahrattas,' said Kirpan Singh. 'Yes, Augustine, those were wars in which forts and borders were taken. I know that the English cannot be trusted, and by God I hope that Ranjit Singh knows it, too.'

'Then help us,' said Augustine.

'But what is the point in aggravating my friend Ochterlony? What will he say if I defend a renegade bandit against his army? More important than that, what will Ranjit Singh say?'

'Webley is not a bandit. He has an army and a fort.'

'But no legitimacy,' said Kirpan Singh.

'And where did you get yours?' asked Augustine angrily.

'We acquired it.'

'And so will we, if you give us the chance,' said Augustine.

'No, I'm afraid not, Colonel. The die is cast. It is too late. Now you must remain bandits instead of kings, and it is our duty as kings to destroy you.'

Augustine stood up abruptly. Kirpan Singh said nothing, brushing his beard down over his neck. Augustine lifted the flap of the tent.

'Colonel,' said the Sikh general suddenly, 'know that I admire you. Know that I would help you if I could. It is painful for me when I realize that you are too late. I wish we still lived in an age when Webley could have been a king, when your army could have swept brilliantly across Hindustan. Know that I would have done anything to help you. But the time is up, Colonel. Such ages must become history.'

Augustine said nothing. He went outside the tent into the hot sunlight. The camp was alive. Kirpan Singh's army was full of energy and activity. Yellow and blue flags rippled in the wind. The tall, erect soldiers in their tightly wound turbans and loose uniforms sauntered by in groups, holding hands or with arms around friends. There was raucous laughter from the tents and drum-beats from all corners of the camp. There were fights and harsh words, gaiety and wild games. Soldiers with their beards flying over their shoulders came galloping through the lines of tents, slashing guy ropes and trampling baskets of produce in the travelling bazaars.

But as Augustine crossed the Jumna that afternoon and looked back at the camp, he felt strangely moved. An emotion of loneliness and fear took hold of him as he thought about what Kirpan Singh had said. It was as if the Sikhs had been defeated. The camp with all its animation and pride seemed to Augustine more like a camp of prisoners. Kirpan Singh had said that such ages must become history. And what begins now, thought Augustine, something other than history?

Augustine hated the English. They had raped and killed his mother! Augustine's father was a Rajput general, a man of wealth and stature in the court at Chittoor. The English killed him in battle and then murdered his wife in her tent.

Charlotte Knowles, called Bibbi Charlotte at Chittoor, had sailed for India to become the wife of a subaltern in the Company's army. Her fiancé was killed before her ship arrived at Calcutta. She landed in Bengal without money or friends. There were a dozen other young officers who would have married her. She was pretty, with bright red hair and skin as smooth and white as ivory. But India excited her, and when the Englishmen promised her a quiet life in Sussex once they had made their fortunes—all they could talk about were the fortunes they would make—she turned them down. After a few months she became the mistress of a Muslim trader. He gave her heavy jewellery that pulled at her earlobes and strangled her neck. The opulence, the greed, the gaudiness dazzled her at first, but she became bored by it after a while.

The merchant dragged her with him when he travelled and they happened to be in Delhi at the same time as Trisuldas Thakur, who was there as an envoy. On hearing about her, he had Charlotte kidnapped from the trader's apartments. Trisuldas's servants carried her to Chittoor, hidden away inside a palanquin, a smuggled jewel wrapped in silk and velvet. From behind the curtains of the palanquin she watched the tawny deserts of Rajputana slide past. She did not know where she was being taken or by whom, but she was glad to be rid of the trader and his uncomfortable luxuries.

Chittoor delighted her. The suite of apartments given to her was in the palace zenana. The rooms were built for luxury and comfort. They were cool and spacious, with rugs and quilted divans. She was dressed in soft muslin gowns which covered her body as gently as cobwebs. The servants were all delicate women whose fingers had a satin touch. They oiled and massaged her. Bibbi Charlotte's fiery hair was combed until it felt like strands of silk. The food and sherbet was subtly spiced for her English tongue.

Whenever Augustine thought of his mother, he remembered what a Sufi had once told him. 'What we can imagine always disappoints us; what we cannot gives us pleasure. Our delights lie not in dreams come true but in surprises.'

The daughter of a London barrister was now a lady in the Rajput court. But for her the most important thing was that she was the wife of a soldier. She had come to India for that reason and it was what she was meant to be. Charlotte Knowles, Bibbi Charlotte, decided to give her Rajput general all of the devotion and honour which she had hoped to give her English subaltern. She was a proud woman.

When Trisuldas Thakur walked into her apartment the first time, a tall officer in a brocade uniform, his steel-coloured moustaches brushed up on his cheeks with bristly defiance, Charlotte Knowles broke down in tears. The General thought she was afraid and tried to calm her. He held her gently. She was not crying out of fear, though, but from an emotion of pride. She saw him as a hero in a drama. It was not purely happiness either that made her cry, but a hollow feeling, a sense of greatness. She clutched his waist and dug her head into his chest. With a soothing hand he brushed her red hair down over her shoulders. With the other hand, he gestured her attendants out of the room.

Bibbi Charlotte became devoted to Trisuldas Thakur and he loved her very much. Between them was an understanding of each other. They both believed in honour and bravery. Each one was vain and they played a part in each other's vanity. Shared vanity binds lovers together more strongly than shared modesty. A woman sustains a man's pride, Augustine had thought to himself. He could remember the fights that took place between his parents, how they would taunt each other, throwing insults back and forth, clawing at each other with words. Their pride fought with itself because they were not proud as two people but proud as one—a soldier and a soldier's wife. And when they made love you could hear them through four sets of walls.

The English killed them both, with ruthless brutality. Trisuldas Thakur was shot off his horse by a cannonball which tore him in two. Bibbi Charlotte was discovered in her tent. She had accompanied her husband into battle. Two English captains stripped her. They were drunk and said they'd spare her the shame of going back to England a whore. While one raped her, the other cut her throat.

Augustine was eighteen then and had been fighting beside his father. He came back to his mother's tent to tell her that Trisuldas was dead. He found that the English had taken the camp and were burning and looting, but he did not think for a moment that they would dare lay hands on his mother. The sight of her corpse and the two English captains covered with her blood made him go mad. He screamed and went at the men with his sword. They were cut to pieces. Augustine rushed out of the tent, his sword dripping. He leapt onto his horse and raced away from the camp and battlefield. Roaming for months, he never once put his sword back in its sheath. He didn't clean it but let it rust, the orange flecks appearing like fresh drops of blood on the stained steel of the blade.

ᔑ

The Colonel woke. For a moment he could not remember where he was. Then the motion of the palanquin reminded him of the journey. He coughed and spat.

'All right, we'll stop here for a rest,' Augustine said softly.

The palanquin bearers lowered the heavy weight and stretched. The soldiers dismounted and tethered their horses. The torch-bearers turned their torches into a fire and began to heat up what was left of last night's meal.

'It's going to rain, Colonel Sahib,' said one of the guards.

'When?' asked Augustine, as if he wanted a prediction to the minute.

'Maybe two hours from now. Maybe three.'

'The fort is two hours away from here.'

The soldier nodded.

'Then I'll go ahead now, for I don't care to get wet.'

The soldier shrugged. Someone had lit a chillum of tobacco and the sweet smell swept through the air. Augustine took his jacket out of the palanquin and put it over his shoulders. He wore no hat and let the curls of his hair fly loose. He found his horse and saddled it himself. Mounting, he turned and spoke to the soldier again.

'If you are wrong, Bhandari, and it rains before I get to the Bijilli Gargh, then I will have you stripped of your uniform.'

The soldier laughed.

'Don't worry, Colonel Sahib, I will be happy to take it off, for it will be soaking wet as well.'

His voice was casual but it contained respect for the officer, a respect not beaten into the man by punishment but put there carefully by the Colonel. He invested his men with loyalty as delicately as a jeweller setting a precious stone.

Though the horse had been walking all night it carried Augustine lightly. The Colonel cantered through the jungle humming to himself a Punjabi folk tune he had heard in Kirpan Singh's camp.

It was still dark, though there were hints of dawn. The forest was thinning out. He knew where he was.

Suddenly there was a brilliant flash and the sky was white, as if the darkness had been smashed open and the dawn had instantly spilled out. In that moment of brightness Augustine saw the outlines of the lower ridges clearly. A few seconds later there was a crack of thunder, like a great whip being snapped in the air, and then a low rumbling. The clouds growled like watchdogs. There was another flash of lightning just at the edge of the clouds, followed by more thunder. Then another brilliant flash lacerated the darkness closer by.

The Bijilli Gargh, named because of the lightning which always struck around it, was a small, squat fort perched on the peak of a low hill. It was built in an oblong shape with a roof that slanted in on the central courtyard. There were two square turrets guarding the main gate. In those few seconds of blinding illumination Augustine could make out every detail. The trees had been cut all around the fort and there was a stockade on three sides above which the hill was bald. Below the stockade the forest was dense. On the side of the hill facing west, Augustine could just make out the cliff which fell directly from the walls of the Bijilli Gargh. The earth of the hill was a red clay and when it rained the water ran down the hill in orange streams.

It was a dismal sight, like a wart on top of the naked hill. The walls were of grey stone and the roofs and floors tiled with slate. At this season of the year the moisture seemed to be absorbed by the walls and oozed into everything. A few lights flickered inside the fort.

On a clear day, with the mountains standing tall above it, the Bijilli Gargh had a romance about it. But it had been designed not for beauty but for war. It could withstand a siege for weeks. The hill was too steep for cannons to be easily dragged up, and though the shots could be lobbed from a distance, the walls were like iron. There was no approach to the Bijilli Gargh. It was built for defence, to protect an army.

Augustine shivered as another bolt of lightning struck close to the fort and again it stood out brightly. It remained silhouetted in his vision even after the flash had subsided. He hated the building. He hated its permanence, the way it had withstood a century of disuse. When they had taken the fort, it had been ruins inside, though the walls were firm. The men had spent days clearing rubble and making the barracks habitable.

One of the cannons on the ramparts was struck by lightning and it seemed as if it was being fired. The sound was echoed back and forth along the ridges.

Augustine did not want to go back into the fort. He hated having the walls around him. The dank rooms smelled of bats and rodents. It was a depressing sight and he was glad when the lightning began to move farther east, the thunder becoming lower and more distant. A slight shower, more mist than rain, began to fall. Augustine pulled his coat up around his neck and stooped in his saddle.

The dawn did not seem to break at any one point. Instead, a faint light filtered through the bank of clouds, as if falling with the rain. Outlines in the forest became more distinct. The darkness which had seemed so complete and primordial gradually lost its presence and faded. It was as if the night was robbed of its dignity. The serene quiet disintegrated into the soft sounds of animals and birds stirring at the first light.

The rain had stopped when Augustine reached the edge of the dry riverbed. The naked boulders stood out white and stark in the morning light. This river of rocks spread up to the foot of the mountains, which were hidden in the mist. Where the river came out of the mountains stood the Bijilli Gargh, sullen and grey, with the clouds sometimes sinking so low that they furled around the turrets.

A track ran along the edge of the riverbed for a few miles and then crossed to the other side, a short distance from the fort. There was no movement along the river. Augustine rode toward the mountains. He felt sure that he could make it to the fort before any more rain fell.

There was an ominous feeling in the air, a sense of expectancy. Silence always bothered Augustine. He had been feeling on edge since the lightning had started. He looked around for signs of life. Usually at this time of the morning animals were crossing the riverbed, sounders of boar and herds of spotted deer. One day he had seen a leopard and her cubs tumbling across the dry boulders, chasing each other in a game. Now there was not even a pine martin or a jackal. The Colonel felt suspense in the jungle as if even the trees were waiting for something. He loosened the leather thong which held his pistol in place and adjusted his sword. For a moment he wished the escort was with him, but then he pulled himself erect in his saddle and smiled at his own fear.

It was raining in the mountains. He could see the blue sheets of water draped from the clouds. Soon it will spread down to the plains, he thought.

Augustine reached the crossing without any trouble and hurried his horse down the embankment and onto the sandy trail across the dry river. The horse was uneasy and kept starting and wanting to turn around. Augustine pressed his knees into its sides and moved on. Almost halfway across, he heard a rumbling sound, as if all the boulders had begun to speak at once. At first he thought it was thunder. The clouds seemed to be sagging lower and lower. They had dropped so low that even the Bijilli Gargh was shrouded in mist. A black shadow settled on the forest.

With a sudden impulse, Augustine prodded his horse into a run. The animal eagerly picked up its pace to a gallop. The whole earth began shaking. Augustine glanced upstream and felt his heart stop. Far away but rushing down on them was a dirty grey wave of water, rolling over itself. The horse was going as fast as it could, with its neck low and its hooves spattering sand in all directions. The flood roared down from the mountains like a stampede. The sound and magnitude hypnotized Augustine. He could not take his eyes off it. The wave grew higher and higher, swallowing up the boulders and tossing them into the air like pebbles. As he watched, Augustine saw the embankment a hundred yards away collapse and trees growing along the side were uprooted and thrown into the air as if they weighed nothing. The horse was going as fast as it could, not watching the wave. Its eyes were fixed on the track and the embankment ahead. Augustine finally turned his head. It was hardly twenty yards to safety, only a second or two. They had to climb the embankment and get into the trees before they would be completely out of danger. The horse stumbled as it began to climb the sandy bank, but it regained its footing and lurched to the top, plunging into the trees just as the wall of water swept past, taking a huge mouthful of the embankment. Augustine reined the horse to a stop. It was quivering all over. He could not get it to turn round. Finally he dismounted and led it back towards the river. Where ten minutes before there had been only sand and boulders, a roistering torrent filled the wide expanse. Augustine watched as huge rocks were turned over, lolling on the surface like whales, and massive sal trees, already stripped of their branches, were thrust out of the current like monsters from the past. Entire thickets of bamboo floated by, dipping and leaping out of the water as if they were alive. The flood had a natural force behind it which Augustine could feel strongly. It frightened him. It was something unpredictable. Rain had fallen in the hills, streaming down the slopes, collecting in the valleys. From there it had built up into a torrent, fed by hundreds of muddy tributaries. It came down from the mountains without warning, like an army breaking out of a besieged fort.

The horse was still shaking. Augustine walked it up the road for a little way. His own fear had finally caught up with him and he could taste it in his mouth. It was as though he were biting lead, a cold, sour, metallic taste. He felt the sweat running down his back. If we had been caught in that, they would have found me a few miles south of here, cleaned to the bone, thought Augustine.

∽

The rain began to fall heavily just as Augustine reached the gate of the stockade. The guards let him in quickly and one of them took his horse. He ran up the dirt trail to the wide flagstone steps of the fort. The mist was all around him. It was as if the flood had washed everything away. Only the fort was left, floating in a sea of clouds.

Augustine stepped inside the brass-studded doors. There was a dark corridor which twisted its way into the fort and finally opened onto the central courtyard. Augustine moved along the inner wall, trying to escape the rain. He reached the slate awnings of the main pavilion.

James Webley had just woken up and was dressed in only his breeches and a pair of slippers. He came out to greet Augustine and embraced him warmly. The two men grinned at each other and walked back inside.

Webley was five or six inches shorter than Augustine. He had a frail body, light-boned, and with the flesh drooping on him. His strength lay more in the stamina of his mind than in his body. If he was determined, he could do anything a man twice his size could do. His skin was pale. He had very light blond hair and was balding. He hid it by combing the long strands of hair over his forehead, which was broad and speckled with sunburn. His face was old, betraying his age. He was fifty-three. The back of his neck was always a bright pink, the skin constantly peeling. Webley's eyes were like fire opals, changing colour depending on the way he turned. They were sharp eyes and their paleness had a haunting quality. Set in a face that was pallid and ugly, those eyes seemed to overwhelm the man himself, so that when you looked at him you were not looking at the scrawny body, the balding scalp, the twisted pink nose, but only into those eyes, their gaze fixed and perceptive.

Augustine looked at Webley carefully. Somehow, the Englishman seemed more stooped. From the back he looked like a walking corpse, his ribs jutting out from under his skin, his spine knotted and curved. When he walked, his head bobbed up and down. Augustine followed Webley into his apartments, noting a stiffness in his walk.

But when Webley turned around, his eyes flashed at Augustine and for a moment he seemed to be the same man Augustine had met eleven years ago in Baroda. He was not a man but a temperament contained in a loose bag of skin.

'Thank God you're back, Augustine. Nothing but a confounded bore without you,' said Webley.

'I almost got killed getting here …'

'Who was it this time?' asked Webley with interest.

'No one. The sot flooded as I was crossing and almost swept me and the horse away.'

'This sot, right here?'

'Yes,' said Augustine. 'Just fifteen minutes ago. While you were sleeping soundly, dreaming of soft thighs and breasts, I was racing for my life across the damned sot.'

'You know I only dream of clothed women. It's one of my great disappointments in life. All other men dream of them naked, but I must have them bundled up to the neck. You know, I don't think I remember even a bare ankle in my dreams. My imagination refuses to undress them.'

'How is our hideout?'

'God! Worse than ever,' said Webley. 'What a terrible place to be holed up. Can't you find me a better fort?'

'Is it wearing on you?' asked Augustine.

'We've been here almost two months. There are scorpions and the roof leaks. The monsoon has barely started.'

Webley was fondling a crystal bottle. Augustine recognized it as the one his friend had stolen from the house of a rich Hindu merchant in Benares. Webley had a habit of pocketing small things in other people's rooms. He never stole anything of value and in most cases the person probably never missed the object. If they did, it was blamed on the servants. Webley used to make Augustine nervous when they were visiting other officers or even rajahs. He would casually pick up a trinket when no one was watching and drop it into his pocket.

The room was filled with objects he had stolen, inkstands, stone carvings, letter-knives, paperweights, and many other things that had caught his fancy from time to time. As they left a place Webley, without fail, would produce something and show it to Augustine, a mischievous pride glinting in his eye. One time he stole what he thought was a piece of cut glass from a prostitute in Kanauj and when he got back home he realized that it was an emerald the size of a dove's egg. It was discreetly returned, for Webley was not that kind of thief. 'It's a hobby with me,' he would say.

Sometimes he is so petty, thought Augustine.

'And what do the Sikhs mumble in their beards?' asked Webley.

'They mumbled about everything and refused to give me a clear answer to a single question. I spent ten days there and each hour they changed their minds.'

'They will support us?'

'Only if there is something in it for them,' said Augustine.

'There is everything in it for them, damn it!' Webley shouted, his pale cheeks turning a blotchy red.

'They are scared of the Gurkhas,' said Augustine.

'They should know the Gurkhas will never leave the hills. They hate the heat as much as anyone.'

'The Sikhs don't trust you, either.'

'What do they say?' asked Webley. Augustine noticed a tired expression spread over his face and dull his eyes. Suddenly he looked very old.

'That it is a trap. That no Englishman is going to challenge his own people.'

Webley hurled the crystal bottle across the room. It shattered against the stone wall. The short man stood up, his stringy hair falling in disarray over his freckled forehead. Augustine watched him and gauged his temper quietly. He knew Webley as well as anyone and could judge his anger as some people predict a storm.

'Damn it, Augustine. Didn't you tell them that it wasn't I who challenged them? The Company challenged me. The English hate me even if I am their own countryman.'

'I explained a hundred times, but they did not believe me. They say that you are luring them into a trap and that once they send an army here, you will join forces with the English and the Gurkhas to destroy them.'

'The English will destroy the Gurkhas before they destroy the Sikhs.'

'The English will destroy all of us,' said Augustine in a soothing voice.

'How is Kirpan Singh, my old friend and enemy?'

Augustine smiled. 'He called you the finest general in Hindustan. He said the English were fools to get rid of you.'

'Kirpan Singh is as full of compliments as his beard is full of lice.'

Augustine's glass eye was fixed on Webley. It made the Englishman irritated to be watched without being seen. The blindness of that eye had a curiosity which was never satisfied. Nervously, Webley paced around the room, half-naked and looking more like a wizened hermit just woken up from a winter's hibernation than the finest general in Hindustan.

'Damn the Sikhs!' cried Webley, 'damn the Gurkhas! They're all frauds, they're none of them soldiers. The only army in Hindustan that I could trust besides my own is the English, and they are the ones I have to fight against.'

He crossed to a low table filled with the things he had stolen and snatched up a silver nail-clipper, taken from the dressing-table of a wealthy courtesan in Indore. On one end of it was a spiral gimlet. Nervously Webley trimmed his nails.

He's a petty man, thought Augustine. When he should be sharpening his sword for a fight, he's daintying his fingers like a woman. What does he need the Sikhs for, or the Gurkhas? He has the finest army in the north, Arabs, Rajputs, Afghans, and Rohillas all regimented together like a patchwork quilt, as vicious as a pack of dogs. They are not trained in systems of war like the English Army. Each man in his saddle fights with instinct, which is a stronger thing than training. They are loyal to him as well. No matter what the numbers or the odds, they will die to the last man. What is he scared of the English for? It is as if he is scared of himself.

'We can hold off the English by ourselves,' said Augustine.

'You underestimate them, my Colonel, because you hate them. That is the greatest mistake a soldier can make, to let his emotions spill into his reason.'

'They are not as invincible as you think,' Augustine said insistently.

Webley turned on his friend, holding the nail-clipper in his hand, with the gimlet pointed at Augustine. 'The English will come at us once and we may repulse them, but they will come again, as persistently as a screw, cutting into us deliberately, slowly, and with each turn deeper and deeper, until they kill us. The English do not strike and then run away. They are stubborn, Colonel, stubborn as a gimlet, and once they have embedded themselves in Hindustan, nobody will be able to pull them out.'

Augustine was leaning against a bolster pillow. There was a wooden chest behind him. Webley stepped towards him and thrust the gimlet at his stomach. Augustine only smiled and did not move. Webley held the point just above his navel and pretended to skewer the Colonel. Then impulsively he pulled it away and drove it into the chest next to Augustine's head, twisting the handle furiously, so that the screw drilled a couple of inches into the wood.

Augustine glanced at it and said nothing.

'The Company's forces will be here within a month,' said Webley.

'Not that soon. They will wait until after the rains. In October they will be here.'

'So we have three more months in this damn fort, three wet months of mildew and scorpions, waiting for those red coats to come marching up and wipe us out. God, Augustine, I don't want to wait. I want them to come now. They would be too cruel if they made me sit out the monsoon before they attacked. I will die before then.'

He's scared of his own kind, thought Augustine, making sure his glass eye caught Webley in its vague stare. If it were the Afghans or the Gurkhas, he would not flinch. He would have no qualms and would laugh at precaution. But the English ... he is scared of them. They make him restless.

'You trust your men a great deal to keep them here for three more months without pay,' said Augustine.

'Other armies mutiny, not ours,' said Webley.

'I hope you are right.'

'They have lasted until now. Surely none of them expect a fight during the rains. There are quarters here and plenty of food. When the rains break we will be in money again,' said Webley.

'Who shall we rob?' asked Augustine.

'No, no, my Colonel. We aren't robbers. We collect taxes,' said Webley. 'But I feel like a bandit, hiding out in this hole.'

'You have always enjoyed being a bandit.'

'That's true,' said Webley. 'And would you have preferred to be a general?'

Augustine shrugged his shoulders and then shook his head.

'There is always money east of here if we care to take it,' said the Colonel.

'There is money to the west as well. But I would rather save it until after the rains,' said Webley, aiming a toy pistol at Augustine's forehead. It had been the plaything of a prince. Webley had stolen it from the nursery in the palace at Farrukhabad.

'We could hit Saharanpur and be back here before a drop of rain fell,' said Augustine.

'No, I told you. We will wait until after the rains.' Webley's voice had become shrill with irritation.

'You're scared that the English will take it as an affront and send troops from Bareilly. But what can they do? As soon as they set siege to the fort, down will come the rain and they will all catch fever. It is better to hit Saharanpur now instead of later. The monsoon will go by faster if the men have loot in their pockets.'

'No,' said Webley, with abruptness.

'What is it in the English that you fear? Your own blood? They aren't cannibals. You're one of them. They won't eat your flesh. If they catch you they will be gentlemen, one to another, and put you on a comfortable barge to Calcutta, from where the first ship will sail you home to dear, dear England. But what will happen to us? God knows. Maybe we will all be tied across cannons and have our bellies shot out?'

'Don't talk like an idiot, Augustine. Of course I'm not scared of the English. There's just no point in aggravating them.'

'But they've threatened you. If your army isn't parading in front of Delhi within the month, your sword in Ochterlony's lap, they will come up here and punish us. They have called us bandits.'

'Well, aren't we?'

'I know what it is that bothers you, James. It eats at your insides like a parasite. You don't want to be known as a criminal. You are what you call a gentleman. A strange word, no? Especially in a country like India. You are not a Robin Hood. There would be romance in that. Ah, if only the English would think of you as Robin Hood, but they won't. Instead, you are a Robinson Crusoe.'

'I didn't know you read books, Augustine.'

'My mother told me those stories.'

'Doesn't it make you feel even the slightest bit guilty to hate your mother's people?'

'I feel guilty being a part of them.'

Webley walked over to a small window which looked out on the plains.

'Tomorrow I've called for a shikar. Will you join us?'

'Of course,' said Augustine, rising and leaving the room abruptly.

~

On his way out Augustine met Pratap Bahadur scurrying across the courtyard. The little Gurkha was a comical man, hardly five feet tall and with a jaunty air about him, like a little boy dressed up as a soldier. Though Pratap Bahadur wore a wide grin and walked with almost a skip in his step, he was a very serious man. Too serious, Webley had said. Pratap Bahadur was the emissary from the Rajah of Nepal and had arrived at the fort soon after they had occupied it. Since then he regularly sent intelligence back to his generals in Almora, describing Webley's army and its discipline, its latest moves and alliances. Though the Gurkhas controlled the entire range of Himalayas as far west as Jaunsar, across the Jumna, they tolerated Webley's presence at the Bijilli Gargh. They knew he was a renegade and a desperate man. He was like a cobra in the house, dangerous but protected by his reputation and the aura about him. Pratap Bahadur was there to keep an eye on him. Occasionally there were discussions about alliances between Webley's forces and those of Nepal, but Pratap Bahadur and Webley were too suspicious of each other for anything to come of the suggestions.

Augustine stared down at the little man. Personalities are as flimsy as kite paper, he thought, and yet they challenge more than the wind. Pratap Bahadur was a small packet of vanity, but he was also a fool. His bravery drove him to make an ass of himself. Though he held the fate of Webley's army in his hands, no one in the fort took him seriously. They mimicked him to his face. They laughed when he tripped. Jokes were told about his wife. He would challenge men to a fight, but they would just laugh and send him away with chiding abuse.

'Colonel, Colonel, I am glad to see you. Where have you been? You left without saying goodbye.'

'I went hunting,' he lied.

'You are a keen shikari.'

'It depends on the game.'

'What luck?' asked the Gurkha.

Augustine looked down at the emissary and smiled. He was not clever with words. Turning, Augustine walked away. The rain had stopped and the slate flagstones were mottled with puddles of water. The tall man strode through them without noticing.

~

Webley had chosen his position well. The Bijilli Gargh offered him protection, not only because of its solid walls and inaccessible location on top of the hill, but because it was situated in a political backwater, into which the British dared not venture. The hill stood about four miles from where the Ganges left the Himalayas, in a broad valley between the high mountains and the lesser range of the Siwaliks. Dehra Dun, as the valley was called, remained part of the Gurkha empire, but a small band of eccentric Sikh mystics, headed by a mahant, had settled in the centre of the valley about fifteen miles from the Bijilli Gargh. Beyond the Jumna the Sikh armies stood guard, ready to protect their isolated settlement. The Gurkhas tolerated the Sikhs so long as they stayed in the Dun. In the same way they allowed Webley to hide out in the abandoned fort, provided he did not enter the Himalayas.

The British were on the verge of starting hostilities with the Gurkhas, but until they did, Webley was safe in his hideaway. The brunt of the Gurkha army was garrisoned at Almora, a fort farther to the east and set back in a shallow range of foothills above Bareilly. Rumours were already filtering through about plans for a British offensive against Almora, but no one had certain information about when it would take place. Webley had stepped into a precarious but protected position. He was safe for the moment, but unless he moved out within the year, he would find himself in the midst of a confused and chaotic conflict, in which he would surely end up the victim. If the British succeeded in defeating the Gurkhas, they would certainly crush Webley in the process. If the Gurkhas repelled the attack, they would strengthen their forces along the foothills, especially in Garhwal, and they would think twice before allowing an English army within their perimeters, even if it was a renegade army of deserters. But for the time being they were safe, and the British officers who had been pursuing Webley for the last year and a half had retired to Meerut to wait out the monsoon.

The Sikhs had been their only hope, and that too had been dashed with Kirpan Singh's protestations and claims of an alliance with the English. For Augustine it was like nesting inside the muzzle of a cannon, waiting for it to be shot off. He knew that sooner or later they would be chased out, and into what. They could not survive much longer. The army would split up into small bands of marauders. The glorious memory of their achievements would fade. They would be hunted down like vermin, shot by the victors, whether English or Indian. They were not a part of this conflict, only a disruptive and foreign element in this struggle between nations. They were a part of the anarchy which had broken loose from the past. For them the time was coming when they would face destruction.

The Bijilli Gargh was a part of that vanished age as well. It had been built by one of the first rajahs of Tehri, as a guardhouse for the Dun. Those Rajput rulers were chased out by the Gurkhas and fled into the arms of the English, who absorbed them into a benevolent bosom, like a kindly nanny suffocating them in the odours of perfume and stale sweat. England was like an enormous wet nurse, suckling the destitute and helpless maharajahs of Hindustan, fondling them with a firm disciplinary hand.

The army was contented with the fort, unlike Webley. The men were cheerful and went about the fort making it comfortable and enjoying the change from their usually nomadic life. One or two men deserted, but it was either because of arguments among themselves or women in other places. In fact, the Bijilli Gargh, now that it had been renovated and was being lived in, exuded a peaceful stagnancy, as if these were not the same men who razed and murdered villages, swept through innocent towns, and robbed the merchants of their money and wares. There was no trace of melancholy over their recent defeats, no fear, only the vague restlessness which you find in men who are not used to sitting still.

Chittoorgargh, where Augustine was born, had a very romantic history. The story had been told to Augustine over and over when he was a child, by his mother's servants, 'the nymphs,' as she called them, and by the courtiers that attended his father. The fort was under siege for several months. The Rajputs inside held the invaders out, but they could get no supplies and soon they were without water and food. As the situation became desperate, the defenders took an oath to die fighting and not to allow any of their women to be captured. The women also took the oath, preferring death to the indignities they would suffer at the hands of their captors. They were a proud people and would bow to no one. When all hope was finally given up, an enormous bonfire was built inside the fort and the ladies of the court, the officers' wives, every woman within the walls, threw themselves into the flames and died. Then the men, frenzied with grief and anger, dressed themselves in scarlet and made a suicidal charge out of the fort into the siege cannons. No one survived, but they had defended their honour, for there were no women in the zenana to be carried away. The moral was obvious and Augustine was told the story so many times that he began to feel as though he had witnessed the event.

Bibbi Charlotte loved the story, the horror of the siege, the tragedy of their deaths, and the melodrama which surrounded the fort. She wept whenever she heard the story told and would hug Augustine to her, as though tomorrow he would ride out of the fort into the cannons and die.

From the time he was old enough to understand the stories and legends that were told to him, Augustine was fed a diet of heroism and tragedy. Everyone around him had a story to tell, from the soldiers in his father's regiment to the maidservants in his mother's apartments. He listened with wide eyes and absorbed all of the tales of battles and charges, exaggerated stories about all the Rajput heroes, some of whom were looked on as gods.

Bibbi Charlotte also told him stories, though hers were different. They were set in a world that Augustine could not imagine, a world of medieval darkness, a world of woods and snow, very different from the deserts surrounding Chittoor. Even the cast of characters was different, though they embodied the same heroics and codes of honour.

For Augustine the stories about the Rajput heroes were far more real and exciting, and he would often imagine his mother's stories to be set in the deserts surrounding Chittoor, rather than in that strange, cold land, and her English heroes to be swarthy Rajput warriors.

Filled with an awareness of Rajput heroics, Augustine had begun to develop a pride in his father's heritage and came to look on it as his own. He saw himself in those heroes and felt a blush of pride when told of their exploits. Still, he was not sure who he was. Trisuldas Thakur was a Rajput. But Bibbi Charlotte, though she admired the world at Chittoor, remained an Englishwoman within.

'Mother, am I a Rajput?' Augustine finally asked her.

Bibbi Charlotte's answer was confusing and it upset Augustine. First, she began to cry, as she always did, sobbing all over him.

'No,' she said, 'you are something better, a part of both worlds, mine and your father's. Never forget that. You will never quite be a Rajput. Nor will you ever be an Englishman. You are yourself, Augustine.'

He did not understand. His sense of belonging to those heroic stories and carrying on those noble traditions fell away from him, and as he grew older he realized how alone he was. There was nothing at his back, no tradition, no history. His father had rested on a reputation hundreds of years old. Every part of him spoke of those dead heroes, the defenders of Chittoorgargh. Trisuldas Thakur was a hero by name and association. By being a Rajput he was immediately a warrior as well, and a hero.

Augustine had to create his own reputation, even though he lived in his father's court and was brought up as a Rajput. In time he began to look at it not as a disadvantage but as a challenge. His mother's tears had not been those of regret and sadness but of pride. For she hoped that her son would rise above these legends and stories and become a hero in himself.

Though Augustine spoke little out loud, he was verbose within himself. If he was nervous or excited, the conversations inside his mind would flare up to such a pitch that his ears would ring.

He was worried. The Sikhs had tangled him up with indecision. Webley, too, was undecided. He did not like alliances. He did not want to tie himself to other armies, especially Indian. If the English offered him a treaty which let him keep his army, he would go in with them. But they have promised him only safe conduct to Calcutta and a ship home. He is too proud and petty a man to accept, thought Augustine. But he is also too proud to join the Sikhs or the Gurkhas and seriously ask for their protection. They are Indian armies, a part of the land. Natives, he calls them. There is something in that word he hates, as if it stood for evil. Native armies, native princes, native tongues, he hates them all.

The Colonel was cleaning his guns. There was a row of them along the wall. Augustine enjoyed cleaning them. It was a long, dirty job. The black powder gummed up the barrels, and if they were left uncleaned for more than a few days, the steel would begin to corrode. Pride in his guns, in all his weapons, made Augustine take care of them as though they were children. He broke down a four bore, double-barrel gun made by Knock and looked down the wide Damascus barrels. This wretched weather, he thought to himself. Already there was a speckling of rust around the breech. Dipping a rag in oil, Augustine pushed it inside with his finger. With a ramrod, he thrust it back and forth through the bore.

Webley frustrated him. He had become too cautious. There was a time before when no danger could deter him. He was stubborn. Before, he had been stubbornly impulsive, now he was stubbornly cautious. It was his mind which had changed, not his character. He was the same man, only older and defeated.

Webley had defeated himself. Augustine could see it in him. The way he sat, the way he moved. Before, when Webley walked, he would try to disguise the stiffness in his leg. Now he exaggerated it. His temper was still there, but now it struck out at Augustine's eagerness, while before it would attack his hesitancy. His moods, his speech, his expression were all the same, for his personality remained as powerful as ever. But it was like a weathervane. The silhouette was the same no matter which way it pointed, only its direction changed with the wind.

Was it his age? Had that defeated him? Augustine could hardly believe it. Only a few months ago, he had been as young as twenty, despite his age. Perhaps he was sick. The damp could have soaked into his bones and rotted the marrow.

Except for the two guns Augustine had taken with him on the trip, all the rest had been left in their cases. Now he had them out and was inspecting each one carefully. With a wire brush he scoured the rust out of a matchlock he had taken from his father's arsenal at Chittoor. It was a beautiful gun, with an inlaid stock and hunting scenes etched onto the barrel. Handling the weapon soothed him. The smell of oil and wood and steel mixed together had a warm and comforting effect on him.

Despite where they were and the situation they were in, Augustine knew that he would have preferred to be nowhere else but with Webley. He tried not to think of the battle at Deoband. Webley had made fools of all of them. They could have defeated the British, but instead they had withdrawn at the last minute and retreated helter-skelter, like a pack of scared monkeys. It had been Webley's fault. They had taken most of the cannons, and the English had fallen back in among their own tents....

But there was no good in dredging it up. Webley had not said anything about it, and neither had anyone else. He had brought them here to hide, like rats afraid of a sprung trap. Every man in the army felt the insult. But no one was bitter, only disappointed.

Wiping down a pair of duelling pistols, Augustine noted

blotches on the barrels. The browning was wearing away.

'Everything in this damned fort is corroded. Our guns, the walls, the roofs, and we ourselves,' said Augustine out loud.

It was sad. The army was still a fine force, but there was a flaw in it. Augustine had known this from the beginning. The army was sparked by one man, Webley. He was the core, the coal of the army. The men are too loyal, thought Augustine. Their loyalty is focussed on him, when it should be diffused among the other officers, among themselves. Webley was now destroying himself through his own caution, his own fear. He had kept his men locked up in the Bijilli Gargh for three months without any action. They were not used to it. They were restless. His fire would never go out. But it would take a lot to kindle the former spirit in the men after such a long time in the damp fort. Loyalty when disappointed can easily turn to bitterness. If they become bitter towards Webley, thought Augustine, the army will splinter into a hundred pieces. He wondered within himself whether he could hold even a part of it together. Augustine got on well with the men, but he knew that the inspiration lay in Webley.

To protect the army, I must protect Webley. If he goes, we all go. He must be kept alive.

Holding the barrel of his favourite flintlock between his knees, Augustine rammed a wad of oiled rags in and out of the thin bore. It was a heavy weapon, designed for hunting geese. The barrel was extra-long and tightly choked. Augustine used it in battle. He was accurate with it up to seventy-five yards.

Augustine remembered the early days with Webley, when they were both officers under the Gaekwad at Baroda. Neither of them had been happy in another man's army. Finally there was the incident over Mehboob Rashid's execution. Webley, Augustine, and Mehboob Rashid had marched out with a small army of mercenaries. They left the protection of Baroda to become bandits.

For years they lived by robbing caravans and villages. Slowly the army grew, with renegades added on here and there. In those days Webley was impulsive and would go into battle with an insane rush of confidence. The men inside the Bijilli Gargh held in their minds that image of him galloping blindly into the smoke with his sabre pointing straight ahead and his scream piercing and inhuman like an animal's cry.

Their band travelled all over the north of Hindustan, through the Punjab, the Doab, and right into Bengal. Nobody could stop them. They were small enough to move without detection and attack with surprise. Their reputation grew until villages would come out to meet them with baskets of tribute. Many maharajahs, nawabs, and their generals tried to destroy them, but no one could catch Webley and his men. They would vanish without a trace, and a few weeks later reports would arrive that they had sacked a town to the east. They could cover thirty miles in a day and after a few hours move on by night.

At that game Webley was a genius—a master of deception and mischief. But over time the army grew too large and conspicuous. It had to fight pitched battles, and Webley, though he was never defeated, lost more men than he would have liked. Their defeat came at Deoband, but none of the men would call it a defeat, for they had already beaten the British by the time Webley gave the order to retreat.

The times have changed. Kirpan Singh is right, thought Augustine. India is now a country of large armies and confederacies. The British put together their Grand Army. The Mahratta chiefs joined together with other rajahs so that it was no longer one general against another but a web of commanders-in-chief and those under them. The dimensions of war have become exaggerated, and instead of four cannons and a couple of galloper guns, the armies move with hundreds of artillery pieces.

These wars have no place for us, thought Augustine. There is no use for personalities and individuals. No use for genius, either. An army of renegades cannot stand up to an army of faceless infantry in their neat mechanical lines. We are obsolete. Some of us could blend into those armies and fight those wars. But not Webley. James must be on his own. He cannot be a part of a machine. There is something in him which rebels. He cannot be a part of anything; he must be everything. Even if the English let him fight for them, he would not last under their system.

2

At Deoband the English had chosen their ground poorly. There were few places that offered any protection on the flat plain. It was white with saltpetre, dotted occasionally with a scruffy cluster of palm trees, looking like shaggy-headed giants from a distance. There was a muddy tank, almost emptied by the hot sun. Two or three egrets bobbed up and down, and snipe scudded over the water. The English had dug rows of trenches next to the tank, neatly laid out like flower beds. Their pioneers had also constructed a jagged line of redans on the far side of the tank. A battery of cannon were put in place behind the trenches. Their wheels had already begun to sink into the mud. Officers in their bright uniforms looked very busy from a distance. They scurried back and forth between the trenches, like anxious insects. Beyond the tank and the redans, the carts for baggage and supplies had been lined up as a makeshift barricade.

Augustine and one of his men, Kishan Chand, had ridden up to watch the preparations. They were out of musket range, and though some of the English sentries fired at them, the slugs spattered up white puffs of saltpetre far short of the two horsemen. Augustine held a stubby telescope to his good eye and scanned the battery. They had twenty cannons. Not many, he thought. The sepoys were seated casually at a distance watching the engineers constructing the ditches into which they would be planted, like rows of wheat. 'Ready for the harvest,' said Augustine out loud.

'What, Colonel Sahib?' said Kishan Chand.

'Nothing. I am just counting.'

'There are at least six hundred men, Colonel Sahib,' said the soldier.

'But no horses,' said Augustine with a smile. He gave the telescope to Kishan Chand.

The soldier laughed and squinted through the eyepiece. He laughed some more when he saw the tank directly behind the trenches, and the cannons sinking into the mud.

'We will not have to do a thing, Colonel Sahib,' he said with a chuckle. 'The water will rise in those trenches within an hour or two and the English will all drown.'

'Then we will have to attack shortly, to make a good fight of it,' said Augustine, turning his horse around and starting off in the direction of their camp. He rode across the plain like a dust devil, the saltpetre and sand swirling around him. It was the end of March and the sun had begun to scorch everything. Kishan Chand caught up with Augustine and they raced back to the line of tents, where Webley and the men were waiting for their report.

'It will be like slaughtering sheep,' said Augustine. 'They have a tank of mud behind them. Their trenches will be full of water within a few hours.'

Webley said nothing. With a dry twig he was scratching the crusted sand between his legs. His head was bowed so that Augustine could only see the pink, bald surface of his scalp.

'You are sure there are no more of them hidden somewhere?' asked Mehboob Rashid. The Arab's face was turned. He had his eyes fixed on a line of palm trees far off against the blinding white of the sky.

'There is nowhere they could hide,' said Augustine.

'A desert has more hiding places than a forest,' said Mehboob Rashid. 'You make the English into fools, Colonel.'

'Go see for yourself, if you do not believe me. See what their engineers have done.'

Webley raised his head slowly. His face was tired. The English had been chasing him all winter. He had avoided them with skill and frustrated their officers. But they were persistent as ants and kept coming after him. It had forced them to keep moving without more than a few days' break in between marches. The men were exhausted. They had not been able to attack towns for fear of being ambushed by the English. Spies among the men kept them exposed. Webley had two men executed because they had been sending information out of the camp. But there were others. The English seemed to know every move they made and could predict where they would be. The army had become too large now, and long, fast marches were impossible. The Arabs had their women with them and so did some of the other men. There were carts full of supplies and baggage.

'We've grown too damned large,' Webley had complained.

But they could not leave anyone behind now. The English would cut them to pieces. Webley had no fort, no place to leave the women and baggage, no place to escape to. He drifted over the plains of saltpetre and dust, like a wind that has been separated from its storm.

Now they had a chance to finish the English off, to kill those that pursued them, at least for the time being. It was a perfect opportunity.

'Are you sure they are as foolish as we think?' said Webley. 'I know you are eager, Augustine. You want to hack the English into kebabs and roast them over a fire. But don't you think it is peculiar that they have chosen, of all places on this tabletop plain, the one dangerous position? Doesn't that make you nervous? When a woman takes off her bodice without hesitation, don't you stop a moment and wonder about her? When a tiger walks towards you, is he coming to receive his bullet as if it were a medal, or is he going to spring on you? They have been chasing us for fourteen months now. Don't you think they're frustrated?'

'Frustrated enough to make a mistake,' said Augustine. 'They're tired out.'

'And now is our chance,' said Webley, finishing Augustine's argument for him. 'But stop for a moment, Colonel, forget your hatred and realize that they have twice as many men as we do. If you were in that position, wouldn't you be confident that in a pitched battle you could destroy these men?" He waved his hand behind his head.

'But we have horses,' said Mehboob Rashid softly.

'The English believe in their own two legs. I think they are drawing us into a trap, tempting us with an easy victory. They could not be such fools.'

'You have become cautious suddenly,' said Augustine.

'I have found occasionally it pays. We are not fighting idiots.'

'If you don't think so, go see for yourself.'

'Fall into the trap, Colonel, but I am not falling in with you,' said Webley.

Mehboob Rashid suddenly stood up and turned on the two men, his hands held out to them in a gesture of pleading.

'The one of you is as eager for English blood as a mosquito. The other is afraid of them. If Augustine is right, we have an opportunity to end their pestering. If he is wrong, we can stay out of range and then run away. Remember that we are on horseback and they are on foot.'

Augustine laughed. 'He has called me a mosquito and you a coward. We had both of us better make him eat his insults.'

Webley bowed his head again and Augustine could tell that he was worried. He had never seen the Englishman like this before. There had been worse situations. It was not even full summer yet, no time to be exhausted. But Webley's exhaustion seemed deeper. It was as if he was exhausted with his way of life, exhausted with being followed, not by the English, but by a force which urged him on and on mercilessly. It was an excitement. But the thrill seemed to have died. Could Webley have been tired of living? Only a man who had lived as fully as Webley had could claim the right to kill himself. But he didn't want death, Augustine was sure of that. It would have been too easy for Webley.

He was not scared either, like Mehboob Rashid, just worn out. He had wrenched life apart, squeezed it like a lemon. He was the rind of a man. His energy had emptied out of him. Webley had squandered himself. Did he regret any of it? Probably not, thought Augustine, he probably enjoys the end as much as the beginning.

You are English, Augustine said within himself, you are a gentleman, a hero to yourself. Your vanity is English. It contains no emotion but pride and it is all pride. But my vanity is every emotion pooled together and erupting inside of me. You are cold and brutal. You feel no pain. You feel nothing but pride. You are too vain to admit that those English officers and engineers have made a mistake. You are one of them, even though they are out to kill you.

~

The army marched across the plain in a random formation, each man beside his friend. Webley rode at the head of the centre column, Augustine in front of the left-hand column, and Mehboob Rashid at the head of the right. But there were no regular lines and the columns spilled into each other from time to time. The men spoke among themselves and there were shouts from one side of the army to the other. In all, there were over three hundred horsemen. A broad fan of dust filled the air behind them as they advanced on the English position.

Webley stopped the army just out of range of the cannons. With his telescope he scanned the area. Augustine and Mehboob Rashid rode up beside him.

'There are only twenty cannons. They had over a hundred when we last saw them,' Webley muttered under his breath.

'That is in our favour, isn't it?' said Augustine.

'They have gone mad,' said Mehboob Rashid.

Augustine laughed with relief. Webley kept scanning their works meticulously. The three officers remained silent for the next five minutes.

'All right, Augustine. You want the English. You can have them,' said Webley, turning and staring right at him. 'Do I have to point you in their direction or do you know the way?'

'I know the way.'

'We'll follow you in,' said Webley, turning and giving orders to his men.

Augustine pulled away and returned to his column. The orders were muttered back among the men. Augustine had been waiting for this moment. Casually he took his cummerbund off his waist and wrapped it carefully around his head. It was a bright blue. Then he checked his pistols and adjusted his sword. His horse moved in slow circles in front of the column. It seemed to sense the excitement. The men in the column had stopped talking. Some were tamping down their muzzle-loaders. Others sat erect and silent. Each of them felt Augustine's emotions. They seemed to be in contact with him. Their eyes followed his movements.

The English were still and silent, waiting for the attack. Only the soldiers' heads were visible along the tops of the trenches. Gun barrels spat reflections back at the sun. The tank seemed grey and stagnant. The air was full of the burning smell of saltpetre, pot fires, and matches.

Finally Augustine stopped. Throwing his head back, he shouted to his men: 'Turn those red coats into a carpet beneath your feet!'

A yell burst out of the column, something between a scream

and a laugh. Augustine whirled about, unsheathed his sword, and headed for the English cannons. His men swarmed behind him.

A few muskets popped, but none of the men fell. Then suddenly the cannons exploded one after the other, with a tremendous noise and storm clouds of smoke. The smoke engulfed the trenches in a second and came rolling across the plain like a flood. Augustine felt his lungs suddenly choke up. They seemed to be on fire. He held himself low against his horse's neck, with his sword pointing straight ahead. It seemed to cut through the black folds of smoke. The wind was from behind the English and swept the smoke right into Augustine's column.

Augustine cleared the first trench. There were no men in it, only a few feet of water. The second trench was also deserted. It was peculiar. There was no second round of cannon fire. He had heard no sound of shots, no whine, no screams, only the dull thud of the report. And there had been so much smoke; it seemed strange.

He had never known the smoke to be this thick. By the time he reached the cannons he knew what had happened. They were deserted, too. He seemed to be moving through a fog or a mist. His men were behind him. He could hear their shouts but he felt suddenly alone in the smoke, as if he would never find another man. It was like a deserted battlefield after a war, but without corpses or men, only the ghostly sounds of musket fire, but no bullets, no death, only the thick, dense smoke which left your lungs raw and burning.

In a moment he was through the smoke. His horse leapt into the tank and then floundered. He saw the last of the English soldiers scuttling around the edges of the tank and hurrying into place behind the redans. The baggage and supply carts had been dragged to either side and there, seeming to glow in the sunlight, were the rest of the cannons, two lines of them, staggered across the plain. Beside each one stood the gunners in their tight uniforms. On the redans, Augustine could see the officers in their black bearskins, crying out like jackals. He felt his horse sinking further into the mud. With trouble he turned the animal around and got on solid footing. By then his men were all around him, some of them already mired in the tank. It smelled foul and diseased. The mud clung to the horses' legs and flanks.

The English muskets began to chatter, and Augustine saw two or three of his men tumble into the water. He began screaming orders at the top of his lungs. His voice seemed to tear his chest apart. The few men that heard his cries turned with him and plunged back into the smoke. Others blundered on into the tank and fell under the heavy fire. Augustine remained exposed until most of his men had dodged back into the smoke. As he turned to follow them, he felt his horse suddenly stiffen and lurch forward. Instinctively, Augustine threw himself off and landed in the soft mud. The horse fell heavily, its legs still churning. A stream of blood flowed out of its side and mixed with the grey ooze. Augustine picked himself up and ran for cover. He ducked behind one of the abandoned cannons and then looked about frantically. Still clutching his sword, he ran madly through the shallow water, his boots sinking into the mire. A horse stood frozen over its dead master. Augustine recognized the man.

The horse was jittery, and once it felt a man on its back, it hurtled back into the smoke. Ball- and grapeshot were spattering up fountains of water around Augustine.

His men were bunched together inside the cover of the smoke. A few stray shots swept past them. Augustine heard their voices and rode toward them. When they saw him, their group opened up to let him ride in. They were only half of the column, but as Augustine began to speak, more drifted in from all sides. He figured that he had lost a third of his men.

Quickly and without hesitation he gave them their orders. He had no idea what had happened to Mehboob Rashid and Webley. The cannons continued to blast into the smoke. Augustine took his men to the right of the tank. This time the smoke was in their favour. It had begun to thin. The wind seemed to have died down and was filtering off to the sides. The fire from the cannons across the tank had also helped to make that part of the plain into a soup of gunsmoke.

Again Augustine pressed himself against the horse's neck and levelled his sword in front of him. The men skirted the tank at a gallop and were in front of the redans before the English knew what had happened. The horses dashed up the embankments. One or two of them fell. The English infantry was ablaze with muskets, spattering fire all along the redans.

Augustine could not understand why Webley had disappeared. He wondered if the rest of the army had been wiped out. It seemed impossible. With hardly sixty men Augustine jumped the redans and swept in among the English. The sepoys retreated behind their cannons, turning and firing as they ran.

One of the English officers was on horseback. He was riding back and forth in front of his own guns, shouting for his men to keep their ground. Augustine fixed his eye on him and rode directly at him. The officer was so concerned about getting his men to hold their ground that he didn't see Augustine until the last minute. His pistol exploded right beside Augustine's ear, but the sword had already gone through him and the slug went over Augustine's shoulder. Their horses collided. The English officer, his eyes still wide with surprise, rolled out of his saddle. Augustine's blade slid out of him as he fell.

His ears still ringing, Augustine charged the cannons. The fire was thick around him, but he was past the front line before the first volley was fired. His horse tripped on the chains of the second line and sent Augustine over its head. He felt himself hit the ground, but he rolled and was on his feet in an instant. One of his own men swung Augustine up behind him.

'They say that the General has retreated, Colonel Sahib,' shouted the soldier over his shoulder.

'He wouldn't have,' said Augustine.

'Yes, they realized that it was a trap as soon as those cannons fired. They were filled with nothing but powder, just to produce smoke. The General saw them evacuate the trenches and take the carts from in front of the real cannons. He ordered the other two columns to retire.'

'Damn it! We've got them!' Augustine said with frustration. 'Why the hell is he running away?'

The English gunners stood by their cannons and fought off the horsemen. Augustine pistolled two sepoys as they came at him. They were both carrying swords and looked astonished when he fired at them. Gradually Augustine and his men cut out an area for themselves. The horses trampled the corpses underneath their hooves as they jockeyed back and forth within the crowd. Many of Augustine's men had fallen as well.

'You were right, Colonel, we have made a carpet of them,' said the soldier riding in front of Augustine.

At that moment a slug caught him in the neck, killing him in an instant. He had been about to say something else, but all that came out was a gruff rattle, like the sound of a hookah. Blood spattered all over Augustine, smearing the side of his face. The man fell back in his saddle and landed heavily on his Colonel. With all his force, Augustine pushed the man out of the saddle and took the horse's reins himself. Without a flank attack or reinforcements, they would all be cut to pieces. Augustine could see his men fighting ruthlessly around him. With a shrill cry which rose above the musket fire, Augustine called his men back.

Most of the English had clustered themselves behind their carts and were firing accurately from cover. High in their saddles the men were easy targets. Augustine unwound his turban and tied the blue sash to his sword. Then, racing among his men, he yelled for them to follow him out.

The blue cloth streaming behind him, Augustine jumped the two lines of cannons and headed around the tank. His men took a few last cuts at the English and then followed him.

Augustine had the heel shot off his boot, and his horse was grazed along the left flank. Once out of range, what remained of the column was drawn up. About thirty men had survived. The smoke was a thin veil over the battlefield. The English had stopped firing and Augustine could hear their voices and shouts from across the tank. The sounds seemed to skip over the surface of the plain like rocks skimming across a pond.

The other two columns had vanished. When Augustine looked back, his heart took a skip. They had driven the English far back behind their redans and killed three times their own casualties. If Webley had just sent Mehboob Rashid to flank the English, or even done as he said he would, followed them on in, they would have finished off the English with ease. As it was, they had left half their men dead and run like rats from a flood. There was little said among the men as they moved off slowly in the direction Webley had retreated.

∽

'You're limping,' said Webley when Augustine entered his tent.

'It's only my boot. The heel's shot off.' Augustine spoke without knowing what he said. He only answered Webley's questions.

The Englishman was lying on the ground, propped up against a bedroll. He was immaculately dressed in his velvet coat and gold-studded bandolier. On his head he wore a peaked hat, like a riding helmet, with a pink cockade pinned in front. His trousers were swan-white and his boots shone in the half light of the tent.

'I thought you'd see their game and retire,' he said lamely, drawing smoke from the coiled pipe of his hookah.

Augustine was covered with mud and filth from the tank. It smelled rank and stagnant. The grey mud was caked along the sleeve of his coat. The blood was still smeared down his cheek and stained the blue colour of his coat a deep purple. That morning both men had ridden out perfectly dressed. The one remained untouched, the other seemed to have been buried in the mud and then resurrected again.

'Is that your own blood?' asked Webley.

'You could say it was,' said Augustine.

He hadn't the heart to explain. He only wondered whether Webley cared. Of course he cared. Seventy of his men had died to no purpose. He was guilty. Not of their lives. It was Augustine's eagerness which had led them into the trap. But they had overcome the trap and almost succeeded. It was Webley's caution which had cost them the battle.

As Augustine left the tent, Mehboob Rashid stopped him.

'The men say you would have destroyed the English in another hour of fighting.'

Augustine stared at the Arab. His robes were spotless as well.

'How could a hundred men hope to wipe out that army?'

'He was frightened. As soon as you charged, he began to shake. I was standing beside him and I could see it in his face. That pale skin was streaming with sweat and looked whiter than ever. His horse felt his fear and began to fidget. I told him to follow you in, but he shook his head and bit his lip. Never have I seen him like that before. Not even in the most dangerous situation. But he was like a child before a beating, Colonel. My God, he was scared. I told him to let me chase you in, but again he shook his head, and in a voice that was as painful to the ears as metal scraping rock, he said that you'd never survive the battle.'

'And why didn't you follow me in, anyway?' asked Augustine.

The Arab curled his lips and frowned. 'Before you were halfway to the guns we knew it was a trap. We saw them moving the carts away from the batteries behind the redans. When the cannons went off, with that dull sound, I knew they were not loaded. Then we saw the English soldiers dashing out of the smoke and heading for the redans. Webley began to shiver all over. He said he didn't want to watch. Before you had even got clear of the smoke, he turned away from the scene and we rode back to camp.'

Augustine pushed his way past the Arab and headed for his tent. The smell of the mud seemed to be soaking into him. It nauseated him. He went behind his tent and vomited, with great heaves which seemed to suck out everything inside him and leave him just a shell.

The next morning Webley pushed the army north. After two days' marching they reached the Siwaliks. They climbed the range of low mountains and then dropped into the Dun. Webley knew of the Bijilli Gargh. It was deserted and they did not even have to break the hasps on the doors. He parked his army within those walls and let his fears and frustrations ferment.

~

Augustine's father had been ruthless. He could remember that. One of the stories he heard at Chittoor a few years before Trisuldas Thakur and Bibbi Charlotte were killed had made his spine coil tight like a spring. It wasn't fear or admiration, but a feeling which only a son can have towards his father, a sort of awe, an emotion both of pride and disgust, a contradictory feeling.

It had been a short battle, on a plain south of Chittoor. The enemy was a band of Pindaris, Muslim raiders who had intruded into the Rajput domain and refused to acknowledge the superiority of anyone. Trisuldas Thakur had ridden down on them with vengeance, killing them to a man, chasing the stragglers like rabbits and beheading them where they fell. The General had the corpses gathered together into a little pile in the middle of the plain, where there was a stone cairn about ten feet high, on top of which the Rajput colours had flown during the battle. Trisuldas had a monument erected on that spot, a cylindrical shrine, dedicated to one of the Rajput heroes. The wall was made of the stones of the cairn and the heads of the enemy. The mud was made from the blood of the Pindaris mixed with the urine of the Rajputs. A few of the survivors were kept alive to build this monument, and on its completion they were beheaded and thrown on top of the shrine. Trisuldas Thakur left this gruesome monument in the middle of the plain as a warning to all other intruders. The courtier who told Augustine this story said that the mud had washed away but there remained a cairn of skulls and stone, which could still be seen from a distance. The plain was supposed to be haunted by the ghosts of those Pindaris and Rajputs who had died. They fought on each night in a never-ending battle. Anyone who rode across the plain at dusk was killed and added to the pile.

The obscenity of that act, which his father had committed before Augustine was born, had always thrilled him in a peculiar way. He did not, revel in the memory and wish to emulate his father, but that cairn of rocks and skulls remained in his mind, far more vivid than the image of his father himself. Somehow the bloody details of that story, told to him long ago when he was sixteen, had imposed themselves on Augustine's memory of his father. It stood out much clearer than any of the battles they had shared or the atrocities he had witnessed. Those deaths and the horror of Trisuldas's revenge blended with the hatred Augustine had felt over his mother's death. It was like a many-layered passion, built out of the bloody details of his life, all stacked together like that cairn of heads. It was a brickwork of terror.

~

After the flood and the heavy storm the air cleared, and the mists seemed to be sucked up into the valleys. In the mountains behind the Bijilli Gargh there was the laughing sound of streams and springs which had broken out of the hillsides. The water stuttered as it fell on the rocks. The forests were green, a shiny green. The first ferns were coiling out of the ground like tiny green serpents. The moss had a dank smell, like wet fur.

There was a ridge overlooking the Bijilli Gargh, about two thousand feet above the fort. Above the plains, above the army of soldiers and hangers-on, there was a remote silence. It was like being out of range of everything.

An old trail curled up the ridge. Often Augustine would ride to the top for the view and the solitude. There were villages in the mountains but he avoided them, making his way through the jungle and underbrush which had overgrown the trail; sometimes he walked, sometimes he rode. He would leave his horse tied a hundred yards from the top and scramble up alone to sit for a few hours by himself. With the air clear he could see far off across the plains. The Jumna was spread to the right, in a lolling, twining course. At that distance all movement was arrested and the Jumna seemed asleep, suspended across the forested plains. To the left was the Ganges, wider than the Jumna and not as contorted. Its surface also shone like glass. But the Ganges seemed to be sheer power and movement. Though the individual currents, eddies, and rapids were indistinguishable, the river seemed to burst out of the mountains with force and determination.

The Ganges was all masculinity and the Jumna was like a woman, thought Augustine. Their sources were in the snow-covered Himalayas—massive peaks in a haphazard panorama. Beauty has no regularity. The sources of the two great rivers were hardly thirty miles apart and yet it took them hundreds of leisurely miles across the flatlands of Hindustan to meet at Prayag, or Allahabad, as the Muslims had named it. Their union was like two cobras mating, the waters swirling into each other. The rivers moved aimlessly across the sandy flood-lands and seemed to reach the ocean, not through destiny or any force of symbolism, but by chance.

From his seat on the ridge Augustine could see them running parallel into the horizon. It was like a detailed map, the sun highlighting certain places, the clouds shadowing others. The geography was intricate, the distances clear and stunning. Augustine felt he could almost reach out and draw in arrows and routes for the army. In his imagination he could see them manoeuvring back and forth across the plains.

The Siwaliks stood out firmly like a reef of mountains. They were a pale blue. Beyond them stretched the plains of the Doab, a strip of land bordered on either side by the two great rivers. It was a part of Hindustan that had seen endless skirmishes and battles. The farmers in the Doab had been well off at one time and the towns prosperous, but this attracted bands of outlaws and marauding princes eager to consume the wealth. Webley and his army had roamed through this territory and collected revenues from every village they passed. Until recently a northern part of the Doab had been their illegitimate jaghir. They swept back and forth across the land, exacting tribute from the landowners and small rajahs.

The farms were regularly razed, whenever the zamindaris could not come up with money as tribute. The zamindaris themselves became bandits and joined the roving armies of Jats, Gujars, and Pindaris who preyed off each other in vicious packs. They killed for anything from a few silver coins to a sack of flour. There were legal and illegal jaghirs all across the Doab, administered through brute force rather than politics. There were powerful rulers as well in the Doab: Begum Sombru, the Bharatpur Rajah, the Nawab of Farrukhabad ... At one time the Moguls had controlled it all with a legitimate and powerful government. But that empire had crumbled like plaster and its remains were strewn across the land, monuments of rubble.

To the west, across the Jumna, spread the Punjab, the fertile territory of the Sikhs. Augustine could almost make out the place where the Bata Naddi joined the Jumna. From a distance it looked so peaceful and green. But though the Sikhs controlled most of the land, and held it firmly, there was constant threat of invasion from the north. The Afghans from time to time swarmed down from the Hindu Kush and plundered the Punjab all the way to Delhi.

To the east, on the far side of the Ganges, was a heavily forested tract of land, the terai. Here there was little stability, little of anything except herds of elephants, deer, and wild boar. The tiger was supreme in the terai and roamed with his wild sovereignty, killing with instinct, as did all other rulers in Hindustan. In this area and to the south of the terai was Rohilkhand, where the Rohillas, ruthless tribes of warriors, plundered, fighting like animals with rapacity and instinct.

Other men seeing that landscape would have been filled with an ambition to control those lands, to own the Doab and administer it from a fortified capital, to build an army that could fight huge wars and campaigns, to accumulate wealth and foster progress. But Augustine was different from most men and though when he saw the panorama and the vast distances of the Doab, which seemed to be so close and immediate from the ridge, though he felt strongly moved, he had no desire to conquer that land. In fact, he regretted that it was parcelled out among the few rulers there were. He wished that all of that land were free, empty of government and laws. He hated forts and palaces, courts and the men that ruled from them. He wanted the land to be left naked and unravished, for his own purposes. Augustine saw those distances and wanted only to move across them without perimeters and borders, without legality or illegality, with only his horse and his sword. It would be a land of no politics. Violence would foster violence and there would be only the arbitration of the sword. In that world of chaos there would be true nobility, fostered by the vanity of each man to himself.

Augustine began to make a sound, like a child learning to form its first word. Inside him was an animal roar, of fear and frustration. Before it left the hollow of his stomach he heard it echo through the mountains, gathering force like thunder. He stopped himself and listened to his own voice. It was still trapped inside him, like the sound in a drum, pulsating, as if ready to burst him open. But like a drum it was also outside him, bombarding the immense territory of the sky. He felt as though he was the centre of the sound, the silent source of the noise. It made him feel so small and yet so powerful. It was not the roar of an army but the roar of one man, alone and remote, isolated on the ridge.

∽

Augustine learned to cry from his mother. She was a strong woman, tall and red-haired. Her skin was pale, and when she darkened her eyes with kajal, she had a ghostly beauty. The fire of her hair seemed to burst about her. Augustine remembered going to her room often and finding her with her hair teased out around her head, her eyes sunken from crying, and her teeth yellow as old ivory. But she cried not from loneliness. She loved the court at Chittoor. She loved the ladies that waited on her. She loved the clothes her husband bought her, the yards and yards of silk and linen and gauze. Bibbi Charlotte cried not because she was lonely or because she wanted to return to England, but because she loved everything she had. She loved her son, her husband, her apartment in the zenana. She loved the colours and lights, fireworks, and kites on the wind. She loved the dust storms of Rajasthan, that umber colour that filled the air, the clouds of sand sweeping around the fort, blotting out the sun. She loved the heat. She loved to lie in her room in the lightest cotton robe and feel it cling to her body. She loved to drink sherbet from the tall silver decanters and feel the soft breeze from the fans of peacock feathers, which her maidservants swept back and forth over her as she lay in complete languor during the summer months.

All of these things brought tears to Bibbi Charlotte's eyes. Whenever Augustine would enter her apartments, she would grab him and clutch him to her breasts. The tears would roll down her white cheeks and baptize his forehead with a mother's emotions. Augustine, who never cried when he was knocked down or hurt himself, who never cried when there was a death in the court—there were many—would look up at his mother and feel the tears gush out naturally. The two of them would sit and cry and all the while be laughing and playing. When Augustine's father would march his army out, they would watch through the intricate screens in the zenana and see Trisuldas Thakur, with his grey moustaches puffed up on his cheeks, riding out ahead of his men. Bibbi Charlotte would begin to cry and so would Augustine. It was not out of fear, but out of vanity and pride. What made some men sneer and cock their heads made Augustine weep.

With other women, so much crying would have made them ugly. But Bibbi Charlotte was not miserable and the tears gave her a look of raw beauty. Her hair never stayed combed and would spray from all sides of her head. Her face, long and finely sculptured, had no lines on it but was like a carved face. Her lips and mouth stained red with paan had a cruel beauty to them. But those wet, red eyes in the midst of all the fury and passion of her face seemed to be child-like and innocent.

It was a sense of melodrama which brought out the tears in Bibbi Charlotte. Within the pampered atmosphere of the zenana, only her imagination could experience her husband's life. What she saw through the filigree of screens was a world of grandeur and nobility. Her separation from it gave her a distant and romantic vision of the Rajput armies. Even when she travelled it was in the seclusion of her palanquin, with the thick brocade curtains around her. The dark perfumes seeped out of the cushions and filled her tiny universe with an artificial atmosphere. Her tents were thickly walled and the insides were lined with patterned materials of bright colours. Tapestries were hung inside the flies of the tent. It was a world of cloth, layers and layers of cloth, from the fine muslin petticoats she wore to the heavy, stiff canvas of the tents.

Bibbi Charlotte filled Augustine with a sense of melodrama. He found that his vanity took the form of tears. A mixture of emotions would overwhelm Augustine. Often he would hear his mother's sobs in his ear, as if she were crying with him. At that sound he would heave with an impulse of drama and sentiment. It was not a simple, flimsy emotion but something huge and important. It was not a woman's emotion either, for Bibbi Charlotte was not an ordinary woman. She would not have cried if someone insulted her or a needle pricked her finger. Her tears were like the rain from a storm, full and heavy.

Vanity controls a man completely. No one can quite master his own pride. It determines the style in which a man carries himself, on which side of his head he parts his hair, whether he holds his pipe between his thumb and forefinger or by the bowl or between his first and second fingers. Vanity governs his fashions, whether he conforms to those around him or whether he contradicts a trend. Vanity controls everything about a man from the smallest habit to the most enormous sin.

Augustine's vanity was swollen. It was so large that it tried to swallow time and history. His vanity was bred in the illusory world of Bibbi Charlotte's apartments. He set himself up in relationship to a world which did not exist, the world beyond the filigree and patterns of the carved screens through which his mother saw nothing but grandeur and pageantry. Augustine was not a little man. He was tall and powerful, but he had set himself up against impossible giants. He had decided to face realities as something greater than what they were. He believed that history was as great in the making as it was in retrospect; that the process of history had the magnificence of its accounts. Reality defeats most men, and only a few dare challenge it with their own imagination.

Augustine learned nothing but disappointment. He had to leave the zenana eventually. He had to leave the ridge from where he could see all of Hindustan spread out in its great distances and go down to the decrepit fort with its mildew and damp. Distances trapped him with a vision of infinite possibilities. He wanted to roam like a marauding tiger, but those distances were hemmed in by conflict and politics.

His emotions were like tinder these days and it took all his strength to control them. In the middle of a conversation he would find himself crying. It was not out of any fear, hatred, or sorrow, but just a current plunging into his body, a current which made him fill his lungs with a gasp of air, made him sit erect. The emotion was like an auger reaming its way up his spine.

∽

Augustine had known nothing but war. His father had died

fighting. From his earliest memories he had been taught to fight, taught to hold a sword and fire a musket. His toys had been scale models of his father's weapons. He had duelled and fenced with playmates and staged mock executions. As a boy he had been treated as a miniature man. What had been expected of him was what his father expected of every soldier in the Rajput army.

When Augustine turned six, his father assigned him a teacher, a dwarf, Somdas. He was exactly Augustine's size, hardly three and a half feet tall. Somdas was a vicious man, frustrated and bitter. He clung to himself furiously and hated any man taller than he. Between the boy and the dwarf developed a relationship which could have existed only between two men of such different ages. Somdas was sixty, a taut package of muscle. He had a bristly grey beard which sprouted out in all directions. His eyes were like live coals and Augustine could remember being hypnotized by those eyes as the two of them fought. Somdas would fix his eyes on Augustine and trap his vision. Once he had the boy caught with his stare, he would slap the sword out of Augustine's hand and then fall on him with abuse and blows.

'Don't look at me,' he would scream, his voice like a parakeet's. 'Don't look at me, boy. It will cost you your life.'

So Augustine learned to keep his eyes moving over his opponent, only fixing his stare on a man when he was ready to kill. Now that he had only the one eye, it was easier. The glass ball would hold whomever he fought in its unblinking gaze. It frightened the fiercest men. Augustine had learned to use it.

From Somdas he learned many things. He learned wrestling. The stocky dwarf loved to throw Augustine over his shoulder. His size allowed him few opponents, and now that he had the boy as his student, he took every opportunity to use his strength on someone his own size. The dwarf was tough as a gnarled scrub oak. His muscles stood out on his stocky body, each one round and hard as a stone. He and Augustine would put on langotis and fight for hours. The dwarf never let the boy win, but always threw him off with all his strength. There was no feeling of sympathy, and Augustine learned not to cry at pain. He learned pride from the dwarf. He was proud of his teacher and proud of himself. When his father would come to visit, Augustine and Somdas would stand beside each other, the dwarf dressed in a gaudy uniform of sequins and badges, with a miniature sword at his side and an enormous turban on his already oversized head. Augustine wore a replica of his father's uniform, a flowing shirt, with a velvet tunic, a bandolier, and a tight salwar pleated over his legs. He also wore a turban, a small tight turban, a peacock feather pinned in front with a jewelled brooch. Whenever Augustine's father had a set of clothes made, he ordered a duplicate for his son, in the same style.

Augustine saw his father seldom, and when they were together there was very little affection between them. He saw his father as a general, as if always through the filigree screen, marching his men under Bibbi Charlotte's window.

Augustine grew up quickly and his height almost doubled in eight years. Somdas taught him until he was twelve and then told him to teach himself. By then the dwarf was a foot shorter than Augustine. Augustine felt guilty, as if in this way he had surpassed his teacher. The little dwarf remained in the court and always had a smile for Augustine. But his furious pride grew into a hatred for the boy, who now towered above him.

It was obsessively on Somdas's mind that Augustine, this boy of six, had become a man while he, now over sixty, still had a body as squat and restricted as Augustine's had been when he first came to the dwarf for lessons. He was too proud to show his resentment. He had had other students and they had all outgrown him. But it was as if he had hoped that this last time, just once, the boy would remain a boy so that he could go on fighting with him, using miniature swords, so that they could continue wrestling forever, so that Somdas could always look his student in the eye and sear him with a stare. That frustration, which pumped the dwarf up like a bladder and then exploded him, once again swelled him up and then destroyed him. A year after Augustine's father brought his son a full-sized sword, Somdas lay down on his bed, complaining of pains in his ankles and knees. Within a few weeks he was completely crippled. It was as though the muscles which he had built up and hardened had all seized him and now pinned him down. His body, as always, had betrayed him.

Augustine went to see the dwarf before he died. Lying on his tiny cot, his little form covered by a quilt, Somdas seemed all head. It was as if his skull had expanded. Augustine could make out the small outline of his body under the quilt. But he had never realized how enormous Somdas's head was. The eyes were the same, the nose bulbous, the lips flat and wide.

His whole life he had been mocked, made a fool of in the court. With the vanity of a whippet, he would pull out his sword and challenge whoever insulted him. The challenge would never be taken because it was not cowardly but instead generous to let Somdas off with only a cruel word and a look of disdain. The tiny sword would flash arrogantly, but no one would cross it with theirs.

Somdas said very little to his pupil. He looked up at him with a tired expression on his face. 'What have you come for?' he asked.

'To see you,' said Augustine.

'To see me finally defeated,' said the dwarf. 'You tried since you were six to beat me. You tried to throw me, tried to knock the sword out of my hand, tried to shoot better than I. That is what a student must do. He must laugh behind the back of his teacher, and you have. A teacher must give a student vanity, and the only way he can do that is by letting the student defeat him in the end. It is rubbish what they say about a student's respect for his teacher. Who believes that? A student must hate his teacher. He must destroy him.'

'No,' said Augustine. 'For me you are still my teacher.'

Somdas struggled under his quilt and with difficulty pulled out his gnarled hand. 'That is what you came to see, isn't it? They are talking about me in court, are they not? You heard them say that I couldn't move, that I am now a cripple. Well, it is true. You see that hand. Remember how it held a sword? I can no longer open it.'

Augustine spun around on his heels and walked out. Behind him he heard the dwarf's brittle laugh.

3

The hunting party had left ahead of Augustine. In the distance he could see a cluster of horses, followed by a throng of men on foot, beaters and servants. The party waded through the underbrush. He urged his horse after them. The sharpness of the morning made Augustine feel as though he were riding through a pane of glass. He and the horse seemed to shatter the air around them. At a gallop, they gained on the hunting party. The beaters were loping behind in an awkward sort of run as they tried to avoid the thickets of brambles and thorns.

Augustine gave a shout as he came in range. The party stopped and turned to watch him ride up. He cocked his head arrogantly, focusing his blind eye on the horsemen. He rode erect, with one hand on his hip and the other holding the reins loosely. The other riders were all postured as well, as if posing for portraits. Their horses waltzed in place impatiently.

'I didn't think you were coming,' said Webley.

He was dressed in a pink jacket and had tied a turban of the same colour silk around his head, covering his baldness and giving him the appearance of a tight-faced spinster. The turban seemed to have pulled the skin on his face taut over the bones of his skull. He carried a short Mahratta lance thrust in a notch in his stirrup, with the blade on a level with his face, so that it gleamed along with his eyes and made them seem even brighter and more evil.

On one side of Webley rode Pratap Bahadur. His horse was larger than any of the others, a clumsy animal he had chosen from the stables. Pratap Bahadur was not used to riding and he sat with an air of uncomfortable arrogance, like a boy king on his throne.

On the other side of Webley rode Mehboob Rashid, dressed in a billowy robe of soft muslin embroidered with gold thread. He wore a head scarf which hid most of his face, except for his Semitic nose. His eyebrows were heavy and low on his forehead. His beard was trimmed close to his face and came to a sharp point. He did not look at Augustine but stared off at some point in the distance.

Each of us has his style of vanity, thought Augustine. For Webley it is a nervous, agitated arrogance. He moves like a stone skittering across the water. In him there is a taut spring which can explode at any moment. He is excited by himself. Mehboob Rashid has a clipped vanity like that of a cat, with no recognition of others, save a challenge or an insult. Pratap Bahadur has the vanity of a little man. He is as exuberant as Webley. His height is everything, and like a little boy among adults he is always jumping up and down, trying to reach their level and attract attention.

Augustine knew nothing of his own vanity. Perhaps he was the most vain among them, though no one would have supposed it. He had dignity and never made a fool of himself, but he was familiar with his men and only cut short those he knew well and disliked. New acquaintances were always met with a quiet, unassuming manner. But behind that, there was a vanity as jagged and sharp as the crystals inside a geode. Augustine's vanity was not the sort which attached itself to specific things. It was an all-consuming pride. It swelled inside him like the roar he had heard come from within himself that day in the mountains. He had no race or king to be proud of. He was loyal to Webley and admired him. He despised Pratap Bahadur and Mehboob Rashid. It was not a blind vanity. He did not compare himself to others. Augustine's vanity consisted of a strong confidence in himself and an exaggerated impression of the world. He saw the tawdry, minor parts of life as great things. For him there was melodrama in all relationships. Augustine's vanity placed him among great things and great occurrences, so that he himself was great.

At the edge of the forest the horsemen stopped. The syces riding spare horses dismounted and squatted down in the shade of a leafy tree. Spears were chosen, guns loaded, and girths tightened. No one spoke and the only sounds were the impatient breathing of the horses and the squeaking of leather and metal. At a signal the beaters moved into the trees, single file. They disappeared as silently as a herd of deer.

Each of the four men was excited in his own way. Pratap Bahadur's horse stood perfectly still, but its rider squirmed in the saddle, turning about eagerly and waving his hands to stop the shaking. The other three showed their anticipation by being completely calm. They were like leaves waiting for the wind.

A low cooee sounded far inside the forest. The beaters began to move towards the hunters, driving game ahead of them as they came. There was a tense moment in which the sounds of the beaters' voices and the noise of sticks and axes hitting the trees echoed across the grassy plain. Then there was a shriek and the noise increased. An animal had broken cover. It doubled back and dashed through the line of beaters, escaping farther into the forest.

'Sambar,' said Webley. 'They have lost him.'

A few seconds later there was a crashing in the forest and a sounder of six wild boars rushed into the open. The riders waited until the pigs were a safe distance from the trees and then all four of them galloped out in pursuit. The grass was high and none of them could tell if the ground was safe or not. There were old wells and ditches hidden under the scrub, but the horses avoided what dangers they sensed, all racing madly together. Augustine pulled ahead by a few yards, keeping himself low in the saddle, his eye fixed on the ground ahead. He gained a little with each stride. Pratap Bahadur fell back. Webley and Mehboob Rashid were side by side.

A large boar broke away from the others and began to cut across to a thicket on the left. Augustine veered after him. He was not more than twenty yards behind the boar. Webley and Mehboob Rashid followed at about the same distance behind Augustine. As the boar began to slow up, Augustine changed his grip on the lance and braced himself in the saddle. Without warning the boar whirled around, its hooves skidding in the dirt and the grass flying to all sides. Augustine was almost on top of him. The boar charged at the horse, meeting the lance-head a little low, at the base of his neck. The force of the charge and the speed at which the horse was going drove the blade completely through the boar, lifting its feet off the ground. The spear broke a few inches from Augustine's hand. Webley and Mehboob Rashid hurtled past him, carried on by the momentum of the chase. They pulled up a distance ahead and then rode back to meet Augustine. The boar was quivering in the last fits of life, its blood staining the trampled grass. Augustine raised the broken lance above his head and laughed. Pratap Bahadur rode up next to him and slapped him on the back. Webley smiled. Mehboob Rashid was looking into the distance again. This time he was watching a herd of spotted deer disappear into another stretch of jungle.

It was the way Augustine liked to kill, at full speed, and with only enough time for instinct to guide him. He liked it to be over fast, the animal dead, everything complete in a few seconds. Those seconds went by so quickly that his memory could never catch them. For Augustine speed erased time. His actions had to be furious ones in which he lost control of himself. Like an epileptic, his memory never retained those seconds during which he spun into madness.

The next stretch of jungle produced another sounder of boar, larger than the first. Pratap Bahadur killed a heavy sow. It happened by chance. He was riding behind again, not able to keep up with the other three. They chased the boars out into the centre of the plain and were riding close behind them when the sow whipped around and reversed direction. Mehboob Rashid was a length ahead of the others and his spear went over her back. She dove between the legs of his horse, sending it sprawling forward. The Arab went over its head and landed unhurt in a clump of elephant grass. Augustine and Webley had no time to react and had to turn aside for fear of trampling Mehboob Rashid.

Pratap Bahadur was struggling to keep up, thirty yards behind. The sow, after tumbling Mehboob Rashid, came right for the Gurkha. He was surprised to find himself alone with a chance to kill the pig. Brave, despite his size, he pressed his legs into the broad flanks of his giant horse and leaned with all his strength, placing the spear far back on the sow's body, just ahead of her haunches. She squealed madly and crashed into a bramble bush, the spear still sticking out of her side. Dragging herself through the thorn bushes, she dislodged the spear and headed off in the direction of the forest.

Pratap Bahadur unsheathed the silver blade of his kukri—sixteen inches of lethal steel. With a Gurkhali war cry he galloped after the sow. She was losing blood and limping. Pratap Bahadur gained on her and, pulling his horse to one side, swept past her, leaning as far down as he could and taking a vicious swipe at her with the kukri. A red slice opened up on the sow's shoulder and she squealed again.

With some trouble Pratap Bahadur got his horse turned around and came back at the sow, who had gone mad with pain and was running in tighter and tighter circles, painting the high grass scarlet with her blood. Another cut from the kukri knocked her down.

The little man was off his horse in a minute. He ran up to the dying sow, her maddened eyes like poison berries. The kukri, no longer silver but stained red, glinted dully as it rose and fell, hacking the animal to death.

He kills like a little man, thought Augustine. There is fury in the way he rides but no grace or style, only frustration. If he had not killed that sow, he would have killed himself. For a man like him, death is all that matters. He is like a mongoose battling a cobra. The cobra strikes with vanity and sways in an arrogant dance. The mongoose bares his teeth in an ugly grin and fights viciously, without beauty or nobility. There was nothing noble in the way that Pratap Bahadur cut the pig to pieces.

Mehboob Rashid stood where he fell. He did not brush the dirt off his robes but stood poised, watching the spectacle of the sow's death.

The next kill was Mehboob Rashid's. He took a musket from one of the men and, carrying it in one hand, rode out alone onto the plain. The next beat produced more boar but he ignored them, sitting erect in his saddle, his white robes blowing casually in the wind. A few seconds after the boar, three blackbucks soared into the open, leaping high over the elephant grass. Mehboob Rashid was after them without hesitation. He was on a fresh horse. The other had been ruined in the fall.

The antelope were a hundred yards from him. His horse was a chestnut stallion with a pale mane. As they chased the antelopes, the horse and rider looked like a cloud racing across the field. The plain was about a mile wide in all directions and soon the Arab was only a white speck against the background of mountains. Suddenly Augustine saw him wheel. The antelopes had turned and were circling around, almost as if they were taunting the hunter. Mehboob Rashid grew larger and larger. He had gained twenty-five yards on the antelopes. He was in range now, but it would be an impossible shot from horseback, trying to aim at the antelopes as they soared through the air with great arching leaps.

The blackbucks swept past where Augustine and Webley were standing. Pratap Bahadur had not left his precious sow and was standing guard over it, recounting the story over and over to the syces, who listened with dumb enthusiasm.

Mehboob Rashid waited until he was directly in front of Augustine and Webley. They saw him raise the gun to his shoulder and fire carefully but without effort. One of the antelopes folded in midair, collapsing on the ground, a tangle of legs and horns. It let out a low groan and died, still kicking in an imitation of its run. The other two blackbucks stopped at a distance and then raced on. They were out of sight in a few seconds. Mehboob Rashid did not even look at his kill but turned away indignantly, as if it was a rat he had killed, or a spider. He rode over to the group of syces and gun-bearers, handing the empty weapon to one of them, ignoring their praise.

'He shoots well,' said Webley, 'as if he was certain of every shot. He had to shoot it, too, if he cared for his dinner.'

'He is missing something when he refuses pork. That antelope will be dry and tough,' said Augustine.

'Well, we won't see any of that sow. The little man is likely to keep it as a pet.'

Webley killed a chital stag in the next beat. They hunted all morning until noon. Mehboob Rashid's buck was skinned and butchered. The beaters built a fire and roasted the meat over its coals. Webley, Augustine, and Pratap Bahadur ate first, washing down the dry meat with swigs from bottles of port and claret. Mehboob Rashid took a shank of meat and went off a distance. He ate with his back to the group and drank only water. When they were finished, the beaters and syces attacked the carcass, and before long it was nothing more than scattered bones.

Augustine went over to inspect the morning's kill. There were five boar, two chital, a sambar stag, two porcupines, a barking deer, and several brace of jungle cocks.

The first beat of the afternoon produced nothing.

'We haven't killed them all, have we?' Webley asked.

'They say there is a leopard in this next strip of jungle. The men saw it sneak in there this morning,' Augustine said.

The four hunters chose their lances. Augustine took a lighter one this time. If it is a leopard, then I must be quick, he thought. Only the beaters with axes and spears went into the jungle. They were nervous and some of them even turned back at the edge of the scrub. Pratap Bahadur left his sow for a chance at the leopard. Even he stood firmly beside his horse without moving. Everyone was stem except for Webley. Augustine could tell that he had chosen the leopard as his kill. Nothing would stop him in this chase.

Webley flung himself into his saddle and grinned at Mehboob Rashid, who paid him no attention. Augustine decided to trade his spear for a musket. One of the men came running through the grass and handed it up to him.

'You are a cautious man, my Colonel,' said Webley.

'Occasionally I have found it pays,' answered Augustine.

Mehboob Rashid looked at both of them and then glanced at his sword. It was the same one he had used to murder a courtier in Baroda. The sheath was of tooled leather, frayed and cut in places. There were gold and silver ornaments, tarnished almost black, decorating the sheath. The Arab's expression remained as solemn and as dignified as ever, and distant as the horizon. He must be thinking about us, Augustine said to himself. Perhaps he is thinking of Deoband. Did he argue with Webley about following us into the smoke? Was he frightened? Behind his cold stare there is nothing but fear. He could have taken his column into the smoke and together we could have chased the British from there to Delhi. But he stayed with Webley and retreated with him, leaving us to our fate. Mehboob Rashid is a coward, though he fights himself valiantly. He is unable to show his emotions, not because he has none, but because he is afraid of them.

Images from the battle at Deoband flashed in front of Augustine. He saw Webley sitting on his horse, with the telescope in his hand. Now he looked so different, waiting for the leopard, defiant and joking. The danger seemed to animate him. Few men were as brave as he was. But then why had he cowered in front of the British? They say that a man can sense his own death. Had he smelled it in the English powder?

The leopard did not leave cover until the beaters were almost out of the jungle themselves. It came out stealthily and ducked into a patch of grass. One of the beaters followed it out, unaware, looking puzzled. He carried a scythe in his hand. Augustine was about to shout to him when he saw the leopard re-emerge from the grass, like a phantom. The man was standing with his back to the leopard. It crept up in a few quick strides and then, rising on its hind legs, took hold of the beater by the back of the neck. One bite and the man dropped without a sound. The leopard was gone before he touched the ground. They had all seen it and a cry started up among the beaters and syces. But no one dared go to help the man.

'He'll be dead for sure,' said Webley. Then without warning he was off in the direction of the leopard. Pratap Bahadur raced after him, followed by Augustine and Mehboob Rashid. Webley had a wide lead and lengthened it over the distance. Augustine and Mehboob Rashid passed the Gurkha and left him in their dust. Pratap Bahadur pulled up and stopped.

The leopard had moved from the grass to a stand of shisham trees. Webley saw its tail disappearing and followed boldly after it. He was about fifty yards from the trees when the leopard came out at him. It jogged into the sunlight, its dappled coat glistening. Webley lowered himself and rode directly at it, dropping his spear to a level with the cat. It sprang without warning and was in the air, a maddened comet of yellow fur. Webley's horse was a very steady hunter, but it lost its nerve and ducked aside just as the leopard took to the air. Webley's spear went wide of its mark and the leopard brushed his shoulder and passed over the horse.

Augustine and Mehboob Rashid reined up a little distance away and watched nervously. Webley pulled his horse back under control and turned on the leopard. It was gone.

Very slowly the Englishman moved forward. His horse stepped gingerly, lifting its hooves high as it walked. There was no sound. Augustine scanned the field for movement, but there was none. The leopard was the colour of the grass and seemed to have melted into the landscape. Webley edged forward, his lance sticking out a few inches in front of the horse's nose. Augustine could tell Webley was frightened, but he disguised it well. He threw a smile at Mehboob Rashid and cocked his head.

He looks like a spaniel, thought Augustine, with his hair hanging down like ears on either side of his pink turban. He was the opposite of the leopard. The cat blended into the scene while Webley clashed with the colours of the jungle and stood out brightly, with an obnoxious vanity, a disregard for nature, as if he expected everything to conform to his fashion. There was no thought of disguise or camouflage in his costume. The pink coat and headgear could be seen for a mile. The way he rode, too, was obnoxious. Mehboob Rashid had seemed to move over the field as if he were a part of it. When he rode he, the horse, the wind, the grass, and the dust were all one. It was as if he burst from the earth, Webley was the opposite. He rode well but it was always as a rider. Never did he seem to be a part of his horse or his surroundings. Augustine had realized when the Arab was chasing his blackbuck that he had almost become a part of his quarry. Not Webley. He was aloof. His vanity separated him and distinguished him from that around him. He burst onto the field, as if he were going to level it. In him there was the spirit of strength and destruction.

The air seemed to have been stretched taut over the landscape. Augustine felt as if he were looking through waxed paper. The yellows and tans of the landscape all merged out of focus and only Webley stood out sharp and clear. The leopard seemed to have become the landscape. Every blade of grass was a whisker, every shadow a rosette of spots, every dusty patch a part of its underbelly, every pebble an eye.

With a hoarse cough the leopard exploded out of the bushes behind Webley. It had circled around and attacked him from where he least expected. He was completely vulnerable. The horse had not time to turn. Webley swivelled in his saddle, trying to spear the leopard. But the cat had taken hold of the horse's rump and had dug its claws into the horse's flanks. For an awful moment it hung there, with an awkward expectancy. The horse lashed out with its hooves, trying to dislodge the leopard, but this only brought the cat to life again. Clinging to the horse's haunches with its forepaws, the leopard began to claw wildly with its hind legs, cutting the horse's thighs to shreds. The poor animal began to buck and it was all Webley could do to hold on. Augustine saw him vainly trying to unsheath his sword. There was no chance to shoot the leopard without endangering Webley, but Augustine pressed the musket to his cheek and waited.

Mehboob Rashid prodded his horse forward. His sword, a curved and shining crescent, glistened in his hand. He broke into a gallop. The leopard had crippled Webley's horse and brought it to the ground. Webley tried to roll off but his foot caught in the stirrup and his leg was pinned under the weight of the horse. Augustine could see the man and leopard glaring at each other. The horse's eyes were frantic. Webley was still trying to get his sword unsheathed, but it, too, was pinned under the horse.

The leopard whirled on the Arab at the last moment, but the sword caught it just below the chin and clipped its head off as neatly as though it had been a melon. The decapitated body went into a contorted dance, the tail striking out like a serpent, the claws flashing in the sun, and a steady stream of blood vomiting from its neck.

Webley extricated himself from under the horse and limped away, not taking another look at the leopard or Mehboob Rashid. His leg was dragging but not broken. Augustine walked his horse over to the dead leopard. The dance was over and the body lay ten yards from the head, blood spattered around. Augustine raised his musket and killed Webley's horse. It was the part of hunting he disliked—ruining the horses.

There was the sound of galloping. Augustine looked up to see Webley racing across the plain, the bright pink of his clothes flashing away into the distance. He was heading towards the Bijilli Gargh.

The animals were gathered up in a short time and Augustine led the party back to the fort. They moved slowly now, in single file, the dead animals slung on poles. Even Pratap Bahadur kept silent on the way back. A syce had stuck the leopard's head on a spear and carried it aloft like a standard. The excitement was over, the blood spilt. The long grass swished around the legs of the riders. It had a dry, crisp sound, menacing.

∽

'That damned selfish Arab!' screamed Webley.

'He saved your life,' said Augustine.

'So what, I saved his. He could have let me save my own, damn it. Now look at me. Just look at me. I couldn't kill a leopard. Do you know what the men will say? I am a coward. The Arab had to rescue me.'

'No one will say that. Though they may call you a fool.'

'You're calling me a fool?' Webley's voice was like a rusty hinge.

'Yes, I am. A drunken fool.'

'Get out of here. I'll have you all killed. All of you. I'll feed you to a hundred leopards and let them tear you apart. You're the coward. You had to carry a musket. Why did you carry a musket, Colonel? Were you afraid? Why did you carry a musket instead of a spear?'

'To shoot your horse,' said Augustine, turning and walking out of Webley's room. The Englishman was spread out on a hillock of pillows. He was drunk. Half a bottle of arrack stood beside him. His pale hands clutched it frantically and lifted it to his lips. He glared at Augustine, who turned briefly at the door.

'You tell that Arab I'll have him shot out of a cannon,' said Webley. 'I should have allowed it to be done back then. He took my leopard from me. He killed it like a coward, with that sword of his. At least he could have let me die like a man. A leopard kills well'—Webley's voice became hushed and childlike. 'You saw how it killed that beater. A noble death. I can feel its teeth on my throat. I can feel it embrace me. I can feel my neck snap between its teeth. Goddamn that Arab! Goddamn him!'

ᔑ

The best friend of the Gaekwad's heir raped the youngest of Mehboob Rashid's wives. Without hesitation the Arab lopped off the young courtier's head. It happened in daylight, in full view of everyone. The Gaekwad's son had Mehboob Rashid taken prisoner and within a few hours he was tied across the mouth of a loaded cannon to be shot to pieces.

Webley was in his suite when he heard the news. He rushed up onto the ramparts. There he found the Gaekwad's son standing in front of Mehboob Rashid, who had been stripped naked and bound with his back to the cannon's muzzle. The Prince was spitting and cursing the Arab. Webley stepped up from behind and casually put his sword between the Prince's legs. The guards drew back. Webley hooked an arm around the Prince's neck and told one of the gunners to untie Mehboob Rashid. The Prince, fearing for his genitals, stood stock still, shivering. Once the Arab was cut loose, the three of them walked to Webley's suite.

Augustine had received news of the incident and hurried out just in time to see the strange procession moving along the battlements. Mehboob Rashid, walking naked and proud, led the way, followed by the Prince, stepping gingerly because of the blade between his thighs. Webley prodded him on from behind.

The insult to the Prince endangered all of their lives. That evening the Gaekwad made his mercenaries prisoners in their rooms, threatening to execute both Webley and Mehboob Rashid. Augustine arranged an escape. The men guarding him were from his own regiment. They agreed to let him go and escape with him. A mutiny was started, and early the next morning Webley, Mehboob Rashid, and Augustine rode out of the gate with a small army behind them. Mehboob Rashid's wives and those of his men also rode out in palanquins. There was a short skirmish with the Gaekwad's bodyguard but the mutineers escaped unharmed. From then on, the three officers were their own men. They fought for themselves. Webley was older than both Augustine and Mehboob Rashid. He had been their senior under Gaekwad and became the leader of their band.

When Augustine checked on Webley the next morning, he was asleep. He woke around noon and began drinking again. Nothing would stop him. Servants brought bottles of arrack, port, brandy, and local liquors up to his room. Webley sat transfixed for hours like an imbecile alchemist, measuring out his liquor patiently, stirring in sugar and other spirits. He would then drink his concoctions carefully, with a blurred but judicious eye. He did not seem to notice anyone who came into the room, and mumbled to himself like a baby.

It was not like him. He had had drinking bouts before, but they were always orgies, full of laughter and other friends. Everyone would fill his tent and lounge around in a stupor for days. Those were gay parties and Webley was the centre of them, full of jokes and puns. The alcohol seemed to animate him and he would giggle without stopping for hours. There would be women and young boys, dancing and serving the guests. All day music would shake the tent and pitchers of punch were poured out like water into the emptied cups. Once the gaiety had become so wild that Webley's tent had collapsed, the central pole toppling over like the mast of a sinking ship.

The orgies were always over in a week and Webley would be sick for a few days and then sober again. While they went on, Augustine and Mehboob Rashid handled the army. The soldiers expected it and would laugh about Webley's drinking without malice. Augustine knew that Mehboob Rashid despised these parties and drunkenness. They never spoke about it to each other.

This time it was different. Webley was alone. He never laughed. His personality faded with the liquor as though, instead of sparking the fire in him, it drowned it. His mind was diluted and he had to be taken care of like an invalid. He vomited on the cushions and then lay in his own filth. He urinated in his trousers. When Augustine pointed it out to him, he giggled with embarrassment.

4

It was about ten o'clock in the evening when Webley's bearer came to Augustine's room. He said that Webley wanted him to come immediately.

The Englishman was lying on a couch, propped up by two pillows. He was still drunk and smelled of vomit and urine. His faint blue eyes seemed to have sunk far into his skull. When he spoke he drooled.

'It's not good to be alone,' said Webley. 'I mean, it's different in a fort like this. The walls, Augustine, the walls. It's like a prison. I think I'll pitch a tent out in the courtyard and stay there. I can't take the walls. They drip and ooze with the damp.'

Augustine took the bottle away from Webley and then sat down on a stool.

'Yes, take it away,' said Webley. 'Take it all away and then hang me out to dry. What can a man do but drink in this place? Go tell them to pitch my tent, Augustine. I won't be able to sleep unless I have canvas around me. I want to be able to tear down my walls in the morning and put them up at night. I want to ride all day.'

'There's nothing keeping us here,' said Augustine.

"Only the rains and the British.'

'We've spent every other monsoon in tents, and what will the English do to us?' asked Augustine.

Webley ignored him. He lay on his back and stared at the ceiling.

'Augustine, why do you believe in things? You're so goddamn gullible. I've learned to distrust everything. India teaches you that. What seems exotic is nothing but plain things polished up. All that glitters … what are we doing here? We're nothing but bandits. Scum. You think we're an army.'

'You could be the finest general in Hindustan,' said Augustine, 'if you weren't afraid of the British.'

'Me? What do you know about me, Colonel? How do you know what frightens me?' Webley coughed. 'The Company Bahadur … hah, hah, the Company … Bhanchod!'

~

Eighteen years ago an East Indiaman docked at Calcutta. It was filled with young officers for the Company's army. Webley was among them, older than the rest by five or six years. As the cadets spewed off the ship into the muggy Calcutta air, there were cries of horror and dismay at the filth, the crowds of Bengalis, the kites and other birds swooping viciously through the air, and the atmosphere of diseased torpor. It was as if nothing moved without effort. The air was thick and the sun seemed to melt everything into an ooze. The cadets pulled off their jackets and loosened their collars, watching helplessly as their bags were dragged off by coolies in different directions. This was not the India any of them had expected. The India of their imaginations was filled with dancing girls with tails which twined around you when you made love to them, and diamonds which grew in pods on vines, like peas.

Webley was beginning to go bald even at that age, but he had his hair plastered arrogantly over the spot. He stood there and waited for his bags to be taken down. You would have thought he was a general from the way he stood. On the voyage over he had kept aloof from the other cadets.

The freedom of being off the ship was exhilarating. Augustine had never been on a ship. He could not imagine what it was like. 'It's hell, like being in the belly of a monster, the air foul and the deck slippery,' said Webley. The tropical air, the muddy smell of the Hooghly, and the noises made his emotions surge. This was Bengal, a place he had heard much about. He was not disappointed by the docks. It was hot and his silk collar chaffed at his neck, but he hardly felt it. The sweat collected on his eyebrows and trickled down into his eyes. But he didn't undo even a button on his jacket, nor did he wince at the sight of a leprous beggar minus his legs, tugging at his boot. Webley stood calm and firm as if he had seen the docks a hundred times. But inside him the excitement threatened to erupt like a volcano.

'My uncle had come back from Bengal with a fortune and two brown sons. He had bought a house in the country, not far from ours. This uncle was something of a black sheep. He had lost his inheritance in America. But he was more of a Jew than a gentleman, so instead of shooting himself, he borrowed money and sailed for Bengal. Wits and a fast tongue landed him a job with one of the rajahs and he was soon earning, embezzling, and enjoying the pleasures of a vast amount of money. He returned to England four years after he left, emaciated and pale from malaria, but with more money than anyone else in the family. Jealousies within and without the family dubbed him a nabob and he was received with some cruelty by the women and no little amusement by the men.

'I was just six years old when my uncle left and fourteen when he returned. For a young boy like me, my uncle had hundreds of stories about exotic animals, royal courts, and strange occurrences. I listened to the stories with thirsty curiosity. My mother told me not to believe him. But the warning encouraged me. I would listen raptly to stories about emeralds as big as your fist and fish that could swallow a boat.'

Webley's uncle would slouch down in his chair and with an air of secrecy pull the boy close to him so that he could whisper in his ear. And then with each word a wheezy sigh, he would recount his stories. He told of his arrival in India, the confusion, how for a month he had no idea where to turn, how he went into debt to a Bengali merchant and had to leave Calcutta in secret. He told of his travels across deserts, through the hot sun, of mountains and icy winds, of weeks when he ate nothing. He told his nephew these things confidentially, as if talking to an adult—it made Webley feel twenty years older. He said the first few years in India had been like hell and he had thought he'd never make it. But then at last he reached a spot not marked on any map, a hidden place, guarded by monks in ochre robes and a high wall. The uncle described it in detail, his brandy-laden breath surrounding Webley in its warm stench.

'I rode up to the main gate and asked the monks what was protected behind the walls. And they told me ... said it was the great Pagoda Tree. I'd only heard tales about it, never imagined it to exist. The monks went on to say that it was a tree with a trunk so large that it took twelve men to encircle it. The branches of the tree were not laden with fruit but instead bore a crop of golden pagodas, a coin the size of a guinea. Each one was worth a fortune. The monks had been ordered by Lord Krishna ... that's their god ... when he was last on earth to guard the place and only allow the bravest and the strongest men to try their luck. They said that whoever shook the tree was allowed to collect whatever pagodas dropped to the ground. But if the man could not shake the tree, he was tortured and then killed by the monks.'

'Malaria and dysentery had reduced me to almost a cripple. I was as fragile as a woman and could hardly stay in my saddle. But I was desperate and asked the monks if I might try my luck.'

'They laughed at me and said that only a few of the men survived and walked out of the gate wealthy. Men three times my size had tried in vain to shake the tree, and they had failed and been put to death. The monks grinned and told me to go away and try my luck at dice and cards, where all that was at stake was my pocket instead of my life …'

'My pocket is empty,' I said, 'all that I have left is my life and no one will take that. Let me have a chance.'

'The monks laughed even louder and told me of the tortures they inflicted. They described how they cut off men's fingers and toes, feeding each one to their victim as they cut it off. They told how they made men swallow live cockroaches and handfuls of tapeworms, which ate out a man's stomach slowly and painfully.'

'I was arguing with the monks, to let this be my fate if I chose it, when the abbot came walking out to see what was happening. He was an old man in a vermilion robe, with his hair dyed the same colour, a beard to his waist. When he heard my plea, he nodded wisely and told the monks to give me a try.'

'I was so weak, I could hardly walk. Two of my servants supported me on either side as I stumbled towards the tree. It was a grand sight, glittering with millions of pagodas, each one reflecting the sun in a blinding flash. It dazzled so brightly that I had tears streaming down my face. The servants helped me forward and placed me against the massive trunk. Everyone stood back at a distance from the tree. I was so weak that I slid down to my knees and my head dropped to my chest.'

'But then, just as I was about to faint, I felt the ground tremble under me. At first I thought it was my own delirium. Then I heard a gruff rumbling below my feet and the ground shook violently. The monks screamed and fled into the monastery. The sound increased and I felt the trunk shiver, as if it were alive. I realized only then what was happening and began to laugh … full of relief and excitement. The earthquake gathered force and the tree felt as if it was going to be uprooted. Part of the monastery collapsed. I kept laughing, slouched against the trunk of the tree. Pagodas began to rain down around me, and after a few minutes the ground was covered with them. My servants rushed forward and began filling their pockets. One of the heavy coins fell on a man, hitting him at the base of his neck. It killed him instantly.'

'The earthquake finally subsided and I lurched to my feet. My men filled a palanquin with pagodas and I threw out all my belongings, filling trunks full of the coins. I set off for Calcutta with this fortune, saying farewell to the vermilion abbot and his monks.'

~

Augustine looked at his drunken commander and saw disappointment and failure in the man. He wondered to himself whether it had been the fortune he had come in search of, or the glory, and had he found either of them?

'As I grew up, I realized my uncle was lying,' said Webley, 'I went to school and learned that four-horned antelopes do not exist and that men cannot walk over fire. I learned about civilization and machines. But I believed the story about the Pagoda Tree, even though I knew it was a lie. I wanted to believe it because of a passion inside me which overcame my rationality. I remembered the story not in my mind but in the pit of my stomach. Whenever I think about it, even today, my uncle's voice comes back to me and I feel the excitement ignite my imagination with dreams.'

'Standing on the dock at Calcutta, I watched my trunks and bags coming down the gangplank, I wondered if when I left India those trunks would be full of golden pagodas instead of clothes.'

Webley's father was a country gentleman. He became heavily in debt as a result of high living in his younger days. Fortunately, he was able to marry off his two daughters and re-establish his estate to the point where his eldest son, if restrained by a sensible wife, would be able to live comfortably on his inheritance. There had been a good living available for the second son, who happened to be religiously inclined and was glad to take Holy Orders. The younger of the two remaining boys became an alcoholic at fifteen and died of a failing liver before he was twenty. That left James. His father knew that the boy wanted to go to India, and approved, but a commission cost more than he could comfortably afford. Finally, with the help of several friends among the Company's directors, a lieutenancy was secured at the very cheap price of five hundred pounds.

The money was wasted, for Webley did not even report to the Town Major in Calcutta. Instead, he bought horses and supplies on credit and set off into central India. It was an idea which he had been playing with during the long, tedious days aboard ship. He realized quickly that there was no hope for him at his age. Perhaps by the time he left India he might be a major, or with luck a lieutenant colonel. But there was no money in the Company army. There were too many men younger than he with a better chance to grow wealthy. They had five years on him. He realized that if he was to find the wealth his uncle had talked about he would have to leave Calcutta and set out in search of a career in the princely courts.

In two months he reached Hyderabad and presented himself to the Nizam. But his name had gone ahead of him and the British Resident forewarned the Nizam. Webley had to escape under cover for fear of being captured. Then began the long journey into the Deccan, fighting dust storms, the barren plateau, the bands of plunderers, and disappointment.

Webley offered his services first to Sindhia at Gwalior but then withdrew when he was offered only the rank of lieutenant. He found that Sindhia's court was infested with Frenchmen, vicious mercenaries who fought among themselves, Catholics and Jacobins. He knew that an English lieutenant would find no place in this army and was likely to be dead within the year.

He hated the French, besides. It was a drawn-out hatred. His father once had a French mistress and spent most of the year in Paris with her and only two or three months with his family and wife back in England. Englishwomen, like English cooking, are only good for breakfast, he used to say. Webley had a half-brother in France, whom he had met only twice. His father had openly brought the boy to England and proudly displayed him as one might display a Louis XVI chair—the boy did have well-turned legs and a padded seat, Webley's mother used to say bitterly.

In Sindhia's court there was an emissary from Baroda. The man drew Webley aside one day and suggested that he might find a worthwhile commission under the Gaekwad, who was looking for European officers, especially English. With a letter from the emissary, Webley continued west to Baroda.

It had been five months since he had left Calcutta. He had been healthy except for his stomach, but that was one of those things you put up with in India, like the heat. His uncle had said that India was a country of loose words, loose women, and loose bowels.

The Gaekwad took Webley on as a captain, with the promise that if he served well, he would be a major within six months.

Baroda was not a bad place. There were plenty of women for Webley to enjoy and there was drink and pageantry. He loved show, and the more gaudy the decorations at a party, the more exotic the costumes of the courtiers, the louder the music, the more Webley delighted in it. At Baroda he joined a regiment under a doddering officer, completely alcoholic and incompetent. Webley did not help the man; instead, he flattered him, sent him presents of liquor and women, so that he was thoroughly incapacitated. In that way Webley took command of the regiment. He drilled and paraded the men. He inflicted discipline without consulting the drunk commander. He led the men into skirmishes while his superior, back in the lines, tried hard to stay on his horse.

Webley was ambitious and foolhardy. The courtiers called him names behind his back, but they were all frightened of him. The Gaekwad was very proud of him and soon retired the drunkard above Webley and placed the young Englishman in full command.

Webley had pride in his regiment. He loved to see their lines straight, their legs moving like pincers, and their drummers beating out the pace with violent precision. While he was in Baroda nothing meant more to him than his regiment. It was the regiment, though, not the men. He had a streak of disdain in him. For a man who was such an individual himself, it was strange that he never respected the individuals under him. They were only rows and columns, rank and file, troops—never men. When he inspected his troops, he looked at his sepoys as a farmer might look at a row of corn. He never looked a soldier in the eye.

Some said it was because he was English. Others, that he was embarrassed because he had become an officer through fortune and not patience and training. Others said he was the sort who wanted to do all the fighting himself and resented the fact that he needed a regiment behind him. He wanted all the glory himself. But no one denied that he was a good officer and no one in the Deccan except for the great Benoit de Boigne had inflamed his men with such loyalty and pride. 'Treat a man like a puppy and he will coddle up to you and whimper and then pee on you. Treat a man like a dog and he will stand proudly beside you with his head high,' Webley once told Augustine.

∽

It was right after Webley had been given command of his regiment that Mehboob Rashid and Augustine arrived in Baroda. Augustine had come from Delhi, where he had been serving under the Mogul Ishmael Beg as an officer in the imperial bodyguard. He had been disappointed with the sad state of Delhi, the ruined buildings, the ghost-filled town, and the blind Emperor, Though it was the most prestigious service in Hindustan, the Emperor's bodyguard was like a poor joke. Their uniforms were in tatters. They had no ammunition. Their pay had been withheld for months because the Emperor and his family had been robbed of everything, even the jewels inlaid in the tiles of their walls. The Afghans had swept down on Delhi and left it a hollow shell, a brittle empire on the edge of destruction, with only its reputation and titles to maintain it.

In desperation, Augustine had left the service of the Emperor and, hearing that Baroda was full of opportunities, headed for the Gaekwad's court. Webley met him there and liked him immediately. He joined the regiment as a captain.

Mehboob Rashid arrived two days after Augustine, coming north from Mysore. He had been fighting under Tipu Sahib, but the politics of the court and the French mercenaries under Tipu had driven him out. He arrived at the head of a band of thirty Arabs. The Gaekwad hired them as part of his own private army.

For five years the three men fought for Baroda. They won many battles for the Gaekwad and each of them accumulated money. Webley became more and more wealthy in his command, until he was one of the richest men in the court. He was first in line to become the Gaekwad's commander-in-chief when the incident occurred between Mehboob Rashid and the courtier. Webley gave up his chances under Baroda, gave up his chance of shaking the mythical Pagoda Tree, and left the security of the Gaekwad's court for a life of banditry and plunder.

Many people said that he was a fool. He gave up luxurious quarters and fine furniture for a tent and a cot. His money was spent paying the troops during lean periods—there were many times when villages were so poor that hardly enough could be robbed from them to feed the army for one night. Augustine could remember one village clearly.

A pale wisp of smoke rose above the mango tope. There were no sounds save the chuckle of frogs squatting in the mud of the tank. Egrets stretched out in loose formation above their heads, flying west into the sun. The plains of Hindustan extended beyond the limits of Augustine's vision. Hoofbeats were muted by the dusty ground.

The village came in sight, a low line of buff-coloured walls huddled together. Outside it stacks of manure rose in tall mounds. Nothing moved, except for the creeping smoke which slid towards them over the surface of the tank. The riders skirted the marsh and broke into a gallop as they hit the higher ground. No sound came from the mud walls, not even a barking dog, a lone musket, a cry of fear. It was eerie, thought Augustine, as though they were charging a deserted fort. They jumped the thorn bushes which formed a pathetic barricade against marauders. The noise of their attack suddenly crescendoed as they entered the narrow gully together, at full speed. A peepul tree stood in the middle of the village, around which a mud dais had been built. The horsemen stopped here, their mounts snorting and jittery.

Augustine called out in a loud voice: 'Where is the headman!'

There was silence. After a moment, he called again.

From out of one of the ramshackle huts, a young man stepped slowly into the open. He carried no weapon. He wore only a torn dhoti.

'I am his son,' said the young man.

'Where is the headman?'

'Dead, Huzoor.'

'Who killed him?'

'God knows, Huzoor. Any one of you, your kind. There have been so many, we have lost track.'

'We ask for tribute, not death. Be quick with it, money and food,' said Augustine.

The young man smiled and then laughed. His laugh had a hollow note of hysteria in it. From out of the houses in the village there came other laughs, a chilling echo of the young man's cackle.

'Insolent bastard,' cried the man beside Augustine. He prodded his horse forward, and as he came abreast of the young man, he reached down and hit him hard with the palm of his hand. The laughter stopped. Slowly the headman's son picked himself off the ground.

'You are welcome to take whatever they have left for you, but I assure you there is nothing. They came every week, day after day, one band after another. "Give us your tribute," they said, and then took everything. They killed most of us, the men. My father died defending his zenana.'

'Who did this?' asked Augustine.

'You did,' said the young man. His lip was cut from the blow and the blood trickled down his chin.

Augustine restrained the sepoy beside him. 'We have never been here before.'

'You have come many times. I do not see your faces. I do not care what uniforms you wear. It was you, time and again.'

'This is the first time we have come to your village.' Augustine spoke softly.

'All right, it is the first time, what does it matter? Perhaps it is also the last time. What are you waiting for? Take it all. Take the jewels we have hidden away, the siccas buried in our walls. Do you see any cattle? They have all been killed. We do not know who comes. It is like a plague. Grain? It was taken the first time you came. We have eaten nothing for months but what we can scrape off the ground, filth, refuse. You are welcome to share that, frogs from the tank, mud.'

'We will see for ourselves,' said one of the men, dismounting. He ran into one of the huts. There were no protests, no cries from the women.

Afterwards, Augustine had thought about that village many times, how its people had been so completely defeated, destroyed. None of them could resist. Their spirit had been shattered. It was true what the headman's son had said. Nothing was left. The waves of marauders, plunderers had washed away everything of value in the village. Women let themselves be raped without a struggle. 'It is a village of bastards,' said the headman's son, wandering about as they turned the huts upside down, searching for money. 'No one knows his own father. Our women have mothered the children of bandits for years.' It was hard to believe the state of the village—complete desolation. Not an animal moved. Even dogs had been killed and eaten. The men were weak and feeble, their pride drained out of them, the survivors of a terrible disaster.

Two years later, when they were passing through the same district, Augustine stopped in the village to see what had become of it. The walls had collapsed. The inhabitants were gone. Not a sign of life remained. Another two years and the walls would be nothing but a part of the level plain, destroyed by the chaos, the storm.

Augustine knew Webley and he had realized as soon as he heard what had happened at Mehboob Rashid's execution that this was the chance Webley had been waiting for. It gave him reason to leave the court, to leave behind a regiment and march out with an army. It gave him independence and a sense of adventure. Baroda was a place for soldiers who spent more time between women's legs than in the saddle. Perhaps Webley was afraid that he would become like the officer he had taken over from, an alcoholic without judgment, only his rank.

Hindustan's vast plains gave Webley the possibilities he wanted. They left him with a horizon on all sides. He did not have his back against a wall. There was nothing permanent, nothing of value, save himself and his personality. Roaming wild over Hindustan, he cared nothing for what would remain. He kept nothing but spent it all. He moved like a dust storm spitting out whatever he collected.

∽

'Our commander is going mad,' said Mehboob Rashid to Augustine.

The Colonel did not answer, but ran his glass eye coldly up and down the robed figure. He had been standing on the ramparts, watching swifts dodge and dive in the air. They were nesting in the crevices of the walls. One or two of the cannons had even been taken over by the birds. Their shrill cries filled the air. Like scissors their wings snipped through the mist.

'Come, Augustine, no secrets between us,' said the Arab. 'We are both silent men, but today we must speak. I have noticed that the Englishman has not been well for some time. He is like a dog going mad, edgy and frustrated.'

'He has always been like that,' said Augustine.

'But this time it is different. The English are driving him mad. If he fights them, he betrays his own blood.'

'My blood as well,' said Augustine.

'You are different,' said the Arab. 'Your English blood makes you hate the English the more.'

'How do you know my blood will not betray me in the end?'

The Arab smiled. 'We need money,' he said. 'Not now, not yet, but in a month or so, when the men begin to feel the damp in their bones, when their empty wallets begin to fill with mildew, when their lungs clog with phlegm. Then we will need money and won't be able to get it. We must get it soon. He will not get it for us.'

'He will be sober in a week,' said Augustine.

Mehboob Rashid raised his eyebrows and worked the muscles in his jaw so that his bearded chin jutted out sharply.

'Have you ever watched a dog go mad?' he asked, 'it is a terrible sight. So terrible that one must shoot the animal in the end.'

'You are plotting mutiny,' said Augustine without emotion.

'No, there is no man I am loyal to save myself and the Englishman. He thinks I am loyal only because he saved my life. He fears me.'

'Like a bear fears a yapping dog.'

'I did not hear that, Colonel,' said the Arab. 'My ears are plugged with thoughts.'

Augustine stepped past Mehboob Rashid and then stopped with his back to him.

'What are your loyalties?' he asked.

Mehboob Rashid scratched his teeth with a fingernail and then spat.

'The Englishman thinks that I lopped off the head of that leopard to free myself from an obligation to him, that by saving his life I paid back the debt for mine. I am not that kind of a man. Debts are never paid back. Tell me, Colonel, do you love James Webley?'

'I do,' said Augustine.

'So do I,' said Mehboob Rashid, his mouth splitting into a smile. 'But beyond that we are different. You admire him.'

'Yes.'

'You dream great dreams for him, like a father for his son or a son for his father. You have ambitions for him. In your mind he is invincible. I think you would give your life for him, which is nothing, except that you would do it for his glory not yours, to give him a chance to live on and win more honour. A man cannot become great through another man's sacrifices. No matter what you do, he will amount to nothing more than himself. Webley will destroy himself, either quickly or through a long-drawn-out agony.'

Augustine's glass eye stood out in its socket, as if about to burst. The good eye squinted almost shut. The cannons were lined up pointing south over the forest far below. The walls fell thirty feet and then from there the dirt cliffs of the hill dropped another two hundred feet. It was late afternoon, more than a full day since the leopard had been killed.

The Arab leapt out onto one of the cannons and waved a hand grandly across the open air. He walked along the smooth barrel, which protruded a few feet over the battlements. Standing two hundred and thirty feet above the ground, the Arab twirled about like an acrobat and faced Augustine, his back to the expanse. As he talked he walked back and forth along the slippery barrel, stepping nonchalantly, as if he were on a broad road.

'Let him fall apart, Augustine. There is nothing you can do. He is not as great a man as you think. You imagine him to be more than himself.'

'I do not admire him when he is drunk,' said Augustine.

'Don't blame him, it is not his fault. They say all English need alcohol to survive.'

'My blood does not cry out for it,' said Augustine.

'I think you have drained out every drop of English blood in your veins, Colonel.'

'How can a Muslim as pious as you are admire a drunkard?'

'Did I say I admired him? I think there is not a better soldier in Hindustan. He, more than any man, deserves to drink. No, I do not admire him. I love him, though. I admire no man, not even myself.' Mehboob Rashid leapt from the end of one cannon to the next, across the empty air between them. They were nine feet apart, but he seemed to step across the space effortlessly, with a disdain for danger. Without stopping, he jumped to the next.

'Tell me, Augustine. Should I have let the leopard kill him? That is what I ask myself now. I saved the Englishman because I love him, and now I regret it. He wanted to die, I think. It was not a noble thing for me to do, but it was out of my love that I did it.'

'If you admired him, what would you have done?'

'Let him die.'

'Love is a strange thing between a man and a woman, but between two men it is noble,' said Augustine.

'No, it is ugly,' said Mehboob Rashid. 'It is dangerous.'

'You saved his life. That is neither ugly nor dangerous.'

'But foolhardy, selfish. I could not stop myself, though. It was an emotion, an ache inside me. Every moment I saw him come closer to death, the emotion swelled up larger and larger like a boil. If I had let the leopard kill him, I would have let it kill me as well.'

'What is wrong with feeling that?' said Augustine.

'Because a man must never take on anything more than himself. He must be his only loyalty. He must be savage as a leopard. We are herded together, Colonel, like cattle, but in each of us is a desire to be alone. We have families, groups of friends, regiments and armies. It is all an attempt to lower each man to the level of others. Our emotions drag on us, pull us down. I do not trust them. When we kill we should not feel anything, neither hatred nor love. There should be no pleasure in it, no revenge, no vendettas, no bitterness. We must kill, for it is in each one of us, the desire to destroy everything but ourselves. We are hunters and the urge has been there from a time before we were herded together by our emotions, from a time when men roamed as wild as cats.'

'Is this the angry philosophy of your desert?' asked Augustine, with a laugh. 'I do not believe a word you have said.'

The Arab had his sword out in a second. It hung over his head, a cold gleaming crescent.

'Perhaps you will believe this,' said Mehboob Rashid. 'I could kill you now, just to be alone.'

Augustine gave a laugh, but it had a nervous edge. The sword which had killed the leopard swung down through the air. Augustine hardly had time to fall backwards. The blade cut his cheek in a thin line from the lobe of his ear to the corner of his mouth. Beads of blood appeared along the line and then dribbled down Augustine's chin.

Mehboob Rashid leapt from the cannon onto the wall of the ramparts and then walked slowly away, the sword swinging in his hand. Augustine felt his fear catch in his throat. He knew that the Arab would have killed him. The sword had not hesitated, cutting the air where his neck had been. He thought about the words Mehboob Rashid had spoken, but they did not seem to make sense. What returned to his memory, though, was the tone of voice, the bitter smell of his breath, and the dark shadows in his eyes, which passed back and forth across his vision like clouds.

Augustine felt a sudden panic inside himself, a sense of abandonment and disillusionment. He felt like a child, like Webley cooing and muttering over his drinks. In his memory the soft melancholy voice of his mother began to purr. He felt innocent and exposed. The blood seeped out of the cut in his cheek and stained his collar. He put his hand to the wound and brought it away red and shaking. His nerves sputtered like fuses, burning up his spine.

It was as if someone had shattered the filigree screens, broken open that world of illusions and dreams, torn down the curtains and let the harsh sunlight stream into the zenana. What lay outside was suddenly exposed in its brutal reality. He saw his father gored by a cannonball and his mother raped.

The tears blurred in his good eye and he began to cry, gently at first and then with loud sobs. It felt as if huge gaps were opening up inside of him. His chest seemed to split apart. It was like being hit just below the ribs. Augustine doubled over and dropped to his knees, the sobs heaving his body. On the checkerboard slate slabs of the battlements under the enormous sky, he rocked back and forth as if in pain.

It was the time of evening just before the sun begins to plummet and the light is amber-coloured and falls in streams. The dust particles in the air shine like flakes of gold and the green of the trees is an emerald hue. Contours and shadows break into abstract shapes, patterns. The earth is a liver colour in the sunlight and the sky like soapy water.

Augustine felt no warmth, no possibilities. His thoughts were like stabbing pains and he held himself back from thinking. But as each individual thought was restrained, the force of all those fears and emotions pent up behind his pride overwhelmed him and burst the barriers of his rationality like a flood.

∽

Webley appeared like a ghost. The pale-blue eyes, so faintly tinted with colour, their brilliance spent, under jutting brows wrinkled with curiosity, and the nose, beak-like, sharp and pinched, the mouth, firm and cynical as a squeezed lemon, a jawline stern and unflinching, and surrounding the face the strands of stringy blond hair, seemingly pasted onto his balding skull; a look of tired depression, beyond day-to-day sadness, an eternal mood of slaty melancholy; the skin transparent as wax, white as dirty sheets, white as ice, white as lard, white as the underbelly of a dead fish floating upside down on the surface of a stream, white as semen, white as the scum on milk …

The Englishman staggered forward and lost hold of the bottle in his hand. It shattered on the stone slabs, and the yellow air was filled with the sickly sweet odour of arrack. Augustine caught him as he fell and took his thin body in his arms. The Colonel dwarfed his friend. With a wide hand he brushed the hair out of Webley's eyes. They looked at each other, both of them crying now.

'A few more days, Augustine, a few more days and I'll be all right,' Webley said softly. He spoke in such a quiet whisper that Augustine bent closer to listen.

'Don't do this to yourself. Don't do it to all of us,' said Augustine.

'It's all over, all over,' said Webley, no longer a place for us. We are dead men … dead men.'

This was the way it was supposed to be. The heroic commander fell back in his faithful Colonel's arms and expired with a sigh or a quotation from the classics. Were these last lines? They were on the ramparts, among the cannons. Webley muttered a few words and then dissolved into incoherence. This was the way it was supposed to be. But Webley was not dying, only drunk. It was not blood that trickled from his mouth, but drool. He began to snore. Augustine let him sleep, sitting silently beside him as it grew dark. The swifts moved through the air around them, coasting and gliding, returning to their nests in the cannons.

The sense of melodrama was revived in Augustine. He began to feel the passions his mother had passed on to him. This time he cried not out of fear and loneliness but from a sense of greatness, an overwhelming feeling of destiny.

For Augustine, Webley remained a figure of great importance, despite what Mehboob Rashid had said. He was not only a friend but a symbol. He stood for what Augustine lived, the life of heroic action, the careless and uncomplicated life of a soldier. The glorious style of an officer. The quest for the mythical Pagoda Tree. The pure energy and action of the man drew Augustine to him like an insect drawn to a light. His energy animated Augustine. The Colonel was determined to preserve that energy, to keep that flame burning. He would stand by Webley, support him, not let him destroy himself. His own honour was tied to Webley's.

~

Bibbi Charlotte lay propped up with pillows on her bed. Augustine sat beside her. He was almost thirteen, tall and gangly, but with a mature face. The way he sat, with one leg cocked over the other, gave the impression that he now thought of himself as a man.

They were talking, sharing stories and gossiping about the people in the fort. Trisuldas Thakur was away on an expedition and hadn't returned for several weeks. Augustine had stolen into the zenana, with the help of his mother's servants, who wrapped him in a burka and brought him past the glowering eunuch guards. Since he had turned twelve he was forbidden to enter these apartments, but Bibbi Charlotte conspired to have him near her and he would often enter secretly to spend an evening with his mother.

The moon had just risen very bright over the desert, which stretched like a frozen sea beneath the windows. The two of them sat facing it, through the screened window. The latticework was etched against the cold white of the moon, patterns of geometry and flowers carved together. The screens were black, as though they were made of coal instead of sandstone.

Suddenly, as they were watching the moon, a triangular head and two long-fingered hands appeared at one corner of the window. A forked tongue seemed to be lapping up the moonlight as though it were milk. Bibbi Charlotte stopped in mid-sentence when she saw the monster. It moved forward across the screen.

Augustine whirled around. By the time he had drawn his sword, the entire length of the dragon was exposed, from the licking tongue to the long tail. It stopped there, standing out black and bold against the moon, almost as if it had been carved into the screen. But then its head poked through the latticework and its two beady eyes flickered in the candlelight.

Augustine, sword in hand, stepped forward bravely and, without hesitating a moment, drove his blade through one of the carved flowers and sank it into the dragon's chest. Bibbi Charlotte screamed and there was a horrible scratching sound as the creature scrambled out of sight.

At the same moment Augustine dashed out of the room, his sword dripping blood on the carpets. He ran up to the roof and there killed the monster as it came climbing over the railing.

The lizard was about four feet in length. To Augustine it seemed to have been preserved out of the past, a prehistoric creature. He knew that it was harmless but had heard stories about these monitor lizards. They were very strong and when the Mahratta armies were fighting the Mogul emperor, they used these lizards to scale the walls of forts. They would tie themselves to two or three of these lizards and be hauled up to the battlements. The armies kept cages full of them for this purpose.

Augustine often imagined a Mahratta warrior being dragged silently up the walls and then creeping over the ramparts to kill the sentries.

For Bibbi Charlotte it was a moment of fear and pride as she saw her son defending her like a man. From that day on she looked on him as a man. There was also a sadness in the realization, a regret on her part, that she had lost him to the world. By defending her, he had shrugged off her protection, a mother's concern and fear for her child. By killing the dragon, he was now free of her, and she was under his protection, that of a son for his mother.

~

Though the wound had not yet healed on Augustine's cheek, Mehboob Rashid seemed to have forgotten the incident. He stopped the Colonel in the courtyard and spoke to him with clipped sentences. 'How is our drunken commander?'

'He will soon be out of his stupor,' said Augustine, ignoring the hand on his shoulder.

'Your week is up, Augustine. Is he sober yet?'

'No.'

'Then we must act on our own,' said Mehboob Rashid. 'We must march against someone before it is too late, before the mud gets too deep. It has begun to rain daily. I have been watching the clouds. They are moving in circles over the mountains. Soon they will besiege us. They will roll in across the plains like a line of war elephants.'

'I know what will happen,' said Augustine.

'Webley fears the English. I fear the monsoon.'

'That is because you come from a dry place, an endless desert.'

'We need money, Colonel.'

'Then get it, damn you!' said Augustine, walking away.

~

That evening Mehboob Rashid left the fort with a small army, a hundred men. They were all mounted. The Arab had no time for infantry. He said that the English put men on foot because they had no respect for them, because they feared a man on horseback. In the saddle a man does what he pleases. On foot he is part of a column, a number, a faceless tool. Mehboob Rashid led the army riding the same chestnut stallion he had killed the leopard on. He cantered out of the gate and down the steep trail, twenty yards ahead of the others. The horse was jittery and pranced around on the rocks, setting off small landslides but never losing its footing.

Behind Mehboob Rashid rode his eighteen Arabs, what were left of the thirty men who came with him from Baroda. They rode proudly, each in a different coloured robe, some with muskets dangling from their saddles, others with lances, some with only swords and perhaps a pistol tucked under the folds of cloth.

The rest of the army had been chosen at random from Webley's men. They rode in loose patterns, sticking close to friends. Their horses scattered across the slope of the hill, leaving the trail and making their way down to the bottom without concern for order and discipline. Their uniforms were their own, each of a different cut and fashion, some of them taken from the bodies of men they had killed. There were Mahrattas, Jats, Sikhs, and Afghans among them, each man a renegade, some of them bandits, some deserters. They rode as individuals and not as an army. Each carried enough food with him for a week.

Augustine watched from the parapet above the gate. He thought about Webley and how many times he had led this army into battle. Usually Mehboob Rashid and Augustine would ride out beside him in front.

There were no banners or drums; those, like the lines and columns, had disappeared when the army left Baroda. But there was a pageantry to the army's departure, a colourful and grand mood among the soldiers. They were cutthroats, villains, and thieves, but they were also an army. Each one of them knew that Webley was on one of his periodic binges, but as they rode out he seemed to be there, ahead of them all, ahead of Mehboob Rashid, riding like a phantom, darting in and out of the trees. It was that image which rose up like a spirit among the soldiers. It was Webley who inspired them, even in his absence.

'Where are they headed?' asked a voice behind Augustine.

Pratap Bahadur stood with his hands behind his back. The faint line of his moustache followed the curve of his upper lip in a smile, but the moustache curved down at the ends and added a cynical touch to his cheerful expression.

'They are going to Delhi to celebrate the Emperor's birthday.'

'Ah, I had heard otherwise. Someone said they are heading across the Siwaliks to sack Saharanpur.'

Augustine smiled. He disliked the Gurkha. Earlier, the little man had been harmless, pestering them like a fly with his frenetic curiosity. But now that the wound had opened, now that Webley seemed to be going under, Pratap Bahadur was dangerous. He was still a fly, but now he was buzzing around the wound, settling down and feeding off the pus. When things were not serious, he was tolerated, but now that the situation had come to a precipice, he was more than just a nuisance.

'A spy should never make mistakes. They are going to Delhi.'

'I am an emissary,' said the Gurkha quickly.

Augustine wanted to get rid of him. 'Since the rain is coming, you will need new quarters, my dear ambassador. Perhaps an underground room would suit you?'

The Gurkha was quivering. His mouth leapt up and down like a puppet's.

'You wouldn't dare,' he said. 'My King's armies would be here in five days to flatten your fort.'

'But if you are a spy …'

'I am an ambassador.'

'There is no difference,' said Augustine. With a quick sweep of his hand, he unsheathed the Gurkha's kukri before the little man could reach it. He threw the knife over the wall and then picked the Gurkha up under his arm and carried him struggling down the steps into the courtyard.

'They will come down here and murder every one of you! You will be wiped out!' squealed Pratap Bahadur, flailing his arms.

'I think they will forget all about you,' said Augustine, handing Pratap Bahadur over to one of his men.

The Gurkha was taken underground and thrown into one of the dungeon rooms. It was a dank cell full of scorpions and spiders, with two or three high windows like arrow-slits, so narrow that even a hand couldn't reach through them. The light entered the room in shafts.

Augustine hated little men. Anyone shorter than five feet made him bristle with irritation. It was not just their size but their gestures, the compact economy of their limbs, which could never stride out or reach, stretch. They moved with the jerkiness of puppets. Their inadequacy bothered Augustine, possibly because they struggled against it. It might have been that though he could cross a room in four long strides or had to stoop while going through a door, there was in him that same tightness, a nervous tension. When he held a sword or swung out to hit someone, his muscles and tendons seemed to hold him back. The casual lankiness of his body hid a short squat torso, stunted arms and legs. It was as if within his body there was another, much smaller body which limited his movements and cramped his vanity.

Augustine struggled against that body. It was as if on his death Somdas had entered Augustine and their wrestling, their swordplay, their quarrels continued within one man. At times Augustine felt as though he were being pulled apart, as if half of him were clenching up like the dying dwarf and the other half were stretching out farther, growing larger, more gangly and uncoordinated.

Because of this, Pratap Bahadur had always irritated Augustine. Ever since the Gurkha had come to the Bijilli Gargh, he had felt his presence at the back of his neck, a tickling itch of annoyance.

He wanted to pick Pratap Bahadur up by the scruff of hair which protruded from under his tilted cap and toss him over the wall of the Bijilli Gargh. It was an irrational hatred, not influenced by the piping voice, the irritating arguments, the subtle questions, or even the spying presence of the man, but by a vague distaste, merely due to his size.

Augustine felt lonely again, as he had that evening on the battlements. He caught himself as he ran up the stairs to the parapet above the gate. There was no sign of the men. The forest had swallowed them up. No one was in sight, neither in the fort nor on the plains below. The heavy clouds hung limply, suspended like a drooping canopy from the top of the Siwaliks up to the ridges behind the fort. Their low cover gave the scene a claustrophobic atmosphere. In the distance Augustine saw the blue sheets of rain slanting out of the west. Streaks of lightning began to spark in the distance. A bass thunder gathered force, like the lowest octave on an organ. The clouds swallowed up and then regurgitated the roar, again and again. The storm was moving across the plains towards the east, from the Jumna to the Ganges. The bolts of lightning danced across the valley, like harlequins doing cartwheels and handsprings in front of a carnival procession. Augustine felt the force of the storm long before it arrived. The air was charged. A wind picked up and the leaves of the trees below him rustled like voices.

Suddenly, there in the distance, he saw movement. The clouds had darkened and the storm was black, but there at the edge of the forest, two miles away, the army appeared. The horsemen rode out onto the shadowy plain, and as they did, Augustine felt a cry rise in his throat. He heard himself utter a startled sound. They moved slowly but with determination, in a cluster. Augustine could not make out the individuals. They were like a swarm of maggots. Augustine watched as they moved towards the storm. Mehboob Rashid seemed to be challenging the monsoon. The wind would be blowing his robes behind him. All the men would ride into the lightning. Maybe some of the flashes were from their muskets. There were sharp cracks and cannon shots of thunder. As the two forces met, the army seemed to spread out, almost in a line, and appeared to race faster into the rain. Augustine felt himself shudder as the two met. The army disappeared into the black curtains of rain. In a second not a man remained. Augustine realized that his hands were clutching the parapet. He released his grip and rubbed his palms together. They were hot and feverish, and he could feel a dry current pass between them.

∽

Webley's drinking caught up with him the day after Mehboob Rashid left. He remained ill for three days, vomiting, with severe headaches and a sharp pain below his ribs. On the fourth day he recovered enough to call Augustine to his apartments.

Augustine found Webley dressed in a clean uniform. Even his boots were polished. The brass buttons on his coat shone. But he lay stretched out on his couch like an invalid, and when he raised his hand it shook noticeably. The whites of his eyes were an amber colour and his face paler than usual. He had bathed and his hair was pinned down to dry.

'Well, I think I've survived,' said Webley.

'How do you feel?' asked Augustine.

'Like hell. It'll take a few more days to rinse it out of my system.'

'Mehboob Rashid took some of the men and went to Saharanpur. We need money,' said Augustine.

'That's a good idea, before the rains knock us to hell.'

Augustine was surprised.

'I would have thought you'd be angry.'

'Over what?' asked Webley with a weak smile.

Augustine shrugged and picked up a gilt cherub which was lying on the floor.

'Do you remember where I got that from?' said Webley.

'I think it was Delhi.'

'No, I stole it from the tent of the Portuguese monk. Remember him? He was travelling from Goa to Calcutta. It has a hole in its head for burning incense. Maybe I'll drill a hole in my head. That might get rid of this hangover.'

'Eat something. It will cure it,' said Augustine.

'Nothing stays in me. It all comes up like a volcano.'

Augustine toyed with the gilt cherub. It fit in the palm of his hand and felt smooth. The gold skin, moulded over the dimples of its buttocks, its belly button, and the stubby penis gave the cherub a demonic tint, as if it had been fried in oil. The Portuguese monk had told them that cherubs were the souls of children that had been aborted or killed when very young by their parents. They became the little people in heaven. He was a mad monk, wandering across India without any purpose but to save the souls of murdered children. He said that India was a cruel country and he prayed fervently for the souls of little girls killed by their son-hungry parents. Augustine wondered if aborted children came out gilded from the womb or whether they were dipped in gold once they got to heaven.

'We'll go to Lucknow,' said Webley.

'When? What for?' asked Augustine, surprised.

'As soon as Mehboob Rashid gets back from raiding. I know many people in Lucknow who can help us. You see, all the time I was drunk I was thinking. I don't remember when I decided, but it was very soon after the first day—alcohol helps me think—I knew that we had to go to Lucknow. There we'll find the money and the means to drive the East India Company out of our territory.'

'You are going to challenge the English?'

'With the finest army a man could dream of. You'll see.'

'Who in Lucknow will you go to?' asked Augustine.

'Ah, leave it all to me, my anxious Colonel, and stop handling that cherub, anyone would think you were a molester of children.'

'But Lucknow is full of English,' said Augustine.

'It is also full of people who hate the English. They are my friends despite the colour of my face.'

Augustine was puzzled. He put the cherub aside absent-mindedly and tried to catch Webley with his glass eye, to get the truth out of him. But the Englishman was clever and spun around on the couch. With effort he steadied his legs and stood up. The blood rushed to his feet and he had to grab the edge of the couch to keep from fainting. But after a moment he recovered, cursing slightly under his breath.

'You didn't think I'd ever face them, did you, Colonel?' said Webley. 'You thought I was scared of my own race. Well, perhaps I was. It's a little like taking your own life. Takes getting used to the idea.'

'We don't need money from Lucknow. We only need your determination.'

'I'm flattered,' said Webley grandly. 'And of course I am above money, but it is the means towards our end. We need weapons. Some of the muskets our men have should have been thrown away long ago. They are patched with wire and the bores are blowing out at the ends. Lucknow will provide us with everything, even a little pleasure. It will be good for both of us, Colonel. Of course you're coming. You will be a changed man once you get out of these gloomy walls. I am tired of dreaming about women with their clothes on. Come with me and we'll unharness a dozen whores and ride them all night, bareback.'

'The English will find us out. We are wanted men.'

'A bandit has a hundred faces, an honest man has only one. We will be disguised with alibis. Come, Colonel, you can surely be something other than a soldier for once.'

'And who will stay here with the men?' asked Augustine.

'The Arab with his hooked sword, Mehboob Rashid,' said Webley, with a faint bitterness in his voice. 'No amount of pleasure would help him. He is made for this sort of life. That of a snake.'

'He should be back within a week. You'll be recovered by then, enough to travel,' said Augustine.

Webley lowered himself back down onto the couch and lay there for a moment. Augustine thought it best to leave him for a while until he was stronger. The excitement might start him drinking again. He himself wanted to get outside. Augustine's passions flowed with his blood. He could see their army now, facing the English and trampling them under the hooves of a thousand horses. He could feel his muscles tense at the thought of killing an English captain.

Mehboob Rashid had to camp on the far side of the river for two days before he and his men could cross over to the Bijilli Gargh. They arrived tired and dejected. None of them spoke much about what had happened. Augustine finally got the story out of one of the men.

He said that they had attacked Saharanpur after three days of marching through steady rain and knee-deep mud. Most of their powder was wet, and when they charged the town, only a third of their muskets fired. The rest either went off with a dull thud or else wouldn't fire at all. The town was ready for them and its army had set itself up in a cluster of houses guarding the main entrance to the city. Mehboob Rashid was wounded in the hip by grapeshot from one of the cannons, and at least twenty men were killed trying to get past their battery. The horses were tired and many of them were sick.

They finally took the town and had most of the men executed, but what money there was had been secreted away and they got only a few hundred rupees and some jewellery. The city was hostile to them and two of the sepoys were murdered during the first night they were there. The women had to be raped, for there were no whores, or none that admitted to being whores.

Mehboob Rashid marched them back almost as soon as they had got there, and the trip back was just as miserable. Their clothes were sodden and spattered with mud. Their spirits were soaked.

PART TWO

5

The river emerged from the sparse forest and began a slow arc eastward for about half a mile before it washed up against the walls of the city. Lucknow was built along the Gumti. It was a lush tangle of trees and architecture. From the edge of the forest it had the appearance of an ethereal city. The swollen waters, reflecting the sheen of the sky, separated it from the bare plain, so that it seemed to rise into the air. It stood on the horizon, which was rimmed with clouds, giving the whole scene an enchanted aura—a vision of a fanciful world.

Each of the palaces and mosques was surrounded by shade trees, tamarinds, mangoes, and palms. Stands of bamboo lined the river, arching over the chalk-white buildings. From where Augustine first caught sight of the city, it looked uninhabited, overgrown. The cupolas and havelis, domes of every shape from an onion to a woman's breast, protruded above the gardens and groves. For Augustine cities had always been squalid places, full of ragged children and lame dogs, garrisoned with miserable swarms of flies, smelling of fecal sewage. But this city, at a distance, had an appearance of poetic splendour.

Travelling on the river was a slow but steady process. The morose boatman squatted next to the tiller, gazing at the shore. He had not moved from his place for three days, except to urinate over the side or accept food from his two passengers. The horses stood in the stem, tethered to the oarlocks.

Augustine and Webley had amused themselves on the journey by firing at targets from the boat. Just after dawn on the second morning, Webley noticed a corpse stuck to a tree root along the bank. A crocodile—one of the huge muggers that lived in the river—was feeding on it. Webley took a shot and missed. The crocodile threw itself backwards and vanished under the current in a whirl of silt. Augustine shot a brace of Brahminy ducks, which they ate. At dusk the air would be filled with swifts swooping at insects and skimming over the surface of the river. They fired at these as well. Webley knocked down six with one shot.

When there was nothing to kill, Augustine sat with his legs over the side of the barge, watching the flecked silt swirling in patterns beneath the surface of the water. Bits of mica flashed in the sunlight. When it rained the surface of the river became covered with whirligig designs—the smoothness scattered with rings all spinning in and around each other.

Webley pointed out Ashgar Hasan's house as they coasted towards the city. It stood by itself, on the opposite bank, about a quarter mile back from the river. There was a wall enclosing it and a dense garden. Around the wall, stretching down to the river and in all four directions, was a lifeless swamp, a grey marsh, where the river had flooded and then receded. Ashgar Hasan's palace and garden was like an island in the midst of a sea of mud. The air was filled with decaying smells, and as their barge touched the shore, Augustine could see the carcasses of drowned animals strewn about, with mists of flies filling the air.

The residence was extravagant, a sprawling building of many levels, decked with cupolas and minarets. The roofs were flat, with elaborate railings. Each of the windows was screened with a fine latticework of carved stone. There were long balconies and terraces, colonnades and arches, as if a dozen different buildings had collapsed into one, forming an outrageous combination of architectural styles and moods. The overall effect was one of chaos, though the stark white plaster gave it a unity, however eccentric.

What had awed Augustine at a distance disgusted him when he saw it up close. The vision of an exotic and mysterious city vanished from sight, and for his entire stay in Lucknow, Augustine was to feel nothing but disappointment and horror.

A young man dressed in white muslin and an embroidered vest of red velvet led them through the garden to a pavilion hidden behind the dense growth of flowering shrubs and bowers sagging with leafy vines. The pavilion was marble, constructed of subtle forms, beautiful in contrast to the garish palace.

Lying on a vast couch of mauve velvet was Ashgar Hasan. He did not even try to move when the two men approached him, but a smile dimpled his enormous face, so that it looked like an overripe fruit poked a number of times to test its softness.

He was a vast man and seemed to crush the divan. His clothes were richly patterned, layers of embroidered silk heavy with gold thread. There was no collar to his shirt. It was buttoned with a single pearl at the neck. From there a slit ran halfway down to his waist, exposing a smooth chest and his left nipple. His breasts were full like a woman's. The nipple, staring out at Augustine, gave Ashgar Hasan a debauched and lecherous appearance. His body looked like a pile of cushions with a head protruding from one end and at the other end an incongruous pair of English stockings stretched to breaking over bulbous feet and ankles.

There was no shape to his body, only bulk, a loose arrangement of fat. Augustine thought of the wax which collects at the bottom of a candle when it burns low—round indefinable shapes. Ashgar Hasan was the meltings of a man.

He was the most respected eunuch in the Nawab's court, a prince in his own right, with wealth and reputation. Around him hovered a flock of admirers and dandies, fawning to please him.

Augustine saw one of the eunuch's hands emerge from under the folds of material like a slug, moving with slow and ponderous effort. Webley stepped forward and took his hand. Augustine saw a helpless look in Ashgar Hasan's eyes. The lips moved, but no sound came out. A young boy leapt up onto the dais and thrust a silver spittoon under his master's chin. The red paan juice dribbled out of the puffy lips and trickled down into the silver cup. When the trickle stopped, the boy pulled the cup away and wiped Ashgar Hasan's mouth with a silk cloth.

The voice was low and husky, as if it had to reverberate through many caverns and chambers in the eunuch's chest before it emerged from his mouth. The tongue was red and Augustine could see it moving between the stained lips with a poisonous obscenity. Webley spoke to him respectfully, without his usual vanity. After a little while he introduced Augustine. Ashgar Hasan moved his hand faintly towards the Colonel, who jumped forward and took it in his. The wide palm felt sweaty and feverish and seemed to wrap around Augustine's fingers like soft clay.

'Welcome,' said Ashgar Hasan, 'Webley miyan is my dear friend. So are you. This little house of mine is yours. These servants as well. Tolerate my feeble hospitality as long as you can, my beloved Colonel.' His Urdu was complex and filled with Persian expressions.

Augustine's room adjoined Webley's. They had been given a suite on the second floor, facing the city. The Colonel had fallen asleep after a heavy lunch and plenty of wine. Ashgar Hasan was an extravagant host and fed his guests as if he wanted them to balloon out to his own proportions.

On waking, Augustine's head seemed to be filled with a raspy, irritating chatter, as if a fly had been let loose in his sinuses. He couldn't locate the sound. The room was dark and humid. The curtains were drawn over the balcony window. Shaking his head furiously, Augustine stood up. The noise seemed to be all about him now, not just inside his head. It was as if he were going mad. Stepping over to the window, he threw back the curtains and went out onto the balcony. The sun was setting over the city and tinged each of the minarets and domes with a soft pink colour. The rain clouds hovered about, stained a dozen different shades of red. The sun seemed violent and gory, the colour of Ashgar Hasan's spittle. In Augustine's ears the unabated screams and hoarse cries grew louder.

Then he saw where the sound was coming from. Hundreds of mynahs were roosting in the palm trees. Their incessant arguments filled the air and each of the bushy palms seemed alive, as the birds fought amidst the branches, darting in and out of the scuffle. They were fighting over their places for the night.

The commotion did not seem to come just from the palm trees but from the whole city spread out in the distance. Augustine felt a frenzy inside him, a terror almost. The arguments of the birds seemed to be a symbol of the city, like the theme in a piece of music, persistent, echoing over and over again, setting the mood. But this was not music, instead a mad jabbering of crowds, of bazaars, of merchants, of politics. The noise hurt Augustine's ears. He felt as though he could not stand it any longer. The city frightened him.

Taking one of his muskets, which was propped in a corner of the room, he stepped out onto the balcony. The flame and smoke from the barrel flashed brightly in the half-light. The palm tree exploded, first with a scattering of bark and bits of branches and fronds. Then a terrified flurry of mynahs erupted out of the tree, filling the air for a moment with the frightened sound of their wings. The other palms chorused in. Dead and dying birds tumbled out of the palm. Some fell with a soft thud, others with a flutter and cries. The few that were wounded hobbled about frantically as if they had forgotten how to fly.

There was silence for a moment and then Augustine heard

beyond the garden, beyond the sludge of the riverbank, the noises of the city indistinct but with a menacing rumble. As he turned away from the balcony, Augustine heard the throaty call of the muezzin, shrill and melancholy. He wanted to leave immediately, to escape the treacherous streets, the crowds and filth. He wanted to ride his horse into Lucknow at full gallop at the head of an army, trample the city, scatter the produce, the trinkets, murder the shopkeepers, destroy the buildings, the slums and the palaces. He wanted to level the city, leave it an open wound on the surface of the plain. In time the sludge of the riverbed, the dust and saltpetre of the plains would cover it like a scab and hide it from sight.

A servant padded into the room with a tray of pastries and sweets, along with a pitcher of iced sherbet. Augustine knocked on Webley's door. The two men sat on Augustine's bed, ate and drank.

'It's good to be back among civilized people again,' said Webley.

'The air is bad here. That swamp is full of disease; the city must be full of cholera.'

'Ah, but inside this garden, isn't it the very perfection of luxury?' Another servant entered as Webley said this and placed a lit chillum on the hookah, which stood on the far side of the room. The tobacco had a rich, fragrant smell, faintly scented with cloves. The servant brought two nozzles over to Augustine and Webley.

'You see what I mean,' said Webley. 'This is the way to live.'

'Yes, and in a week we'll be as sedentary as your fat friend.'

'He's only that way because they cut his balls off,' said Webley.

'Does he regret the fact?' asked Augustine.

'I suppose he is used to it by now.'

'He never talks about it, I suppose,' said Augustine, drawing a bittersweet cloud of smoke from the hookah.

'Not unless he's drunk.'

The two men sat silently for a long time. The smoke wrapped itself around them in loose circles, like webs spun by phantom spiders. Augustine felt his senses relax. The mynahs had become silent after returning to their roosts. They did not seem to notice the casualties they had suffered. He felt the restlessness flow out of him. The palace and the adjacent city felt less constricting. He still wore his travelling clothes, but Webley had told him that Ashgar Hasan would have his tailors working busily at making them comfortable garments, suited to courtiers, not mercenaries.

'I wonder how Mehboob Rashid is doing,' said Augustine.

'Oh, God,' said Webley, 'don't remind us of that damned fort. It was like a rat-hole.'

'It is a safe place.'

'There we were animals. Here we are men.' Webley spoke the last few words into the nozzle of his hookah. The hookah rumbled across the room, the water hubble-bubbling in its pot-belly as they drew the smoke through it.

'I can't spend any more time here than necessary,' said Augustine. 'This life is for men who have lost their genitals.'

'You have the stubborn pride of a bull. Come now, my Colonel, shed your manliness. We'll soon have you dressed up like the most effeminate courtier in Lucknow, with your hair oiled, your face shaved as smooth as brass, and your clothes reeking of rosewater and musk.'

The thought of dressing up in silk and satin disgusted Augustine. He imagined himself with one nipple exposed.

'When are you going to do your business here?' asked Augustine.

'Business?' said Webley in alarm.

'I mean the money and the arms. We are at war, let me remind you.'

'Ah, in good time. Until then don't spoil the fun by reminding me about that damned fort.'

Webley had always been impulsive and petty, ever since Augustine had known him. The slightest inconvenience could trigger his temper, while he might at the same time ignore a far greater danger. His mind worked only in the present, attaching itself to things momentarily and then skipping on to the next. He could never focus his attention on more than one object at the same time, but he could very easily forget the one when his mind travelled on to the next. It had been that way with clothes, women, guns, swords—he had a new one every month. If he liked something he had to have it. He did not have the patience to wait and took what he desired, casting off what bored him. He was irritated by things which no longer interested him. One moment he would be playing with an ornament he had stolen and the next moment he would throw it away, as if it were nothing more than a stone he had picked up off the road. Augustine had seen Webley throw a pocket watch off the ramparts of the fort at Baroda. It had been a perfectly good watch, gold-plated, set with jewels, in a finely tooled shagreen case. But the fact that the hour hand did not quite follow the time properly upset him. It irritated his precise genius, and in a fit of pique—probably there was something else bothering him, a love affair, an intrigue in the court—on finding the pocket watch in his hand, he simply tossed it over the parapet wall. It dropped a hundred feet and smashed on the ground below.

The following is an extract from the journal of Dr Thomas Marlow, an Orientalist scholar who died in India in 1813, while on a tour of the northern provinces.

The society of Lucknow is sufficiently pleasant for us to tarry here a few more days than we had planned. In fact, have taken a bungalow just outside Baillie Guard Gate with a fine view of the river, the cool breezes of which we enjoy even on the most scorching of days. Servants we have hired in excess, though my wife seems to think there could never be too few of them. The most impressive of these are my two soontah burdars, burly fellows with horses' tails for moustaches. Their sole purpose is to follow me about on errands, guarding me with two awesome bludgeons of ornate silver, more for ceremonial purposes than for any real martial quality, though I do not doubt that a fib from one of them could break a man's skull as if it were a dove's egg. It was an idea of Martin Rogers's. He has four of them, at each corner of his palanquin. When he rides through town it looks as if the Queen of Sheba is on tour. As for the other servants, I cannot recall all of their designations, or their duties, but it seems to me they are paid in great part simply for sitting in the shade and passing the time of day with games of ludo and dice in the dust. There are Mossaulchees, Kitmagars, Khansomahs, Hookahbdars, Hirkarrahs, Poadas, one or two syces, a Chauskot, and a Dorreah.

Lucknow is a city of early breakfasts and late dinners. The gardens are lush and lovely, a verdant paradise of blossoms, shrubs, and trees. The city has a mood about it of languid splendour, where men and women concern themselves chiefly with only the arts of jollification and petty intrigue. The natives, of course, live in ribald luxury, having no discretion in their tastes. It is an orgiastic life, glittering with baubles and tinsel. The English of this city, most of them merchants, have all too freely adapted themselves to the virulent but oh so sweet pleasures of the city. It is a wonder that any of them still stand firm on their feet. I think the city should have been depopulated by this excess, but no, it thrives like a disease, with a false flush of health on the cheek and a deceptive hop to its step. One can only wonder when this will all collapse.

I have found few people of any intelligence in this city, however, with whom to carry on a productive conversation.

The bazaars in Lucknow are supposed to be worth seeing. I am not a man of the marketplace and my gods are more pastoral, so I have avoided these parts of the town. Ameenabad bazaar is the best shopping area, according to my wife. The fine embroidery and lace work of these craftsmen deserves mention, as well as the ornate brass work and silver filigree.

Of course there are many sights of interest for a scholar and I have taken in the mosques a number of times, and carried on conversations with the pirs of these mosques. They are shrewd men and love argument, but their minds are barricaded with laws and catechisms. Yesterday, for instance, we bargained over the divinity of Christ, like shopkeepers fighting over the value of an item. The pirs believe that Christ was born, but as a prophet, not as the son of God. I felt obliged to take the side of my tradition as these bearded Methusalahs began to dismantle the temple brick by brick. We bantered on for a good two hours, until my wife sent a servant to fetch me, saying it was time for tiffin. It says little for the Oriental mind that it is warped by its ancient predilections. This happens in such an ancient society, where ideas are boiled down with time to a hardened mass of aphorisms, laws, and creeds. India, however, is more than that. It is a crossroads as well as a nursery for art, culture, and religion. There is something buried in this country, in the soil, in the winds which breathe life across its dusty face, for whatever comes to India is changed, altered, turned into a more eloquent and lyrical expression of itself.

Take for instance the intricate art of miniature painting. I have seen this style as it is done in Persia, from where it was imported to this country. The figures in a Persian miniature are lifeless, merely flat motifs on the paper, decorative, impersonal, and without emotions. However, as soon as this style of painting reached India, via the Mogul courts, it was transformed into a vibrant celebration of life, the characters in those drawings animated and dancing off the page, with as much emotion in them as in a canvas by Goya or Velazquez. Here in India that crude art became a splendid form of creation. The artists imbibed the spirit of this country and their creativity was enhanced.

One has only to look at the music of India, and then to where it came from, and the same comparison becomes obvious. The lute in India is as expressive as the human voice, whereas in the Middle East it serves only to twang and warble like a child's toy violin.

The only importation into India which I believe has failed is that of the English Gentleman. Perhaps, as many would argue, he could not be improved upon, and the usually beneficent climes of Hindustan turned against his subtle and civilized nature, reversing the trend. Could it be that the English Gentleman has lost something in India, a subdued perfection of character, which is replaced by the frenetic excesses of life in places like Oudh?

The English in Oudh, for the variety of their life, are really quite the strangest birds in this aviary. They have adopted many of the Indian manners, such as smoking their pipes—hookahs—with the regal pose of any native potentate. A dinner party in any one of the Anglo-Oudh households is certainly a smoky affair, for everyone brings his own hookah and hookahbdar to light the pipe along with his private assortment of chillums, spouts, scented waters, and mouthpieces. Again it was Martin Rogers who showed me his hookah collection. He has drawers full of elegant smoking gear, everything from jade and emerald mouthpieces to chillums made of good English clay. He buys his tobacco from a little shop in Ameenabad, where the tobacconist stocks Turkish blends, Virginia leaf, and even some exotic Chinese tobaccos laced with opium. Everyone in Oudh has his private fancy, not like hobbies really, more like harmless private perversions. There is a fellow who is expert in the making of paans. He eats over fifty a day, a different one for each time of the day. Some have pearls ground into them, some diamonds, others are made with bhang and opium, sweet jams and currants. And remember that these are Englishmen, not natives, who have taken to these habits with such enthusiasm. It is as if the atmosphere of the town creates in them a frenetic imbalance.

Drink is by no means the least of these habits, though it cannot be blamed on Lucknow, for among the gentlemen of our race there is no mean degree of tolerance when it comes to wine. But this tendency is exaggerated in Oudh, to a dizzying degree. The parties I have attended, of which there have been too many to count, demand of the gentleman a strong, veritably immune constitution, a liver like a sponge, and a tongue with the diction of a hammer. I have none of these attributes, and on most occasions, after having taken my fill of wine, which by the standards of Oudh is miserly, I have fallen down unconscious and spent the night on my host's couch. I do not say this out of any desire for self depredation, or a perverse habit of insulting my own manliness, but simply to illustrate the amount these gentlemen of Oudh consume. Four bottles of claret are a minimum, and I have seen gentlemen still standing after eight and carrying on the most animated and perfectly genuine conversations with ladies of this society, who themselves are stout drinkers. No wonder the symbol of Oudh is the fish.

∽

Later that evening the tailor arrived, as Webley had said he would, with a bundle of clothes under his arm. He was a thin, gaunt little man with a white beard cropped neatly against his face. Augustine dismissed him abruptly, saying that he would try the clothes on in a little while. The tailor bowed and pranced out of the room, muttering softly to himself.

The Colonel toyed with the fine material, turning it over in his hands. It embarrassed him, as if he were looking through a pile of ladies' underclothes. Who would wear these petticoats, he said to himself. Nothing would make him put them on, or even hold them up against himself to check the fit.

A few minutes later two young men entered the room. They were effeminate and waved their hands in the air as they talked. From their appearance they looked like courtiers, but they introduced themselves as barbers and began to spread their combs and scissors out on Augustine's bed. The Colonel watched them suspiciously but did not send them away. One of them drew a chair into the middle of the room and asked Augustine to please sit down. He eyed the two men with mistrust. They were very smooth and oily and their moustaches seemed to have been trimmed every hour, to exactly the right length. While one sprinkled scented water on Augustine's hair, the other held a mirror up in front of him. The Colonel looked at himself in the glass with a stern embarrassment. The barbers' hands felt as if they were going to steal something at any moment. They were as gentle as a pickpocket's. The fingers ran swiftly through his long hair and massaged his scalp. All the time the mirror darted back and forth in front of Augustine, giving him views of his face from all angles.

With flashing scissors, the barber clipped away at the long strands of hair which hadn't been cut for months. Augustine felt like a pet dog. He was uncomfortable. The young man with the mirror put it down gently and went over to the bed. He returned with a paan for Augustine. The Colonel took it in his mouth, though he did not care for it, and chewed sullenly. All the time he kept wondering to himself why he let them do this to him. The tobacco had a bitter tang and the lime made his gums and lips feel numb. A mild intoxication overcame Augustine and he began to relax. The mirror was in front of him again and he was able to see his hair being styled to a fashionable length. The barber seemed to know what was proper and did not even ask him how he wanted it cut. He felt foolish. When the barber finished, he oiled Augustine's scalp with a greasy pomade which smelled strongly of magnolia. The Colonel remembered having smelled the same perfume on a prostitute in Baroda. The thought of her comforted him and he settled back in his seat. One of the barbers had begun massaging his face with another oil and then lathered his bristly cheeks. The man's hands seemed like a woman's, but Augustine began to ignore his senses. The paan lifted him out of the room. He was dreaming about the prostitute in Baroda. She had been a lovely woman, lithe and playful. Augustine had kept her for a while. There was a feeling of insanity about her, a desperation. She was temperamental, would rage for hours with him over the smallest matter. She was possessive in a strange way, not jealous, but Augustine always had the feeling that she was holding on to a part of him.

This madness of hers took the form of a curious habit. Augustine discovered it only after he had known her for some time. In a trunk which she jealously locked in her room were kept the pits of every fruit she had ever eaten. It was a hoard of mango seeds, apricot pits, pips from oranges and grapes, each carefully put away, like coins, something of value. They had more worth for her than anything else. Augustine finally got her to open the trunk for him and he watched with amazement as she ran her hands through the collection of cherry stones, which were arranged in a shallow ivory box, separate from the others. It reminded Augustine of Webley's collection of objects which he had stolen. There was something in this perversion which Augustine could not understand. It was as if the courtesan were savouring the refuse of all her affairs, as if she enjoyed not the fruit and its sweetness but what remained. She was a miser with love, stowing away the seeds, not for any purpose, simply out of an urgent desire to preserve and not to spend.

When he left her she said nothing, asked for nothing. But he knew in a queer way that she had kept a part of him, just as she hoarded the pips and seeds.

Augustine thought about her in detail. His mind drifted back and forth between a hunger for the woman and a detached realization of the room and the barbers. He remembered how easy it had been for him to leave her. All he had to do was walk out of the room. She did not begin to cry or follow after him. He did not have her clinging to his shirt and begging him to take her with him. She just lay there naked on the bed, with the calm detachment of a woman who has always been left, discarded. And he had felt nothing himself, only a faint sensation of distaste, more exhaustion than anything else. She was spread out on the sheets as if she were a part of the bed, as if the servants would come in the morning and roll her up with the bedding, along with the pillows, and put her in the cupboard. When the next man came, the bed would be made for him and she would be there, spread out as usual, with the inviting softness of a pillow.

The razor scraped off his beard. The young man's hands moved quickly, with an enthusiastic skill. Augustine felt someone holding his hand. He glanced down to see the other man manicuring his nails. A current of revulsion ran through him, but the paan seemed to have pinned him to the chair. His mind swam inside his skull like a fish in a glass bowl, with a trapped irritation. He wanted to give the two barbers a kick each and send them scurrying out of the room, but his whole body was drooped in the chair and refused to move. He felt as obese as Ashgar Hasan, as immobile. He kept trying to convince himself that the paan gave a pleasant sensation, but he was not enjoying it. He wanted to regain control of himself. A sense of frustration threatened inside him. He felt it fighting off the effects of the drug.

There is a point at which luxury outdoes itself, thought Augustine, where it becomes so lavish that it is obscene and perverse. It tries to disguise the animal in us. Women paint their faces, dress in yards of bright material, plait and braid their hair into complex arrangements of curls and curlicues, until they are dolls instead of people. Augustine felt himself being rearranged, turned into another creature, not human, not even animal. He considered this level of luxury, in which men were transformed, made so delicate as to be vulgar. Sex was the element in which they lived, not the hot and sweaty moments of copulation, but the cold, dry moments of desire. It was like ice that never melted. The luxury of Ashgar Hasan had a stamina which could only be sustained through the complete denial of fulfilment, a desire ever present but never fulfilled. What was there in that luxury but frustration disguised as pleasure?

The man who was manicuring Augustine's nails began to slip his hand under Augustine's shirt and remove his upper garments. At first the Colonel sat still and let himself be undressed. Once he was naked to the waist, the barber began to whet a razor in front of his face. As the blade was run up and down the leather strop, it made a sucking sound. The two men together oiled his chest and shoulders. It was only then that Augustine realized what was happening. He stood up suddenly, the paan forgotten and his mind clear and angry. With a shout he sent the two men scuttling out the door. He shook his head like a dog that has sniffed pepper up its nose and looked around him. Picking up the barbers' scissors and razors, he tossed them through the door. A nervous hand reached out and collected them from beyond the sill.

Augustine ran to the door between his room and Webley's. Throwing it open, he found his friend sitting in a similar position to the one he had been in a few minutes before, with one arm raised above him like a gibbon hanging from an invisible branch. Another barber was shaving his armpits with care. Webley grinned at the Colonel, with a stupid look of dazed bliss.

'What are you letting them do that to you for?' asked Augustine.

'It's quite nice. They say that in Lucknow women won't sleep with a man until he's shaved,' said the Englishman.

'They won't touch me,' said Augustine, looking down at his chest with horror.

'Oh, come on, my Colonel. It's all for the good. The women like you to shave your privates as well. You'd think they had something against hair.'

'You're mad. Let the women shave themselves if they want, I don't care. But a man …'

'Do you think a woman wants to go to bed with a bear?' asked Webley. 'Look at you. With your shirt off you have the appearance of some jungle animal, a monster. These women are delicate things, my dear, not the usual flotsam you've slept with in the past. They demand style. They have standards. What are you afraid of, that if you lose your hair your manliness will go as well? You're not Samson, damn it.'

Augustine looked with disgust at the Englishman's bald chest. Even his armpits were blond and there was hardly any hair to shave off. His balding head, nevertheless, had been carefully hidden under his forelock. Without saying anything more, he walked out of the room, leaving the Englishman to complete his grooming. Looking down at his hands, he suddenly noticed that one set of fingers had been cut and cleaned, the other was still dirty and the nails ragged from being torn and chewed. The creases in that hand were black with grease and grime, while the other hand was a ruddy brown colour.

Augustine was irritated with Webley. Why didn't he shave his head clean as well and be done with it? The Colonel could not understand this frivolous vanity. For him pride was something which involved armies, courage, skill. He did not pamper his vanity. Instead, he exhausted it in long chases after boar. His pride led him to risk his life. It was relentless and had no patience admiring itself in a glass mirror. He liked to see his reflection in greater things, against the panorama of battle, on horseback. His vanity rebelled against grooming and dress. He liked his hair chopped unevenly, his uniforms rugged and practical.

Ashgar Hasan had sent word to Webley that he was having a celebration in their honour that evening. The two mercenaries went down to join the party. Webley wore the white flowing outfit of a Lucknow courtier, looking the part except for his pale skin and withered-looking face. Augustine had changed into his uniform, which made him look twice as tall and broad. The rich blue jacket was festooned with gold braid, and epaulets protruded from his shoulders. From their rooms they could hear the music of lutes and drums. All day the smell of roasting lamb and curries had been rising from the kitchens behind the house.

The room they were directed to opened onto the garden. It was a long hall, with arcades running along the entire length of one side. The garden was lit by tapers as well as by a swarm of tiny oil lamps. All of this light gave the sky an even more perfect blackness. Each flame was dilated in the night and cast about it a faint glow of illumination, absorbed by the shadows. The palm trees, with their hidden flock of boarders, stood like sentinels, hoary clusters of branches massed about their tops.

The room itself was ablaze with lights. A tremendous chandelier of candles was suspended in the middle of the room, with two similar but smaller hanging lamps on either side. The glass chandeliers were stained a variety of pastel colours, soft blues and reds as well as a jade green. These colours gave the room an artificial atmosphere. The silver stem on which the exotic blossom of light hung was a thick chain of polished links. There was no delicacy to the chandelier, no spray of crystal facets. It hung from the ceiling like an awkward flower, one of those rare flowers which blossom once every hundred years.

It was a glass world, fragile and transparent. A lone musician sat in one corner of the room. In front of him was a jal tarang, a line of glass bowls filled with water to different levels. He tapped them with silver mallets, producing a light sparkling sound. But there was a sadness to the music, too, a soft sound like the chink of bangles or the melting of icicles, tears falling on a mirror.

A crowd of people filled the room. Their eyes turned on the two officers as they walked in. A rustle of voices filtered through the room. Augustine and Webley walked in boldly, their heads cocked, like two stags stepping out of cover. The uniform surprised everyone, with its stem, military cut. The man wearing it surprised them even more, partly because of his size, but also because his features were so truly his own. He looked like no one else they had ever seen. The blind eye glinted in the barrage of light, seeming to have a supernatural vision. Everyone knew who these two men were. Some in the crowd had probably heard stories about the Englishman's army. But there were no soldiers in the crowd, and if there had been, they would have been the sort of soldiers that carry jewel-encrusted swords and pose for portraits.

Ashgar Hasan dominated the room. He seemed not to have moved since the morning. It was as if his servants had picked him up as he lay there in the garden and carried him in the same position back inside the house. He seemed to have his own pedestal, a living sculpture. Two chairs, copies of European furniture, stood vacant on either side of the eunuch. One of the men sitting near Ashgar Hasan rose and gestured towards the chairs. Webley led the way. Both men sat down and crossed their legs in the same motion. They sat without looking at anyone in particular. Two hoses from the hookah were put in their hands, and trays of sweetmeats and spiced pastries were offered to them. Beakers of wine were also brought round and both men drank them to the bottom quickly. Once they had been refilled, they stood untouched for a long time. The hospitality, their manners, all seemed to be in accord with some unwritten text of etiquette. But it was not as though actions or the host's specific gestures had been dictated. This was a more subtle game. Its rules depended on each man's opinion of himself, for the most binding rules of etiquette stem from vanity.

For almost an hour nothing happened. No one in the crowd said anything out loud. The jal tarang whimpered like an abandoned child. It was as if the two guests were on display. Wild animals captured in the jungle, thought Augustine to himself, as he rolled his glass eye over the rows of guests. The chair was uncomfortable, and he crossed and recrossed his legs a number of times. Webley and Ashgar Hasan spoke in hoarse whispers and the Colonel could not make out what they were saying. From time to time a young boy squatting in front of the eunuch would lift a crystal goblet of wine to his master's bloated lips and tip exactly a mouthful into the enormous cavity of the eunuch's puffed cheeks. There would be deep gurgling sounds as the drink flowed into the formless body, and then a soft sigh would fill the room. Everyone fixed their eyes on the giant when he drank, as if they expected him to gobble up the saqui boy, the goblet, and all.

While he waited for the entertainment to begin, Augustine concentrated on fixing an expression on his face, somewhere between complete disdain for the crowd and a patronizing stare.

What he wanted was to stretch the effect of one glance over the period of an hour. He wanted the guests to remember only that fraction of a second which he would grant them. With patience he manipulated his face so that it formed the image of himself that he wanted those people to remember. They were all watching him. He had them captured and it was his job to convey to them that he was a far greater man than any of them, that he could spare only one glance for them and no more, being caught up in a much more important world. And yet while he tried to look distracted, he realized that he had nothing else to do. His mind at that point was not concerned with anything but looking and being looked at.

Augustine finally caught some of Webley's conversation with Ashgar Hasan.

'At war?' said the eunuch. 'But isn't that always the case with men like you?'

'Ah, but this time it is different,' said Webley, with a note of condescension in his voice. 'The English have challenged us.'

'But you are the English.'

'No, that's just it. I'm not. I've been thrown out of their camp, or rather, I left it. You see, they hate rebels even more than they hate the French. We are a separate race as far as they are concerned. You might call us another nation.'

'I don't understand,' said Ashgar Hasan. 'You are both conquering India, and in the end, no matter who succeeds, this land will be English, no?'

Webley nodded, with some thought.

'Well, put it this way, said Webley. 'I am conquering India for the King, my King. The Company is conquering it for the Prime Minister.'

'I see. But that makes them the rebels, doesn't it?' said the eunuch.

'You might say it does.'

The eunuch clapped his hands, almost as if in delight at this realization. The pudgy palms came together with a muted, hollow sound, but it had the effect of sudden thunder in the room. All whispers ceased. Silence seemed to echo through the hall, as if the sound had left a gap in the air and that vacuum reverberated with a hollow emptiness. Then in the quiet was heard a faint, far-off tinkle, the jangle of ankle bells, the sound of someone walking. The jal tarang stopped its music. As the sound grew louder, all heads turned to the garden. The tapers seemed to burn with a richer colour. The bells seemed to be the sound of the oil lamps. It was as if the silence had brought them to life, just as the darkness lit their flames. Just as the absence of light animated their colour, the absence of sound thrilled their voices.

The dancer entered the room, and as she did, the orchestra of lutes began to tune their strings. She moved across the room, wading through the crowd of men, a lone woman in their midst. And yet she did not surrender to them but cut a path to the centre. The crowd swept away, leaving a portion of the floor empty, for her to dance upon. She bowed low and reverently to the eunuch, her hand fluttering in front of her forehead as she dipped three times, once to Webley, once to her master, and once to Augustine. The Colonel caught in her eye a mischievous sparkle. He did not return the look but stared at her sternly.

The drums suddenly exploded and the dancer cocked herself with alarm. Standing there still and composed as if of stone, she waited for the correct beat to hurl her into the dance. The nautch began with a flurry, her breasts, her arms, her thighs jiggling about in animation. She was plump, though her curves were smooth and inviting. Her skirt stretched to midcalf. Her bodice was cut low, exposing the billow of her breasts. Two mirrors glinted to suggest her nipples, and a long veil was tucked into the niche between her breasts, the other end wrapped about her waist.

Augustine was relieved to have the gaze of the crowd off him for a while. He shifted in the chair and stared about him. He was glad to be the audience for once. The dancer did not excite him, even though she tossed her body about with an abundance of suggestion. Augustine sucked on the nozzle of his hookah and waited patiently for her to finish. When she did, the lutes whined in dismay.

Another dance was performed by the same woman, and then, at a signal from the eunuch, she was escorted out of the hall. Some of the men applauded, others jeered. The eunuch turned to Augustine and asked him what he thought of her.

'She was pleasant enough,' he said.

'The next one is far better. She is a curious woman. I have seen her dance once before and have brought her especially for you to see.'

Augustine bowed cautiously.

The second dancer was grotesque. She was tall and her body seemed to have been pulled and stretched, so that nothing was in proportion to anything else. Her breasts were enormous. Her legs had no shape and were flabby. Her belly was narrow, almost squeezed into a knot. Her hips swayed and her shoulders were as broad as any man's. But the most outrageous part of her was her face. It was speckled with smallpox and her nose had a twist to it, unbalancing all her other features. She was wall-eyed. Her lips completed her ugliness, painted crimson, the lower lip bulging out as if it had been bitten by a mosquito.

Webley laughed out loud when he saw her, and the rest of the audience joined in. Augustine could see Ashgar Hasan heaving with amusement under his voluminous clothes. The woman did not seem to notice the laughter of the audience. Instead, she smiled, as if they were paying her a compliment. Augustine searched her for a hint of sadness, but she covered it well. The snickers moved about the room and men leaned out to pinch her wide buttocks.

Her ugliness seemed to be her only trait, for she danced poorly, twitching about the floor like a cat in heat. The men were far more excited by her oddity than they had been by the former dancer's beauty. She seemed inhuman. Her body was as absurd as Ashgar Hasan's. While he seemed to have no shape, she was all contours and protuberances. Augustine wondered whether she might be a hermaphrodite, but there was a distinct feminine aura about her. She was almost a caricature of a woman. Augustine felt embarrassed, not because of any morality curdling in his mind, but more out of his inability to laugh at her. She was not even obscene. She was gross. In a peculiar way, he was fascinated by her, but she angered him as well by flaunting her ugliness. The very fact that she was a woman was what struck him most of all. His image of a woman was either motherly or sensuous. This woman was neither. She seemed to have no charm, no sympathy. She inflicted her ugliness on the world. Her dance might stimulate the other men in the room, but it only upset Augustine.

The evening went on and the audience refused to let the dancer leave the floor. Perspiration sparkled on her upper lip and streaked the powder on her face. When she spun around, spittle flew into the crowd of men. Augustine could hear her heavy breathing, a panting sound, low and husky. She became almost intoxicated and her wall-eyes rolled around in their sockets like white knuckles. Finally she fell, exhausted, writhing on the floor. Two of the men carried her out amidst jeers of disappointment.

Augustine noticed that Webley was the most disappointed of them all. He cried out loudly and shook his head, demanding more, yelling to the men to revive her and bring her back again. Ashgar Hasan was delighted at the success of his dancer and emptied most of a goblet of wine in a few deep swallows. The saqui refilled it. The uproar continued. Augustine sat sternly in his uniform. He wondered whether it was boredom or dissipation which excited these desires in the men. Were they all so satiated that they had to turn to grotesque women instead of beautiful girls? Had they seen too much beauty, or none at all? Did opulence breed bad taste? Suddenly the room disgusted Augustine. The chandelier was nothing but a glass monstrosity; its colours clashed and the light it cast hurt his eyes. The men with their clean oiled faces, their shaven armpits and smooth chests seemed repulsive to him. It all had a mood of degeneracy about it, of coarse scandal. There was no pleasure involved, only desires heightened by the bizarre and grotesque. Nothing was genuine. It was a world of glass: glass lamps, glass beakers, glass pitchers, glass jewels, glass music. Augustine felt clumsy in this world, in his heavy boots, with his sword and cummerbund. He felt that if he moved at all he would break things. He saw himself stepping on the jal tarang, shattering the tiny bowls under the heel of his boot. He saw himself knocking into the chandelier, having it burst in fragments about his head.

As Augustine was thinking about these things, he suddenly realized that the hall had become silent. Beside him, Ashgar Hasan had shifted his position. Servants were propping him up with pillows. He let them lift him with unconcern and smiled gently over the crowd, their beneficent patron, a symbol of their degeneracy.

The hush was broken by the sound of the eunuch clearing his throat. In a hoarse but mellifluous voice, he began to speak, first welcoming 'Webley miyan and his dear Colonel Augustine.'

He said that in honour of the occasion he had composed several lines of poetry, and with their kind permission he would like to recite the couplets. Augustine and Webley bowed slightly and gestured for him to begin.

Again the eunuch cleared his throat. He recited only the first phrase, then repeated it, recited the first line, repeated it, and then finally the entire poem in a gush of words, each syllable full of symbolism, meaning. Urdu is the language of poetry, thought Augustine, it is so subtle and complex.

In honour of my friends, Hasan will have another glass of wine,
For his throat is dry from talking about times that have passed.

A dry throat is the curse of either one who talks too much
Or him that cannot pay for wine. Words are spent like coins.

My fingers closed about this cup contain a secret,
As I drink the wine pries my fingers open.

Hasan, you have compared a woman to a chalice. Is it true,
Or is that simply your mistress's face reflected in the wine?

You ask yourself, How can such a fat man speak of love and women?
Oh, Hasan, from a distance you cast a thin shadow.

The warrior has two beds at night. One on the cold battlefield,
The other in a woman's arms. He goes to either life or death.

6

From Dr Marlow's journals: We are all awaiting eagerly despatches from the Continent as to the progress of the war in Spain. General Wellesley is said to be doing extremely well. Brigadier Wolsey made the point last night, at a small dinner given by Mr and Mrs Proctor, that should Wellesley succeed in routing the French, it would make an enormous impression on the Indian Army. There is a very strong feeling among the fawjis (the military) here in Lucknow that it is one of them doing the fighting over there. Of course Arthur Wellesley was a darling of the army here in India at the battles of Assaye and Argaum. The stigma which the Indian service languishes under, that they do very well at pounding the natives but wouldn't stand a chance against a noble enemy like the French, may soon be erased.

No dinner table is complete without conversation of Boney and his generals, the Spanish campaigns, and the proposed invasion of England. It was only a few months ago that we received full reports on the battle of Salamanca. Anglo-Indians throw the names Bussaco, Talavera, Vimeiro about as though they were Seringapatam, Laswari, and Aligarh. There is a feeling of being a part of the campaign. Only two years ago the Company armies attacked and conquered the islands of Bourbon and Mauritius, and insignificant but much talked of victory.

We have all been warned that Lucknow is full of French agents, each with his own wiles. The native courts are supposed to be overflowing with these scoundrels, peddling Bonaparte's wares to the perfidious rajahs. When each mail comes up the river, news spreads quickly among the Europeans of new gains and losses, of alliances and reinforcements.

The morning after Ashgar Hasan's banquet, Augustine and Webley rode into the city to explore the streets and gullies. It was early and the clouds had drifted to the corners of the sky, leaving an enormous canvas of empty blue above the city. Embroidering the canvas with the intricate stitching of their wings, vultures, hawks, and crows circled with leisurely deliberation over the carrion below. The smell of rotting flesh was mingled with that of the other refuse and the rank odours of the swamp. Even at that hour small groups of people were slogging through the mud in search of food and valuables. A cluster of chamars had grouped themselves around the carcass of a young buffalo which had died the night before. One of the men was skinning it, his hands moving quickly, his head swathed about completely in his turban.

They reached the ferry after wading through a patch of floodwater. On their side of the river, Webley pointed out a pack of dogs running across the open land to the north of the city. There must have been at least thirty of them, loping together in unison, without effort, almost as if they were floating over the ground. The two horses stopped and the men listened. A distant sound of baying reached them, faint and almost musical. But the sight gave Augustine a shiver of uneasiness and he kept his eye on the dogs until they were out of sight.

'Are they hunting hounds?' asked Webley of the ferryman as they were crossing.

'No, Huzoor, they are wild dogs. They have stolen children, killed farmers. Each of them is vicious and I have seen them bring down a full-grown ox.'

'Why have they not been shot?' asked Augustine.

'Men have tried and several have been killed, but they gather numbers, Huzoor. They will only die when one of them goes mad and bites the others. Then we will be rid of them, Huzoor.'

The city was a filthy maze of tiny streets. There were occasional gardens planted here and there amongst the jumble of houses. The two officers admired some of the buildings, the palace, and the tank. The great Imambara with its high gates carved with the designs of fishes and crocodiles stood facing west. But neither Augustine nor Webley was impressed. They had seen far grander monuments in Baroda and Delhi, with more intricate carving than any displayed on the buildings of Lucknow. The city seemed ready to crumble, though it was still a young capital. The mood inside the city was derelict as well. The pageantry was all there—in fact the streets seemed to have been prepared for a procession and a festival—the gates of the city had been painted gay colours at one time, but it had all faded. The decorations had been blown down by the wind and rain. The monsoon hung over the city with an unpleasant closeness. People walked about as if in a stupor. Augustine wondered whether the night before they had all been to celebrations like the one at Ashgar Hasan's palace and were all suffering from a common hangover.

These were not the swamp people. These were the city people, but they seemed to be dredging through their own swamp of transactions and mercantile pursuits. Was it a swamp of gold in which they were searching for a discarded clod of mud, a sea of jewels in which they had lost a horse's turd? Within all that excess there seemed to be an essential scarcity.

Lucknow was a city of bricks and plaster, whereas Delhi was one of sandstone and marble. Where is the city our armies will build? wondered Augustine. It is of canvas and cotton, the least permanent of all cities, but for that reason the safest.

Shortly after Augustine had joined the Gaekwad's army under Webley, they were sent to Delhi as the escort for an ambassador from Baroda to the Mogul court. The army encamped south of the old city and waited there for a month, until the ambassador had been received and completed his business with the Emperor.

There were no hostilities and the army was simply there for the sake of pageantry and to impress the city of Delhi with its straight lines and smart uniforms. For that month, Webley and Augustine amused themselves hunting nilgai and peacocks in the countryside around their camp. It was a desolate area, with a scruffy growth of thorn jungle cut up by ravines.

Though no one lived outside the walls of the city, there were extensive ruins of former cities scattered in all directions, a vast maze of rubble, overgrown by the munj grass and babool trees. It was treacherous for riding because of the many abandoned wells and drains, where a horse's leg could easily be broken. The grass hid snakes as well as game birds and rabbits. On one day, riding behind a pack of hounds, they killed over thirty brace of rabbits, and ruined six horses. For miles the crumbling forts and tombs stretched away in derelict patterns of former grandeur. Of all the remaining buildings the most plentiful were mausoleums, built to contain the remains of kings, queens, lovers, and courtiers. Here and there even a saint had been entombed.

These buildings covered the horizon with their silhouettes, hundreds of domes, like a range of low hills, some of them recently constructed, others falling down with age. Augustine could remember vividly riding through this city of tombs—the graves were as large as houses—at sunset, with a ruddy glow hovering around each of the monuments like a halo. The peacocks calling sounded like lamenting bagpipes. They would perch on top of the tombs, etched against the sunset, as if mourning the death of the soul beneath them. Augustine could remember shooting them off the tombs and then sending a boy running to pick up the bird if it was dead, or to chase it through the knee-high grass if only wounded. Once a boy had been lost till morning chasing a wounded peacock.

They had been camped outside Delhi for almost two weeks. Webley was complaining about being bored. They had shot great amounts of game, crocodiles from the Jumna, ducks and geese. He and Augustine were out near Hauz Khas, the great tank and university built by Feroz Shah. Close by the complex of buildings was a line of tombs, older even than the tank. Without explaining himself, Webley sent a man back to camp to bring a canister of powder. It was about noon and the man returned late in the afternoon. Meanwhile, Webley had entered one of the tombs and dug a small hole in two of the walls. He then constructed a mine out of cloth, paper, and powder packed tightly into holes in the wall. He trailed a line of powder from each mine as a fuse and set a match to his handiwork.

One of the mines exploded beautifully, sending bits and pieces of the wall in all directions. A few stones almost landed on top of Augustine and the horses. The other mine flared up with a tremendous cloud of sparks and smoke, but there was no explosion. That side of the mausoleum remained intact. Augustine could remember the acrid smell of the powder, and the sight of the stones and rocks erupting in all directions. He joined Webley and together they blew up four more tombs before nightfall. The two men almost killed each other when they both set a match to separate fuses and didn't tell each other. The tomb burst into the air behind them as they were running for cover, and only through luck did they escape.

Now, as they rode through Lucknow, Augustine imagined the buildings exploding around him, bursting into the air, spewing the wafer-like bricks in all directions. The destruction of those monuments had given them a thrill, as though they were tampering with history. It was more than vandalism, it was an assertion of their lifestyle, the violence of their personalities in conflict with the permanence they found around them.

Returning from their tour of the city, Augustine and Webley passed through an especially narrow gully which opened onto the river. It was just dusk. A haze filled the air—coal and wood smoke from cooking fires. The houses along the gully were ornately carved, with honeycombs of small windows along the top floors. Dogs hunched and diseased, not like those sleek animals they had seen running across the plain, skulked in the drains. Rats the size of tomcats ran between the legs of the horses. Webley was in the lead. Augustine followed a few lengths behind.

Above him he heard the sound of a shutter being opened and looked up to see a braceleted arm adjusting the curtain. It was a thin arm, and it darted about like a graceful dhaman searching for prey. Augustine stopped his horse and stood there watching. In a moment a figure appeared. It was a girl of about sixteen. Her face was oval-shaped and her hair, combed free, swept over her shoulders. The eyes fixed on Augustine were young and curious. He felt an absurd desire to throw something up to her, a token of his surprise. There was a child-like loveliness about the girl, which seemed incongruous in that crass city with its perversions, its flies, its filth. Hurriedly he tore a button from his jacket, and when he caught her eye, he threw it up to her. She held it awkwardly, all the while looking at Augustine. Then her eyes fell to the button. It was simple, made of brass with a pattern etched into it.

She laughed brightly and disappeared. The Colonel smiled and stayed a moment, looking up at the open window. He didn't really know why he had thrown it up to her, except that her innocence had delighted him. He had, up to that point, decided Lucknow contained no one like her. The girl had nothing to do with the city. Perhaps she was from out of town. Then suddenly Augustine realized the rashness of what he had done. Could anyone have seen him? He looked around. The other windows were empty. Her father would kill him if he had been seen. Who was her father? he wondered.

As if in answer to all these questions, a voice rattled up from below him. Augustine looked down and there at a low window, almost on a level with his horse's knees, was a withered face, hoary and diseased. There were pale pink splotches on her skin. The crone repeated herself, as if he could have misunderstood her.

'Do you like the young one?'

Augustine started up in his saddle. A lost feeling took hold of him. Now he wished he had not stopped, had only seen the bracelets on the girl's arm.

'She will cost you plenty,' said the crone. 'There are dozens of cheaper women, more experienced than she. But when you pick a bud, you destroy a flower, and that raises the price.'

Webley had turned his horse around at the end of the gully and stood watching. Augustine spurred his horse on.

'Women?' asked the Englishman.

Augustine nodded.

'Then who's stopping us?' said Webley with a laugh, and rode past Augustine, who followed him back to the window.

'One that has bathed recently,' said Webley to the crone. 'And knows the tricks.'

Augustine said nothing, but dismounted. A boy came out of the main door of the house and took their horses. The two men stepped into the courtyard, ringed with verandas on all four sides. The crone appeared out of a shadow, her twisted body like a gnarled root that had just been dug out of the ground. The courtyard was empty, but there were voices dodging about and the sound of singing, hushed and brittle.

The old woman directed Webley in one direction and told him to choose for himself. She crooked her finger in front of Augustine's nose and then pointed up a staircase to the top floor.

'You will be the first man she has had,' whispered the crone. 'Are you sure you can afford it?'

Augustine did not say anything to her. He followed the bent finger up to the second floor and found the door open. Hesitating a moment, he knocked. There was no answer. He brushed the curtain aside and strode in.

The girl was curled up against the pillows of her bed, examining the button Augustine had thrown to her. She did not even look up when he came in, but let him stand there for a minute while she traced the pattern with her fingernail. Her hands seemed so small to Augustine, so delicate. She was humming softly to herself, with the detachment of an idiot. Her hair was blown around her like a restless cloud, but she still looked unravished, young and pretty. Augustine felt awkward in front of her, and when she raised her eyes he could not help looking away. She seemed to have known that he would arrive in her room. As if the street opened onto her bed, Augustine thought bitterly.

The girl was dressed like any other prostitute, except that her breasts did not fill the bodice as fully as they should have and her skirt was loose around her hips. She had not painted her face, either. It was as if she was acting the part. Augustine tried to console himself with that thought. He only wished that he was somewhere else with her, and hated the old woman for having broken those naive moments.

'What is your name?' he asked kindly.

'Laila,' she said in a sly voice, not looking at him but smiling at the button.

'No, your real name.'

She thought a moment, and Augustine wondered whether

she had a real name, or whether she lived under a dozen names.

'Khasturba.' This time she looked earnestly at Augustine and he believed her.

'Are you old enough to use musk?' he said as a joke.

'It is only a name, but I do use musk. Would you like to smell it?'

He came closer and sat down next to her. The scent was there, faint and yet powerful, so that Augustine wanted to keep on breathing it, deeper and deeper, until it overwhelmed him. She was not self-conscious at all and laughed at him.

'You snuffle about me like a pig in a garbage heap.'

'Don't say that.' Augustine took her hand away from the button and kissed it. 'How old are you, Khasturba?'

'Thirty-five,' she said with a laugh.

'The old witch downstairs told me you'd never slept with a man before.'

'She lies. That way she can charge you more. Virgins are scarce in Lucknow.'

'Don't say that,' Augustine repeated.

'Then what would you have me say, that I am your daughter?' She spoke impetuously, with a distilled maturity, giving her an impish air.

'Is this for me?' she asked, pointing at the button.

Augustine nodded. He turned away from her and stared at the floor. Hating himself for ever having stopped in front of her window, he lifted himself off the bed and began to leave. She was on her feet in a moment and pushed him away from the door. He was surprised at her strength and let himself be dragged back to the bed. She was still laughing, in a lighthearted warble. The sound of her voice held him there.

'Would you rather I lied and said that you were the first, and cried out in pain when you put yourself inside me? Would you have me tell you I did not enjoy it because it was the first time, but promise that tomorrow I would explode with pleasure? I have lied about these things so many times. What is once more? They say that even a whore is supposed to be committed to the first man to come inside her. I don't believe any of that. I don't think it matters. I am eternally a virgin. Love me now and I will love you as if it were the first time. When it is over, will it be any different for you or me from a dozen other times before? Or is this your first time?' she asked with cunning.

Augustine had to laugh.

'But I will not make love to you tonight. We'll just sleep beside each other,' said the Colonel.

'She will charge you the same.'

'I will pay her double the price.'

'You're mad. Are you afraid that afterwards it will be like any other time?'

'No, it could never be that way.'

Khasturba sighed gently and went to a chest of drawers in the corner of the tiny room. Augustine fought with his boots until they came off. As he watched her, she prepared an opium pipe, heating the resinous ball over an oil lamp. She went about the process carefully, using only what she needed of the drug, not wasting any of the gummy substance. The smell it gave off was bittersweet. She offered Augustine the pipe, and when he refused, she shrugged lightly and inhaled the opium herself. He had not expected this and it shocked him. But he let her finish the pipe without saying anything.

She came to him, with her eyes blurred over with what he wanted to imagine were tears. But she was not crying and clutched Augustine with passion, not remorse. Her arms, her mouth, her legs, every part of her tried to seduce him, but he wrenched himself free and laid her down on the bed.

'Listen to me. Let us just sleep together.'

'What? Have you lost something more than your eye in war?' She was teasing him.

Augustine threw her an angry look. 'No, I don't want to make love tonight.'

'But that's what I'm for,' she said.

'Just let me hold you.'

She let him pull her to him and lay sulkily, sucking on the tips of her fingers. The Colonel brushed her hair flat down on her head and kissed her forehead. She squirmed.

'Oh, well,' she said finally, throwing her head back and looking at him with a frown. 'It's just as well. I'm still sore from last night. He was enormous.'

Though it hurt him, Augustine said nothing. After a while Khasturba spoke again. 'Are you not jealous?'

'Of course,' said Augustine with a smile.

'I don't understand. Did you come here to sleep with a whore or to find a wife?'

'I did not mean to come here at all,' said Augustine.

'Then your friend dragged you along. Who is he?'

'A friend,' said Augustine.

'You are soldiers?'

'How did you guess?' asked Augustine, kissing her again. She had quieted down and now spoke in a drowsy voice, soft and melancholy.

'And who do you fight for? The Nawab or the English? Your friend is English, no?'

'We fight for ourselves,' said Augustine.

'Bandits?' she asked with wide eyes, mocking astonishment.

Augustine said nothing.

'How did you lose your eye?' she asked bluntly. 'By a sabre cut, or a musket ball, or an exploding mine?'

'A spark from a cooking fire,' said Augustine quietly.

'No, don't lie to me,' she said, laughing. 'It must have been something more heroic than that. A tiger clawed it out or maybe another whore like me.'

'It was just a spark, a splinter of light. How old are you?' he asked her again.

She eyed him suspiciously. 'I am fifteen, or sixteen. I'm not sure exactly. I can only guess.'

'You have parents?'

She threw herself away from Augustine and glared at him, with the fury of a cat. 'You did not have to come here to feel sorry for me. You have no claim to me. I will sleep with you because it is my business. But do not feel sorry for me.'

Augustine reached over and took her arm. With a firm hand he dragged her off the bed, undressed her, and then put her under the sheet. He did not say any more, but extinguished the candle flame between his fingers. The two of them lay there in the blackness of the room, neither of them moving, not touching each other. All that Augustine could hear was the girl's breathing, quick and panting. He wondered if it was the opium. What dreams did it tie her up with? He imagined the drug taking her like a man. She gave herself to everything, to the drug, to the darkness of the room, to the night. Her life focussed around abandoning her body to the world. She knew no desire. The money went to the old crone. What presents she gets, from old men like me, thought Augustine, she keeps. The presents mean nothing to her, except that her childish features have fooled another man, so vain as to feel sorry for her. But then Augustine realized that she had not lied to him. Somehow the frankness of her admission comforted him. She had not treated him like another lion after a lamb. She knew that her virginity meant something to him, and that was why she had told him the truth with all the brutality of a shattered innocence.

Augustine thought about Webley. He must have chosen a woman like the one that danced at Ashgar Hasan's. Maybe that same woman lived here in this brothel. He could not help but imagine their lovemaking. Coarse and ugly, like an old wrestler doing his exercises. Webley's body reminded him of a white radish. The whore would look even more exaggerated and inhuman with her clothes off. The thought disgusted him. When he shut his eyes in the darkness, it was brighter than when he opened them.

Khasturba rolled over against him and put her face in his chest. He held her gently and let her fall asleep. They said nothing more. Her perfume seemed to put him to sleep, like a drug, like the opium she had taken. When he woke it was light. The window she had opened the evening before gaped at the morning. Augustine dressed quietly, while the girl slept in a heavy trance-like sleep. Augustine did not wake her, kissing her on the forehead gently before going out.

Webley was still asleep but rose quickly at Augustine's knock and left his woman, lying bleary-eyed, clutching a few coins in her hand. The crone caught the two men as they were leaving and took her money from them, before sending the boy to fetch their horses. This morning she was less friendly and spoke to them as if they were nothing more than boys who were up to mischief.

As they rode down to the river, Webley reached into an inside pocket and produced an enamel brooch in the shape of a peacock.

'It's rather nice, isn't it?' he said jokingly.

Augustine smiled and handed it back to the Englishman. 'Do you think she'll miss it?' asked the Colonel.

'Not unless it was of sentimental value, and I don't think anything in this city is.' Webley spoke lightly and with his fingers combed the hair over his bald patch.

From Dr Marlow's journals: Yesterday we attended the funeral of Major Ridgeley's wife, Clara. The poor woman had suffered terribly and her death was merciful. The surgeons could not decide on what it was that killed her. Some said fluxes, others called it a malignant fever, someone suggested cholera. They are still not sure what took her, but I imagine it was one of the dozens of tropical diseases these climes are apt to spawn.

Death in India has a peculiar suddenness about it, and it is uncommon for anyone to go on for months before dying, as in Mrs Ridgeley's case. Usually the disease hits you one moment and you are in the grave the next. I remember the very sudden death of our hostess in Allahabad, the widowed Mrs Cartwright. The night previous she had presided over a sumptuous dinner with all the graciousness of a dignified lady. She went to bed with a slight fever, my wife says, nothing uncommon. The next morning she was suffering severe chills and by noon was unconscious. It took hardly seven hours to kill her. The surgeon diagnosed it as a putrid fever.

Living under such uncertain, nay, tenuous circumstances explains to a degree the character of Anglo-Indians. They enjoy life to the fullest, knowing that tomorrow they too may well succumb to some such dread disease. As for the military, their plight is worse. In camp and on the battlefield, even in European wars, infection and gangrene take a heavy toll. But in India the dangers are a hundredfold. The slightest cut, the lightest wound, can become septic within an hour, causing the loss of limb and sometimes even life. A bullet in the stomach is as fatal as one in the head.

Death is viewed here with a certain nonchalance. It is such a common occurrence. People attend funerals with hardly a wet eye among them. At poor Mrs Ridgeley's burial, only her husband looked distraught. The others were as composed and serious as if this were just a simple vespers service in the chapel. Whereas in England I have seen hysterical kin being led off to carriages and a melancholy gloom settling over all the mourners, here in India it is a routine, not quite a picnic, but certainly not a cause for much concern. And though at first I was shocked at the impassivity of these people, I now realize that if I were to attend four funerals a week, every week, and many more—as many as three a day—during the rains, I too would lose all emotion.

Death is a way of life here. The graveyards stretch on and on, their carved monuments like a miniature model of the city. There is a wall around the cemetery, and inside there are one or two struggling trees. But otherwise it is a plot of land completely divested of life. There is no grass, no moss, no pleasant bird, not even a wriggling gecko. The tombs are elaborate but their marble has a deathly quality about it. The miniature angels and crucifixes, the tiny domes and parthenons, the Roman columns and copies of native temples and palaces, all add an unreal touch to the graveyard, an unbelievable jumble of culture. Mrs Ridgeley was buried under a tiny bungalow, a copy of the one she had lived in all her stay in Lucknow. It had been a request of hers and the carvers had been working on it for months, completing it only a few weeks before she died. The graveyard is situated on the banks of the river Gumti, poorly placed, for every year the waters of the river overflow and flood the cemetery. The white saltpetre has made its way into the wall and has crept over most of the tombs, eating away the masonry and bricks. It gives the whole place an eerie sort of look. I heard one lady remark that this was the closest any of them would get to lying in an English churchyard covered with good English snow. The saltpetre resembles snow, but is crusted and yellow in places. It crumbles under your feet with an abrasive sound. Some say it eats the corpses up like acid, others claim it preserves the bodies with its chemicals. I heard that one time a grave which had been covered with saltpetre was dug up years after the burial, and the corpse was perfectly life-like, unchanged by time.

∽

Webley ordered the barber to come shave him and told the servants that he would not receive anyone until he had prepared himself. Augustine bathed and then took a light breakfast on his veranda overlooking the garden. The day was deceptively bright, for though the sun was out with tremendous force, shadowy patterns of cloud were moving in to shutter it off. Augustine watched the scenery about him change as he ate melon and sipped almond sherbet.

He thought about the girl persistently, as if she were an unsolved sum, an answer which nothing added up to. Cautiously he wondered whether the crone would part with her. He could always kidnap her. Khasturba was like one of those flowers which blossom at night. They give themselves to the moon instead of to the sun. She is an eternal virgin; Augustine wanted to laugh at the thought. The crone had called her a bud. Every night, like one of those exotic flowers, her bud opened and she gave herself to the falling stars, to the comets, to the sickle moon. Daily she returned to a bud, shrivelled up like a tight nipple, waiting to be opened by the eager darkness. It is beautiful, thought Augustine, while it lasts. But she will wither quickly and the crone will throw her out. Perhaps the crone was once like her, fresh to the touch. Augustine shivered. Now she is like a black and wrinkled tuber that has been uprooted by hungry pigs.

In his mind he idealized the girl. He thought about himself, twice her age. He felt ashamed. And yet his vanity stopped him. He was still a man and the night before he could have made love to her violently, with fury and stamina. What frightened Augustine was the thought of other lovers. She will have them all clinging about her. And worse than that, those nights beside me, when we are alone in the darkness, she will still be unfaithful, giving herself up to the stars. Lying there on her back, embracing the night with all the pent-up desires of her imagination.

He realized the futility of his desire for her and yet he could not stop the plotting in his mind. He wanted to kidnap her from the crone and take her with him back to the Bijilli Gargh. Augustine wondered when Webley planned to return to the fort, and he guessed it would be a while. He didn't want to leave her with the witch another night, to have her virginity taken the hundredth time.

Webley knocked on the door and walked in. He was combed and dressed, as if for another one of Ashgar Hasan's parties.

'Come, my Colonel. They say a gentleman waits in the garden below. Shall we go have a look at him?'

'You've no idea who he is?' asked Augustine.

Webley shook his head. The two men stepped out into the hall and headed downstairs. The building was still. Asghar Hasan never rose until three in the afternoon. A few servants moved about cleaning up the remains of last night's party.

The garden seemed empty. The grey cover of clouds gave it a mysterious atmosphere, as if haunted. The half-caste and the Englishman walked towards the pavilion at the end, between the sentinels of ragged palms. Nothing moved. They climbed the steps up to the marble platform on which Ashgar Hasan had been lying the first time Augustine had seen him. There was no one there today. The marble gave the pavilion an eerie feeling, like a tomb or a monument. They turned and stood looking back at the house.

'I wonder where he's gone to,' said Webley. 'The chuprassie said he was waiting in the garden.'

Just as he said this, as if it had been a cue for his entrance, a man stepped out from behind a lattice covered with vines. He was about a hundred feet away. They had passed right by him without noticing. Behind him followed a boy of about nine or ten, an African, black as obsidian.

Augustine guessed the man was French, though his costume was Indian. He was very thin inside the voluminous clothes. Within all the layers of petticoats and outer garments the figure moved as if it was naked, with a self-consciousness, a mincing nudity. On his head he wore a tightly tied nawabi turban. An orange crest of feathers was pinned in front with a jewelled brooch. He wore gold earrings. His coat had a richly patterned border woven in gold on a silk background. It was full-length and fell in tiny pleats from his waist, which was wrapped around with a sash of the same material. His shoes were brocade and turned up at the toes. To Augustine he was the perfect, ludicrous image of a European affecting the nawabi style, overdressed and uncomfortable.

The African boy, too, was fancifully dressed. He wore a red velvet jacket with lace cuffs. Instead of trousers he wore a pair of pink satin breeches, which seemed to harness him uncomfortably. As he followed the Frenchman, the boy's face carried a hurt, almost belligerent expression.

As the two outlandish figures came towards them, Augustine caught the first whiff of perfume. They both seemed to be bathed in it. There was nothing discreet about the scent, like Khasturba's perfume. The attar, for Augustine recognized it as the perfume made in Lucknow, reeked as if to disguise something. The two figures, one slippery as an eel on ice, the other cross and petulant, seemed to float in the fragrance. It was their medium. They seemed preserved in it, like cherries in brandy.

'James!' the voice, a violin tuning up: 'I wouldn't have recognized you.' The arms were thrown out to embrace Webley, but the Englishman bowed slightly and stepped aside.

'Jules. What in hell are you doing here?' asked Webley.

'Is that any way to greet a brother after thirty years?' the Frenchman asked Augustine with familiarity, and then to Webley: 'Introductions, my dear, introductions. Who is this Solomon?'

'His name is Colonel Augustine. This is my half-brother, Jules Antigone.'

'My inexpressible pleasure,' said the Frenchman, blinking his eyes at Augustine.

'And why the blackamoor?' asked Webley.

'This,' said Jules, with a flick of his wrist, 'is Domingo, a young man of great potential. He will soon take the world by storm. In fact, I call him the black Napoleon. Hah, hah!'

'Lucknow, of all places to find you,' said Webley with a sneer.

The Frenchman pranced through six beats of a waltz step and then bowed. 'I love the wickedness but I can't stand the filth,' he said.

At this moment Domingo, the black Napoleon, spouted out a stream of French. His pink lips burst open over white teeth, and when he spoke, it seemed he was saying twice as much as actually came out. The Frenchman patted his furry head and laughed.

'He says he does not like you—' to Augustine. 'That your glass eye is demonic.' The boy stepped forward, to offer his own translation by kicking Augustine in the shin.

'Monsieur Domingo, it will do no good to kick him. He is a soldier. They feel no pain.' Jules laughed at his own joke.

Webley spoke. 'You haven't changed in your tastes, I see, little boys and rouge. Do you still drink your cognac out of a crystal slipper?'

'Ah, like a good brother you remember,' said the Frenchman, taking Webley by the arm. 'Come, James, there is a taint of bitterness in your conversation. Are you still cross about when I threw you in the fountain? I got a black eye in return, so isn't it quite settled?'

'You found us quickly,' said Webley. 'Who told you of our arrival?'

'Lucknow is a city of whispers.'

Webley and his half-brother drew aside and walked away from the pavilion, leaving Augustine facing the black Napoleon. The Colonel tried to make friends with a smile. The boy frowned and seemed to turn an even darker black.

'Come, let us be friends,' said the Colonel, patting the boy on the back.

Another swift kick to the shin made Augustine move back a step. Bonaparte could not have looked more defiant. Domingo resembled the general. He was fat. Obviously the Frenchman overfed him. His eyes seemed to sear everything he looked at. His stance was that of a toy soldier, a miniature giant.

The two brothers were walking on the far side of the garden. They did not seem to be getting any friendlier, and once in a while Webley's voice grew loud enough for Augustine to hear. Meanwhile, he tried to entertain the boy, first showing him his sword. Domingo turned it over in his hands, feeling the smoothness of the steel. Then, without warning, he made a jab at Augustine, almost running him through. The Colonel leapt aside and wrested the sword out of the boy's hand. With care he sheathed it and decided to play safer games with the boy. He noticed a small gecko stuck to the roof of the pavilion. Very slowly the Colonel reached up and then, with a sudden lunge, grabbed the lizard in his fist. It squirmed frantically but he held it firm between two fingers and thrust it towards the boy. Domingo's teeth flashed in a snarl of fear and his eyes bugged out. He howled and was off like a rabbit after the Frenchman, tripping over a creeper as he dove off the steps of the dais. In complete terror, he blundered through hedges and flowering shrubs until he landed gasping at his protector's feet. Jules looked startled and gathered the boy into his arms, cooing to him like a mother. Augustine looked down at the lizard and shook his head. He was almost glad the boy had been scared away. Gently he put the gecko back on the wall and went inside.

~

Webley had mentioned Jules two or three times before, when telling Augustine about his family and childhood in England. It was one of those things that Webley liked to talk about, just as he liked to discuss women or horses.

The English have a certain amount of respect for their childhood, Augustine had decided. It is a nostalgic longing to return. In fact, when they grow up they live an imitation of that childhood. And in that childhood Jules had always been the villainous half-brother intent on destroying their fun, trampling their sand castles, invading their games. The way Webley talked about his younger days, it seemed as if he still hated Jules for throwing him into the fountain, and that he was ready to black his eye again. Somehow those days seemed more important to Webley than what he was doing now. He talked of school and his friends with a longing to retain some of that boyish excitement. He still wished he could cause mischief, steal the masters' books, throw ink at 'Gobble' Fanning, who was twelve stone and looked twice that. Each of the boys dreamed of becoming a soldier, of killing Frenchmen and conquering Spain. And now, those dreams come true held no excitement for Webley. He wanted to recapture that childhood, not because those things he had dreamed of were less adventurous in actuality. No, he had surpassed his imagination. What he wanted to return to was a reckless immaturity, a virginity. It was that world of sweaty boyish glory, a copybook existence, where everything was more than real. His adulthood robbed him of that rosiness, that wild irresponsibility.

For Augustine it was difficult to understand, because his childhood was nothing but a space between birth and maturity in which he was taught the things he would use later on. There were games, a gay time, his mother, dreams and illusions of being a soldier. And yet now that he was thirty-five, he had no desire to return. It had tried all his patience to coax some warmth out of Domingo. Augustine was a man. He had dignity. Even when he was a boy, it was as if he had been a miniature man. His father took little notice of him until he was old enough to hold a sword. And yet there was nothing unkind about his childhood, no lack of love, no neglect. In fact, his mother would have wept at the thought of sending him to boarding school for nine months of the year. She would never have been able to console herself for that. His childhood, except for moments, was forgotten, blocked out of his mind. It was as if Augustine's life had begun with the death of his mother.

∽

The three men lay silently in their palanquins. Ashgar Hasan rode in the lead, six men carrying his enormous weight, instead of the usual four. Each of the palanquins was curtained with rich brocade draperies. Augustine felt like a woman in purdah, amidst all the tassels and mirrored cushions. The only light which entered the palanquins came through two fine-lace windows. Augustine squinted through these to get a view of where they were being taken. Outside were the sounds of the street. The bright sunlight fell in patterns on the Colonel's clothes.

Both he and Webley were dressed in their uniforms. They were being hidden from the crowds in the street, to avoid suspicion and rumour.

After a good hour of riding they reached the palace and Augustine could feel the palanquin tilt as the bearers carried him up a flight of steps. They seemed to wander through the rooms of the palace for several minutes before they finally set Augustine down.

He crawled out and stretched himself. The room was a narrow passage, hung with dismal pictures and tapestries. Oil lamps with pastel-coloured chimneys lined the walls. Webley emerged and brushed his hair down with a hand. In the crook of one arm he cradled his helmet. Augustine thought to himself: How much more dignified he looks in a uniform. The flimsy silks and laces of Lucknow made him look older, more fragile. As he stood there, looking about the hall, there was no mistaking him for anything but an officer.

Ashgar Hasan's palanquin was not in sight. The two officers waited to be instructed. Augustine felt a strange mood in the palace, a haunted feeling, as though everything were about to vanish. The oil lamps gave the room a dull light, and there was also the faint smell of their burning, thick and stale. The palanquin bearers had disappeared and the only other person in the room was a lone sentry at the far end of the hall, guarding a double door. He held a lance in one hand, but there was nothing impressive about him. He was as tawdry as the room, the worn silk carpets and the badly painted portraits. The sentry slouched as though he were asleep. He had no dignity and Augustine despised him.

They had come to have an audience with the Nawab. Ashgar Hasan had arranged everything and had instructed them on etiquette. The Nawab was supposed to be a very effeminate and nervous man who was easily insulted. If the slightest detail was missing, or even a hint of disrespect showed in a man's face, the Nawab would fly into a temper and all chance of winning his favours would be destroyed.

'He is like a high-bred stallion,' said Ashgar Hasan. 'He is unpredictable, quick to take offence, sudden in his judgments.

He can change his mind four times in an instant.'

Augustine was faintly nervous that Webley might offend the Nawab with his vanity. He could not bow and cringe too long. If things went badly, all hopes of getting aid from the Nawab would be lost.

No mention was to be made of the Bijilli Gargh or their army. The politics of the situation were not to be discussed. They had come to be seen, to present their nuzzer and leave. Ashgar Hasan would do the rest. If the two officers were well received, then in time all would be arranged. This was a formality, merely a ritual. Their nuzzer, the gifts they would offer the Nawab, had already been prescribed by his secretaries. They had requested English watches, a jewelled belt, and a wig, which Ashgar Hasan explained was something the Nawab had once seen an Englishman wearing and desired for himself. All of the requests had been carefully purchased by Ashgar Hasan and lay ready for presentation.

Augustine felt as though the fate of their army lay on those silver trays. He was nervous not because of the Nawab's reputation or the grandeur of the rooms. He felt uneasy about the Bijilli Gargh and wondered how the Nawab could arrange everything for them, when he himself was nothing more than a puppet of the English. Everything he did was watched. Ashgar Hasan had explained that this was why they had to be especially secretive about the meeting. They should not have met at all in that case, thought Augustine. But the Nawab would never give them arms and money without receiving their nuzzer and taking a good look at them.

The double doors opened suddenly and startled the sentry. A plump man and two servants came down the hall towards them. He greeted them in flowery Urdu and directed the servants to carry in the trays of gifts. With a mixture of obsequious humility and practiced manners, he then led the two officers towards the double door, turning every few steps and bowing, as if to make sure that they were following.

The audience chamber was ablaze with lights. Candles and lamps burned in every corner and a heavy chandelier of oil lamps hung very low from the ceiling, as though it was about to drop. A few servants crouched in the corners, staring at the Nawab. He was a thin little man without a beard or moustache but with long hair curling over his collar. Augustine could see that he was mad just from the expression on his face.

Augustine and Webley performed their ceremony perfectly, bowing, each touching his hand from heart to forehead with a fluttering movement. They never looked the Nawab in the eyes but tried to appear as humble as they could despite their uniforms.

After a moment or two the Nawab spoke to Ashgar Hasan, who had suddenly appeared beside him. Augustine had raised his head from one of his deep bows and found the eunuch before him, erect for the first time, standing there like a plumped pillow with his head tilted toward the Nawab.

'So these are your soldiers of fortune?'

Ashgar Hasan introduced them with a long string of compliments, calling Webley a western star that had risen in the east, the commander of the finest army in Hindustan, brave as a tiger.

'You enjoy Lucknow?' asked the Nawab, cutting his eunuch short.

'Huzoor said Webley, 'it is a paradise. May it always be so. There is no more beautiful place in the world.'

'I am having an entertainment, the fighting of animals, which I am told the English take great pleasure in watching. Perhaps you will join us.'

'With pleasure, Huzoor.'

'Animals must be driven to fight,' said the Nawab softly. 'Men fight without provocation. Perhaps someday I should put men in the arena and watch them fight.'

He laughed with a shrill hiccough, and the others in the room roared in unison at the joke.

There were more pleasantries. Augustine said nothing but let Webley do all the talking. It would have been rude for a subordinate to speak out.

Finally Webley gestured to the servants holding their trays of gifts. The first came forward with the watches. They were uncovered and displayed. Hardly interested, the Nawab brushed his ringed fingers over the watches and then with the same movement gestured that they be taken away. Next came the jewelled belt and he received it with the same boredom, not even pausing to look at the jewels.

The final tray contained the wig, lying there like a sleeping cat. This gift intrigued the Nawab and he lifted it off the tray and fondled it, a delighted grin spreading over his face.

Removing his crown and carelessly letting it fall to the ground, the Nawab placed the wig over his long black hair. It made him look ridiculous, like a clown. He waved his hand impatiently and one of the servants, as though he could read the Nawab's mind, scuttled forward with a mirror. The Nawab grinned at himself in the mirror, tucking the wig daintily into place.

'Now I can dance with the English ladies,' he said. 'I am a jain-tul-men.'

Again they all laughed with him.

Putting the wig aside, the Nawab beckoned to one of his servants crouching in the corner of the room. The man hobbled over to a table on which there lay a tray filled with paan. Augustine and Webley were given one each, the signal to leave. They bowed again and were ushered out of the room.

How strange, thought Augustine, that our fate should lie in

such trivial things. It is as if it were a game. But he was pleased, for the Nawab had obviously been delighted with their gifts and his pleasure would certainly be converted into aid for their army, weapons and supplies.

7

—So Blakewell takes the Moor by the scruff of his neck and shakes him till his teeth rattle like anklets at a nautch, and then he tears the bills out of the circar's hand and rips them into pieces, saying, 'There's your precious debt!' The circar scuttles off, his tail between his legs, without a sicca to show for his troubles …

—Harriet says the ayah's had a red-haired child that looks like Robert, poor dear …

—The magistrate asks Blakewell to pay up after the circar and his babu lodge a case. Blakewell tells the magistrate he's damned if he'll pay a sicca to that Hindustani …

—No wonder Shepley's feeling so glum. He lost six cases of Madeira on the Euphrates. Word just came in …

—First it's the heat, then the rain, then the dust, and then the cold …

—Just got a letter from Clifford, he lost an arm at Bussaco, but he's back with his regiment, the 88th Connaught Rangers …

—I hear Boney's having a rough time of it. Seems so damned far from Lucknow. I wish I could hear the guns at least.

—Don't think we're removed from it, plenty of French in India.

—Won't do any harm. India will never be theirs.

—So we hope.

—They say the Nawab himself is being taken in by a flock of French agents … never could trust him, could you?

—There he is, coming in now … the Resident Sahib is bowing down like a confounded pariah … the impudence of these Moors! I tell you, let the army have him and we'd turn him into a sepoy, all the natives are good for …

—When's it to begin?

—An hour late as usual …

—So Blakewell's sentenced to the next ship home and disappears that evening. They say he's gone south, to Arcot or Tanjore. He'll make good soon, if he doesn't go bad …

∽

The English voices drifted and mingled in the humid air. Though he could not catch many of the words and phrases, Augustine recognized a quality in their speech which was at the same time both melancholy and blustering. They were all bluff, and yet they were like tired old liars who have fabricated a mansion of untruths which threatens to collapse on top of them. In that sticky, half-baked atmosphere, the wet earth actually steaming under the bold sun, they muttered on like a troop of monkeys out for an afternoon's gambol. How could there be so much to talk about, when they were together every day of the week, within the protective walls of the residency compound? Augustine could detect a strain in their voices, the tension of retold stories and guarded truths. The only way they could spin out the truth, to occupy themselves through the long dreary months at Lucknow, was to lie bit by bit, until they had constructed the complex structures of gossip, intricate globes, spheres, pyramids of lies, precariously balancing on top of each other, a false security.

To Augustine the voices brought back his mother. For her, too, India had been a fantasy, in which she was a fairy queen. The gilt and glitter of her apartments at Chittoor had deceived her. For the English, even for Webley, it was a land of outrageous possibilities. Even the steaming earth and the moist air, thick enough to choke you, gave it all an unreal atmosphere. This was the land of fire-walkers and four-horned antelopes. And yet, what made it most like a dream was the isolation, the loneliness. It was a land in which anyone could disappear overnight, taken by a fever or a sudden urge to make a fortune. Characters appeared and vanished, as if the thick air were a medium in which they could levitate and move invisibly about.

But his mother had not had that dreary, nostalgic tone to her voice which filled these conversations. Somehow the English accents and intonations detached themselves from the words. What they said was not important, as long as it sounded English. Even a hoarse Cockney would have mixed in well with those voices. To Augustine all these accents were the same. He could hardly distinguish a Somerset burr from a Cockney twang, but he recognized the same loneliness in all of them. Each struck the air like a separate chord or note, slightly out of key. Their speech had that moaning quality of an instrument not in tune with the others, that isolated honk. His mother had no accent at all. Her voice was soft and always with a waver of emotion, as if she would never be able to get the words out. When she read to him, he would watch her carefully to see if she was crying. He never listened to the words. The sound of her voice was more important to him, not controlled and balanced, but quaking and dangerously close to the edge of breaking down. Her speech always had a suspense to it that kept him listening. And now what returned to him were not the stories she used to read or the words she had used to explain something to him, but only the music of her voice, like an accompaniment without the song. There was a difference between the bursting emotions of her speech and the insistent loneliness of these English voices.

They were all waiting for the spectacle to begin. Where the English were sitting was an enclosed area with chairs and sofas under a row of garish canvas pavilions. Farther on was the main pavilion, of even brighter colours, furnished with carpets and plush velvet divans. Punkahs swung back and forth over the heads of the guests, circulating the torpid air. In the main pavilion sat the Nawab, with a few of his favourite ministers. Ashgar Hasan was close to him, still in his reclining position, with a bolster under his arm. He was in deep conversation with the English resident, a squat puffin of a man with a squashed pink face.

There were a fair number of Englishwomen, dressed in pale muslin, their long dresses not too different from the outfits worn by the Nawab's courtiers. They were certainly more sensibly dressed than the men, who stubbornly wore the same clothes they would have worn in England, sweating copiously under their coats, waistcoats, and cravats. Augustine felt his scalp itching as an elderly gentleman passed by wearing a wig. The back of his coat was covered with a hemisphere of white powder, where the tails of his peruke had swung back and forth, leaving a dusting of pomatum. Each of them had a peculiar stork-like stance, which even Webley assumed when he was thinking. Their stockinged legs seemed too thin to support the weight of their bodies, and they appeared almost rigid, even at the knees, as if their limbs had petrified in the heat. There was something grotesque about them, a wild incongruity with the scene. Even the younger men had that look of stooped and beleaguered age. Some wore spectacles and looked like wizened owls, unaccustomed to being out at this time of day. They paced back and forth, pausing only occasionally to have a word with another of their peculiar race. They seemed to have some humour, but it was dry and halfwitted. They rattled off the stories mechanically, and even their laughter had a windy falsity to it.

In contrast, the ministers surrounding the Nawab seemed to be nothing more than coagulations of the humid atmosphere. They were all fat as melons. The way they moved, those of them that had the energy, was like sluggish algae drifting about on lazy currents, never of their own accord. They seemed to bump accidentally into those around them, not with any intent of fellowship, but only because they had been blown in that direction by the punkahs. They did not walk; they floated. One of these figures glided into the pavilion, where Augustine stood leaning against a bamboo support. The minister bobbed up to a clutch of English ladies and paid his respects. They snubbed him bluntly. He went off smiling, though, as if they had each kissed his fleshy jowls. As he watched the ladies, Augustine thought to himself: They get rid of him with a few curt phrases, but the hours they'll spend telling each other how beastly awful he was!

The Nawab's pavilions formed a semicircle, part of a vast arena, the rest of which was made up of a tremendous crowd of people. These were the townspeople, the swamp dwellers, the river men, villagers from outlying districts, bunches of Eurasians, and a few clusters of the less fortunate Europeans, who had not been invited to sit with the more important guests. It was a seething crowd of dark bodies, all shoulders and heads. They were pushing and shoving, packed tightly together, despite the wide expanse of the flat plains stretching out in all directions. They were huddled as if afraid of the animals which would soon be let out into the arena. On the far side of the circle, directly opposite where the Nawab was seated, stood a line of bullock carts. From that distance Augustine could just make out the animals and hear an occasional roar or grunt. The grey shapes of three elephants loomed up in the distance. One or two camels raised their heads occasionally and groaned at the crowd. Finally Augustine spotted the rhinoceros. They were being kept separate from each other, held down by a web of chains and ropes. Each stood seemingly docile, among the Lilliputian creatures swarming around them. Animal roars, cries, squeals arose from that side of the ring, and with each sound the crowd grew more excited.

Finally a man on a white horse galloped into the ring. He

was dressed flamboyantly and turned his horse this way and that, spitting mud into the air. He stopped abruptly in front of the Nawab's pavilion and dismounted ceremoniously. Then he bowed almost to his knees and stood up slowly, with a bobbing motion, his hand gesturing respectfully from his forehead to his heart. The Nawab flicked his wrist and the man spoke. He had a booming voice which carried over the sounds of the animals and the crowd. He announced the order of events, which animals would fight which. When he had finished, the Nawab made another perfunctory gesture and the man galloped out of the arena at top speed, saluting the crowd. They cheered him violently, as if he was their general.

The first to fight were two dogs, a bullying mastiff and a thin vicious whippet with a speckled coat and a high-pitched bark. The whippet circled the mastiff and lunged at the larger dog, taking bites at its legs and body. The mastiff lumbered about clumsily, waiting for a chance to grab the whippet. The fight was uninteresting and the two dogs never tangled. Finally the mastiff took hold of the whippet and shook it by the neck until it went limp. The crowd was disappointed. The English ladies feigned disgust but seemed to be enjoying the brutality of the fight.

Webley had wandered off in the direction of the pavilions beyond the Nawab's area. Augustine saw him come sauntering back, spinning his knobbed cane and whistling 'Money in Both Pockets.' He fitted in perfectly and had even affected the stork look, his shoulders bunched around his neck. The way he nodded to everyone, he could have been mistaken for a local.

'I've seen a better dog-fight in Chor bazaar,' said Webley, coming up beside the Colonel.

Augustine nodded as he watched two men in loin-cloths drag a hyena out into the ring. The mastiff stood nervously guarding the dead whippet. The two men finally released the hyena close to the dog and ran to a safe distance. The hyena laughed, as if in mockery of the shaggy dog. It, too, circled the mastiff, its body hunched as if with rabies, its teeth showing in a painful grin.

'Some nice necks in the crowd,' said Webley. 'One or two young widows and a loose wife here and there. What do you say?'

'Go ahead,' said Augustine. The hyena had just leapt at the mastiff and, taking hold of its hind leg, snapped the bone with its powerful jaws.

'It would be a lovely change after all this local fare we've been living off. These are dumplings, not chapattis, mind you,' he said with a wink.

'Cold dumplings, if you ask me,' said Augustine.

The dog was limping and losing blood. The hyena sat patiently down on its haunches and waited for a few minutes. The mastiff was brave and charged him. The dog had no chance. Augustine glanced over at the main pavilion. Ashgar Hasan was ignoring the fight. He and the Resident were still talking with great earnestness.

'Come along, there's a lovely girl. I'll introduce you to her if you promise me the first shot. Her husband's a bore, but we can handle him.'

'Leave me out of it,' said Augustine.

'No, you have to come. I've told her all about you. Do you realize that you're an Italian duke who has just sunk his wealth into the indigo trade?'

'What are you talking about?'

'I mean, that's what I've told her and her husband, whatever his name is,' said Webley, tugging at Augustine's sleeve.

They were dressed like planters. Augustine had agreed to shed his uniform for the sake of disguise. But he was not ready to play the fool for Webley.

'Do it for me, will you,' said the Englishman. 'I haven't had white meat for nearly ten years.'

'I thought you preferred the dark,' said Augustine, giving in.

'Good show, now slouch a little. You can't stop looking like a colonel, can you?'

As Augustine followed Webley through the maze of chairs and bodies, he felt a surge of hatred for these people. Their pink faces leered at him. Their fragile features, their painted lips, their yellow teeth. The smell of their European perfumes, their English sweat; the sound of their voices, the accents; their stance, like a flock of storks in a puddle, all of these things made Augustine cringe inside himself. They seemed so ugly and trivial.

Webley seemed to have given in to their petty world, reduced himself to mediocrity. He had no image, no vanity, only the thought of sleeping with one of those chalky-faced women. The limits of that society choked Augustine. He wanted to get above the gossip, the lies, into an atmosphere of boundless possibilities, in which the little items were only part of tremendous ideals, tremendous actions. Here it was like the dogs fighting, a disappointment.

The crumpled forms had been dragged off the field. The hyena had been put back in its cage. It was as if the drama of the spectacle had to be first tempered, dampened by the ugliness and pathetic struggles of the smaller animals. It was as if these first few fights were supposed to disappoint the audience, so that the real battles between the larger animals would take on a magnificence proportionate to their size. Somehow the tragedy of the spectacle would not have been complete if the whippet had not barked so shrilly, and the hyena had not snapped the mastiff's hind leg so quickly and then finished him off with such sudden murder. The crowd played up to the event, crying out for more excitement, bored by the first two fights but thrilled at the prospect of what was to come. It was a subtle violence, brutal and frank in its first image, but underneath the blood, the snapping bone, the flying fur was something of a grotesque violence which played on only the black keys of the emotions, so that there were no perfect feelings, nothing but a vague marginal sense and partial perception of the scene. The crowd groaned like an organ. There was no scale, no development, only these haunting tunes, running along your nerve ends.

'Mrs Jane Marlow, may I present Mr Augustine Carlos Vinetti. And this is Dr Marlow,' said Webley with a flourish.

'How do you do,' said Augustine, with a bow, before he had even seen the woman.

He looked up to find her simple-faced but pretty. Her husband was a wiry, snake-like creature whose eyes darted about with viperous curiosity.

'You're Italian,' said Mrs Marlow, very pleased with herself. She was at least ten years younger than her husband.

'Have you ever been there?' asked Augustine cautiously.

'No,' said Dr Marlow, 'but I've read Addison's *Letter from Italy* and I'm a confirmed papist. My sympathies are all with Rome.'

'My goodness!' said Mrs Marlow, 'he usually doesn't let that drop until later on in a conversation.'

'I suppose it's not quite the thing in India, being a papist,' said Marlow.

Augustine had no idea what they were talking about. Webley realized and took the helm of the conversation.

'I hear in England it's quite the fashion,' he said quickly.

'No, not really,' said Mrs Marlow. 'He's ahead of his time.'

'I suppose you'll convert?' asked Webley.

'No, of course not. I would not go so far. Call it a hobby.'

'And where in Italy are you from?' asked Mrs Marlow, a blush on her cheek.

Augustine fumbled and then said, 'Athens,' with a nod of his head.

'Oh,' said the lady, not thinking anything wrong with the answer.

'I see, an expatriate,' said Dr Marlow. 'Have you ever attended an Orthodox service?'

'No,' said Augustine, squirming.

'They're quite fascinating, lots of pageantry and very little religion. It's quite remarkable, that they can believe so little and do so much.'

Fortunately, Dr Marlow was one of those people who thought he knew more about the world than anyone else. Augustine let himself be filled in on Latin literature and the architectural genius of the Colosseum. Meanwhile, Webley had seated himself next to Mrs Marlow and was gathering her glances up like posies.

A wild boar had been brought into the ring, a tremendous beast with a bristly back and short stocky legs. His beady eyes seemed to flash in the sunlight and there was something very wild about him. He waited in the centre of the arena impatiently as an ox was dragged in. It took four men to keep the ox steady. When he saw the boar, he bellowed and broke away from the men holding him. At top speed he came after the grey boar, who waited solemnly to meet the white giant. Just as they were about to collide, the boar grunted furiously and ducked to one side, hurling his body into the air and plunging a tusk into the white flank of the ox. For a moment the ox stood still, surprised at the pain. Assuming the gentleness of a dairy cow, it licked the wound with its long pink tongue. The blood flowed quickly and stained the white hide a rich scarlet. The boar charged this time, but had to lunge aside when the sharp horns of the ox swept at him. The two animals exchanged blows for a few more minutes, and then suddenly the ox turned away. All of the bluster and bravado which he had brought into the ring with him had vanished, drained out of him. His white hide was smeared with mud, and the red stains on his belly had spread across the length of his body. He staggered once or twice and then began to trot off the field in the direction of the carts and cages. The boar crouched in the centre of the field and his heavy breathing could be heard all around. He waited for his next challenge. A few minutes passed and a bear was let into the open. It killed the boar in a few furious minutes of fighting. There were no tactics to the bear's fight. He blundered in like a drunken soldier, swaying on his hind legs. When the boar hit him in the body, he fell forward on top of the pig and disembowelled him with a few playful swipes of his claws. He began to eat the boar self-consciously and defended his kill three times, once against another boar, once against a gaur, and finally against a cringing leopard that refused even to come close to the dead boar or the bear. But there was nothing heroic to the bear's fights. He had no style, no wildness about him, only a blunt strength. Two men came out with chains and a cage, to drag him off the field, but he charged them as well, almost mauling one of them. Finally the Nawab ordered him shot.

One of the English party was given the honour of finishing the bear off. A slender gentleman with an exaggerated stoop and a nervous smile staggered out onto the field under the weight of a heavy musket. He tried to aim standing up but could not hold the gun steady. Finally he sat down in the mud, soiling his satin breeches, and fired at the bear from about thirty yards. The bear died with a resentful grumble. A pathetic cheer rose from the crowd as the Englishman, not even a stork, more of an egret, pranced off the field in glee.

'That's the Resident's nephew, quite a griff,' said Dr Marlow.

'Don't you think the bear deserved a better show than that?' asked Mrs Marlow.

'No, he was ugly and took up time. He had no style,' said Augustine. 'They had to get rid of him.'

'But the least they could have done was let one of those rhinos or an elephant loose on him.'

'I suppose so,' said Augustine, 'but it's not their turn yet.'

Augustine thought to himself how important the death of the bear had been. He had been watching the crowd, not the English, but the rest, those forming the main part of the ring, the anonymous mass of bodies. They had become restless with the bear. He had insulted them with his way of fighting, the absence of style. The boar had speed and fury, a definite wildness. The ox had a vanity which thrilled the crowd, and the hyena was a villain. But the bear was nothing but his strength. He was crude and the pain he inflicted, the blood he spilled, had no drama attached to it. He was like a poor comedian. More important was the Englishman who killed him. The Nawab had chosen him well. It was an honour but it was also an insult, an insult to the crowd, to the bear, to the whole drama itself. For a man to intrude on the fights between these animals was unforgivable. This wasn't sport, it was a spectacle. And to have chosen the weakest and most incompetent among the English to finish off the insult of the bear's performance gave the spectacle a tawdry dimension. It created a disappointment, a let-down which would only be relieved by the more majestic animals.

'What are you doing in India?' Augustine asked Marlow.

'I'm writing a book. At present I'm collecting material.'

'May I ask the title?'

'You may. It will be called *De Religionibus Indiae,* a monumental work deserves such a title.'

'And what will be the subject of this book?' Augustine asked, trying to avoid his Italian lineage.

Dr Marlow looked at him suspiciously and decided he actually didn't understand. So he took it on himself to explain the matter from the beginning.

'From the look of you, your bearing, your physique, I'd say you were a sportsman. And there's nothing wrong with that. But I'm at the other end of the line, an intellectual, a man of books and eyeglasses. What I come to India for is much much different from why you are here. Of course you've invested in the indigo trade—a risky gamble, if you want my opinion. But be that as it may, you're also here for the sport. Splendid hunting, much opportunity for adventure, a paradise for men like yourself. India for you is a playground. Not for me, however. For me it is a vast library, a store of knowledge, of curiosities, of quaint customs and beliefs. Religion is my hobby as well as my occupation—which is why I am not a particularly devout man. You mustn't be if you're going to be true to your subject. Objectivity, that's the word which must ring in a scholar's mind like a church bell. My life is built on a litany of facts. I have studied Christianity in all its forms, from the bizarre to the mundane, and I am frankly bored with it.

'Ah, but India. It is a land of religion. Don't you find it so? Perhaps not. You don't look deep enough. There is a religion, a piety, a surging faith in this country which excites me. It's not like in England, where going to church is like having the linen washed.'

Dr Marlow rattled on as if nothing would stop him. Augustine glanced over at Webley. Mrs Marlow had her hand on his sleeve and was whispering in his ear. They had grown intimate remarkably fast. It surprised Augustine, for among the Englishwomen he had noticed an outward show of icy coldness, enough to freeze any man's advances. But they were not coy, only flirtatious in a crude sort of way. Their eyes followed you and stuck to you. At one moment the look they gave you was curious, then admiring. But if you turned on them, they became immediately cold, until you had been introduced, and then it all became a mush of pleasantries. Mrs Marlow disgusted him. She was so blatantly unfaithful that the affair lost all semblance of a game and turned into a transaction.

Augustine thought back on Khasturba. She was completely different. She was coarse and frank, but there was a good humour about the whole thing, and a seriousness as well. There were emotions involved. But with Mrs Marlow, despite her laugh and the look of amusement in her eyes, it was nothing but a crude transaction. She was more of a whore than Khasturba. Dr Marlow's voice droned on like a wasp trying to escape through a closed window. He listed the places he had visited, the saints and mendicants he had met, the maharajahs who gave religion a flagrancy and style so completely different from the ascetic simplicity of Sufis and sadhus. 'I usually work on two books at the same time, so that if I'm of two minds about a certain point, I can put one opinion in the first book and the other in the second.' Augustine no longer cared whether he was mistaken for an Italian duke or not. In a sense it didn't matter any more. Introductions are the only point at which lies count.

'Ah, the tigers!' said Webley, turning away from Mrs Marlow. Augustine had noticed that the first few fights had not interested Webley. In fact, he ignored them, as if they were only an excuse for the crowd being there.

The first tiger was brought out in a cage and carried into the centre of the arena, glowering at the crowd from behind the heavy iron bars. It tried to pace back and forth within the cage, but there was enough room only for a sharp circle and the tiger looked as though he was chasing his tail. The crowd was amused.

A wild buffalo was led into the ring of spectators. It came patiently, without tossing its head and pawing the ground. The men bringing it out into the ring edged forward until they were about twenty yards from the tiger's cage. One of the men then dashed forward and opened the gate to the cage. Like a spring which had slowly been tightening in those cramped quarters, turning, turning, the tiger burst out with a cough, almost as if it were clearing its throat. The men released the buffalo and scurried for safety. The buffalo snorted, flared its nostrils, and its red eyes almost glowed. But the tiger ignored the black shape with its wide spread of horns, and as if it had a brewing vendetta with one of the men, pounced on a running figure and began mauling him with its claws. Augustine saw the Resident's nephew leap out of his chair and start into the field with his musket, hoping to repeat his former bravery, but someone caught him by the shoulder and held him back.

The buffalo saved the man's life by charging at the last minute and hooking the tiger with the tip of its horn, picking the orange-and-black body into the air and flinging it aside. The buffalo didn't give the tiger a chance to recover but was on him again, butting the furious cat with its horns. Two men hurried out and rescued the wounded man, dragging him away to safety. The tiger by this time had latched itself on to the buffalo's forehead between the horns and was shredding the great black hump of neck which shook back and forth painfully, trying to dislodge the tiger. Ribbons of blood garlanded the buffalo, and the tiger's flaming coat was also covered with patches of redness.

The centre of the field, where most of the fights had taken place, was now a swamp of mud, a foot or two deep in places. Even the hot sun could not dry it up, and as each of the animals flung itself into the fray, the patch grew larger and more mucky. The animals that were killed seemed to soak into the ground, and if they had been left there overnight, the ground would probably have swallowed them up. Those that went out of the ring alive were caked in mud, their legs heavy with it, their underbellies dripping water and blood.

The crowd hugged the arena as the tiger and the buffalo tangled. There was no stockade, no wall, nothing to protect them. They clung together in that broad arc of bodies, giving each other a false sense of security. They formed the wall themselves and were as vulnerable as if there had been only a few of them scattered about. The calls, cries, and laughter of the crowd served as mortar holding the wall together. When the animals began to edge towards one side of the ring, the wall on that side would begin to buckle, shift back ten yards, and those in the back might run for safer ground. The crowd had only the illusion of safety. Any one of the animals could have turned on them and burst through the wall, scattering people to all sides, and escaped without any problem into the wasteland stretching north from Lucknow. But for some reason, instinct or fear, the animals did not try to break through the wall. Perhaps the barricade of human scents deterred them. Their spirit had been broken in the cages. Hunger, and a madness bred in confinement, made them fight. It was a wild violence, a frustration, alien to the jungle. Here on the vacant plain, with only the wall of people around them, the animals vented their wildness on each other. For them it was not combat, not sport, but a drive to destroy one another. Augustine wondered whether it was an instinct, self-pity. For them death was their only alternative. Captivity kept them alive when they would rather have died.

The tiger finally brought the buffalo down to the ground and mercilessly killed it.

'Where else in the world would men forsake their families, their fortunes, the comfort of their homes for a life of complete abandonment, living off charity, grovelling for their existence, and yet happy in the knowledge of God?' Augustine realized that Dr Marlow hadn't stopped talking during the entire fight. He seemed oblivious of the whole scene, even his audience. Augustine's mind strayed in wider circles as the Orientalist expounded. 'It is their heritage—from the earliest days, when they were cowherds in the forest. It was a land as well ordered and structured as that displayed on Hephaestus's shield. But in these people is a genuine belief in God. Their idols have more life to them than any act of imagination our church or yours, for that matter, can produce. Faith, that is what their scriptures profess, a universal love. These people are inhuman in their capacity for belief. Every moment of their lives is taken up with worship. From their morning squat in the fields to their lovemaking at night. It is all part of an elaborate ceremony and ritual, which confesses their human inadequacies before God and asks for forgiveness. Can you imagine that? Can you imagine that fervour in England? Can you imagine hymns being sung from every household in London? Religious processions down Leadenhall Street every other day of the week? I suppose you can't. But just think of it, why, that is real dedication. Their lives, castes, and obligations are ordained by God, not by the economy. It is the words of saints, prophets, and priests which make the people shudder, not the forces of politics and wealth.'

Mrs Marlow and Webley were giggling over a joke between them.

Something close to jealousy overcame Augustine. He did not mind Webley flirting with the Englishwoman. Let him sleep with her, he thought, and find out whether he prefers dumplings to chapattis. He wanted nothing to do with the English, despised them, hated them. Their voices grated against him. But for a moment he wondered whether he wasn't jealous of Webley for being English. He could escape into that world, another stork in the puddle. Augustine hated him for having grown up in England and having had English parents, having brothers, and the childhood which he was always trying to preserve.

In a sense he was jealous of his manners. Augustine had always been stiff in company. It was from his days in Chittoor, where the hospitality and the etiquette had all borne the stamp of soldiering. He knew the correct way to greet a lady, even kiss her hand and bow. But there was something in him that revolted against this social charade. He was used to dealing with men around the dinner table and women in the bedroom. These women with their gay colours and beaked noses, their high-pitched laughs, like birds raiding a cornfield, bothered him. They lacked a modesty which his mother had embodied, a flaming modesty which could excite men. You could respect a woman like that. Khasturba would be that way, he thought, if I take her out of that brothel and give her fine apartments. But then he laughed to himself. There were no fine apartments in the Bijilli Gargh. It was like a prison. He thought of her wasting away in that dank fortress, like a moth trapped in a bottle.

The afternoon had spilled into twilight and an ochre tint spread over the horizon. The shadows of the crowd stretched out into the arena, like a ghostly parade. It was late, time for one more fight. The Nawab leaned over to a courtier and whispered in the man's ear. He bowed and vanished in the direction of the animals.

A low moan of excitement and tension rose out of the crowd. A rhinoceros was brought into the centre of the field. Twenty men held him with ropes and chains. He grunted belligerently and tried to charge this side and that. The men dug their heels into the soft mud and braced themselves against his weight. When he was released, he galloped in a circle two or three times, snorting and shaking his head. Then, with self-satisfaction and a docile idiocy, he lowered his enormous body into the middle of the mud patch, wallowing in it with delight. But when his opponent appeared, another rhino slightly smaller but more energetic, the great armoured body rose up out of the mud and stamped the ground.

There was something prehistoric about the two rhinos. They seemed to have been transplanted there out of a former aeon, cast up out of a forgotten valley where time had not been able to spread its shadows. Each was a Goliath, a thundering mass of hide and horn. The folds of skin overlapped on the haunches and shoulders, and as the rhinos moved, their thick skin moved also, scraping against itself. It was like the bark on a tree, that coarse pebbled texture. The heads were small in comparison with the heavy bodies; the skulls long and slender but thickly boned. The eyes blinked—tiny eyes, the only vulnerable part on the massive animals. Two ears jutted out from the top of the head, small and leaf-shaped, flicking to every sound. Then there were the horns. Each of the rhinos had two, a dull yellow colour. The larger animal's were splintered, the other's were sharp and menacing.

Everyone in the audience had stopped talking, even Marlow. Heads turned and a silent tension descended over the twilit field. The time of day, the preceding medley of fights, the crowd's appreciation of the violence, had all given this final combat a mood of drama. This was the climax of the drama. Everything before was superfluous. It was not excitement or a thrill which this last fight instilled in the crowd but more of an emotion of culmination, almost a nostalgia, the last battle. What it conveyed was a mood of melancholy. This was not the best fight of the day. There were ones with more excitement, more violence, more blood. But it was the size and the blundering wildness of those animals which created the final emotions which silenced the crowd. It was their bulk, their ponderous movements, the sway of their bodies, that primordial aura about them, as if they had just pushed their way out of the swamp ooze where they had been buried for thousands of years. There was nothing mammalian or human about them. The rhinos were almost mechanical.

With a numbing crash the two collided. At first impact, the smaller animal slipped in the slick mud and landed on its knees. With a furious churning of legs it tried to gain its feet again, but the older animal with the shattered horns nudged it over onto its back and sank its horn into the tight skin of the belly right under the hind leg. The cry also was primordial, between a scream and a roar. The horn came out gory, the blood streaming down onto the rhino's face. The smaller animal lurched upright and threw itself against its opponent. This time both animals withstood the shock and battered against each other without any effect. Finally, the younger one ducked and brought its horn up under the other's chin, catching its jaw with the sharp point of its horn. This time it was the other's turn to scream, bitter and frightened, but full of rage and desperation.

They fought on and the crowd now broke into voices, whispers, shouts, cheers. The gamblers shouted their odds. Augustine wondered whether it was the death of the animals which attracted these people. It was what they bet upon. But it was not the morbidity of the conflict, the inevitable death of the one animal and usually of both. The death inflicted by the horns, the teeth, the claws, even the musket in the cowardly hands of the Englishman; it was not the finality of the battles, for this was not a tableau with any symbolic content. That was not what excited the audience. There was none of that kind of emotion in these killings. The death was unimportant. Once it was over, the carcass was dragged away and given to the vultures. What was valuable, the horns and tusks, were stolen, sometimes the skin was preserved and tanned.

What was important to the crowd, the human stockade, was the danger, the pain, the agony of the fight. They were caught up in the fury of the two animals. What they wanted to see was blood flowing, teeth bared, and frightened exhaustion in the eyes of the animals. Those people wanted to see wildness, irrationality pitted against itself, a mad, delirious combat, destructive not in its inevitable death but in the infliction of pain. The mutilation, the brutality. They enjoyed hearing the cries of wounded animals, those dumb meaningless sounds. This was not a stage where all the killings took place out of sight and were reported to the audience by the characters. In fact, there were no characters, no reporting, only the immediate, sensuous experience of watching the animals tear each other apart.

Suddenly the smaller rhino cried out again and turned away from its opponent. The night was close and at places flares had been lit. Augustine could see cheroots glowing all around the field. The two great shadowy forms suddenly broke out of the centre, where they had been held for so long, as if by gravity in a fierce orbit. One chasing the other, they plunged directly into the crowd, spattering those in their way to all sides, trampling one or two, hurling others into the air. In a furious chase they disappeared into the darkness, out into that plain of saltpetre and grey mud. Perhaps the ooze would swallow them up again for another thousand years, until they emerged again to fight once more.

Lights now burned where the rhinos had smashed through the wall of men, and the crowd had clotted around the spot to see what wounds had been inflicted.

Webley invited Dr and Mrs Marlow to come for dinner at Ashgar Hasan's palace, and together the four of them rode off in that direction. It was dark and many shapes passed them in the night, riders, carriages, groups of men walking together. But the rhinos were gone forever. People were returning full of the fights, the diversion of an afternoon. Before they reached Ashgar Hasan's, the word caught up with them that four men had been killed and six wounded by the rhinos in their flight. As Augustine rode back from the animal fights, he thought about the Bijilli Gargh. It seemed so remote from Lucknow, both in distance and in the atmosphere of the place. He wanted to return, partly because he was worried that the English might learn of their being away from the army and try to attack, partly also because he was restless in Lucknow. He wanted the familiar comradeship of his soldiers, the simple pleasures of riding and hunting, instead of the starched manners and ungainly style of the courtiers.

In the city there was a feeling of conspiracy. Webley and he were at the centre of it. As he rode through the darkness, he imagined all around him spies and assassins. It was a world of subterfuge and intrigue. What kind of death waited for him behind the mud walls and in the narrow gullies of Lucknow? An ignoble death, a death without meaning or tragedy. He imagined a thug leaping onto the back of his horse and strangling him with a silk scarf, or a flash out of nowhere, and even before he heard the report of the pistol, that awful groan which he knew was his own—or perhaps something as simple as a knife thrown from behind, cutting through the darkness silently, arching towards him and bedding itself up to the hilt in his back. For a moment he even imagined, with horror, Khasturba pulling a dagger from under the quilt and stabbing him, all for the price of a few rupees. Augustine was not afraid of dying but of the insult of an ignoble death.

He had a nightmarish vision of the city, like a giant cage filled with many varieties of birds: the English storks and egrets, water-birds, migratory birds winging in droves, setting up a deafening cackle all about him; the birds of prey circling over the carrion, the ruthless, cut-throat world of petty cheats, assassins, and thugs, the crows and kites and vultures. Then there were the effeminate songbirds, the delicate, flighty birds, so beautiful and yet so ugly. Together they set up such a din, like the mynahs in the palm trees, that Augustine wanted only to fire his cannons into their midst and scatter them.

In the centre of all this babble, he saw Webley's half brother, Jules, in brilliant plumage. There was something disgusting about the Frenchman. He carried himself like one of those exotic birds, so heavy with coloured feathers that they can fly only with a frantic beating of wings. Jules and his black Napoleon flapped about him with an unnerving flutter of lace and silk.

More and more the thought of the Bijilli Gargh troubled him. He imagined the British armies coming down on the fort like a migration of birds, attacking the defenders with their beaks, swooping down on them with their claws and talons extended. They came in flight upon flight, and as soon as one was shot down, another flight appeared over the horizon, strung out in a thin, wobbling line. He could see them, almost as though they were hovering, not seeming to move forward or backward and yet menacing. Then as if in an instant, they were larger, the outline of their wings visible, their long snake-like necks curving up and down with the motion of flying. Then the sound of their wings, thumping the air, shuddering the silence.

Though Augustine hated the Bijilli Gargh, with its squat silhouette and gloomy rooms, he loved the army inside it, the men he had trained and lived with for years. How could the fate of the Bijilli Gargh, the fate of Webley's army, be put in the hands of such men as the eunuchs and courtiers of Lucknow? Augustine could not believe that Webley was allowing himself to be sucked into that chaos of politics. They might get their arms and munitions, but they would lose their freedom.

Augustine distrusted any man who was not a soldier. Jules made him uneasy. He had arrived with too much coincidence. His flattery had a false note to it, hinting at sinister motives. Inside himself, Augustine knew that Jules had some purpose. He wondered to himself what Webley and the Frenchman had spoken about in the garden and whether they had met together in secret to make some plan behind Augustine's back. He did not trust Webley in this city.

He trusted Ashgar Hasan even less, despite his disarming hospitality. The eunuch had welcomed the Frenchman into his palace and given him rooms on the same floor as theirs. What cards did the eunuch hold? Though he was in the Nawab's court, he was a power in himself, more powerful in some ways than the Nawab.

Where did the English stand, and how much did they know? Had Webley been recognized? They should never have attended the animal fights and displayed themselves for all to see.

Augustine had the feeling that when the Nawab and the Resident were speaking together, it was about them, about the fate of Webley's army. Had they walked into a trap? Augustine felt an irrational distrust of everyone, even of Webley, boiling inside him. He wanted to escape with Khasturba and return to the Bijilli Gargh, to move on. He hated the thought of the men sitting inside those walls, waiting for the inevitable siege. There was danger in stagnancy, in staying at one place for too long. Only in movement, in travelling about, was there safety, a sort of momentum which carried you out of reach of danger. Once you stopped moving, you were dead.

He distrusted Khasturba as well, though he knew that she was innocent. What if one of her lovers coaxed the story out of her? Who was this tall soldier who was said to be a recent favourite of hers? Had he spoken of himself? Why was he in Lucknow? Perhaps the opium would make her boastful and unwary and she would spill the story to them. Or perhaps in her jealousy she might offer his story to a lover, as a taunt, as a flirtation.

In the darkness the faces leered at him, the pale and cunning Jules, his eyes no more than creases on his face, the enormous jowls of Ashgar Hasan, Webley, the Nawab with his English wig, the Englishmen, Khasturba, and behind them all, standing up like an evil fetish or relic in the shadows of a dingy tomb, the Bijilli Gargh. Those faces appeared to haunt the fort. He was afraid for the army and for himself.

From Dr Marlow's journals: Made the acquaintance yesterday of two very peculiar gentlemen, the one English as a pork pie and the other rather indeterminate, possibly a Eurasian. They claim to be indigo planters, though neither of them quite fits the mould. They carry themselves like soldiers and I am inclined to think they are deserters or mercenaries. Both men are friendly, the Eurasian fellow, who really looks like an Italian count and has a glass eye—certainly not the mark of an indigo planter—is a curious fellow, brooding. His friend and obviously his superior is quite free with the ladies, a dandy sort of fellow despite his age. He would be about ten years older than myself. He is a gentleman, despite his appearance and protestations to the contrary. The other, the sullen fellow, appears to feel uncomfortable in the company of these hedonists, and I must say that I am attracted to him because of it. There is a lucidity in his silent demeanour, an expressiveness of character which is fascinating. He seems to ooze with personality.

Friends of mine have warned me against such men. They infest Oudh like termites, supported by the fancies of the natives. They may even be Bonapartist agents. It is said that the Nawab is the patron of twenty or thirty such freebooters, each with his own army of brigands. They live a desperate life, preying on innocent towns and counties, destroying more than they take, and generally giving our army a bad time. The difficult thing is to know one when you see one, for they are very good at disguising themselves and presenting alibis as if they were the credentials of the King's own minister.

A man I know from several dinner parties, Captain Longsworth, told me some of the most gruesome stories about these men, how they massacre whole villages, women and children. They are more of a nuisance than thugs and the native bandits. Many of them, it is also said, are papists and Jacobins. I don't begrudge them that, but it is somewhat unnerving to think that such men exist. You never know who they might be.

I cannot say for certain what these two are doing here. After they have been around, the rumours will be sure to circulate and I will certainly find out their real identity. Until then they are not bad company, in a social sense. I mean, even the sullen chap has manners, though a little blunt and uncertain.

Captain Longsworth told me about one fellow, Pohlman I think was his name. He went by the name Sombre among the French and Somru among the natives. He had an entire cantonment of English murdered for the Nawab of Bengal. It was a dastardly affair, cruel and malicious. No one can really offer any explanation for the killings except a fanatic bloodthirstiness on the part of this mercenary. The Company offered rewards for him and the army was put on the alert, but he has escaped them all, I believe. Captain Longsworth said he died peacefully on his estate near Meerut. His wife, a Moorish woman who adopted Catholicism, is now the commander of his army and a very respected and dignified friend of the Company, not at all in the frame of her husband.

∽

The British in Lucknow lived apart from the city, in a society so much in contrast to that of the Nawab that it startled Augustine. Webley got himself invited to the Marlows for a few days and took Augustine along, 'as a diversion for the old man'. This meant that he was supposed to distract attention from the liaison between Mrs Marlow and Webley. It was not difficult, for Marlow, being the bore he was, revelled in having an ear bent in his direction, no matter whose it was. Obviously he had found no one else in the city with whom he could 'carry on a conversation of any substance'. In other words, the gay and lighthearted people of

Lucknow had no time for his ponderous observations. He spoke at long stretches, only pausing to quaff a beaker of pale ale. His conversations were always one-sided and Augustine could let his mind wander without the fear of having to agree or add his own opinion to the stew.

Marlow's bungalow was set on a knoll, slightly west of Baillie Guard Gate and the residency buildings. There was a long veranda in the front from which the two men could see the river and beyond, framed by trees. For the three days that they were there it rained steadily, so that Augustine and Marlow were trapped on the veranda.

'I hope you don't mind my talking to you, but speech always seems to loosen my thoughts. I can't write a word down unless I've said it to someone, tried it out, you might say. When there is no one to talk to, I speak to myself, the conversation rattling on inside my head. Speech is not words, sir, speech is a hot wind within you, like the draught of a fire. Words ride the wind like sparks. Inspiration, that is what speech is, sir, the heat of inspiration … Ponder, if you will for a moment, the source of inspiration, that furnace from out of which blows that wind. The Western man, that is, the two of us, would place it in our minds, somewhere behind our eyes. The savage races locate it between their legs.' Marlow chuckled at his own daring. 'The Indians, and I do not throw them in with the savages for a reason, would say their inspiration came from the navel. Note if you will the progression, from genitals, to abdomen, to head. It cannot fail to strike you that it shows the ascension of the intellect from the animal to the sophisticated man. Ha ha!' he laughed.

Augustine sighed and smiled, whispered something into his beer and nodded for Marlow to continue.

'India, and I think I am the only man with a mind generous enough to allow it, I place halfway towards civilization, just as their skin is not as black as that of savages, neither is their intellect completely divested of illumination. Though it is still as backward as a cloven hoof in comparison to the five fingers of my hand, there is something afoot among these people, akin to culture. I am a student of history and I know that it has not always been so, and though I hate to admit it, the currents of time signal regression among these people. They, too, had their Greece and Rome, their Socrates and Cicero. But whereas England and Europe built upon those traditions and enhanced their history with their present, India has tumbled from its past, and threatens to fall still farther into the pit of degeneracy. The fires in their furnaces have died low, and the forge wherein their ideas and beliefs were tempered and tested has ceased to function.'

Augustine wondered where Webley and Mrs Marlow were. He imagined them in one of the back rooms, the spatter of rain drowning their voices. He hated Mrs Marlow. She was desperate. Her husband probably spoke to her about religion instead of making love. You could see it in her eyes, a passionate desire. She was overripe. Her attraction was not in her beauty, nor her manners, but in a heavy sensuality, a crass instinctive animalistic desire for sex. And Webley had responded. It amused him. She gasped for sex like a fish on land gasping for air. Marlow was oblivious. He did not seem to notice it in his wife. He was like a eunuch. His mind made him impotent. Augustine listened half-heartedly as he ran another leafy idea up a trellis of words.

The water streamed down in front of them like a curtain, the spray landing just short of their feet. Two servants squatted at the end of the veranda, huddled in conspiracy. Augustine thought back on the animal fights. He thought of the Resident's nephew and the death he had inflicted. He thought about the men killed by the escaping rhinoceros. The beer and the cannonade of rain made it all a dream. He felt his body, heavy as lead. Marlow's words droned on and on, persistently chasing themselves in circles.

'Compare our heroes to theirs. Take Achilles, sir. It was Homer's genius that created a hero like him, but it was the Greek mind, the predecessor of the modern mind, which in truth brought Achilles to life. And how different he is from the champions of the Hindu epics. So much in contrast! The Hindu heroes are blackguards, sir. If they were in the British Army, they'd be courtmartialled immediately. They shared their wives ...'

Augustine remembered his father and wondered for a moment whether he had been a hero. He had fought with distinction and his soldiers trusted him, but that was all. To his mother he was the greatest soldier, but she was his wife. Augustine had admired his father but he had never felt anything towards him. In fact, his father bored him. Despite his courage and flair, there was something ordinary about him. He was not a legend, only a good soldier.

The first time he had ridden into battle with his father, it was against a renegade tribe of Pindaris that were causing depredations among the villages around Chittoor. With two hundred men at his back, Augustine had felt proud and excited. He glanced at his father and tried to imitate the stern look on his face, the casual pose, but in his boyish excitement he could not stop looking around at the soldiers, from this side to that. He could not help but start at the bark of muskets from the corn. They defeated the bandits ruthlessly, killing most of them and scattering the rest.

Something disappointed him, though, and he could not describe it. It was his father. He lacked the qualities which Augustine had admired in him for so many years, those attributes which his mother wept over. Trisuldas Thakur did not disgrace himself, but neither did he impress his son. When he ordered the charge, he rode part of the way with his men and then veered off to one side, taking Augustine with him. They drew away from the fighting, out of range of the shots, and watched as the horsemen dashed into the corn and routed the Pindaris. There had been danger, excitement, vanity, but somehow for Augustine there was not enough of it. His father did not ride into the corn waving his sword. It was as if the enemy was not worth the risk.

All of the battles they fought together Augustine and his father won, except for the last one in which Trisuldas Thakur had died. But that battle was not over for Augustine. It continued in his mind. Trisuldas Thakur did not have the character of a hero. He was vain, but his bravado had a false quality to it. As if he did not quite believe in himself.

'There is certainly something more noble about Achilles than about Arjuna, would you not agree?' Marlow said in a confidential voice, though he waited for no reply. 'The Greek hero ponders his role in the battle, whereas the Hindu simply kills his enemies by the droves. Of course there's the Bhagavad Gita, but if you ask me, that's a later addition to the epic, a sort of tagged-on afterthought. And beyond that there is no notion of the noble enemy, which is in fact a reflection of the hero's character. That he looks on his opponent, in Achilles' case Hector, with respect, confirms my point that the Greek hero is a far more admirable man than the Indian ...'

Trisuldas Thakur had died in battle, which was noble enough. He fell to the English, who were admitted to be a fine army. But his death carried with it none of the tragedy of a hero's death. He was simply blown apart by a cannonball. If he had died defending his wife instead, there would have been some glory to it, some drama. Augustine could only remember his death as one of the many. It was overshadowed by his mother's. Hers was tragic, pathetic. In her death there was a suggestion of immortality, martyrdom, all the elements of melodrama. Trisuldas Thakur was simply the victim of a chance cannonball, not meant for him.

He died instantly. There were no last phrases. Augustine did not even dismount beside him. He only turned away and rode off to tell his mother, not with a flurry of emotion, weeping as he went, but only with resolution, knowing that it was the right thing to do. He thought he would find her eager and expecting news of victory. He had imagined her breaking into tears again, just as she always did when he mentioned his father. For her it would be the same as if he had come back and told her that the battle was theirs and that Trisuldas Thakur had killed a hundred men instead of being killed himself. But she herself was dead and in his fury he hated his father as well as the two men that raped her. He blamed him for having brought her with him to the battlefield. He blamed him for not dying protecting her. He blamed himself as well.

'The notion of blood guilt, which is central to the Greek tragedy, would seem absurd to the Hindu. In fact, the Bhagavad Gita is nothing but an apology for killing your own family. How do you like that for a philosophy, eh? I'd say it puts the Hindu hero down a notch or two … turns him into a butcher. His valour is determined by the number he kills, not how or whom he kills.'

Webley was a hero, thought Augustine, and he still could be. It was in his bearing. Augustine had never realized what was missing in his father until he discovered it in Webley. He was an erratic officer, whose record was no better than Trisuldas Thakur's. He was a runaway, a traitor. But he was a hero because of his vanity. In him there was that inspiration and instinct which could submerge any amount of defeats and irregularities in a flood of confidence. Augustine had felt it in him from the beginning.

'Strange how there are no tragic heroes in Hindu literature……'

Perhaps it was a belief that Webley would die nobly, tragically. An intuition.

'In truth, Indian history contains no hero, to my mind…..'

Augustine thought of himself. He was not a hero. Suddenly he heard Somdas yelling at him. For an instant that hatred returned, that fear. It came upon him as if it were a reminder of his former fears. He thought to himself how he could never be a hero because of that fear. Though he had submerged it, it was there, imbedded in his mind.

'Indians are of an effeminate nature, subject to the weaknesses of women, the little fears. They are not the stuff of heroes.'

Augustine felt inadequate.

'They are better, far better as soldiers, rather than as officers, and as subordinates they come the closest to being heroes. Show me one good Indian general, sir ...'

8

Khasturba's head was pillowed against his arm. Augustine lay contented, drowsy. The brightness of the thin moon surprised him. How many times had he lain there like that, exhausted, numbed to the bone, played out like a fish that turns over belly-up near the shore. But that night he was not tired in the same way. Rather than having drained his body, he had drained his emotions, pumped every dream, hope, and thought out of himself. The girl had listened to him carefully, without moving. That night she was not restless. In his admissions, his story, there had been a sort of soothing mood which overcame Khasturba. He had broken himself open in front of her, spilled out his life, hidden nothing from her. There was now a tenderness between them. He felt small and insignificant. She felt calm in his arms, as though she had smoked her opium.

'Make love to me now,' she said. 'There's nothing more between us.'

'No,' said Augustine. 'Not in a brothel. It wouldn't seem right.'

'Do you think it will ruin me?' she asked. 'Do you think that if you make love to me here, it will spoil all the future times? If you really cared for me, you'd make love to me anywhere, in a field, in an alley, even in a gutter. The place wouldn't matter.'

Augustine said nothing, but smiled.

'You have not told me about yourself.'

She looked away.

'What is there to tell you,' she said. 'I know nothing. From when I was small I remember the hag. She was younger then and some of the men slept with her. No more.'

'You never go out?'

'No, not unless customers request it, and then we are fetched in their palanquins, hidden inside the curtained box and then returned the same way, after their passions and money are spent.'

'It's an ugly life.'

'Not so ugly as some. There is comfort.'

'As ugly as a soldier's?' asked Augustine.

'No,' she said in a whisper, and stood up. She went to her trunk and found her opium and the pipe. The slate-coloured smoke drifted to the ceiling and hung there like cobwebs. Augustine could smell the sweetness of it. After the pipe was finished she returned to his arms. She threw a leg over him. As if in a trance, her eyes became dreamy. Her voice had a sad honesty to it.

'I said there was nothing between us.' Khasturba kissed Augustine softly on the neck. 'I lied to you about myself. I do know my own story. Perhaps when I have told you, then we can make love. But maybe you are stubborn and will not take me until I am all yours.

'How much of the story is true, I don't know. It was told to me in part by a cousin who liked to taunt me, and also by my uncle, who was a dear, kind man. The cousin must have exaggerated and my uncle hid things from me, the really ugly parts of my life. Over the years, I have pieced it together. I am ashamed of it. Perhaps that is why I have become a prostitute. It is the only profession I deserve.

'I think that my father was a soldier, though I can only guess about that. It is just that inside me is a feeling, an excitement when soldiers come to my room. As I knew you were a soldier when you rode past, even though you wore no uniform. I can see it in other men's faces, too. For that reason, it must be in my blood.

'My mother could only have been a prostitute like myself, no more than that, certainly not a lady. There must have been more between her and my father than there is between most men and women, for she was very jealous of him. My uncle told me this. He knew nothing of my father. I do not think that my father kept her, but visited her as you visit me. This was in Farrukhabad, not Lucknow, a much smaller city where rumours travel faster and most people are known to each other.

'I do not know what happened, but I can guess. My father must have taken up with another woman when my mother became pregnant with me. I was still in her womb when my mother killed my father, poisoned his food when he came to visit her. He must have been a man of some influence, for there was a great confusion over the murder, perhaps embarrassment. He could have been married to another woman, or some such thing. In the end it was taken to the courts. Whether the magistrate was an Englishman sitting under his shamiana with his spindly little desk in front of him and his Hindu secretary sitting beside him, I don't know. It could have been one of the Nawab's officials, a bearded old Muslim with his mind sunk in the laws of the Koran.'

'Whoever it was had a clever mind. The murder must have been easily proved and public opinion against my mother. The sentence could only have been death. That is all a prostitute receives. But the judge was kind. I still had four months to be born, as he could see from my mother's shape.'

'He allowed her to live long enough to give birth to me and then be hanged the morning after. He gave me life, but I cannot decide whether I should now thank him for it or curse him. I was made an orphan by his justice. God knows what led him to decide the case in this strange manner. Perhaps he felt it was only justice to my father, that a part of him should live. The judge could have thought that if it was a son, he would grow up into the image of his father. But a woman is never so lucky. I have become what I am—the only choice I had.'

'I still wonder what my mother thought. Was she grateful for those four months of life, or did she hate me for drawing out the agony? I wonder if she wanted to abort me, whether she prayed that I would be stillborn. Did she plead with the magistrate, begging him to kill both of us? I think that I would have hated to give birth if I were her. Imagine sitting in a cell—a miserable routine—growing larger and larger, more uncomfortable. The very process of giving birth is like imprisonment. And how much worse it must have been for her, knowing that my life meant her death. I do not really feel any guilt. I am selfish, as my mother must have been.'

'But then, sometimes I wonder if she wasn't grateful, if she didn't bless the magistrate. I have never wanted to become a mother. Thank God, I have never been pregnant, despite all these men. But she might have loved me—not that I care. She might have lain there in her cell and imagined my life for me, imagined that I would become the wife of a Nawab, with power and influence in the zenana. Did she know that I would be a woman? I cannot guess. Could she have had the forgiveness in her to hope that I would become a man like my father, despite his deceit? Or did she know that I would become a woman and suffer the treachery of such men? I can only tell you how I would have felt. There was something tragic in my mother, which I can still feel now. It is like a disease passed on from one generation to another. She was crippled and so am I.'

'My mother wrote to her cousin, her only relative, and asked him to take me after I was born and bring me up in his home. That was my uncle, as I called him. He came all the way from Indore and took me away from the prison guards, hired a wet nurse, and, when I was healthy enough, returned with me to his house in Indore.'

'Uncle died when I was ten. My aunt, his wife, tried to be kind to me but the children taunted me with this story. Children can be vicious. Five years ago, I ran away and came to this city.'

'But when I think of what happened to my mother, I realize that my life has been happy compared to hers. Imagine, whether she hated me or not, being hung the morning after I was born. They must have taken me away immediately. She probably never saw my face. I, of course, never saw hers, but I can imagine what she looked like that morning when they hanged her. She must have looked like me.'

Augustine felt shattered, as though the tragedy of his own mother's death was somehow linked with that of the murderess, Khasturba's mother. Why did there have to be so much drama in life? He longed for the mundane, the simple deaths, and yet he felt himself inexorably drawn into a world of pageantry, in which all the events were tragic, the characters trapped by fate, as though someone was telling his story and he could not escape the inevitable melodrama of his life.

For Augustine there was a relationship between Bibbi Charlotte and Khasturba. They were not the same woman. In fact, they were two extremes of womanhood, a mother and a pubescent lover. But apart from the broad differences, there were many subtle contrasts, so subtle as to be similarities of a slightly different shade. Their closeness and yet their disparate personalities acted inside Augustine like a mixture of wines, each inflicting its unique intoxication and yet both combining to cause a dizziness, a disturbing confusion, so that his mind could not focus on one without the other becoming fuzzy. Their images blurred, sometimes superimposed upon each other. It was as if one eye, Augustine's good eye, saw Khasturba before him, but there in the other eye, the glass one, was an opaque vision of his mother. And then in an instant the relationship was reversed and Bibbi Charlotte lay before him, while Khasturba floated about in the distance. He could not think of one without recalling the other.

Their personalities were completely different, one had the body of an adult and the mind and reasoning of a child. The other had the body of a child, winsome and fragile, but the hard realistic mind and tongue of an adult. Bibbi Charlotte lived in that vacuum within which there were only her imaginings. Khasturba was so hardened, so tempered with the ugliness of her situation, that she had to escape into the infused world of her opium, in which nightmares became pastoral thoughts and the awful truths of her life were nothing but vague memories, terrible but distant. It was as if the drug took her beyond the present, lifted her up and put her forward, into death almost, a world in which there were no lovers, a sexless world, an innocent world of childhood, the infancy and youth which she had not experienced. One day she said to Augustine, 'I was never a child and I think that I will only become a child when I die. That will be forever—the most wonderful thing that could happen.'

For Bibbi Charlotte it was not a hundred lovers but one. Her husband made love to her and she imagined that he was all her childhood heroes come to life: he was Sir Galahad, St George, and Robin Hood put together. She did not need opium to set her dreaming, to sweep out the terrors of her life. There were no truths to hide. In a sense it was a confined madness, the world of the zenana, a return to childhood with Augustine, the fascination with imaginary people, the fairies, the dwarfs, the giants, the centaurs. And through it all rode her husband, the noble hero. The delicate balance of her innocence was protected within her rooms, her tents, her palanquin. It was destroyed only by the gruesome nightmare … the two British officers …

Augustine wondered to himself what she had thought as they raped her. How had she greeted them? Had she screamed, or had it become just another part of her fantasy, like fear in a dream that makes you wake up sweating?

Augustine's fantasies had been destroyed by that incident. The heroes seemed to dissolve into the nightmare and become frightening images of themselves. Yet he fought on, in a belief that though that world had died he still remained, champion of his mother's fantasies. He fought and lived to recover that intricate and fragile innocence which had existed in his mother's apartments.

In Khasturba he had found someone he believed could reconstruct it for him. For this reason he hated the bitter core of her personality and attempted to dig it out. He wanted her child-like innocence to flow out of her like milk.

She resisted him, fought off his dreams, his images of her. He wanted her to become a child forever. And as she said one night, 'You can do that only by killing me.'

He hated the opium, and yet it brought her closer to Bibbi Charlotte, seemed to soften her angry words, dull that cruelty which he could not love. Now that she had told him about her mother, he felt at first that he had lost her, that she was in fact a symbol of everything he was trying to destroy, the reality. But then he thought of the baby, still wet from its mother's juices, being carried off in the arms of a jailer, and she became again the woman he was searching for. He wanted to hide her away from other men, give her back the innocence of her birth.

~

From Dr Marlow's journals: We got news this morning of the strange and macabre murder of Mr Cullen at the hands of his servant in Kanpur. The incident took place two days ago. Cullen was evidently a well-to-do John Company wallah, dealing in taffetas and silks. He was well liked and generous with his servants. No motive for the horrible crime has yet been unearthed.

It appears that Cullen was engaged in his morning toilet, a customary routine of his. He sat in a plush chair before a full-length mirror and had his servant, a young Mussulman, groom him, manicure his nails, brush his hair, wash his teeth, and shave his whiskers. A peculiar and essential article of a man's toilet in India is his tongue scraper. Most gentlemen use it themselves without the aid of their servants. Why Cullen allowed his servant to scrape his tongue for him I cannot understand, but on the fatal morning this ritual was being observed and the servant, in a fit of frenzy, plunged the scraper far down Cullen's throat, choking him to death. It must have been an awful death. The other servants heard the sound of gagging and entered just in time to apprehend the murderer, who was making a quick exit via the roshandan. He had stolen nothing and when questioned refused to give a satisfactory answer for his conduct. He was shot the next morning. Cullen had no kin, hence the articles in his house have been given over to the Company for auction. They say he had some lovely Chinese porcelain which might be worth the trip to Kanpur.

A party of our friends joined us for a picnic on the estate of the late Major General Claude Martine. We took four barges down the river from the point in front of our bungalow and drifted slowly down the Gumti, a truly delightful ride. There were many escapades. Young Galsworth pushed his lady into the river and then, as he was hauling her out, fell in himself. There was a surfeit of gaiety and the whole affair ended as happily as any party can. We had arranged for musicians, who wafted us away with the gentle notes of their music, such favourite numbers as 'Kiss My Lady' and 'Brightly My Lady Comes to Me, Her Hair All Flaxen Tangles'. They were players from the army band and looked fine in their uniforms. The day, thank God, was lovely, with only a vague suggestion of clouds. There has been a brief lull in the monsoon. Though pleasant now, this forebodes heavier weather to come.

In addition to Galsworth and his lady, Miss B——, a fine

creature with the handsomest figure in Lucknow, there were the two gentlemen, Mr Wainscot and Mr Vinetti (perhaps he is Portuguese), whom we met at the rhinoceros fight the other day. The former of the gentlemen was in fine form, full of stories and a basso accompaniment to the older songs. He was unacquainted with the latest numbers, a sure sign that he's been in India for some time. Mr Vinetti stood firm in the bow of his barge, looking not unlike Nelson at Trafalgar. I asked him if he was keeping a lookout for the French fleet and he said, 'No, crocodiles' which I thought was a rather dull thing to say when there were ladies around, but it seemed to animate the gentle sex and they began to titter. There were six or seven other ladies, whom my wife had invited. I knew only one of them, a Miss Plebish, the daughter of a magistrate. She seemed very fond of Mr Vinetti and shrieked the loudest at his mention of the crocodiles. Bryney of the Company warehouses joined us, along with Mumford and Dickens and General Wolsey, who swore he was getting seasick. He was so afraid of the crossing to India that he came overland by caravan to join his regiment. 'Can't stand the sea,' he says. 'It's imprisonment with the chance of drowning, not to mention the seasickness.'

We reached Constantia just after noon and went immediately into the shade of two magnificent neem trees, where the khanna had already been laid. We'd arranged for it to be taken by carriage, as that is faster. Of course there was beer and hock aboard the barges and all of us were elevated by the time we reached the estate, though it wasn't anything to deter our drinking the late General's health, as well as that of the Nawab and the band, the King, and the variety of other toasts which are customary in this Oriental exile, not the least of which is a drink to the gentle ladies.

Constantia, General Martine's palace, is one of those excessively ornate structures which stud the desolate plains of India with their garish silhouettes. It is part of what could be called a Gothic renaissance, if that is not a contradiction in terms, a vast tangle of moulding and arabesques in plaster. There is a hint of the Baroque in it, with elements as diverse as an English church, a French cathedral, a mosque from Constantinople, and a Hindu temple, all muddled into one, a combination so inaesthetic as to be pleasing in its quaint curiosity.

After the meal, which lasted a good hour and a half, General Wolsey and I stretched ourselves out under the trees and fell to snoring. We were wakened as the evening cast a soft glow on Constantia, giving it the atmosphere of a fairytale palace. The waterbirds winging their way home overhead, the pigeons with their soft rumbling, and the circling kites and hawks gave to the scene the tranquillity of a utopian dream.

And Claude Martine deserved such a palace. He is buried in the basement of the palace, to scare the Mohammedans away, so I am told. But neither the confused extravaganza of architecture nor the brilliant evening light can quite match the splendour of this man's life. He was an adventurer par excellence, a genuine freebooter in the most complimentary sense of the word, and a gentleman to boot. Everyone that knew him found him pleasant company and an honest businessman. He made a fortune in the indigo and silk trades, as well as being the chief adviser to the Nawab of Lucknow. Moreover, he was in the East India Company's service as their political agent in Oudh. His history is complex and I have been able to piece it together from the accounts of many who knew him. They all speak highly of his merits and swear that no European understood the Oriental mind as well as he.

A common soldier, as the inscription on his tomb reads, when he arrived in India, Martine joined the Company service after the defeat of the French in Pondicherry. He raised a French regiment for the English merchants and over time rose in rank and gained the respect of the Company Directors, who finally sent him to Oudh, at the Nawab's request. They say the Nawab was enamoured of him because of his hot-air balloon, the first of its kind to fly in India. Once in Lucknow, Martine established himself both in the court and in the marketplace, investing heavily in the indigo trade and reaping such a fortune from this lucrative business that he was known as the wealthiest man in Lucknow. He was a personal friend of General de Boigne, the Savoyard mercenary who fought under Sindhia. The two men were of one breed, one of that diminishing class of soldier who can flourish anywhere in the world, with a little bravado and a good sword. There are so few men of that style left. It is as if the world is destroying its heroes.

Martine's begum has moved out of the palace. He left his fortune to be distributed among the poor, and also demanded in his will that a school be set up for the education of young boys. This has been done.

Lucknow still lives in the shadow of this man, and it is said that at his funeral there were thousands present, all weeping unashamedly, poor and rich alike, Europeans and natives, Hindus and Mohammedans. In the light of such a career, the ornate palace of Constantia seems but a humble sepulchre for such a grand individual.

I cannot say what happened while the General and I were asleep, but I feel assured that the party did not break up because of our somnolence. In fact, on waking, the charming giggles of Miss B—— were in my ear. Only Vinetti seemed morose. He stood like a statue on the parapet of the palace, silhouetted against the sunset. There is something in that man, a tormenting thought or idea, a fanaticism which I cannot put in words. He looked for a moment almost like a reincarnation of General Martine, standing on the battlements of that garish building. I am sure he is a soldier, and General Wolsey confirmed my suspicion today by asking who the stiff fellow was and whether he belonged to a regiment in the Nawab's service.

The party broke up just before sundown, and we all rode back to our bungalow for tea, the ladies in jampanis, and one or two in the carriage, while the men rode horses. It was a jolly day, one of that sort of occasion you cannot imagine taking place in India.

'Is Webley a good soldier?' asked Khasturba.

'The best,' said Augustine.

'Then why is he not in the Company army?' she asked.

'He is too good for them. Under them he would be nothing. By himself he is the commander-in-chief.'

Khasturba turned her back to Augustine and spoke into the pillow. 'I saw him only once. That day you first came to me. He looked like an old man, a grandfather.'

'No, no, you did not get a good look at him. He is handsome in an English sort of way—balding, but handsome. His fair hair makes him look older and he has aged these last few years.'

'I like soldiers. They usually get killed before they are too old.'

'Webley will never be killed. He has an instinct for survival. A month ago he was almost killed by a leopard, but escaped.'

'You do not want to be a commander-in-chief?' asked Khasturba, turning back to Augustine.

'How could I? An army is not an easy thing to command.'

'But you are a good soldier, no?' she asked.

Augustine laughed and said nothing.

'Who made you a colonel?' she asked.

'Webley.'

'And what is his rank?'

'He has none. Sometimes they call him General.'

'Would your rank stay the same if you fought for the English?'

'I would never fight for the English.'

'Though you are half-English, no?'

'My mother was English.'

Khasturba stared at Augustine until he looked away.

'Who was she?' asked Khasturba.

'A woman who loved this country. She was from another time, not made for this life. She was too fragile to be a soldier's wife. She could not survive.'

'And what about me?' asked Khasturba. 'Will I survive? A tough old whore.' She laughed, as though pleased with the thought.

'Don't speak like that.'

Khasturba's voice was coarse. Her laugh made Augustine's ears sting. He hated her when she spoke like that, as if it weren't her own voice but that of a demon which had possessed her. She had smoked her second pipe of opium. Augustine wondered if it was the drug which made her speak like that. Then he could not decide whether it was herself, her true self, which the opium brought out. He wondered whether she was really the tough old whore disguised under a soft skin or the innocent girl tortured into ugliness by the drug, by the old crone.

'Does the old woman give you the opium?' asked Augustine.

'What does it matter to you where I get it from?' she asked.

'You must stop it,' he said bluntly.

'Who are you?' she asked. 'First you refuse to sleep with me when that's what I'm for. Now you lecture me on my bad habits. Can't you see my life is one enormous bad habit? Yes, I'll tell you where I get my opium from. I have a lover who comes to me once a week. He supplies it to many people. I get it from him for nothing.'

'For sleeping with him,' said Augustine.

'That is the same as nothing.'

Augustine had just finished bathing. He was dressed and shaving his own beard. When the barbers had come, he sent them away, only taking a razor from them. He was exhausted and wanted to sleep. As he shaved, he thought about what Khasturba had said the night before. She had been like a witch. It was painful for him to hear her speaking that way. He wanted to exorcise the devil in her, kill it. He imagined her lying there in the bed, thrashing about, tormented, surrounded by ashen mystics, each of them chanting a separate hymn in mad harmony. The air was thick with incense. Prayer wheels twirled in hypnotic rhythms. They were driving the spirit out of her. Suddenly she exploded, like an animal shot in the spine. For a few minutes she was like an epileptic. Then suddenly all was quiet. The mendicants withdrew, shaking their matted heads soberly. Augustine saw himself go up to the bed and lift Khasturba into his arms. Her body was feverish, her face white, her hair wild about her head. Augustine kissed her and spoke softly in her ear. When she woke, it was as if she was once again a little girl, smiling uncertainly up at him.

The door burst open and Domingo, black as a cannonball, shot into the room. He was wearing a jacket made out of a tiger skin and kept shouting French obscenities at the top of his voice. Augustine grabbed him as he rushed past. The boy was startled for a second, and then with a sudden impulse he bit Augustine's hand. The Colonel swore at him as he dashed out into the balcony and shinnied down a pillar into the garden.

A few seconds after he had disappeared Jules fluttered into the room, a flurry of silk and apologies.

'My dear Colonel Augustine, has little Domingo come in here?'

'Come and gone,' said Augustine. 'He jumped out the window and disappeared into the garden.'

'Oh damn,' said the Frenchman, throwing himself down on Augustine's bed like an expiring prima donna. 'I can't chase him any more. He's very spoilt, you know.'

'And whose fault is that?' asked Augustine, already tired of his visitor.

'Not mine of course, probably Davigny's. He's the fellow that gave me Domingo as a present on my birthday.'

'How old are you?' asked Augustine, resuming his shave.

'No, no, no. I never admit my age,' said Jules, his fingers drumming out a silent rhythm in the air.

'I see.'

'Shall we have something to drink? I'll call the servant.'

Augustine wiped his face quickly, but the Frenchman had already gone out into the hall and was shouting for the servant. In a few minutes two bottles of mango shrub arrived, along with a bowl of pistachios. Webley's half-brother began devouring the nuts like a starved squirrel, watching Augustine nervously. The shrub was a little sour and very strong. Augustine said little. His eye had trouble staying open, while the Frenchman's incessant voice bantered on.

'Who made you a colonel?' asked the Frenchman. 'My brother?'

'Yes,' said Augustine.

'You are very devoted to James, I would say.'

Augustine did not turn away from the mirror. 'He is a fine man,' he said.

The Frenchman giggled, like a young girl who has just heard her first naughty joke.

'I would not have expected it of you, Colonel. A man of your … dimensions, shall we say, must have ambitions. Certainly the life of a bandit is exciting, but do you find it satisfying? Would you not prefer the life of a general, or even a king?'

Augustine turned to face the Frenchman. Jules sat with his legs crossed, one foot dangling in front of him. By moving his toes he slid the slipper on and off his heel in time to some tune in the back of his mind. Behind the foppery, that glossy finish and gilt personality, there was a menacing character, calculating, perhaps even evil, thought Augustine. The scents from his clothes, his hair, his body, perfumed the air. But it was like the smell from a rotting bouquet. The flowers were withered but the odours survived in the air a moment longer.

'There is some method in your talk. Come out with it,' said the Colonel.

Jules winced. 'How blunt you are!' he said, sucking on his little finger thoughtfully. 'But I suppose a soldier has to be as blunt as his sword is sharp. I'm told women enjoy blunt objects. Who knows. It is a pity, because speech should encase its meanings. It should flow over itself With sheer virtuosity. But here we are all soldiers, blunted by war, maimed in our faculties. Every phrase must be delivered like a command, an order.'

Augustine held the razor out in front of him.

'Get out,' he said, 'before I slice your pretty throat.'

Again Jules trilled with laughter.

'I will be short as well, Monsieur, for the soldier's sake. There is a lot of money I can avail you of. My brother is stubborn. He will not take it because of where it comes from. And yet he has to fight the English bereft of funds, supplies, and ammunition.'

'What do you know of our army?' Augustine said viciously, threatening him with the razor again.

'I know that you have been backed into a wretched warren, like badgers pursued by a pack of hounds. Your army is about to mutiny. And your General will not fight the English because they are his own blood.'

'You are a spy.'

'Wait, dear Colonel. I have not told you all. My brother is surrounded by men who adore him, who love him and cannot see his faults. His second-in-command, a fine and, if you'll allow me, a handsome man, is too much of a coward to take hold of the army and destroy the English.'

'Bastard,' said Augustine. He knew it all now.

'I have more money than you could dream of. In fact, I have the entire treasury of France at my disposal. They have given me leave to negotiate on any terms with you.'

Augustine lunged forward with his razor. The French agent screamed and fell back in his chair, toppling it over behind him. Clutching the side of his head, he swore at the Colonel. Then his eyes stopped suddenly and stared at Augustine with horror. There was a look of bewilderment and fear on his face. Blood was streaming through his fingers, staining his shirt and coat. His mouth opened as if he was about to say something. Then he pulled his hand away from his head. The ear he had been clutching came away with his hand. For a moment he looked at it. Then he held it up to his head again, like a man holding a shell to his ear to hear its whisper. His scream was like a woman's, wild and cringing. The French agent ran out of the room, thrashing his way through the curtains in the door.

Augustine took a handful of pistachios and wandered out onto the balcony overlooking the garden. He felt very little. Even the hatred had left him. Only the squeal of terror rang in his ear. He broke the nuts open and then sucked them out of their shells. The shells had a sour, salty taste, from the brine they had been soaked in. He went back to thinking about Khasturba, plotting out a scheme by which to steal her away from the crone and the brothel. It was very simple. He only wondered whether she would be willing to escape with him. The way she talked, she was resigned to her life, within those walls, between those sheets. Maybe she would not come with him. He decided to take her, anyway. Let her realize the freedom and she would thank him for kidnapping her. Her petulance would give way to gratefulness and he would possess her, protect her fragility. In his mind he turned over and over the thought of Khasturba, forever a virgin in his arms. Each night he would come to her and take her gently. She would whimper, cry softly into his shoulder, and then clasp him to her, wanting more and more until the night was over and the morning came to revive the blush in her cheeks. The hymen would again blossom, her innocence would return.

Webley entered and, after pausing a moment in the centre of the room, came out onto the balcony.

'Whose ear is that?' he asked curiously.

'Oh, that!' said Augustine with a smile.

Webley took a few of the nuts out of Augustine's hand. He tried to break one with his teeth and then spat it out.

'Too much of a bloody nuisance, these nuts. Someone should peel them for us.'

'They're not peels, my dear fellow, they're shells. And as far as I'm concerned, that's the best part.'

'Don't be ridiculous. You don't eat them, do you?'

'Of course not. You suck on them, to get the taste.'

Webley made a face. 'You had company this morning?' he asked.

'Your brother. I'm afraid I got cross with him.'

'Yes, I thought as much … looked like his ear.'

'I hope you don't mind,' said Augustine.

'No, no. He's only my half-brother. If you'd cut off both ears, I might have made a fuss. As long as half of him's intact, I'm happy.'

'He offered me money,' said Augustine.

'What kind of money?'

'French money.'

'He came to me as well and I sent him away. I suppose he thought he'd have better luck with you.'

'Have no fear,' said Augustine.

'That's what I like,' said Webley. 'Loyalty in the ranks.'

It stung Augustine, but he stood it.

'Call it friendship instead,' he said.

'Imagine that bastard even thinking I'd sell myself to Bonaparte,' said Webley quickly.

Augustine said nothing. He was loyal to Webley, but it was not the same loyalty which Webley spoke of.

'The French haven't a hope left,' said Webley. 'Why persist? India is already in the hands of the English.'

'It could be in our hands,' said Augustine.

'You are too ambitious, my dear. Do you think that little army chasing us is all the English have? Look at Lord Lake's Grand Army. See how they destroyed the Mahratta chiefs.'

'Holkar and a handful of men, no more than our army, harassed them for months.'

'Ah, but that was not pitched battle,' said Webley. 'In pitched battle see if the horsemen can challenge the infantry square.'

'Who needs pitched battle? We can march out of that dismal fort and no one can touch us. We can live in the saddle, eat in the saddle ...'

'And poke our women in the saddle, I suppose,' said Webley with a laugh. 'How long can an army go like that?'

'Far longer than it can huddle in a dungeon.'

~

There was something ugly about Webley now. Lucknow seemed to have turned him into a different man. He had become even more disillusioned with himself. If was as though the pleasures and luxury of the city made him question his own nomadic life. He was tired, but there was more to it than that. Augustine saw it in their friendship.

When we were both much younger, less cautious, less thinking, we went where we wanted to go, lived our imaginations. God, it was as if we owned the world. It spun when we told it to and stopped still when we commanded. There is that part of being an officer. You have power. When you are young, as we were, it thrills you to see men stand up straight when you speak to them. Webley still has that thrill in him. He loves to shout at a man and see him tighten around the neck, as if a noose had just been slipped over his head. He loves to see his soldiers' eyes staring straight ahead, perfectly still, unblinking. There is still that boyish vanity in him.

But though the excitement may be there, it no longer means anything to him. His men give him no satisfaction. He looks at them as animals. They are rows and columns, like figures in an accountant's books, to be crossed out, subtracted, added, multiplied, and divided. It makes me hate him sometimes, seeing how ruthless he is. He looks on our friendship in the same sort of way. I, too, mean nothing to him.

I admire him, but it is like admiring a weapon. The workmanship may be intricate and precise, the carving beautiful, the steel of the best quality. It may fire perfectly and shoot accurately. But there is no loyalty or friendship in a weapon. In someone else's hands it can kill you. In your own as well.

9

From Dr Marlow's journals: One of the most publicised and cruel practices in Hindustan, second only in its horror to female infanticide, is the practice of suttee, the ritual suicide by fire of a newly widowed woman on the pyre of her dead husband. For the common Englishman, secure and civilized before the hearth, adjudged moral in his practices and upright in his religion—that amalgam of Greco-pagan and Gothic-Christian beliefs—suttee can be only a dreadful and repugnant ritual of a savage and desperate people.

Though it embarrasses me to admit it, I have witnessed no less than six such horrific events. Now that you have kicked off your comfortable slippers, risen up in disbelief and outrage, taken the sword and scabbard from above your chimneypiece, and sworn that you will cut to bits any gentleman who allowed such a despicable act—'And not less than six times,' you scream ... Perhaps this book will be consumed in the merry flames of your English hearth. But let me assure you that on each occasion I attempted to prevent the horrendous murder but was bodily held back by the crowd of Moors, for whom the violence was an act of religious importance. If only you, dear reader, had been with me, perhaps we could have hacked our way through that crowd and saved the damsels, though I must admit that each of them had such a poor neck that it was not worth saving.

Most vivid in my memory is the death of a minor potentate, who, though his kingdom was small, made up for it in his vast array of wives. He died of a sudden illness while I was sojourning in his palace and thus became witness to the sad but true events that follow. The Maharajah's pyre was prepared on a dais in front of the fort, and surrounding it there was a moaning crowd of commoners, ladies, and courtiers. As soon as the Maharajah's carcass was set alight, one by one his wives came screaming through the crowd, dragged by an army of brutes who bludgeoned them at every step, and finally hurled them into the flames, which rose a good twenty feet into the air. Each poor woman died with a scream on her lips. I shouted from the balcony whereupon I stood and watched the gruesome spectacle. 1 raced down among them, but it was too late. They pinned me down, pummelled me terribly. I wounded a few of them, but I was overwhelmed, and when they finally released me, not less than sixty women had been flung to their death.

∽

Augustine felt like an intruder in Khasturba's life. He felt as though he were stealing something from her, like Webley pocketing souvenirs. He felt as though he were rummaging through her private world, which seemed like a drawer crammed full of ugly and embarrassing objects.

'When I arrived in Lucknow, I was a virgin. The crone took me in, and for the first few weeks, I was treated like a princess. I loved the comfort of this room, the delicious food, the baubles she gave me. But then, of course, the time came when I had to begin earning for the witch. I felt I could not escape. The luxury of this room, the privacy, held me here, though I knew it couldn't last. I knew that soon it would all be taken away to tempt some other girl newly arrived in the city. They auctioned me off like a cow. I remember it so clearly. There must have been twenty men, all of them louts, merchants, smelling of money. They bid for my virginity as though I were an animal. Then I realized what I had become. I cried and they teased me, chucked me under the chin, and told me to save my tears for later.

'I was lucky, though. The crone had some sympathy for me. Other girls my age had their teeth pulled out, leaving them with a line of bare gums, so as not to hurt the gentlemen in their pleasure.'

'Stop it,' said Augustine, 'you spoil things by talking like this.'

'I spoil things, hah!' said Khasturba. 'You are the one asking me to remember. I will remember everything for you, from the first man, twice my weight and like a buffalo wallowing in the mud. It was not a pretty initiation for a girl. They should have had a young and handsome man to come and love me, so that I could always recall him to my memory after the others were let loose on my body.'

Augustine ran the palm of his hand over her breasts, felt their gentle contours. She responded slowly but with insistent urgency. For a moment he thought he would give in, but then he stopped himself. Her hand moving down his chest stopped instantly, as if sensing his decision. They lay poised. Her breathing seemed to have stopped altogether. He rolled away from her and sat up on the bed.

'You're leaving,' she said.

'I should go away forever. You must realize I am a dangerous man,' he said, suddenly frightened of himself.

'I have slept with criminals before,' she said, not understanding.

'No, you are right, you need a young and handsome man.'

'And you are the one I want,' she said.

'I will destroy you,' he said.

She laughed lightly and drew him back to the bed. The fear inside Augustine faded. He was embarrassed with himself for having thought that he could destroy this girl. She was almost like a younger version of the crone, and in her eyes he could see the image of that wretched woman, bent and haggard. The crone would destroy Khasturba, not he. He would save her, protect her, kidnap her back to a second childhood.

Turning back to her, he almost said this, almost offered her escape, but then he became afraid that she might turn him down. He would take her against her will, without warning, so that she had no time to think about it, no time to turn him down.

She mistook his sudden change of mind as giving in to her. Khasturba was once again all about him, with the rapacity of a snake, twining and untwining her legs with his. He kissed her softly on the neck and his gentleness seemed to still her. She fell away in disappointment.

'What fun are you?' she said, pouting.

His eyebrows pinched together as he eyed her. There was something about her body which made him draw back. He felt he might hurt her, crush her, though he knew he couldn't. For a moment the fear again crept into him. He felt as if he would smash her after drinking her wine, like the brutish English officers after their toasts, breaking their glasses on the floor.

Augustine left Khasturba's room early. The crone was awake. She never slept. But the stable boy was not to be found. Augustine saddled his own horse and rode out into the black street, where the night had coagulated like filth in a gutter. He was soon at the riverbank. The boatman had gone home, leaving his flat barge lying sideways against the shore. In the darkness Augustine could hear only the soft murmur of the water. A lapwing woke downstream and called—teet tarra, teet tarra. Another answered it, and there was silence. Augustine dismounted and walked over to the boat. Frogs clustered along the bank suddenly leapt into the river, with a volley of splashes. Augustine started. There was something dangerous in the atmosphere, a building tension which seemed to stretch the darkness to a point of breaking open. It was as if the night would suddenly tear apart, confront Augustine with a frightening brilliance.

Putting his weight against the boat, he nudged it out of the mud into the current. Ropes held it fast. Augustine wished he was back in bed with Khasturba, listening to her whispered breathing. Webley had gone that night to sleep with Mrs Marlow. When Augustine compared the two women, it made him wince at the thought of Mrs Marlow with her scaly skin. She had udders instead of breasts, hips like a cow. Khasturba was lithe and playful as an otter. Her breasts were plump as quails, and as soft.

His boots sank into the mud as he searched for the boat's moorings. He could see very little. The sky was overcast. The boat had vanished, but he knew it was still there, tugging against the ropes. After searching, he found the metal girder where the ropes were tied. With all his strength Augustine tried to haul the boat back to shore.

Still along his spine there was that itch of fear, irritating him and forcing him to work faster. But no matter how hard he pulled, the boat refused to come back to shore.

The horse suddenly snorted and screamed. Augustine turned to see it rearing, a tall, shadowy form. The white patches above its hooves flashed in the darkness. It screamed again. But Augustine could see nothing. He wondered if there was some ghost, or some animal in the water. He ran to the horse. It stood still now, shivering under Augustine's hand.

It was then he heard the first growl, low and sinister. Another slightly higher growl came from behind him. He took his pistol out and then thought better of it. In the darkness his sword would give more protection. The horse screamed again, rising into the air once more, knocking Augustine aside. In a moment it was gone, into the river. Augustine could hear it thrashing its way in the water. Still he could see nothing. The growls started again. He listened carefully, counting how many there were. He still didn't know what these animals were. His sword held ready, he began to back off into the water.

Instantly a shaggy form exploded from out of the night. The sword swept upwards and there was a yelp. Another dog came from the other side and faced Augustine with its teeth bared. It was so close he could smell the foul breath from its open mouth. This time the sword attacked. The dog made no sound. Its head lolled to one side and it sank into the mud. The rest of the pack began barking, shrill and frantic. Augustine moved back quickly. He felt himself step into the water. He stopped when it reached his knees.

Augustine never saw the third dog. It landed on him with such force that he collapsed into the water. The dog was off him as soon as he went under. He came up coughing. But before he had regained his balance they were all around him in the water, yelping, barking, growling. He remembered having watched them race across the plain. There had been over a dozen of them. He wished he had a light, so that he knew where they were. Something like a wave came up against his leg, and then he felt teeth sink into his calf. Augustine's sword struck the dog in the body. It made a hoarse sound, like a man in the last stages of consumption. The dogs backed him farther and farther into the water. The river was shallow for some way out and they swam after him.

Something struck his back. Augustine turned quickly and threw himself into the boat, but he was not yet safe from the dogs. They attacked the boat and came clambering up over the sides like a band of pirates, their nails scraping against the wooden hull with a gravelly sound. Augustine fought them off, killing two or three more. With trouble he found the ropes. Two were tied at the prow and two at the stern. Quickly he cut them. The boat shuddered and then swung into the current. In a few moments the barking was behind him. He lay down in the boat and rested. His breathing ached in his chest, and his leg had started to throb. It felt as if the water was still lapping against it. The pain searched up and down his leg. It seemed to probe every muscle and tendon.

After the boat had gone a distance, he took the pole and steered across the river. The current was fast and it was a long distance. Dawn broke as he reached the other side.

An oxcart going towards Lucknow picked Augustine up and carried him to Ashgar Hasan's house. The horse had already returned and there had been a commotion among the eunuch's servants over where Augustine had disappeared to. Men were preparing to go out and search for him. He was taken to his room and a hakim was called to treat the wound. When it was finally dressed and the burning of the medicine subsided, Augustine fell asleep. He slept soundly without dreaming.

Webley woke him in the late afternoon. They sat and talked until night fell.

'Those same dogs?' asked Webley.

'Yes, a pack of them, almost wild. They would have eaten me and the horse all together.'

'It couldn't have been rabid?' asked Webley.

'No, I think not. But its teeth would be like poison, anyway. I hope to God the hakim cleaned the wound well. It hurt enough.'

Augustine was not tired. He felt only a dull pain in his leg, and a faint embarrassment. There was nothing he hated more than sickness or wounds. Thank God, there was no fever. It made him feel reduced somehow, belittled by his own body, in a sense betrayed. He wanted to stand up and stride across the room. He wanted to ride his horse and make love to Khasturba. He wanted to hunt, to fight, to climb the mountain behind the Bijilli Gargh. But now he was like a bedridden grandmother, wretched, helpless.

'It's lucky you had your boots on, otherwise it would have gone right to the bone,' said Webley.

'I could walk on it,' said Augustine.

'Yes, and lose your leg to infection within the week. Stay off it, my Colonel. The rest will heal it far better than the medicine.'

'And how was your night?' asked Augustine.

'Oh, yes, I forgot to show you.' Webley reached into his pocket and, after a moment, produced a thin bracelet, encrusted with brilliant stones.

'I took it from her jewellery box. It's not precious, is it?'

'No, I don't think she'll miss it,' said Augustine. He watched Webley turning it over in his hands proudly, like a crow that has just stolen a trinket and taken it to its nest. Webley examined it with care, as if it really were precious.

'Was her husband home?'

'No, he'd gone off in search of some exotic shrine a hundred miles from here. He will be coming back tomorrow. And your night? Other than the dogs, I mean.'

'It was good.'

'Don't tell me you've fallen for a whore?' asked Webley.

Augustine was startled. He blinked at Webley and then laughed. 'She's not what you think, not the kind of whore you find most times. She's very young ...'

'And says she's a virgin, I suppose.'

'Oh, no, of course she isn't.'

'Don't be an ass, my Colonel. You should find yourself a good wife, an Englishwoman who can keep your bungalow tidy.'

'I don't have a bungalow,' said Augustine.

'You've never slept with an Englishwoman, have you?'

'No,' said Augustine.

'You don't know what you're missing, my dear fellow. It's like a trip back home, refreshing.'

The worst part of the wound was that Augustine was kept away from Khasturba for two weeks. His leg began to go septic, but the hakim stopped it and it began to dry up. Augustine sent Khasturba a message, saying that he would be unable to come to her for several days. As he lay there, he wondered if she missed him, whether she was concerned or if she thought he had run away like all the other men in her life. Outside her door they were free, able to run wild. Her prison was not theirs. Was Khasturba sleeping with others while Augustine was kept from her? She was laughing to herself, he thought. Everything she had insisted on was true. He could never love her, she said. 'Yes, tonight you love me, cradle me, promise anything you like and I will believe you until morning when you are gone. Do you think I'd be a fool to lie here watching the doorway for your shadow to return? It is easy for you to talk, riding away with the morning fog. These streets are like a maze. You will go into them and never return. Should I be such a fool as to hope? If I did, the doorway would remain empty forever.' He lay there now and hoped that her shadow would fall on the curtain, the sound of her anklets would be like laughter down the hall.

∽

'I think you do not like this city, Lucknow. I think it is because you do not understand it, dear friend.'

Ashgar Hasan lay on his side like a loaf of dough rising in a warm place. The sun streamed in through the open windows and pearls of sweat were strung across his forehead. Augustine and he were alone. The servants had vanished and the room smelled strongly of wet bricks and the garden outside. A caged bulbul sang intermittently above them. Their voices were low, hushed by the stillness of the room. Augustine felt comfortable, the pain in his leg faint and distant. His eyes circled the room from where he lay on the low cot. Two of Ashgar Hasan's men had carried him in and placed him there without explanation. At first he was annoyed and felt helpless, not eager for the eunuch's company. But as they began to talk he realized how lonely he had been, lying in his room. Ashgar Hasan's grotesque size no longer bothered him. He became curious about the eunuch and remembered the poems which Ashgar Hasan had recited on the first evening, the romantic couplets strung together—a ghazal, the cry of a wounded antelope. He remembered the low moan the blackbuck had given after Mehboob Rashid killed it from his horse. The anguish of that call had been in Ashgar Hasan's verses, in the words, the rhythm, his voice. It was an immense sadness, overwhelming, the cry of separation, of death. It was something Augustine could understand. This was not the complex talk of Marlow, an Orientalist's jabbering. Those poems had been the cry of something he knew intimately. It didn't matter if the complexities of Persian grammar escaped him. There was a deeper meaning which surfaced in Ashgar Hasan's recitations, a haunting melody of words.

'You have heard perhaps of the man who planted a hedge of roses because of their thorns, to keep the goats out of his garden. The roses ultimately flourished while the garden withered. Lucknow is not dissimilar to that man's garden. Here we are caged by beautiful buildings and marvellous facades, but inside the garden there is emptiness. In the same way, we have an elaborate system of manners and etiquette to shield our personalities. Eventually, the manners have become everything and the men nothing but empty sacks and bones.'

'Your poetry,' said Augustine, 'is that, too, a hedge of roses?'

The eunuch laughed. 'No, that is shauq. To understand the meaning of shauq is to understand this city. I am not talking about the roses now. You have asked about something far more complicated. It is like asking me to show you the yolk without first breaking the shell.'

'From a distance, as we came down the river, Lucknow was like an enchanted city.'

'It is … it is. But the enchantment is like any kind of magic, it is a sleight of hand. You understand? A trick to deceive the eye.'

'You have lived nowhere else, yourself?'

'First you ask about the city, then about me. Which do you care to know about … tell me that. Our time is short.'

'Both,' said Augustine with a smile.

'You have no respect for time. What I could tell you one day might take from dawn to dusk, but another day it could be explained in a few terse sentences. This is the problem with truth, ah!'

Augustine shrugged and settled into his pillows with a sigh. Ashgar Hasan began, his voice a low rumble, interspersed with the soft whistle in his breath. 'Since you insist, I will first tell you of myself, and then if there is time … 'Lucknow.' He spread one hand in a gesture of offering, as if on the soft pudgy palm there rested the answer.

'My birth was in Bulandshahr, a dusty city of flies and sewage. My mother died giving birth and I know nothing of her. My father was a rogue, much interested in dice. They say that the night I was born he lost two thousand rupees on a single toss and deemed me unlucky. With that judgment over my head, I was given to a woman of the household who was barren. She brought me up, holding me to her dry breasts as if there were some nourishment in them for me. I grew up within the confines of that sprawling house, clutched within the walls of the city, room upon room, so many I never found my way out of one without stumbling into another I hadn't known existed. It was not a family but a confused jumble of women and men sharing each other, an ants' castle of intrigue. Really, I never knew who all those people were. The women lived like vipers in a hole, never leaving their cells. Having been born a man, I could wander freely until I was twelve. There is something about growing up amidst so much uncertainty—the logic of a family escapes you, and you gain an irrational sense of associations.

No mother, only a frustrated shrew, pressing me hopelessly to her sagging breasts. Even when I was twelve I remember her, a frightening vision, calling me to her and opening her bosom to me. I had to suck those black nipples, shrivelled like raisins, in a desperate struggle to draw life out of her.

'A strange thing happened many years later, in the zenana of a Prince in Shahjahanpur, where I was kept for a time, soon after I became a eunuch. The Prince had a young wife, a tender woman, her skin as soft as a magnolia petal. She was the Prince's favourite and he loved her like a fiend, jealously. My job was to guard her from any man who might try to court her. In time she became pregnant. She would talk with me about it, gently, with the shy excitement of a child. I became closely attached to her. And then in the seventh month the child within her aborted. It was a tragedy and the Prince was furious, he threatened everyone for days after, for the child was a son.

'I mourned with the lady, for 1 loved her very much and it was as if the son had been my own, though I could never have had a child. She became sick after this and for days lay in a fever. The midwives begged the Prince to let a child be brought to her so that she could nurse it, for they claimed that the sickness came from having no child to suckle. But the Prince in his jealousy forbade this and the woman suffered. I spent many hours in her company. There were others around and she complained of pain in her breasts. The milk would seep out of its own accord and her blouse was always wet around the nipples. Then one night, as I slept outside her room, guarding the passage, I heard her call. It must have been two o'clock in the morning when this happened. I entered her room and found her alone, crying into her pillow. I asked her what was the matter and she complained that the pain was unbearable and that her breasts felt as if they would burst. She begged me to suckle from them, to relieve the pain. I was embarrassed and frightened lest someone find us, but I loved her and hated to see her in agony, so I lay down on the cot beside the girl and took her swollen nipples between my lips. She had not slept peacefully for days, but that night when I finally lifted my face from her bosom, I found her snoring softly. I was happy and loved her more than ever. The milk tasted sweeter than any sherbet and it seemed to fill me completely, all through my body. The sight of her relieved and quiet also made me happy. I felt strangely fulfilled. Does that seem too peculiar for you?'

Augustine shook his head violently, fascinated by the story.

'I came to her every night after that for three months and she grew healthier and healthier, until the milk stopped flowing and the pain ceased. Many times she wanted me to be her lover and wept over the fact that I could not. She gave birth the next year, to another son, and I moved to Lucknow, where I have been ever since. I hope I do not embarrass you with the details of my life. For a man like me, the intimate moments are all that exist. Except for a little politics—more in recent years— my life has been one of complete sensuality, always within the zenana. My stories are not like those which you could tell, my dear, of battles and shikar. There is a little intrigue which I could discuss with you, gossip, but all my life has been taken up by the fact that I am a eunuch, thrust in amongst the most sensual people, the harems of the Nawabs, but strictly relegated to being an observer and not a participant.'

'You regret being a eunuch?'

'Not any more than I regret the other things in life.'

Augustine coughed with embarrassment. 'Before you became a eunuch, did you ever make love? Don't mind me asking.'

'Not at all. I didn't, before or since,' he said with a chuckle ... hesitated, and then, with a lecherous glint in his eye, said merrily, 'but I've ten fingers, all intact.'

Augustine looked at the bloated hand, freckled with moles and jewels, the nails neatly manicured. There was something obscene about those fingers, as if they had grown there like warts and were not a part of the massive wrists, a kind of fungoid growth.

'Becoming a eunuch is like pruning a rose bush. You flourish. I was as thin as you once—now look at me.' Ashgar Hasan's laugh was lusty and full-throated.

When Augustine said nothing in reply to this joke, Ashgar Hasan sobered and went on with his story.

'I have not told many people about this thing, this being castrated, but in your eyes I can see a curiosity. I think it is the violence of the act which appeals to you, Colonel, because I tell you frankly, never have I met a more violent man than yourself. It is not in your face or in your hands. It is contained inside you, like the wildness in a tame panther. Excuse me for talking like this; you see, I admire my own ability to observe character and personality.

'It is not pleasant, anyhow, but shall we say I describe my becoming a eunuch because, unknowingly, you have asked me to tell you. It began when I was sixteen, my father offered me into service with a nearby prince. For two years I worked as a messenger and cup-bearer in the palace. Then it was the Maharajah of Bareilly who took me from there as a gift. He kept me for several years to supervise his servants, the other young men of the palace. Fond of me, he suggested that I become his eunuch, saying that I was a faithful servant. I hesitated, but before I could say anything two of his hijras latched themselves on to me and crooned encouragement into my ear, promising me power, wealth, and respect in exchange for my genitals. And to tell you truthfully, what they promised me that day in Bareilly has come true. I demurred, but finally the word came that the Maharajah gave me no choice. I was destined to be a eunuch. It was his will and I submitted to it.

'They kept me resting for a few days, fed me cold foods to make me relax, gave me herbs and medicines to calm me. On the fifth day, the two hijras came to me. With them they brought a bundle of instruments. One of them gave me a pipe of opium and they sat there like two hungry pie-dogs watching me inhale the precious drug. Gradually my body slumped. What I remember is like a dream, the details have faded. There was no pain until afterwards. A bamboo was taken and split, so that when it was opened it was like a pincer. After shaving my privates, they took my penis and testicles and clamped them with the split piece of bamboo. A numbness settled over me and I stared hard at the ceiling, not wanting to see the hideous features of the two hijras. The razor must have been sharp, for I felt nothing but a soothing warmth, which was the hot oil they poured over the wound. The bamboo was removed and a bandage wound around my crotch. Then I was taken to another room, where more opium was given to me until I slept. For five days I remained drugged, and when I returned to consciousness, the scab had already formed. It was a month before I could walk comfortably again and two months before my duties in the harem were explained to me.

'It was peculiar, no longer being a man. The women would leave their faces uncovered in front of me. And a great amount of respect was accorded to me from then on. Even the Maharajah was more confident to speak with me on delicate matters, and I was often his go-between in both political struggles and tiffs between him and his ladies. When I succeeded in soothing the ladies' jealousies or calming the fury of an ambassador, he gave me lavish gifts of jewels and expensive cloth. In those first years I did not miss the pleasures which I knew other men enjoyed. There was too much besides.

'Not until I moved to Shahjahanpur and fell in love with that Princess did I really regret the act. All I can say is that I am a happy man. In every respect, what I forfeited I have been reimbursed for in full. Do you not like my splendid house? Is it not worth the sacrifice?'

Augustine laughed. 'Perhaps. I cannot say.'

'True. It's something you will never have to consider.'

'I suppose it's the same thing as having a horse shot out from under you.'

'I couldn't say, but you may be right.'

'Then you came to Lucknow?'

'As a young man of twenty-nine. I found favour in the Nawab's court, began working for him as a secretary and translator, able to enter the harem and keep track of the intricate complexities of women in purdah, their dangerous affection for intrigue. There are more spies in a harem than anywhere else in the world.'

'You never worked as a spy?'

'Who doesn't, once in a while, whether it is for himself or for some other master.'

'Being a eunuch …'

'Being a eunuch helped. There is nothing that inspires more confidence in a man than being in the company of an impotent member of his own sex. It is a curious thing, but ever since that moment which I never felt, when the hijra's blade severed me from my sex, men have felt no shame or danger in me. You yourself, perhaps, feel the same way. I am a comfortable man to be with. I cannot threaten you or your women. For that reason a eunuch has a revered and important role to play in the court of any prince. As a spy I was harmless, giving out information which was obsolete and unimportant; as an adviser to the Nawab I was invaluable. My position gave me access to the opinions of others, which another more virile person would have been unable to acquire.'

'But Lucknow is such a debauched and sensual world. How can you live in this place, of which all four corners are sex?'

'Again, it is my fingers,' said Ashgar Hasan with a lewd chuckle.

Ashgar Hasan stopped himself and then laughed heartily. His speech was quick and efficient. When he laughed it was perfectly timed, so well did his speech synchronize with his thoughts.

'But you asked me about Lucknow, hurrying me on relentlessly. Yes, it is a bold city of carnality in all its guises. I may not be able to love a woman in the same way that you can, but I am full of lust and desire. Because I cannot get rid of it, I spend it the same way I spend my fortune; I am able to savour it and study its variations, its curious habits.'

'What satisfaction is there in that?'

'A poetic satisfaction. The anguish, perhaps, but more so the inadequacy.'

'That is like enjoying pain,' said Augustine.

'Which is the wont of the soldier, is it not?' He gave a clever laugh.

'I disagree.'

Ashgar Hasan shrugged. 'We will not argue. That is a bore.'

'If this is all you are living for in Lucknow,' said Augustine, 'anguish—then I would say you must be very satisfied.'

'Fulfilled, my dear, fulfilled!'

'I am not very clever at talking,' said Augustine, 'but I think you are playing with me. This nonsense about fingers and anguish ...'

'Not at all, I speak with complete sincerity, my friend.' Ashgar Hasan's face had fallen into a serious frown. 'But this is the same as you trying to explain the complicated tactics of an army to me. We are not men of similar occupations. No matter. What I am concerned with is trying to explain myself and this city to you, in your language, so that you will not bear us a grudge. Leave us to our silly games and ride off to your own farcical world, but do not go without sympathy for us. I have known enough soldiers so that I do not hate your murderous activities. I tolerate them, understanding that they are identical, really, to my sensual dalliance.

'Have you never wondered why a chessboard is chequered with black and white squares? They have nothing to do with the game. It could be played as easily on all white squares, or on a totally black board. The game would be unchanged. You see, it is the same thing with us. We make distinctions which have no relevance. It is the pieces, the men, that are uniquely important.

'So let me start again with the hedge of roses. You understand *that,* of course. We protect ourselves against an enemy without and yet it is within the garden that the disease lies. What you love in war is destruction. It is something which was bred in you as a boy, stealing eggs from birds' nests and smashing them on the ground, killing other people's pets. We, too, in Lucknow, believe in destruction, the rampage of our emotions. For that reason we ruin our health, turn our bodies into gross and disgusting factories of waste.

'It is what disgusts *you,* that *we* live for. Perhaps it is boredom, the natural successor to extravagance, which makes this city what it is. You are a man of distances, of broad plains, vast panoramas, the limitless sky. I am a man of closed rooms, full of fusty odours. For me there is security in doors and locks. Just as a man who lives locked within himself becomes a creature of moods and perversions, so does a man who remains indoors. Somehow, our captivity has changed us. Have you ever seen a monkey kept in a cage? He becomes nervous, desperate for entertainment. The swinging about within the bars, the hoots of laughter, the hopeless masturbating in the corner, these are all a part of his madness, something he acquires in captivity. So it is with us, these walls, these ceilings animate us in curious ways. Our behaviour becomes a desperate attempt to fill that room with all of the carnality and lust which is rampant in the world. It is as if we are besieged, stockpiling our desires. Because we are trapped we hoard our pleasures. Whereas you live outside Lucknow, travelling across Hindustan, taking your women from the side of the road, even from the gutter. But for you it is a healthy thing, because you ride on, leaving those women behind. We, instead, wallow in our own mire. There is no escape for us.'

Augustine listened with a smile on his lips. He could sense a desperation in the eunuch's voice, a hopeless captivity, as he called it. The words strayed. Ashgar Hasan had given up trying to draw it all together; his speech was like his palace, a hodge-podge of styles and ideas, blended together by the smooth language and hoarse but pleasing voice. The metaphors lay on top of each other like naked bodies wormed together in an orgy.

Then suddenly, with an abrupt change of tone, Ashgar Hasan stopped his rambling and spoke bluntly.

'You have fallen in love with a woman of this city, a prostitute, I am told. Has she taught you anything about Lucknow? Perhaps. Women are not as intellectual as men, but they are far more intelligent. One movement of her body could probably tell you more than all my tired maundering. But allow me to give you one word of advice. Leave her here in Lucknow, for it will be impossible to take her away from this captivity. She will die under the fierce sun, the bold landscape. Leave her in this garden with its hedge of roses. Let her teach you the pleasures of this evil city and then go away. For you cannot stay here. And she cannot leave.'

'She is not a part of this city,' said Augustine.

'Nevertheless, she lives here, within these confines. To uproot her will mean her death.'

'But she is eager to escape."

'All of us are,' said the eunuch. 'But it is impossible.'

'We shall see.' Augustine felt himself getting stubborn. He did not want to talk about Khasturba, but he couldn't help himself.

'Is she beautiful?' asked Ashgar Hasan.

'In a delicate way, yes.'

'Ah, a child!' His voice was like a gossiping old woman's, curious, eager, flickering.

'A virgin,' said Augustine, not able to stop.

'Oh ho! Surely you have deprived her of that by now?'

'No, I love her in a different way.'

'That is dangerous, my dear, very dangerous.'

They were both silent for some time; neither wanted to go any further. Aggressive as Ashgar Hasan was, he did not wish to offend Augustine. After a while, he began again, his voice monotonous.

'It is all shauq, you know. That is the truth of it. You know what shauq means, I'm sure, but its implications, I think, have escaped you. It is not just a hobby, as you presume. It is a far more violent thing. Shauq takes hold of a man like a parasite, clings to him, refuses to let him go. For some it is gambling, as it was for my father. The dice were his gods, their black eyes staring at him with the hypnotic glare of an idol. He worshipped them. When he walked, his hand was always in his pocket, fondling the two ivory cubes, pocked with the treacherous dots. I have never trusted numbers since then; they have always had that look about them, like the eyes of a devil. For others it is cock-fighting, or the animals fighting in the arena, just as you saw a few weeks ago. For still others it is kites, their shauq gives them no time for anything but struts and paper and glue. They are forever constructing these paper birds, flying them like idiot children, competing with others who share their shauq. For you it is hunting and war, am I not correct? Unless you are wielding a weapon, whether a sword, a lance, or a musket, you are not happy. Blood-spilling is your shauq, and a noble activity, I will agree. The valour, the glory, means nothing to you. It is simply the satisfaction of your shauq … eh? Am I not right?'

Augustine did not answer directly, instead he said: 'And for you it is poetry?'

'In part, yes. I am many things, but mainly I am a poet. My poems are very much a part of me. Lucknow is a city of shauq. Here it is the only purpose in men's lives. Shauq is the idle man's diversion, and as Lucknow is the largest city of loafers, so it is the capital of shauq. Our boredom brings it upon us. We grasp at our diversions furiously, with a pent-up frenzy. It dictates us. We are enthralled by these things.'

~

Several days after his conversation with Ashgar Hasan, Augustine was lying in bed. A crow had landed on the parapet outside his window and he was watching it eating something pinned down by its feet. There was a cruelty in the crow. It was a bird which lived on death. We, too, are scavengers, thought Augustine, going out like crows on the wind, battling kites and vultures, collecting scraps of refuse. The crow had come away with its booty and was feasting in peace, out of reach of the kites that screamed down from the air.

There were voices in the garden—an argument. Augustine could not make out the words, but shouts arose from all around. He could hear a man speaking English. His voice sounded familiar. The crow cocked its head and then, giving a sudden cry, took off, a bluster of wings.

Curious, Augustine pulled his weight out of bed and hobbled over to the window. Beyond the edge of the parapet he could see the bald head of Dr Marlow. His arms were gesticulating like a puppet's whose strings have become entangled.

Two or three servants were trying to restrain him, but he threw them off.

'Take your hands off me, you dusky bastards,' he cried. 'Chhor do, damn it. You go dekko for that planter sahib, the English son of a whore. Tell him to kholo his bolo and get his arse down here. He has to explain some things to me. Chele jao, after him, man!'

The servants acted as if they understood nothing. They pointed dumbly at the gate and tried to push the scholar in that direction. But he had come prepared, and in a flash his hand ducked into his coat and pulled out a duelling pistol, finely engraved and gleaming, obviously one of a pair. He waved it about and then suddenly fired into the air. The ball struck the parapet outside Augustine's window and shattered a part of the masonry. Marlow held the pistol awkwardly, like a boy after his first ejaculation.

There was a hush. The shutters of Webley's windows swung open. He stepped out onto the little balcony as if he were going to deliver an oration. He had dressed himself in his uniform. The flaxen hair had been carefully combed over his head, so as to give the impression that there was more of it. His lip was stretched into a perfect sneer, cold and proud.

Marlow looked up at him with astonishment, all his bravado drained by the sight of the uniform and the slight but imposing figure above him.

'You've come to see me?' asked Webley.

The servants, sensing danger, drew back.

'You are no better than a common thief. Where is that bracelet? I took it off an idol in Tanjore. It means a great deal to me. It's a memento.'

'You mean you stole it?' said Webley.

'I did not,' screamed Dr Marlow, raising his hand angrily. He had forgotten that he held the pistol. Glancing at it in surprise, he hurled it away from him and reached into his coat once again. The second of the pair of pistols was now cocked and ready in his shaking hand.

'You'd kill me because of a bracelet?'

'For the bracelet and my wife's honour.'

'She gave it cheaply,' said Webley. 'I mean her honour, of course.' His sneer became tighter.

'Give me back the bracelet!' screamed Marlow.

'Did you beat it out of your wife? Did she take long to admit it, or was she easy to loosen up? I imagine she cried a lot. It's a bad habit of hers, that. Did you hit her with your hands like a man, or did you use a stick?'

Marlow was ready to explode. Webley played with him, bending his nerves back and forth like a wire that will break suddenly, snap apart in your hands.

'But you want the bracelet back, not her honour. That means nothing to you. I couldn't give her honour back if I wanted. Someone had stolen that before me.'

The pistol exploded. It leapt out of Marlow's hand. He was engulfed in a cloud of smoke. The ball bit off Webley's epaulette on the left side. Augustine was close enough to smell the singed cloth. Webley stood very still.

'No, no, Dr Marlow. You are a scholar and not a man of action. Allow me to instruct you in the fine art of duelling with pistols. It takes a great deal of practice.'

Augustine saw the bald head beneath him. Marlow's eyes glistened like two garnets, but he stood still. Webley drew his pistol from where he had tucked it in his sash.

'Now, my dear Dr Marlow, you will notice that I am standing above you. When you are firing at an angle, either up or down, the ball will tend to rise, so it is first necessary to aim low. You will notice that I am lining up my barrel with your navel. Now, neither should you take too long in firing nor too short a time. Use the tip of your finger, not the second knuckle, as you are wont to do. Exhale and do not inhale again until after firing. Your finger must tighten evenly and with a steady pressure on the trigger. Do not be abrupt and, above all, keep both your eyes on the target.'

Marlow began to turn just before the slug caught him. He completed the motion with a sudden whirl of his body. There were no contortions, not even a cry; he went perfectly limp and collapsed with his face down. Augustine saw Webley reach into his coat pocket and take out the bracelet. He tossed it towards Marlow with an insolent flick of his wrist, so that it spun in the air.

Augustine turned to go back into his room. He felt no sympathy for Marlow, only a slight disgust over how easily he had died. It had been like the bear killed by the Resident's nephew. His foot touched something on the floor of the balcony as he was thinking. Looking down he saw two fingers of a hand, partly eaten away by the crow. It had dropped them in its flight. Augustine kicked the fingers over the side into the garden. They must have come from one of the corpses washed up along the riverbank, he thought.

∽

The last entry in Dr Marlow's journals: You get a feeling sometimes that those Moors are watching us with an abstract interest, like a curiosity in a cage. They seem to know something more than we do, a secret understanding of the future and of the present. When I speak with mendicants and sages on the roadside, they sit there dusty and ashen, half-naked, some totally so, on their deerskin mats, with dented begging bowls and matted hair, and in their faces is a vague amusement, a superiority.

No Englishman would admit to it, and most genuinely mistake it for a dullness in spirit, a lazy ineptitude. But I think the lines which crease their faces are not of puzzlement and idiocy but of humour, the cracks of laughter showing before a grin erupts on their faces. This can only spur me on. I am not offended at being the fool, for though we may know nothing, we are noble fools and go about our pointless errands with a flourish of grandeur, like madmen thinking they are kings. So what if the Moors should look at us as this? My errand, however foolish, is to discover the reason for their smugness.

10

In his enforced idleness Augustine reminisced, played with his memory. He had thought many times that he should have kept journals. Daily, men entered their experiences in volumes, reducing adventures, thoughts, feelings to a tangled scrawl on the page. It gave every incident a permanence, a life of its own. It was a record as well. Augustine wished he had kept notes the time he and Webley went hunting at Bharatpur and each of them shot over seventy ducks, geese, and snipe. He wished he had noted down how many of them were mallards, how many teal, pintails, bar-heads, and brahminies. He wished he could remember exactly who had dined with them in Agra. They had been fighting the British that morning but had invited them to hunt hares along the Jumna. They had been camped in the best area for hares, and the English had felt rather put out that their sport had been spoiled by the hostilities. So they had stopped firing at lunch and sent over an invitation. All afternoon they followed the dogs. One fellow had a fine pair with English bottom. No dogs, not even the finest Persian hounds, could match them for speed and endurance. Course after course they had followed, through the fields of chickpeas and young wheat, the hounds chasing the hares with arching bounds. Their slender bodies seemed to stretch out, becoming even longer and more slender as they ran. Each of the officers on his horse was dressed for the dinner that would follow. There was something about that day which still excited Augustine. He had hunted behind dogs many times, but this hunt had had a special dignity about it. Perhaps it was the green wheat, like velvet patches on the khaki plain. The dogs had been some of the finest. It had been a winter day. There had been beer, which the English officers brought, and ice to chill it with. About it all was a pageantry. It had been one of those glorious days which you wait for over and over again but which never return and are never quite matched. Augustine had hated the English even more bitterly then, but all was forgotten. They had basked in their own masculinity, their pride. Everyone was at his best that day, no one drunk in an unseemly way, no fights. It had felt as if they were all part of one great army, one great corps of officers, each man unto himself. There was a sort of universal esprit de corps among them, for they all loved the same two things, war and sport. That day, more than any other, had made Augustine feel acutely the English part of him. Though he was the only country-born among them, it was ignored. He had felt a part of them, just another shouting, laughing schoolboy. That night they ate and drank so much in Webley's tent that none of the officers was able to go back to his line until morning. Before the first light they were all gone, and suddenly, there in the direction in which they had disappeared, Webley pointed out the dozens of glowing beads of light from the matchlocks. They had dressed quickly and rounded up their men. Muskets were primed, the galloper guns tamped down, moustaches twirled, and at the first cannon shot from the British, sport ended and war began.

Augustine wished he had a journal of those battles, the skirmishes, Webley's brilliant manoeuvres, how he outflanked the English time after time and sent them scuttling for cover in the munj grass. He wished he had described how the tall grass had caught fire, how the grey smoke plumed up, and how the grenadiers could be seen running from the flames, the shot kicking up dust at their heels.

Augustine's mother had taught him how to write. She taught him what she knew and he picked up what he could. He was literate in Persian, which he had been taught by tutors his father employed. Once or twice he had begun journals, deliberately, carefully sentencing out each thing that happened to him, being elaborate in detail and uncautious about any form or argument. But whenever he read his entries over— never was he able to keep up the discipline for more than two or three days—they seemed awkward to him.

Language seemed to reduce him to the most mundane level. It robbed him of his style, which was more of action than of words. He felt like a fool when he clambered over the awkward grammar and construction. Sometimes he himself could not understand what he had meant to say. And worst of all, nothing that he wrote about seemed of any importance. He had realized that he was not the sort of man who could produce volumes of lucid prose on the slightest provocation. He was not like Marlow, with his steady stream of adjectives running on and on.

And now that Marlow was dead, those words remained, what he had said could not be destroyed. It was as if his mind were still alive on those pages. Perhaps someone would edit the scholar's notes and publish them, thought Augustine. They were there, anyway, opinionated, verbose, but definitely a part of him.

Augustine envied Marlow and wished that somehow he, too, could leave such a record.

Marlow's death caused a stir in Lucknow. His body was found floating in a tank outside the city. Mrs Marlow immediately directed the suspicion towards Webley, and the Resident demanded his arrest from the Nawab. Suddenly the two soldiers of fortune became the centre of attention in the city and their true identities were discovered. This made the English even more adamant in their demand for Webley's and Augustine's arrest. The Nawab, however, delayed, procrastinated with all of the artistry and style of an Indian court. He made excuses, acted ill one day, very busy another. Ashgar Hasan had spoken to him even before the corpse was fished out of the tank, requesting him to put the English off. He said that Webley and Augustine were his house guests, and should they be arrested while in his home, it would reflect on his hospitality. The Nawab understood these arguments far better than those of the Resident, who lined his pleas with talk of treachery and murder.

'In fact, dear Colonel,' the eunuch said one day, having dropped in to see how Augustine was recovering, 'the Nawab believes in dealing from both decks. He is interested in your predicament, which I outlined with great care. Of course the death of this man means nothing. We may be able to outfit your army. There is a belief in Lucknow that the English are tiring. They have spent too much on conquering Hindustan and perhaps, if men like you and my dear Webley miyan succeed in trouncing them on a few more occasions—perhaps we will see the last of them.'

'The Nawab is a shrewd man,' said Augustine.

'He plays a game of solitaire, moving the chess pieces against himself, taking both sides. There is neither skill nor honesty in the game. In truth, it is hardly a game. A man of his stature has no opponent, save himself. And no matter who wins, he is sure to lose.' The eunuch cracked his knuckles as if they were walnuts and smiled.

'You are convinced the English will be defeated?'

'I am convinced of nothing,' said Ashgar Hasan.

'Have you told Webley about the Nawab's offer?'

'No. Since last night he has been out.'

'Perhaps they have arrested him,' said Augustine.

'No, no, Augustine miyan.'

'Why do you say that?'

'Because they are still looking for him,' said the eunuch.

'They will try to kill us.'

'Is that something new for a soldier to face? Here in this

house, within these walls, I promise your safety. Outside …' The bulging shoulders shrugged casually.

'I must talk Webley into returning. God knows what has happened to our army,' said Augustine.

'You must persuade him to leave Lucknow. It is not a safe place.'

'With this money our men will fight like hawks.'

'Only because of the money?' The eunuch, who had been reclining on a couch against the wall, gestured to his servants. They hoisted him from under the armpits and carried him into the hall. His feet dragged on the ground.

Full of excitement and anticipation, Augustine rode out of the garden that night. His leg had almost healed. The thought of the Nawab's support, the image of their soldiers carrying new weapons, and the picture of Webley charging into the English lines, with his sabre cutting left and right, thrilled the Colonel. He had almost forgotten his danger. As he rode through the gullies towards Khasturba's room, he kept alert for assassins.

Tonight he would carry her away from the brothel, wrapped in his cloak, riding in front of him on the saddle. They would steal out and ignore the crone's screams, ride furiously through the cluttered streets. He warned the boatman to wait for him and paid him extra. Tomorrow he would send someone to buy Khasturba the finest silks and muslins and hire tailors to stitch her clothes. He would ornament her as if she were a bride, and then the next day, outfitted by the Nawab, they would ride north toward the Bijilli Gargh. He would send word ahead that his room should be specially prepared for Khasturba, curtains put up for her privacy and beds laid with cushions.

The boy took his horse and led it into the stables. The crone came out whining and wheezing as if something was the matter. She tried to stop him from going up to Khasturba's room, but he called her a jackal bitch and brushed past her up the stairs. A candle glowed through the curtains.

Augustine heard laughter and at first he thought it was from one of the adjoining rooms. But as he drew close to Khasturba's room he could hear her giggling. With his sword unsheathed he stepped into the room. Khasturba caught sight of him over the man's shoulder. She looked frightened.

Webley turned and faced his Colonel. His first expression was one of surprise. Then he laughed.

'Colonel, you are better now. I was just telling this sparrow how the dogs had attacked you and you were laid up. Please … she has been asking about you. You should have told her what was keeping you away. The dear thing was worried.'

He spoke in English so that Khasturba did not understand what he said. It irritated Augustine to hear him talk about her that way, as if she were an idiot. Khasturba had turned her face away.

Augustine spun out the door. He felt nothing at first, only a desire to get away from the room, away from Webley and Khasturba, to be alone. The boy was just returning from the stables when he saw Augustine coming down the stairs. He turned to bring the horse. Augustine ignored him and waited in the courtyard. The crone suddenly appeared below him, hovering about his legs. There was something inhuman about her, not just a blackness in the cloak about her shoulders but something shadowy about her form which no light would brighten.

'I tried to stop you,' she said.

'You peddle her about as if she were an attraction at a village fair.'

'She is my merchandise, after all.'

Augustine flew at her, reaching for his sword. But she was gone with surprising quickness, vanishing as abruptly as she had appeared in that dungeon room, with its window at street level, from where she called out to passing men. All Augustine heard was the sound of a bolt being drawn shut and a scuffling noise, like rats under a closet.

Returning to Ashgar Hasan's estate, Augustine brooded over the incident, recalling again and again Webley's face, his words, the way he had spoken of Khasturba right in front of her, just as he would have done with any Chandi Chowk whore. He had probably been there since the night before, having no idea that the English were after him. He was safe, though. The crone ran a discreet establishment. Unless someone saw him entering the brothel, they would never find him.

The garden was still and inviting. The air was moist and seemed to condense on the leaves. All about him there was the sound of water dripping. There had been no rain for almost a week.

It was not as dark as it had been the nights before. People had been saying that the monsoon was about to end. There was no moon, only a few stars searching out the gaps in the clouds. The garden was all sounds and no shapes. It was not a still darkness, but almost alive. Augustine felt as if he was engulfed by a black mist, clouds of smoke. Only the marble pavilion gleamed in the night. It had a sort of iridescent glow about it. As Augustine looked closely, he could see the vague outline of the palm trees.

Moving slowly down the path, he tried to think of Khasturba, but there was nothing left of that image, that fresh and innocent face. All he could remember was her head turned away from him on the bed, almost as if she was ashamed, afraid that he might say something to her. But he had no words left. He had hardly the emotion to cry. It was strange: when tears came so easily to him, why couldn't he cry now? The innocent girl, the eternal virgin—he could not even laugh. But what was different about this time? What about the dozens of other men she had taken to her bed before Augustine had arrived? He had stopped thinking about them. Those nights with her, holding her next to him, had erased all that had gone before. But now she had once again given herself up, violated her innocence … given herself not really to anyone in particular but to the night, to that darkness, to that candle flame, to the resinous opium with its sweet stench. Augustine thought of Webley instead. It didn't really hit him at first that Webley had been the man in bed with Khasturba. It could have been any man, anyone who had happened in off the street. Augustine would have liked to have hated Webley for what he had done, but somehow he could blame only Khasturba. He tried to curse Webley, tried to hate that smile on his face and those foolish words, those taunts. But when he thought about it, Webley had betrayed nothing between them. They had no code. One's whore was another's. Augustine remembered how many times they had shared women. Short of money, they would take one woman, toss a coin to see who slept with her first, and then trade off during the night. What was different this time? Why should Webley have seen anything wrong in what he was doing?

But Webley had known that Augustine loved her. He had said so. Augustine wondered whether he had done it out of spite, or out of a fear that Augustine would follow her instead of him. Perhaps he was jealous of Augustine.

When he reached the pavilion, Augustine sat down on the first step. The marble was cold and translucent. It reminded him of a mausoleum. Marble has a quality of death. As Augustine ran his fingers over the hard surface, he felt a chill riffle his spine. Death seemed nearby. Though the thought hadn't yet touched him, he was very close to taking his own life. It would have demanded very little for Augustine to fire his pistol into his mouth. That moment just before suicide was one of complete solitude. Augustine felt no despair or frustration, simply an emptiness.

Then it occurred to him, not as a last resort, a hobbled thought, but like an inspiration: he decided to kill himself in a furious instant. The idea comforted him. Augustine had been betrayed, insulted, abandoned. He would answer his fate with the most potent response any man possessed, his own death. The grandeur of the idea overcame the sorrow of the circumstance.

Augustine did not act on it immediately. Instead, he savoured the thought, the immensity of the act. Now he wept.

He saw his life leading up to this moment. The tragedy of his mother's death. The precarious life of a soldier, which both he and his father had lived and which he had survived.

The Colonel felt very old and wretched. He could now think of Khasturba only in relation to his own age. She was a picture of youth. The thought that he could have loved her embarrassed him. He felt a fool, a dribbling old fool. If Khasturba were to laugh in his hearing now, he would wither with shame. He wondered how she could have even lain with him. It would have been the same as lying with a corpse. For now he could only think of himself as dead, sprawled out on that white marble, staining it a brilliant red with his blood. The pistol smoking in his hand remained to tell the story. His own mouth was dumb, his tongue shot away, his eyes rolled back in a horrific expression. He wondered who would find him first. Would it be the servants, the gardener arriving at dawn to trim the hedges and weed the beds? Or perhaps Webley would find him. He hoped so. This time it would be the glorious General lifting in his arms the limp body of a trusted officer. Webley would cry. Augustine almost laughed at the thought and wondered if for once the thin fair hair would fall over those pale eyes and expose the bald patch on Webley's head. Would Webley regret having slept with Khasturba? Perhaps he would wish he could have died instead of Augustine.

His mother used to talk of dying as if it was something which kept happening over and over. There were so many ways to die, she used to say, a knife, a pistol, falling, strangulation. Augustine remembered how she would break into tears at the thought. One day his father had told her about the death of a young lieutenant in his army. He had charged with the rest of the men, in fact he was one of the first into the enemy lines, but as soon as he was inside the cannon smoke lie panicked. His friends said that he was so afraid of closed places that he refused to sleep inside a tent. Even if there was a heavy dew, he would lay his cot outside and sleep under the open sky. If it rained, he huddled awake until dawn, refusing to close his eyes in fear that the tent might collapse about him. The smoke was thick and acrid and there were cries from the gunners all about him. He felt choked and surrounded. One or two of his fellow officers had heard him scream. How he had enough mind to turn his horse and charge out of the smoke no one knew, but the next thing they saw was the young man galloping away from the skirmish, into an open field. Someone rode after him, but before anything could be done to stop the officer, he had drawn his own sword and stabbed himself below the ribs. He died calling himself a coward. Bibbi Charlotte had wept for an entire afternoon over the story, and her husband left her bed in frustration, not being able to comfort her. Augustine had crawled in beside her once his father had left, and she drew him against her warm side and stroked his head. The boy had cried as well, and now he remembered feeling his wet tears on her soft breasts.

His memory drew tears out of him again. He felt like the young officer surrounded by the thick smoke. The darkness was close and smothering. He felt he could see nothing. He was nowhere. He remembered charging into the cannons at Deoband, that feeling of total loneliness as you enter the smoke. Even the reports and cries seem muffled. That was exactly the feeling he had had when the thought of suicide had struck him. It had blown away the smoke and exposed everything.

Augustine was not afraid to kill himself. He was not worried about the pain, knowing that it is just the afterthought of the wound. But as he toyed over the thought of suicide, he translated it into such a grand and majestic act that he felt unequal to it. The setting, too, bothered him. He wondered whether the shot might not rouse the servants. Webley must find him. Then, too, he wondered if it would not be interpreted as part of the incident with Marlow. The murder might be blamed on him and his own death said to be a vindication. Rumours would claim that the English had hired someone to kill him and make it look like suicide. That would destroy the dignity of his death. Augustine wanted to choose how he should die and murder seemed somehow inglorious. Perhaps he should wait, wait until Webley was there to take the blame.

Augustine remembered the army. He was worried what Webley might do if he killed himself. He might give himself up to the English, to be hung. Or he might escape to Calcutta and catch a ship home. No, he would never go back, not without shaking the Pagoda Tree. For a moment Augustine felt he would laugh. He imagined Webley walking casually onto an East Indiaman, whistling 'Money in Both Pockets.' There was something incongruous about him. Out of uniform he looked like a clerk or a writer, something of a griffin, new and excited. The only indication that he had been in the country long was his nose, which peeled constantly, layer after layer, always a raw red where he had picked at it.

Augustine realized that he had to live. He had to be next to Webley, fight with him, worry him into attacking the English. If he was not there, Webley might again change his mind, lose his determination. As it was, Augustine felt nervous. The Nawab might give them the money, they might even get to the Bijilli Gargh and prepare to fight the English. But Webley would hesitate in the end.

Augustine realized that he would have to lead the charge. Webley would see those red coats and perhaps, through his telescope, even recognize a face, a friend, himself. He would never have the courage to attack without Augustine there to support him. Mehboob Rashid would be no help. He was a mercenary fighting for nothing but plunder. How could he be expected to understand the emotions which welled up inside Augustine. Mehboob Rashid could never comprehend his ambitions for Webley. The thought of conquering Hindustan for any reason other than to strip it of its wealth was absurd to him. Webley himself could never be a king unless Augustine was there to dream for him. And what was a king without dreams?

After some time another idea began to grow in Augustine's mind. This was a far greater idea, full of possibilities and excitement. Suddenly suicide seemed a cowardly way out of the dilemma. It was over so quickly, and what was there in it but death and a fleeting melancholy?

He would use Khasturba. He would give Webley something to fight for. Augustine remembered his mother, how she had urged his father on. She was a soldier's wife. Khasturba would be the same. At one time Augustine had imagined she would become his wife. She was to be his ideal, the reason for him to come back alive, the reason to conquer Hindustan. Now she would be Webley's wife, or at least his mistress. Augustine was confident that she would gladly go with Webley. He did not stop for a moment to consider whether either of them would refuse. When he had found them a few hours ago, they had been together. Why could they not stay together always? Augustine was still unable to think of Khasturba as a whore. He had discovered her. He would steal her from the brothel. He would give her to Webley as a gesture of respect, a gift. There was no question in his mind that she would accept his terms and that Webley would take her. She would sustain the

Englishman, give him hope, revive his tired enthusiasm. With her help Augustine would convince Webley to fight the English.

It was not a matter of choosing between the two, weighing his loyalties, his jealousies. Instead, he was faced with only one option and that was to keep them together. In both he had a stake. He had ambitions for both of them, and by putting the two together, he would accomplish in one stroke what would have taken him two. Once his initial shock wore off and he could look at it objectively, he realized that this was an opportune occurrence, almost as if he had planned it himself.

He wanted Webley to be a hero, to go down in history with a grandiose story of accomplishment. Khasturba he wanted to save from the ignominious fate which the crone had in store for her, the terrible world of a prostitute. Each needed someone to bolster him up. Until then Augustine had played that part, encouraging Webley, acting as his right-hand man, and bring the true lover for Khasturba, not the customer. Now he would give them to each other and step out of the way. Alone they were nothing, but together they would combine into a bilious temperament, a violent passionate personality, almost as ambitious as Augustine's.

But he felt within him a faint uneasiness, as if he might be creating something which he could not control. This temperament might become a monster which would prove more destructive than he had imagined. Perhaps it would destroy him, or itself. But that was the chance he had to take, and as he lay there on the marble floor, the coldness of the stone seemed to seep into his bones and he felt a chill run through his body, not excitement, but a cold feeling of destiny.

The darkness was now conspiratorial and comforting. Augustine lay back on the marble platform, and where ten minutes ago he would have lain dead and bleeding, he now stretched his body out in contented languor and plotted the kidnapping with pleasure. His suicide was forgotten as easily as his love for Khasturba. Augustine's love for Khasturba had been so firm as to be brittle. It could not withstand the shock of finding her in bed with Webley.

From the stables Augustine took two horses, his own and another, an old and feeble nag which he knew would not be missed. He rode his own horse down to the river, leading the other by the reins. Next to the river, at the spot where the ferry boat deposited its passengers, there was a grove of dwarf palms. Here Augustine dismounted and hid himself and the two horses. He did not have to wait long, for after about half an hour, he heard the ferry coming towards him. He heard Webley's voice speaking to the boatman. There was the sound of hooves on the planks, the chuckle of coins exchanging hands, and then at a gallop Webley was gone along the road to Ashgar Hasan's estate.

The boatman was just about to cast off for the other side when Augustine called to him. They crossed and Augustine told him to wait there for him. The man complained that he had not slept all night. The glint of a sicca rupee silenced him and he huddled down like a sulking child to await Augustine's return. The Colonel mounted the nag and led his own horse in the direction of the brothel. When they were a few corners away from the place, Augustine tied his horse to the railing of a low balcony and rode on.

Everything happened as usual. The crone took her fee, the boy led the nag away, and Augustine climbed the stairs to Khasturba's room. For a moment he felt afraid to enter. A sudden feeling of sadness took hold of him, as though he wished Khasturba was still his. But she was now Webley's. He tried to hide any emotion on his face, and as he parted the curtain for the second time that night, it was as if he were entering the room for the first time. Khasturba had heard him in the courtyard. She lay with her head thrust into the pillow. She was crying. Augustine strode over and touched her shoulder. She turned on him, like a leopard surprised at its kill.

'Can't you leave me alone for once! Let me be what I am, rather than something you imagine. Get out of here … Get out.'

Augustine smiled benevolently. She hid her face.

'I have come to take you out of here,' he said.

'To hell with you, to hell with all of you.'

'I'll no longer be your lover.'

'You never were,' she said savagely. 'You are impotent as an ox.'

Augustine looked at her quietly for a moment. Then he tore the bedclothes from her, took her in his broad hands, kissed her violently and without passion. She was surprised and lay still. He took her without feeling, entering her without a sound. Khasturba cried out, more with shock than pain, almost as if she had been a virgin. It was over quickly and he lifted himself off her deliberately and pulled up his trousers. Her breathing was heavy and she lay with her eyes shut, as if she was unconscious, her mouth slightly open over her white teeth. The candle guttered out, with sporadic flashes of yellow light. The darkness once again surrounded Augustine. He felt her hand slide into his. She said something, but he did not understand.

His voice was harsh when he spoke to her. 'That is all over now,' he said. 'You must listen to me. I have told you everything about Webley, how he steals souvenirs from the women he sleeps with, how he is a great general, and how he is afraid to fight the English. Now tell me, do you like him?'

'He is a gentleman,' said Khasturba, after a silence which seemed as if it would never end. 'And he is older than you, much older.'

'How does he make love?' asked Augustine.

'Well enough.'

'Like an Englishman?' asked Augustine.

'How should I know? He is the first English I have slept with.'

'Would you become his mistress?'

Khasturba's hand froze in Augustine's. He squeezed it, not with affection, but to encourage an answer from her.

'You are mad, certainly mad!'

'He needs you. I need you for him.'

'How many times did you say you loved me? How many times did you touch my breasts and kiss me? You said you wanted to marry me. You refused to be my lover, though you loved me more than any man has ever done.'

'I never loved you,' said Augustine.

'You lie. You lie.'

'It is over.'

'I know that. The way you made love to me, I knew it.'

'You must come with me tonight. I will take you to him and you will be his mistress. You will come with us when we march to the Bijilli Gargh. We will prepare apartments for you to be comfortable in and dress you like a queen. You can stand on the battlements and watch us defeat the English, watch him ride into their cannons with his sabre cutting the air into gleaming arcs, watch the men follow him and overrun the English, plunge in among them and wipe their army out until their blood is smudged across all Hindustan. Then you will travel in your palanquin with the army and watch us conquer the land from the Jumna to the Ganges.'

'Did he send you?'

'No. It is my idea. If you are with him, he will never hesitate.'

'How can I help him?' asked Khasturba. 'What have I got to do with the fighting?'

'You must be there when he comes back, radiant, young, demanding. You must attack him with more force than the English.

You must wound him with your teeth and nails. Excite him, torment him, love him.'

'I could never love him.'

'He must love you, then,' said Augustine. 'He must become your lover in every way. If he does, then the English don't stand a chance.'

'You talk as if the war is being fought in my bed.'

'That's exactly it. The war must be won in Webley's mind, and his mind must always be in your bed with you.'

'You have gone mad. Can't you fight the war for him? You are as much a soldier as he.'

'Don't try to understand me. Forget me. Learn everything you can about Webley, his likes, his dislikes. Be as calculating as a whore. Play with him, trick him into loving you. He must develop such a passion for you that it overwhelms him.'

'He is not a passionate man,' said Khasturba.

'Yes, he is cynical. You must overcome that. You must make him believe in his army, in his men, in himself.'

'What you want me to do is to make him into a fool like yourself.'

'Don't talk about me. Never say my name in front of him. Never let him suspect that there was ever anything between us, or that I have told you these things tonight. He must not suspect our conspiracy.'

'He knows everything that went between us. That was why he came to me, to find out. And I told him everything,' said Khasturba.

'Make him forget it all. Overwhelm him with sex, until he sees nothing but your face, your breasts, your thighs.'

'How is it that you have forgotten these things so easily?'

Augustine did not hear her, or if he did, he ignored her.

'Use your art, your techniques of love, to make him an idealist, a poet, a dreamer, turn him into the biggest sop in Hindustan.'

'Why do you think I would go with you?' asked Khasturba.

'To be free of this place, to be free of that crone, to live like a queen,' said Augustine.

Khasturba seemed so much older now. Gone was her innocence, that childish laugh he had loved. Her hand in his felt dry and wrinkled. The scent from her bed was stale and her breath had a poisonous smell. But when she lit another candle, he saw in front of him that same woman whom he had seen in the window that first day. He knew that Webley would not be able to resist her, for she was cloaked in sensuality. She could melt steel. He watched Khasturba move about the room quickly, collecting a few things from here and there and bundling them up into a cloth. He admired her. She had a confidence and an air of maturity about her which he had never noticed before. He felt strangely proud of her.

Augustine dropped from the window. It was not a long distance, no more than twelve feet. This was the one moment he had been afraid of. Would Khasturba follow him? He stood looking up, hoping the crone had not heard him. Khasturba hesitated at the window, then she tossed her bundle down to him. He caught it and put it on the ground. She jumped quickly and landed beside him. He was surprised, expecting her to be afraid of the drop. Augustine had thought he would have to catch her. But she smiled at him mischievously.

'I have been waiting to jump from there for a long time,' she whispered.

Again Augustine heard that noise, like rats, close to his feet. The little window opened at street level and he dimly made out the crone's face behind the bars.

'Who's there?' she cried, and then when the two of them began to run, she shouted after them: 'Thief, you thief!'

Footsteps rattled behind them, but Augustine reached the horse after a few corners and boosted Khasturba into the saddle. He swung up behind her and urged the horse forward. They were gone before anyone could reach the place.

~

Augustine knew that Webley would come to his room, so he waited. The servants put Khasturba in the room next to his. She said she would bathe and sleep. Late in the morning, Augustine recognized the clipped footsteps coming towards his room.

'My dear Augustine,' said Webley, 'I have good news, splendid news, but before we go into that, let me apologize, from the depths of my consternation. I honestly felt the cad when you found me there with that girl, what is her name?'

'Khasturba,' said Augustine.

'Yes, I knew you had a certain affection for her, but I didn't know how deep it went.' Webley laughed nervously. He was very bad at apologies. There was an embarrassing silence.

'Oh, hang it all, I'm sorry if it upset you,' said the Englishman, picking at his nose with his little finger.

'Don't mind. It's forgotten. We have more important things to think about, such as the Nawab's offer.'

'Oh, you know about that,' said Webley, disappointed.

'Ashgar Hasan told me.'

'Quite. By the way, look what I stole from her room. It looked like one of yours.'

Augustine turned the button over in his hand. It was the one he had thrown up to Khasturba that first day when she appeared in the window. The brass gleamed dully in his hand. He felt like laughing. What had Khasturba called it, a medal? Webley grinned with an impish satisfaction. The button looked more like a coin, thought Augustine. He pocketed it and laughed at Webley.

'I have stolen something for you as well,' he said.

'What? Show me,' said Webley eagerly.

'Come,' said Augustine, and led Webley to the door connecting his room with Khasturba's. Drawing the curtain, he let Webley look inside. Khasturba lay on the divan, stretched out, her head resting on her arms, her hair, still wet from bathing, strewn about her. She was asleep.

'You have exhausted her,' said Augustine.

Webley was sucking on the knuckles of his hand, as if he had just hit someone with his fist. His eyes looked worried. Augustine let the curtain fall dramatically and stepped back. He put his arm around Webley.

'Let her sleep,' he said. 'Tell me what you think of her.'

'My God, man! Why did you have to bring her here? What is it?'

'Aren't you going to thank me? She's a present from me to you.'

'For me?' Webley pointed to himself.

'Yes, you'll need a woman on this campaign.'

'But I thought she was yours.'

'No,' said Augustine. 'All along I was thinking about you. What do you say? You don't like her?'

'She has a fine neck, but we can't take her with us.'

'Of course we can. She's just what you need in the Bijilli Gargh, to keep the chill out of your bed.'

'Don't be a silly ass. How can I have a mistress?'

'What do you mean?' said Augustine. 'You'll learn to appreciate her.'

Webley looked at Augustine curiously, and then he began to laugh. He laughed noisily, snorting at the thought of it. Then suddenly he stopped and looked at Augustine.

'You've gone mad,' he said. 'A present. Her?'

'What? Are you going to refuse?' Augustine tried to look hurt.

'No, I quite fancy the idea. She'll do. But, by God, she's young.'

'Tender.'

'Quite,' said Webley.

'Now, what was your good news?'

Webley shook Khasturba from his mind and thought a moment as if he had to remind himself of something.

'Oh, that? You know about it already. The Nawab is going to fit out a caravan for us, loaded with arms and supplies. He wants us to defeat the English, the two-faced bastard. These native princes, can't trust them. Just imagine, out of one side of his mouth he's paying compliments to the residency, from the other side he's asking us to chase the English out of his court.'

'A game of solitaire,' said Augustine.

'What did you say?'

'Oh, nothing. When do we get the money?'

'We already have it. Ashgar Hasan is purchasing everything for us. He says we must stay inside his compound walls until we leave, some nonsense about murder.' Webley shrugged. He stepped over to the curtain and took another peek at Khasturba. Coming away smiling, he grabbed Augustine's hand and shook it vigorously.

'By God,' he said, 'you really look after your commander-in-chief.'

They both laughed and set about drawing up plans for the march, lists of supplies to be ordered through Ashgar Hasan. Augustine noticed an excitement in Webley, as if Khasturba had already animated him. He, too, felt a thrill as he watched Webley list column after column of powder, shot, grape, ball. He could already see the tumbrils, the supplies being loaded onto the camels, the guns stacked like firewood, the ball-shot rattling inside its canisters; the matches, the flints, boxes of swords. In his mind he saw them setting out from Lucknow, strung out across the plain, a chain of pack-animals and men, the mounted bodyguard armed with gleaming weapons, the silk banners with the emblem of the fish, the standard of Lucknow. He imagined himself and Webley leading the caravan, the white dust puffing out from under their horses' heels, the gentle movement of the walking animals, the creak of new saddles, and Webley occasionally scanning the horizon with his eyeglass. The pageantry of their march filled Augustine with a feeling of grandeur and melodrama.

Amidst all the preparations, Augustine suddenly thought of Jules. Something brought the Frenchman to mind. He asked one of the servants where he had gone. The man looked puzzled and said that he had not left but was in his room. He was ill and food was being taken to him.

On one of his trips past the French agent's door, Augustine decided to find out what had become of him. As he pushed open the doors, the smell overwhelmed him. It was a rank odour of decomposition. Augustine held back at the door, wondering whether he should lift the curtain and go in or turn away.

'Who is there?' came a feeble voice. Augustine recognized it as the Frenchman's.

Lifting the curtain, he was met with the awful sight of Jules Antigone stretched out on his bed, dressed in the same clothes he had been wearing the day he had come to Augustine's room. The bloodstains had dried on his clothing. He hid one side of his face and glared at Augustine with one glinting, frightened eye. The smell was stronger and it was coming from him. The windows were shut, the curtains drawn, and the room had a dismal, cave-like atmosphere. Augustine stepped over to the window and drew the drapes, holding his breath. He opened the shutters to let some air in.

'Don't,' cried the Frenchman. 'Leave me to die, you son of an English whore.'

As he said this, his face became wholly visible to Augustine, who drew back in horror. Where his razor had clipped off the man's ear, there was a gangrenous wound. One eye was completely shut with swelling. The colour of the skin was a sickly blue-green, like a huge bruise, with the luminosity of a butterfly's wing. Here was that perfumed dandy, that foppish coxcomb, who reeked of expensive scents, dressed himself more times than a woman, curled his hair, shaved thrice a day to hide even the shadow of a beard, polished his teeth with tufts of rabbit's fur, and painted the lids of his eyes. He was reduced to this. He was now nothing more than a foul smell. His voice hardly made a sound, it had lost its shrill nasal quality and now was nothing more than a coarse whisper. The smell nauseated Augustine. He had smelled decomposition before. He had fought battles in the heat of June, when if a man fell in the morning he was high by afternoon. But this was different. The man was alive. He was slowly being eaten away by his own flesh.

'Where is Domingo?' asked Augustine.

'He has run away,' Antigone said faintly.

'Do you require anything?'

'Go to hell, you Solomon …' The words were mumbled, incoherent. Augustine left the room quickly, not wanting to see him die. He shut the door tightly and went to his room. The smell stayed with him all that day. He changed his clothes and still it clung to him. He bathed and it did no good. It was as if it had been absorbed into his body, into his mind. The servant came that evening to tell him that Antigone was dead.

PART THREE

11

It was as if Webley had fallen in love for the first time. Perhaps he had. Augustine sensed a new lightness in his mood, a return of some of the dash and glamour he had lost. He even looked younger, and the Colonel was pleased with the effect Khasturba was having on the Englishman. She bled him of his cynicism and he would come out of her tent puffed up like a randy pigeon and slap Augustine across the shoulders. It was as if he was thriving on her youth.

The supply train gathered in a camp behind Ashgar Hasan's palace. No attempt was made to conceal the preparations, for in a city such as Lucknow even the smallest secret could not escape detection. Men and animals arrived in clusters and the area took on the atmosphere of a fair or carnival. Augustine spent every moment absorbed in organizing bullock carts, camels, elephants, packing weapons, powder, and ammunition. Meanwhile, Webley and Khasturba did nothing but make love, toy with each other like children with a new game. Their laughter, hers high and piercing, his older, almost a cackle, filled the gardens and the residence until late at night. Servants were kept busy running back and forth, carrying sherbet and sweetmeats to the couple. Augustine felt relieved and absorbed himself in the task of preparing for the long march out of Lucknow. Ashgar Hasan arranged for all the payments, relishing the excitement of preparations.

But for Augustine this was only the beginning. Ahead of him he saw the coming battle, the lines of British infantry, the eight- and twelve-pounders roaring all day like tigers in the forest. He thought of his revenge, how they would plunge into the enemy lines, their lances and swords blazing the way. He wanted to move, to march towards the Bijilli Gargh, but there was so much to be done. It was fifteen days of hard marching from Lucknow, through the treacherous Rohilkhand, full of marauders, the Rohillas, the Gujars, and others. Augustine collected an armed guard for the journey, a hundred and twenty-five of the Nawab's best men, loaded down with muskets, a brace of pistols each, and glittering cutlery. Their horses were decorated with feathered caps, peacock feathers braided into their manes, and rows of glass jewels on the bridles and stirrups. Each soldier wore a green turban pinned with the silver emblem of a fish. They were Muslims, of Pathan descent, bearded, their teeth stained red with paan. Their commander, Hafiz Rustum, stood as tall as Augustine. He was an elderly soldier who had made his pilgrimage to Mecca. His beard was dyed a flaming orange and he laughed up great gouts of phlegm every time he spoke. He seemed always jovial, though Ashgar Hasan said that he had once ordered the execution of twenty-two of his own men who had dared to argue with his command.

'I hear our noble commander has fallen for a virgin whore,' said Hafiz Rustum with a laugh which rumbled up from inside his lungs and erupted in a loud hawk and a spit.

'He is preparing for battle,' said Augustine, winking his good eye.

'I do not like virgins,' said the Muslim. 'It is like eating unripe guavas.' Again he laughed.

'The English have a passion for virginity.'

'So do we,' said Hafiz Rustum. 'But we demand it of the women we marry and of our daughters, not our mistresses. A mistress should be fully ripened, not sterile.' He waited for Augustine to say something and then added quickly, 'But I am sure that by now he has ripened her.'

The last of the supplies to arrive were the cannons, twenty of them, gleaming brass from the Nawab's armoury. Each gun was drawn by a sturdy pair of oxen. The drivers rode perched atop the carriages, looking like villagers hauling fodder, rather than gunners on their way to battle.

Ashgar Hasan saw the caravan off from the roof of his palace. Augustine and Webley rode past his walls and saluted their friend and patron before riding out into the maidan to join Hafiz Rustum and the mounted guard. They rode slowly across the plain, a long line of men and animals, first the three officers, then the loose formation of cavalry followed by palanquins: Khasturba's and those of the other women, her servants, and Hafiz Rustum's mistresses. He had told Augustine that he could not deprive himself of women for too long, or else he would die of old age. 'It would cripple me, and besides, if they are killed or captured, what is it to me? I can have any woman in Lucknow for the asking.' After the palanquins followed the camels, the elephants, and the oxen, all moving with plodding determination.

Augustine looked back and saw the lush horizon of Lucknow with its margin of river receding into the distance, into the soft curtain of dust rising behind their baggage train. Ashgar Hasan could be seen standing in one of the ornate cupolas which decked his residence, and as they got farther and farther away, he lost all semblance of form and profile, becoming only a vague blur, immobile, sedentary. He blotted out a tiny portion of the sky. Augustine fixed his eye on the eunuch. To him Ashgar Hasan was Lucknow, and as his silhouette became indistinct, so did the memories of that city, the ribald excesses of men within walls of brick and plaster. They themselves became inert and lifeless like the buildings they built, so brilliant and elaborate, with the minute and gaudy details scratched on their surfaces. But as Augustine rode away from the buildings, their complex and ornate exteriors sank into the flat plain and served only to blot out the sky's rim. He held up thumb and forefinger in front of his good eye and the city which had seemed so sprawling and awesome fitted into the space between.

As soon as the buildings were out of sight, the armed guard spread out and scattered back among the slower-moving sections of the caravan. Webley dropped back beside Khasturba's palanquin. She coyly lifted one of the lace curtains and teased him. The palanquin bearers did not smile, staring straight ahead, their breathing only a faint whisper. At stages they laid her down and others came forward to carry the Englishman's mistress. The whole caravan knew who she was and her story. The jokes circulated with hushed amusement among the men, and though the coolies that carried her weight despised her and spoke cruelly of her, they betrayed none of this while they walked steadily on, without a hint of exhaustion or emotion. There was something solemn about the procession, despite Khasturba's lighthearted voice, the noises of the animals and their drivers. From a distance, perhaps from where Ashgar Hasan stood in the cupola, the supply train seemed not just a line of individual men and horses but almost an animal itself, a bizarre creature, a monster inching its way across the barren plain. It was like a worm or a caterpillar. And hanging over it like the pall of dust was the pall of war. The sun blinked from behind the clouds and the brass cannons shone for an instant, both beautiful and harsh at the same time.

Augustine and Hafiz Rustum rode on together slowly, keeping a hundred yards ahead of the caravan. They talked about the subjects they knew, war and sport. Hafiz Rustum had fought against the Mahrattas, the Sikhs, the Rohillas. Only three months back he had returned after chasing a murderous band of Pindaris from the outskirts of Lucknow to beyond Ujjain. He laughed even when he recounted his losses, as though he took none of it seriously. But occasionally Augustine would catch in his yellowed eyes a distant expression as if, though he laughed now, he had not laughed then, as a younger man. Age seemed to have made him jolly. Augustine could imagine him with his beard black and cropped, his body lean and arched in the saddle, fighting earnestly, with desperate seriousness.

As they rode through the babool jungles, clamorous with babblers and parakeets, across the wastes of saltpetre, past stands of palms, Hafiz Rustum spoke of his pilgrimage to Mecca.

'When I was young, you know, I could not tell the difference between my passions and my beliefs. Lifting my sword to cut at some infidel, I would think, I am doing this for God. And bowing to prayer five times a day, I would feel a desire to go out and catch the first kaffir and run him through. In war I felt devotion. In prayer I felt death. I remembered the story which a great pir told me when I was first learning to ride and my feet could hardly reach the stirrups. The pir was a kindly saint. He would sit me beside him outside the mosque and tell me that if I was going to be a soldier, I would have to learn to pray with as much fury as I fought. He told me about a famous Mogul general who served under Alamgir against the Mahrattas. He was a fine officer and a devout man who kept regularly to his prayers. And one day, while he was fighting, the time came for him to pray. He dismounted in the middle of the battlefield, with the carnage all about him, the cries of dying men and those that had killed them hovering about his head. Spreading his saddle-cloth on the ground, he knelt down to pray. One of the Hindus, seeing him defenceless, came riding down on top of him and with one slice of his talwar cut his head from his neck. His body remained as it was, still facing Mecca in the attitude of prayer. Another Mahratta came from the other side and severed his cupped hands at the wrists. He remained fixed there. A third of the enemy chopped his arms off and a fourth cut him through at the waist. Soon he was only pieces scattered on the ground. But after a few minutes, when his prayers were finished, his body came together again, and as if nothing had happened, he mounted his horse and joined the fighting. He killed each of the men who had cut him apart, and many others besides. They said that until he died—many years later, of old age—the scars were still visible on his neck, wrists, and the other parts of his body that had been cut through.'

The old officer with his burnished beard laughed with harsh and throaty hiccoughs, throwing his head back. Augustine laughed as well at the story, which seemed both macabre and naive at the same time.

'Oh, God,' said Hafiz Rustum, catching his breath. 'Only a boy could have believed that story. I swallowed it like a savoury pickle and it has burnt inside me ever since. What you believe as a child stays with you even after you lose your innocence.'

Augustine could not think of anything to say. He listened with interest and curiosity. Though the story sounded ridiculous, it contained an element of truth. It was the stuff of legends. That story had made this jolly old man fight ruthlessly and view death as nothing more than an eclipse. To fear death was to be afraid that the sun would never emerge from the moon's shadow. No wonder he laughs, thought Augustine, remembering his mother's stories and the equally unbelievable but legendary heroes of her world.

'But just as with any story, it was told to me long before I believed it. The understanding came to me when I made my pilgrimage to Mecca. We rode a dhow from Bombay to Jidda and then made the rest of the journey by camel. It was not a difficult journey, far easier than many of the marches I have been on. But as we entered the city, something overcame my companion and me. For the two of us, both soldiers, God had been nearest to us in war. But now, in that holy city, we realized the far more awesome presence of God. We came upon it suddenly in the midst of hordes of pilgrims, wearing our white robes instead of turbans, sword-belts, and cummerbunds. It was more a sudden realization of God's vastness. Here were Muslims from as far away as Spain, Africa—black as the muzzle of a cannon, they were—and from farther east than India. All had come together in that city, soldiers, merchants, and farmers. We realized then how great and various His people were. We became aware of our position in history and how God covered us all like a huge tent. Then that absurd story the pir had told me as a boy came back to me more strongly and I felt its meaning. As we were riding out of the city, back to our corner of the world, I told my friend this same story. We began laughing then and did not stop until we fell asleep that night.'

Or since, thought Augustine. Then out loud he asked, 'And Mecca, what kind of a city is it?'

'It is not the city but the people which make the place holy. There is the rock on which Abraham was to sacrifice his son, tokens of a religion. The houses are dull, the colours of the desert. There are flies and rats, cockroaches and bedbugs, just as in any hundred cities you could find. Lucknow is a far more impressive place, but then of course it is not a holy city.'

Augustine thought about the story and how much a part of Hafiz Rustum's people it was. He thought of his mother's stories, how strange and English they had been and how he had altered them in his own imagination to fit his world. A feeling took hold of him of melodrama and loneliness. He felt as if none of the stories involved him. He had no tradition, no people. In a sense, he was his own legend. There was no one for him to admire and emulate. He did not have a Shivaji like the Mahrattas, or Ashoka and Akbar like the Moguls, or an Alexander, or a St. George. He had only himself.

Suddenly the cumbersome caravan behind him dragged at his heart. He wanted to rush off, to race across the plain towards the Bijilli Gargh and charge in amongst the British, heroically alone.

He wanted to detach himself from the slow-moving oxen, which would take fifteen days to cover a distance he could gallop over in four. He wanted only the armed guard to follow him. He wanted Webley to leave Khasturba in her palanquin and dash ahead of him so that he could chase him over the expanse of Hindustan in a wild race.

Augustine's tears flowed down the slope of his nose and cheeks. He couldn't help himself. Suddenly, out of one of the clumps of palms which were scattered about on the plain, a hare burst into view, scurrying as fast as it could over the loose sand. Augustine dug his heels in and the horse leapt forward, brushing past Hafiz Rustum. Augustine had his pistol out in an instant and leaned down low in the saddle. The hare doubled back just as the horse and rider were drawing up behind. It headed for a second clump of palms to the right of where it had broken cover. Augustine wheeled abruptly, but the hare now had thirty yards on him and was going hard for the protection of the palms girdled with wild ber bushes. Augustine's horse felt the impulse as well, as if their nerves were connected, and it strained forward at full speed, its hooves hardly touching the ground. Thirty yards remained between the hare and the palms. The horse was still ten yards behind. Just as they were about to go crashing into the clump of trees, Augustine was able to lean down with his pistol only a few feet from the terrified hare and fire. As he did, his horse turned sharply, almost unseating him, missing the trees by a few inches. The hare struggled with a broken spine a few moments and then died in a fit of convulsions. Two or three boys came dashing out of the baggage train. They leapt on the dead hare and began fighting over it. Augustine wiped his tears on the sleeve of his coat and turned away.

Hafiz Rustum and Augustine took a party of men ahead with them to set up the camp. They spent the rest of the day shooting ducks and snipe in a jheel while they waited for the rest of the caravan to catch up. In this way they travelled for fifteen days.

~

As a young boy Augustine had hated to kill. He would shout angrily at others who climbed about the fort at Chittoor, robbing pigeons' nests for no better reason than to drop the eggs and watch them smash a hundred feet below at the foot of the walls. In those days he was his mother's son, protected and pampered.

He was taught violence. Somdas, the dwarf, forced Augustine to kill. He could still remember the little man screaming at him while Augustine hesitated before cutting the head off a chicken. 'Pretty lad, mother's baby. Why does it scare you? Be your father's son!' The taunts would rattle on until Augustine finally killed the bird, shutting his eyes as he did so, almost cutting his finger instead. Then he would turn away from the blood, drop the knife, and run. And behind him the clatter of abuse. 'Coward, simpering coward! Come back and watch it die.'

The swordplay and shooting he learned easily, for he was well built and athletic even at that age. He rode with ease. Only the killing bothered him. The dwarf was fanatical. He would bring animals from the palace kitchens and make Augustine slaughter them, one by one. Augustine would gag. He would throw up, and the dwarf would scream and send him running to his mother, his breeches spotted with blood, the tears bursting from his eyes. He was terrified of the dwarf, more frightened of the little man than of his father. Trisuldas Thakur never came to watch his son's lessons.

On one occasion, Augustine stood outside his mother's door, hiding in the fold of a heavy curtain. He listened to his parents speaking about him. His father asked how he was progressing.

'Are his lessons going well?' he asked.

'You've given him to a madman who will drive him mad as well,' she said.

'The dwarf is a good teacher, an angry man. But in anger there are lessons to be learned. The boy will outgrow him both in body and in mind.'

'He's afraid of the dwarf,' said Bibbi Charlotte.

'Why?'

'Somdas teases him. He makes the boy kill animals in cold blood, slaughter them with his sword.'

His father made no answer.

'Augustine is terrified. He does not like to kill. I watch them from the window. He rides well and can hold his own with a sword against his teacher. But when it comes to the blood-spilling, he cowers. He comes crying to me.'

'You should send him back.'

'How can I? That man is a torturer—a maniac.'

Augustine's father grunted. Behind the curtain the boy was crying. He felt both embarrassment and anger. Why had his mother told? He wanted to run into the room and fall on his mother, but he couldn't. When his father was in her apartments, he was forbidden to go inside. He had to wait until their lovemaking was over. Their laughter and soft voices made him cry even harder, until he ran from the door, down the dark stairs, so wide that he had to take two steps to cross each one. The fort was like an enormous prison. He roamed inside it but never left its walls. Inside those walls lurked the dwarf, holding some animal by the throat, waiting to trap Augustine and make him cut its throat. Whenever he moved about within the fort, he avoided Somdas, never turning a corner without looking first, going by another route if there was even a faint chance that his teacher would cross his path. When he went for his lessons, the fear would build in him, spread into his arms. And when they wrestled, or fought, or rode in the courtyard, Augustine tightened himself up, so that his muscles were knotted with terror. Though all their fights were mock combat, the boy fought with a desperate desire to kill the dwarf, not as he killed the animals, with a feeling of nausea and sadness, but with all his frustration building up. Somdas's death would have released him from the terror and frustration. Somdas seemed to know this. It excited him and he fought back with just enough restraint to keep the boy going, all the time taunting him with shouted instructions. In his fury, Augustine would forget his techniques and flail out with his talwar. Somdas would casually turn it aside and send it spinning into the dirt. He was safe for the moment. Finally Augustine succeeded in wounding Somdas. He had learned his strokes well and second-guessed the dwarf. At a point when Somdas had strayed off his guard, the blade suddenly sank into his arm. The dwarf leapt back with a grunt. His eyes for a moment shone with panic. Augustine stopped and laughed. He giggled uncontrollably as the dwarf, puffing with anger, rushed off to bandage the cut.

After that Augustine's frustration ebbed. He had succeeded in frightening his teacher and this assuaged his desperate anger. But the fear of killing those animals wouldn't leave him. He could not face it, and after the accident, Somdas increased the killings, knowing that his pupil was frightened. He did it more out of spite than as a lesson. Augustine could sense this.

Several days after he overheard his mother and father's conversation, Augustine had the opportunity to overcome his revulsions. He killed the enormous monitor lizard which had appeared one night at his mother's window. The impulse to protect his mother freed him of his fears. He killed the monster savagely, chasing it up onto the roof after stabbing it once through the screen of the window.

On the flat roof of the zenana he slaughtered the lizard

heartlessly and efficiently. Only after he had killed it did he realize what he had done.

In the bright moonlight, which gave the scene an eerie texture, all shadows and silhouettes standing out in bold relief, Augustine felt a surge of confidence run through him, a sterile, cold feeling as though all his nerves had been cut through. He felt that he was no longer a part of the softly lit zenana, with its cushions and divans. He felt the dry wind against his face and saw the shadowy desert spreading out from the fort, ribbed with sand-dunes, each cleanly outlined by the moon. It was a colourless scene. Even the lizard's blood was black.

From then on Augustine took to hunting. He would leave the fort and wander through the countryside around Chittoor, chasing chinkaras and blackbuck across the wastes of sand and rock, stalking leopards in the scrub jungle. He learned about the jungle and the desert, the animals. He trained himself to track. Suddenly there was relief for him. His frustrations, the puzzlement of adolescence absorbed itself in killing. In hunting, what Webley fondly called the pastime of destruction, the boy found an escape. What had terrified him now soothed him. Though he still went to his mother's rooms and cried in her arms, Augustine had found something else which calmed him.

Soon Augustine was riding beside his father, in front of the regiment. Somdas had realized that the boy would kill him sooner or later. He told Trisuldas Thakur that his son was ready for war. Bibbi Charlotte realized it as well, and wept over her son with both pride and sadness, with that emotion of melodrama heaving inside her.

There was room for Hafiz Rustum's men to be quartered inside the fort, but the caravan with its oxen and animals had to be left outside the walls. The carts were parked on the north side of the hill, inside the palisades, on a knoll. Here the drivers and servants pitched their tents and set up a comfortable camp. Augustine watched them with amusement, wondering how they could sit so calmly in the face of battle. It was as if they knew more than he did and believed that no danger lay in store for them.

12

The following is an extract from Soldiering in Hindustan, *the personal memoirs of Major Gerald Fitzroy-Morris, formerly of the 16th Grenadier Guards.*

6 September 1813: The Bijilli Gargh. The chase is almost over. We have the fox in his den. Our Grenadiers are baying at his heels like a good pack of hounds. I joined Carlyle yesterday with another hundred of the finest sepoys in Hindustan. The position at first seemed an awkward one, but a despatch from Delhi, from Metcalf's pen, assured us that we are entitled to enter the Dun. So far there is no sign of the Gurkhas or the Sikhs, only Webley's men bobbing about inside the walls of the fort.

The Bijilli Gargh is an imposing structure, situated above us on a steep knoll, protected to the east by a precipitous cliff face. The engineers have scouted on all sides of the fort and decided that the only practical entrance can be effected by storming the main gate. It will be taken only at a great loss, which I am unwilling to assume. The cannons are being set up and we will commence bombardment just before dusk this evening. Our pioneers are hard at work digging trenches and constructing redans for the battery.

Our camp is located on a sandy stretch of a dry riverbed, running to the south of the fort, and is protected from the enemy cannons by the embankment along the riverbed. The trees also hide us from view. We are not certain as to the number of the enemy cannon but suspect that it is minimal. So far they have not fired at us and let us construct our works without provocation.

The fort is an ancient structure and unlikely to withstand

much bombardment. We should effect a breach within a day or two and perhaps storm the citadel on the thirteenth or fourteenth. There is a great spirit among the men. They are working themselves into a fever.

Webley and his second-in-command, a Eurasian styling himself a colonel—his own commission, I presume—recently returned from Lucknow. The Nawab of Oudh's troops are with them and now within the fort, as we were told they would be. The plan is simple, if followed, though I am not one to put faith in these native armies. As soon as our men storm the Bijilli Gargh, the Nawab's troops will turn against Webley and assist us in the rout. Evidently Webley's presence and motives were discovered in Lucknow. The Resident parlayed with the Nawab and the outcome of their talks was this agreement. It seems an expensive plan but Webley has given us too long a chase and the Company is willing to put any price on his head, providing the head is severed from the body. They say he murdered a civilian in Lucknow, which inflamed the city considerably. He has brought back with him a Moorish wife as well. I shall expect to relieve Webley of his sword within the week.

Carlyle has been here seven days. I set out from Delhi two weeks after he did and by forced marches made splendid time. It is pleasant to be camped now in the leisurely yawn of this valley. The breezes are cooler, though the air has a suffocating stillness around midday which lingers on until the evening brings back the winds from off the snow mountains.

We have decided that before attacking the fort we should take a day of rest, and Carlyle has suggested a fishing expedition to the Sone River a few miles to the south of us. He claims it is full of trout and a native fish called the mahseer, which means big head, supposedly a terrific sporting fish. Fortunately I brought my split cane rod and a good quantity of line, so we shall see what the river has in store. The rains have ceased now for some days and the water should be a fine colour and temperature. It has been four years since I cast a fly. Perhaps I have lost my touch, but I have certainly not lost my excitement, the thrill of having a brutish tug at the end of my line. Of course it could never match the pike in Devon or even the speckled trout I used to angle for in the stream behind the Listersons' country house.

Perhaps this campaign will not prove such a bore as I had thought it would, even if the Gurkhas don't show up. I only hope that tomorrow Webley will let us fish in peace. Should the hostilities begin our sport would be ruined.

~

7 *September 1813: The Bijilli Gargh.* This morning, at about an hour past dawn, Carlyle and I set out for the Sone to try a few casts in the river, which is said to be full of fish. The water was lovely when we arrived, a murky green in the pools and very blue and white in the feathered water. Carlyle borrowed a rod and spool of line from me and made his way upstream. I headed down to where I could make out the confluence of the Sone and another smaller, nameless tributary.

My first cast dropped the fly two yards short of a log which was spinning about in a whirlpool. The instant the fly settled on the water, it was snapped up by a good fish which bent my rod nearly in half. It put up a desperate fight and finally broke my line. I had not thought the tension was too great, but it seems the line had sat through five monsoons and had been weakened considerably. I switched to a waxed cord which I had purchased from another keen angler last winter in Hyderabad. He was off home to England and swore by the cord, saying it had held some of the heaviest fish in India. My split cane rod is seventeen feet long and a very fast taper. It is excellent in both accuracy and strength, for you hardly have to think where to drop your fly and the rod, as if by intuition, settles it on the very spot.

Subsequently I landed three more fish in the following hour, one of them over fifteen pounds. I began moving upstream, casting occasionally but enjoying the day. My subedar carried the fish. It was a delightful walk through the grassy forest, alongside a stream which was in all respects an angler's paradise.

We had walked for half an hour and I had landed another fine mahseer, bigger than any of the others, when suddenly the quiet idyll was interrupted by an explosion above us, a report like that of a mine but more muffled and deep-sounding. The two of us stopped in our tracks, suddenly reminded of the ensuing bombardment and battle, wondering how the sound of the siege could have reached us so far away.

Our anxiety was great and we hurried upstream to find Carlyle. As we were walking along the bank, I noticed a white object about a foot long floating with the current. In another moment there were fifty such objects, an entire fleet, some as large as three feet, others very small. My subedar, in what I thought was a sudden fit of madness, dropped the fish he was carrying, stripped to the waist, and leapt into the water. Only then did I realize that these were fish and the whole situation became apparent. The subedar extracted twenty-odd stunned fish from the river, and they comprised such a weight that I had to shoulder my own catch.

We found Carlyle sitting coolly under the shade of a small tree surrounded by fish of all kinds and descriptions. His two sepoys sat nearby, cleaning the fish with great industry. Evidently the quiet pleasure of angling did not appeal to the Captain and he preferred to massacre them by the dozen. He had discarded my rod and reel and constructed a bomb which was then exploded in the depths of a large pool wherein the fish were plentiful. The explosion which we had thought was cannon fire had killed or stunned the poor creatures. The two sepoys, dripping wet like my subedar, had obviously collected the catch while the sportsman sat and enjoyed a leisurely pipe.

I was angry for this interruption. The fishing would be ruined as scared and dying fish rushed hither and thither, upstream and down, warning all their fellows of this scourge, this danger which boded catastrophe. The Captain was very put out at being reprimanded and I am sure he thought me a bore for enjoying the sport of dangling feathers over the water. His method proved far more effective and the sepoys were very pleased. We loaded our horses with fish and headed back to camp.

∽

Mehboob Rashid stood on the battlements above the main gate. Augustine could see only his silhouette against the sun, the edges of his silk caftan burned red, like the skin between the fingers when held up to a fire. The Arab cut an imposing figure and Augustine wondered whether the English could see him from below. Augustine wondered what he was thinking. Was he afraid? He feared the English as much as Webley. Or was he longing to be back in the desert, with his camels and dancing girls, fighting over water instead of blood, the heat and the sand more of an enemy than other men? Augustine tried to imagine the loneliness of that desert. He tried to envision riding across that searing, shimmering horizon.

'You had no trouble while we were away?'

Mehboob Rashid turned slowly and looked at Augustine. The two men were caught in the glow of the sun.

'No. You were away for a long time.'

'We enjoyed ourselves.'

'Playing English games?' asked the Arab.

'Do you think we have enough powder and shot to face the English?'

'Do you think our English general has enough courage?' asked Mehboob Rashid.

'He is eager to fight,' said Augustine.

'Then we do not need powder and shot.' The Arab smiled dryly so that his fear showed along with his teeth.

'They waited for the weather to break,' said Augustine.

'There is more rain to come.'

'The roads are drying up. The Ganges dropped ten feet even as we were coming up.'

'No one can predict the weather. Where is our commander?'

Augustine jerked his head towards Webley's rooms and smiled. 'Feeding pigeons.'

The Arab ran his tongue across his lips. It was a grey colour. His lips were a deep red, the lower one full and puffy. Augustine watched him carefully, wondering when he would run, run like a blackbuck with a cheetah after it, run from the Bijilli Gargh, from Webley, from the English, back to the sea and across that watery desert to the golden beaches of Arabia, where there were no walls to hide behind, to back up against, only the expanse of desert into which Mehboob Rashid could ride, running forever, escaping into an ocean of sand. It would be only a matter of time before he ran, taking his men and his wives with him.

'Who is this palace soldier whom you have brought along?'

'Hafiz Rustum. He has been to your country.'

'He has been nowhere. These men say they have been to Mecca ... pilgrimage, hah! They come like a procession of fleas. But what do they know of Mecca? They have not fought for the city, protected it. They come not out of devotion but for a holiday.'

'Hafiz Rustum is a lauded general.'

'I do not trust him.'

'You trust no one,' said Augustine.

'They say he is in the Nawab's army, a soldier of Awadh. But

Awadh is under the British, or is their ally …'

'It is the same thing.'

'Then why is he here with us, fighting the English?'

Augustine laughed. 'You should know enough about the games of treachery to answer that for yourself. The Nawab is eager to repel his English suitors.'

'There are better ways to accomplish that,' said the Arab, 'than to send a hundred and twenty good men to join a band of plunderers whom the English have cornered like rats. It is like stepping into the quicksand, to help another out of it. Both will drown. He cannot be that much of a fool.'

'We have friends in Lucknow. They recommended us to the Nawab and plotted with him.'

Mehboob Rashid turned away. 'Yes, I have also heard about your friends in Lucknow, eunuchs and drunkards. What good is their word? This man will turn against us when the time comes.'

'He will not do a thing like that.'

'A palace soldier, Colonel,' said Mehboob Rashid, 'knows only two things, politics and treachery. His sword is sharp on both sides. He has no honour. You were fools to bring him.'

'If he was sent to kill us, why didn't he do it on the journey here?'

'The English want your army destroyed as well as you. They are a systematic people, with schemes ranging beyond the present times.'

'Hafiz Rustum is an honourable man.'

The Arab shrugged. 'And this woman,' he asked. 'Who is she? Where did he find her?'

'In Lucknow,' said Augustine.

He would have liked to laugh. Webley had not left her alone the whole way from Lucknow to the Bijilli Gargh. Even in her palanquin he had made love to her, the poor bearers struggling under the weight of two passengers instead of one and trying to compensate for the jostling going on inside the thick curtains, which set the whole palanquin rocking back and forth.

Now that he was back in his own rooms, Webley was with her day and night. He was like a fish that has come upstream for spawning. It was as if nothing could sate his desire.

He has more stamina than a bull, thought Augustine with admiration. Webley would certainly come out as soon as the fighting started. He would come out hungry and full of fire, burning like a god with anger and desire, wild-eyed, his tongue hanging out, smelling of sex. He would enter the fighting with the same determination and eagerness with which he entered Khasturba. Augustine was pleased and wanted to laugh out loud.

'He is compulsive,' said the Arab, 'like a man in a fit. He will kill himself.'

'No, he will not die easily. He will inflict his sting and his venom on the English before he dies.'

'I wish I hated the English as much as you do,' said Mehboob Rashid. 'I would kill Webley first, before any of the others. He is our enemy.'

Augustine laughed, and as he did, a grey plume of smoke rose from the British camp. It rose casually above the trees, and just as it began to spread out, like pipe smoke dispersing, the cannonball bedded itself into the wall of the Bijilli Gargh, just beneath the two men, spattering masonry everywhere. The report was muted. Mehboob Rashid turned and shouted to the sharpshooters located in the turrets, on either side of the gate. They immediately took aim and fired in the direction of the guns. Augustine took the stairs two at a time and began yelling orders in the courtyard, sending men scattering in all directions. Shot landed inside the fort, dropping on the flagstones with a sharp sound, louder than the report, and sending bits and pieces of slate skittering across the courtyard. The new brass cannons, dragged up to the fort by oxen, suddenly bellowed. The gunners ran about their cannons anxiously, lining them up. They answered the dull but awesome roar of the eight- and ten-pound British guns, thumping in the distance like irregular heartbeats. Men raced for loopholes in the wall and began a quick fire.

Webley appeared at the door, wearing only his breeches and boots. He yelled to Augustine. The Colonel ran towards him. Mixed with the acrid gunpowder smells was the faint scent of Khasturba's perfume. Augustine stood close to Webley and shouted into his ear over the cackle of muskets and the sound of cannons and men. The darkness was growing about them and it was impossible to see the English sepoys except when they moved, faint grey shapes among the trees. Only the glowing pinpoints of light betrayed them, the matches on their muskets, the pot fires near the cannons. There were lanterns and fires lit on the riverbed below, and occasionally a running shadow could be seen cutting across the orange light. The cannons stopped with the full darkness setting in and only the lone musket crackled like the sputtering of a dying fire. Two of Webley's men had died, killed by the same cannonball.

8 September 1813: The Bijilli Gargh. The two hours of firing last night have showed us that the Bijilli Gargh is a sturdier fortress than we had thought and that the men inside are determined to repel us. These mud forts are deceiving structures. They look, on first sight, as weak as village huts, but they seem to absorb the shot which, embedded in the mud, reinforces the strength of the walls. Webley has a good number of cannons, most of them brought from Lucknow. I have instructions to return these to the Nawab of Oudh as soon as we have taken the fort. Their sharpshooters have taken their toll. We lost six men to their aim, for they are admirable shots even at that range, and Carlyle was wounded lightly in the hand.

The surgeon has cleaned it and Carlyle, being as strong-willed as any Indian officer (and that is no mean comparison), is already back in the saddle, promising to thrash the man who hit him. They have lost two men, it seems, for in the early hours of this morning we caught sight of their cremation fires up the dry riverbed from us. The smoke was blown down into our camp and it had a strong odour, like charred ham. Burial is so much more civilized, despite the chance of jackals and Gujars digging you up.

We commenced our bombardment after a breakfast of smoked tongue, which Carlyle was saving until he had the appetite. He was hungry as a bear and I'm afraid he'll give Webley no quarter if he gets hold of the fort today. The Bijilli Gargh just seems to swallow the shot without a shudder. We've succeeded in knocking a parapet down to the left of the gate, but it is not part of the main wall and there more for decoration than anything else.

The surgeon is kept busy with our wounded. Their marksmen are again causing some concern. There is nothing more frustrating than having your gunners potted off like vermin. I have ordered my men to remain in their trenches until we have effected a breach. There is no point in exposing them until then.

∽

10 September 1813: The Bijilli Gargh. Today the Gurkhas arrived, not in our camp, but in the mountains above the fort. We could see them at dawn, lined up along the bare ridge, watching us from a safe distance. I am not sure whether this army is on Webley's side or ours. More likely, their own. It seems they are standing by to watch what happens. It gives me an eerie feeling, to think that they are holding back until they see who has the upper hand.

Then they will swoop down and help the victors divide the spoils. Carlyle sneers at them, but I am afraid; there is no vanity lost in admitting it. We have close to fifteen hundred men. Webley has a quarter of that amount. The Gurkha numbers, no one can say. There could be ten, there could be a thousand. Our men are nervous. It is a strange thing: when we fought the Mahrattas and others the men had no fear, for they were fighting against soldiers of their own kind, mercenaries in a sense, and if they lost and survived there would be no retribution. Instead, they could join the victorious side and carry on with their careers. But now it is different. The Gurkhas will kill them to a man. They will not enlist a regiment of men outside their own people. It is a national pride amongst them which is new to India. It was not like this when I first came. I am sure that Webley's men are also scared, for they, too, will be destroyed if they lose. This is like a final battle for both sides, in which there is no escape for the defeated. Perhaps it will encourage our men to fight with more determination.

∽

The siege had smothered the fort in a hovering tension almost as thick as the cannon smoke which filled the central courtyard from morning till night. It was so thick that you could not see one side of the courtyard from the other. The vague silhouettes of men could be seen scuttling about, carrying powder and shot, toting water. It had been going on now for seven days without let-up. Augustine and Webley had seen the Gurkhas and they wondered if their army would take sides or just observe. They seemed reclusive and distant on their mountains.

It was just midnight. Augustine had woken up to make a round of the fort and take the reports of the pickets. He heard the sounds of an argument in the courtyard, and before he could go outside to see what was happening, Mehboob Rashid broke into the room, holding one of the Awadh soldiers by the throat.

'I told you they were traitors. I told you, Colonel, and now, by Allah, I've caught him in the act ... Read this if you still have your doubts.'

Mehboob Rashid handed Augustine a folded piece of leather, the sort which orders were despatched on during battle. On it was a message, written in neat Urdu script. It read: *We still await your orders. If you advance now and storm the fort, it will be ours. My men will cut these brigands to pieces.* It was signed by Hafiz Rustum.

'I caught him as he was lowering himself by a rope down the cliff. He had fastened a rope to one of the gun carriages and had descended halfway down the precipice. I gave him the choice: either he climb back up or I would cut the rope. It is a great distance to fall and he made up his mind quickly. I have been waiting for this, Colonel. If only you had listened to me that day.'

Augustine could hardly believe the truth. The friendliness which Hafiz Rustum had showed him on the journey up had dispelled all Augustine's caution. But it had been as false as his laugh.

'Bring him here,' said Augustine softly, 'and a Koran, please.'

Mehboob Rashid smiled and left the shivering captive huddled in the corner of Augustine's room. Augustine said nothing, but inside he felt both rage and sadness at having been tricked by a man whom he had respected, even admired.

Hafiz Rustum and Mehboob Rashid came into the room silently. The Arab had a sneer on his lips. Hafiz Rustum looked angry. The ever-present laugh had disappeared. He glanced at the soldier in the corner and swore at him.

'My Colonel,' said Hafiz Rustum, 'have this man shot. I demand it. He is a traitor.'

'If he is to be shot, so are you,' said Augustine, remembering what Ashgar Hasan had told him about the twenty soldiers whom this man had executed.

'What! You suspect me?' His voice and his expression were all the confirmation Augustine needed. The laugh rang hollow in the room.

'Here,' said Augustine, lifting the strip of leather into the light so that Hafiz Rustum could make out his own handwriting.

'Who has done this? What do you mean by showing me these things? Here is the spy.' He pointed to the wretched bundle of a man.

'You were going to turn on us at the moment in which we were most vulnerable. I was a fool to trust you, or the Nawab.'

'I swear …' Though he kept his poise, Augustine could see that Hafiz Rustum was nervous.

'Yes, you will swear on this,' said Mehboob Rashid, producing the heavy volume from under his robe.

A look came into Hafiz Rustum's eyes when he saw the holy book.

'Your beard is a pretty red,' said the Arab. 'You have gone to Mecca, I hear. A pious man. Then surely your word, on this Koran, should be all the testimony we need.' He grinned a wicked cat-like grin.

The two Muslims faced each other and Augustine had a feeling he was not a part of this. It was their struggle, within their religion and people. It had nothing to do with the circumstances.

Suddenly Hafiz Rustum reached under his cloak for a pistol. He had hardly got it out when Mehboob Rashid's sword severed his head at the shoulders. It lolled for a moment and then toppled to the ground. The body lowered itself slowly to the floor. In the light Augustine saw the red beard in its pool of blood. There seemed to be a laugh on Hafiz Rustum's face, an agonizing laugh. Augustine wondered if the head would join the neck again, as in the story, but there seemed very little hope of it.

Mehboob Rashid stood over his victim. He hawked and spat. His sword had cut so cleanly that there was not a drop of blood on the blade.

'Have his men taken prisoner, quietly and without a fight. In the morning we will deal with them. Have someone take him out, will you.'

Mehboob Rashid stepped back and stared at Augustine, then left without saying anything.

∽

13 September 1813: The Bijilli Gargh. Our plan has been found out. They executed the commanding officer of the Awadh troops and have tied all of the men to stakes driven into the hill at the foot of the fort. They are in our direct line of fire and I dare not bombard the fort, for fear of killing these men. Our cannons have been silenced. I have sent a message up to ask Webley to treat with us. It is a clever punishment for traitors, exposing them to the guns of their fellows. Over two dozen have been hung from the walls, suspended by ropes. They will die by evening. It is this cruelty which makes Indian warfare such a hateful business. I wonder whether it was Webley or his second-in-command, the Eurasian Colonel, who conceived of the plan. Probably it was the Eurasian, for I cannot believe that any English gentleman, no matter how many years he has spent under this blazing Indian sun, could commit such an atrocity.

13

The Bijilli Gargh was holding up well. Some of the roofs of the inner pavilions had been smashed and at places parapets had given way. The main walls were as sturdy as the rock they were built on. Augustine stood on the ramparts with his telescope. Below him he could hear the groans of the Awadh soldiers, tied to the posts or else suspended like puppets from the gun carriages. They dangled freely. Some were already unconscious. It was a gruesome sight. The English had stilled their cannons, and in the respite, Webley's men were busy cleaning up the fort, while their commander-in-chief took a break from war and pursued love instead.

A hirkarrah came up the path. Augustine had the message brought up to him. It was written in a tidy schoolboy's hand, inviting '*the commanding officer within the fort to come down and treat with us, as surely there must be a peaceful solution to this bloody business.'* It was signed by Major Gerald Fitzroy-Morris.

Webley was irritated that Augustine should interrupt him, but when he glanced at the message, his mood changed suddenly.

'It's Fitzy, by God. Just imagine … I wonder if he still fills his pants when he's scared. Go see what he wants, Colonel.'

Augustine nodded. 'You know him?'

'Of course I know him. I knocked his tooth out in a game of hockey. When you see him, have a look at his front teeth; one will be broken in half. Tell him I'll knock the rest out in a few days if he doesn't go back to Mama.' Webley laughed.

'I shouldn't agree to anything, then?'

'Of course not. Run them in circles a bit and then come back before the pounding starts again,' said Webley.

Augustine sent for a horse and accompanied the hirkarrah down to the British lines. At the bottom of the slope, Fitzroy-Morris and Carlyle were waiting in the trees, both smoking cheroots. Augustine could not stop the feeling of hatred wriggling inside him when he saw their uniforms, their powdered queues topped with enormous bearskins. They sat in their saddles with a casual air, haughty and bored. Augustine rode towards them slowly. They were both small men, at least six inches shorter than Augustine. Their horses were also smaller than Augustine's, so that when he rode up to them, they had to tilt their heads back to speak. The Major was about Webley's age. His white queue gave him a sort of ageless appearance, though his face was lined and a grey moustache curled over his mouth. When he spoke, his throat jumped up and down eagerly. He did not look like the storks in Lucknow, stooped and awkward. There was a swagger in his manner. When he grinned and held out his hand, Augustine checked his mouth. There was a chip out of the front tooth. The tooth itself seemed to have died, for it was a greyish colour.

'Where's Webby, sir?' asked Fitzroy-Morris.

'I beg your pardon?' asked Augustine.

'Your …' The Major hesitated. 'What rank has he given himself, by the way?'

'You mean James Webley. He doesn't have a rank.'

'No rank? I see. I'm sorry for him,' said the Major absent-mindedly. 'You're a colonel. So he'd be above you … Well, that's of no consequence. Except that I hoped he'd come along … for a chat. You see, Webby and I were at school together.'

Augustine nodded.

'By God … I almost forgot,' said Fitzroy-Morris. 'Despatch just came in this morning—rider from Delhi. Wellington has defeated King Joseph, Boney's brother, at Vitoria. Great news, eh. Tell Webby, will you?'

There was a moment's silence. Augustine could feel nothing over the news. It did not touch him in the least. He could think only of Jules.

'Captain Carlyle, may I present Colonel Augustine,' said the Major with bluster, as though they were old acquaintances. 'Captain Carlyle is my second-in-command, a fine soldier, a fine sportsman, and not above a little dalliance with the ladies ... hah ah hah!'

Augustine hated Carlyle on sight. The Captain's fist was bandaged, so they did not shake hands. They nodded to each other, very slightly. Carlyle was the sort of Englishman Augustine despised. He was as cold as a corpse. His face, hard and dark, carried with it a bitterness. There was no emotion in the man. His bloodless lips were sucked against his teeth.

Fitzroy-Morris and Augustine rode together towards the tents.

'Now, you won't tell your wretched gunners where we've pitched my tent, will you?' said the Major. 'We're hidden by the rim of the riverbed. But the truth is, I can't bear sand. It gets into my clothes, my shoes, my hair. So I've moved my tent into the trees. I hope it's not visible from above.'

Augustine laughed. 'No, you're well hidden, I assure you.'

There were trenches among the trees and two or three embrasures for the cannons, but still the army remained in the riverbed, awaiting a breach. Pioneers and sepoys were busy lifting dirt out of the trenches and piling it up for the construction of redans. From the fort they had been able to make out some of the preparations going on below, but the trees hid most of it.

'Here we are, sir. You know the inconvenience of tenting, but make yourself at home, Colonel. A drink perhaps; come on, I'm having one. Port, sir, as tawny as a Moorish hussy ... hah ah hah.'

The three men raised their glasses solemnly.

'To the boar, a finer beast never ran before a horse.'

Augustine saluted with his glass and swallowed a mouthful of the sweet wine. Despite himself, he liked the Major, who had a sense of humour and held nothing against an enemy. The men dangling from the walls and those tied out in the hot sun were forgotten for the moment.

'So, you've chased us a long way,' said Augustine.

'Not I. Carlyle's been on your trail for the past year, I believe. My men and I just joined him a few days back, from Delhi. This is Carlyle's affair, entirely.'

Augustine nodded. He did not look at the Captain. He ignored him. But Augustine knew exactly what he was thinking. Their minds went back to Deoband.

'I didn't recognize the Captain."

'He's the one, but knowing him, he probably put smoke between you whenever he was in range.' The Major charged his glass and toasted the fox, for its cunning.

'You know, I've ridden after jackals, but they don't have the same wit and spirit as a fox,' said Carlyle.

The Major, sensing trouble, changed the subject. 'And how is dear Webby? … Can't imagine him as a deserter, by God. Is he well?'

'Very well,' said Augustine.

'We hear he has a Moorish wife.'

'A mistress.'

'Ah … and did he know it was I who sent him the message?'

'Yes, Major, he did. He said he broke your tooth at hockey once.'

The Major frowned. 'He called me Fitzy, I suppose … hah ah hah. God, so long ago and yet it seems like yesterday we passed out. We were all rogues you know, gave our masters hell. And yet in all that roguish pranking we were chums, for life, we thought. Strange how life turns you back to back; all of a sudden you're shooting at the lad you promised to write to once a week … loyalty is a strong thing in boys, sir.'

'You were good friends with Webley?' asked Augustine, interested.

'Not as close to him as I was to others, but close enough. Strange, isn't it? Tell me about him, Colonel. I'm curious.'

'He's going bald,' said Augustine.

'Hah ah hah! Is he really, by God. So am I, just thinning out, but if I live another fifteen years, I'll be as clean as a boiled egg.' Both the Major and Carlyle had removed their bearskins. Their perukes were heavily powdered, and every time they shook their heads a halo of pomatum surrounded them. 'Does Webby talk about school days often?'

'Occasionally. He told me that I should have gone to school.'

'Did he now? He must have fond memories. We all do. Did he ever mention Potty Larkin, who put on airs because his father was a ship's captain? We threw him in the duck pond and he almost drowned. Or Solitary Woodenham, who had only one ball? Or the day six of us went out in the woods to find a bees' nest which Digby Coope, the only boy that didn't need a nickname, had found in a yew tree? We all came back stung, puffed up as though we had the mumps.'

'And what was Webley like?' asked Augustine.

'He was always at the head of things, led the rest of us into all sorts of adventures. There used to be an old pump organ in the chapel that you operated with your feet. Before evensong one day, he and a couple of us filled the bellows with coal dust so that when the parson's wife started it up for the first hymn it belched smoke as if it was on fire and we exited with cries of 'Run for it!' 'Fire!' and 'Sodom and Gomorrah hath come!' But those were the roguish things we did. There were the serious moments as well, when we all swore allegiance to each other for life, sitting in our beds after the lights were put out, talking in whispers. Webby should have come down, we'd have had a grand time. Tell him, will you?'

Augustine could hear Carlyle scuffling his chair impatiently.

'Sir, if I may interrupt,' he said.

'Yes, Carlyle …' Fitzy was still remembering his school days. Augustine could see it in his eyes.

'Pardon me for bringing up the business at hand, but I think that the Colonel should know that we've enough supplies and men to hold out indefinitely. It would be a waste of effort and life for them to resist any longer. If the walls don't give in, their supplies will give out and I must say that after the chase they've given us, my men will not spare one of them should we take the fort by storm. Besides, the ghastly treatment they've meted out on those wretches hanging from the walls will only serve to put a fire beneath the anger of my men.'

'You heard him,' said Fitzroy-Morris, gesturing to Augustine.

'Captain Carlyle makes no mention of what would happen to us were we to accept his treaties.'

'The same terms, sir,' said the Major.

'Which are?' asked Augustine.

Carlyle sat upright. 'May I remind the gentleman, sir, that no less than six times before I have sent *Mister* Webley a promise of safe conduct to Calcutta and passage on a ship home, in return for the surrender of his men and arms.'

'The question remains,' said Augustine, 'of Webley's fortune. Will it be confiscated?'

'I didn't know Webby had collected a fortune, by God. How much?'

'A considerable sum,' said Augustine.

'I see. Well, I could promise that he would be allowed to carry it with him to England. He's earned it, I suppose, regardless of his methods.'

'And what about the rest of us?' asked Augustine.

'Your men would be free to enlist as Company sepoys. And yourself?' The Major thought a moment. 'I'm sure there'd be a spot for you as well.'

'As a bandsman, or a farrier?' said Augustine bitterly.

'Oh, I see. I didn't quite know.' He paused to fill his glass. Carlyle sniggered. There was a delicate pause.

'There are some country-born units, I believe, rather good, too.' The Major thrust his hand into a pocket and extracted a snuff box. 'You know, strangely enough I had you placed as Welsh ... your voice perhaps ... and you are fair, sir. Take that as a compliment.'

Carlyle sniggered again. Augustine was about to turn on him, but he stopped himself. The Major meant no harm. He didn't mind his drivelling on. But Carlyle worried him, pestered his hatred with every word he spoke, and Augustine knew that he would kill the Captain soon enough. This was not the place.

'That's quite all right, Major. I'm not worried about what will happen to me. I've fended alone before and can certainly do it again. I'm worried, though, about my men. To follow me would be disastrous. There wouldn't be anything in it for them. And I can say they're not the sort that easily changes sides.'

'It's a comfort to find men like that in India. Not like those bastards you've got tied up there.' The Major offered Augustine a cheroot and the three of them lit up. The Captain absorbed himself in his smoke, sitting silently, stiffly, while Augustine and the Major spoke on.

Fitzroy-Morris had come out to India six years before Webley. His father had been able to buy him a commission in the East India Company army. After a few months at the Institution for Gentlemen Cadets at Barasat, he had joined a regiment and gone south to fight against Tipu Sultan. 'Name any battle in India and I've fought in it,' he said, not boasting, but with a reluctant sigh; not satisfaction, but regret and nostalgia. 'Sometimes I wonder if I shouldn't have done the same thing Webby did. I heard about him first after the storming of Aligarh. Another chum of ours, Beau Ridley, told me about him. He was part of the reserves and I was in the storming party. Ridley cleaned up after us. We had dinner together and he was rather hard up for money, being a gambler and a ladies' man, so I bought a horse off him … wretched animal, gave it away as a gift to some rasildar who'd lost a leg at Aligarh. Be that how it may, Ridley says to me, 'Have you heard of old Webby?' and I said, 'No, what's his story?' Then he tells me and we laughed about it. But neither of us imagined he'd live very long or make a fortune … hah ah hah. And who'd dream I would end up pounding him?'

Augustine had put aside his cheroot. 'What do they say about him in the army?' he asked.

'Some call him a deserter, others never heard of him, and a lot of us wish we'd done the same as he. It takes balls, that does, and tough ones as well. Maybe there's not that feeling of pride in it, but you are your own man. Ask Carlyle, for instance. Sir, tell me. Wouldn't you rather be the one doing the running, the looting, the raping, rather than the other doing the chasing, the bickering over prize money, the curtseying to officers of twice your rank and half your ability?'

Carlyle said nothing for a moment. Augustine acted as if he didn't realize the Captain was there.

'Sir, it's not a matter of liking one and disliking the other. It's my duty as a British officer to catch and hang a deserter.'

'You're so awfully stuffy, man! That's not what I asked you. Give an opinion, not a catechism.'

'Sir,' said Carlyle. 'I think I'll take a chukker of the camp. See how our defences are getting on, since it seems we will have to carry this siege to the end.'

The Major waved him out impatiently and then laughed. 'A good soldier. You shouldn't hate him as much as you do, Colonel … ah hah … I could see it in your eyes, sir. By God, he's as shirty as they come. These English, and look who's talking. I'm an Englishman, as English as a mutton chop. Wouldn't have dreamed of coming to India if my father's luck had been better. We're all sort of frustrated gentlemen here. Soon I'll be a lieutenant-colonel and on a ship home, with nothing to show for it but a few debts, a ruined liver, and a tiger skin or two. It's not what we imagined. We thought we'd all be nabobs, sir, our pockets heavy with pagodas. But no, we're just Indian officers, with a little glory and not much more … and the glory isn't worth two pence at home. You have to have fought Boney, sir, Spain, Salamanca, Vitoria, that sort of thing …'

'In a way, I suppose it's better to be country-born, as you call me,' said Augustine. 'At least we don't have to go back.'

'Go back to what? England—I don't mind the place, dear dear England. It's a lovely country. You should go there some time, Colonel. Going back's not the problem. It's leaving. This Hindustan of yours … or whoever it belongs to … it promises a lot, gives a lot, but you always have the feeling that hell, I haven't got enough. The country makes you greedy. You're proud of the boars you stuck, the tushes you won, the tigers you killed, the regiments of sepoy grenadiers … but somehow there's always something more to be done, something more to be taken, something more to be achieved. I suppose it's what keeps Webby here, like the rest of us, until we die or are sent back. There's no consolation in India. It demands more and more of you, like a woman … hah ah hah … a woman that enjoys being bedded down. Leaving's the problem. You keep kicking yourself, sir, keep realizing it's time to go, but there she is wanting more, and damned if you don't give it to her.'

'You're the only one I've heard talk that way,' said Augustine.

Fitzroy-Morris shrugged. 'By God, maybe I am. I'm beyond caring now. Carlyle is young. He's desperately proud, a cock-of-the-rock officer for whom there's still glory in loyalty and honour. He believes in England, in the modesty of Englishwomen—a lie if you'll believe me—wretched women. The widows, sir, you should see them, hanging around the regiments like hawks. 'A fine neck,' you say, 'a good figure/ and 'well-brought-up' … but it's nothing, Colonel, I assure you, except that when evening falls she's always looking for a young officer who'll take her to bed with him. That's why I never married. I thought, hell, if I leave her a widow, she'll be the same as the rest … a disgrace, sir!'

The Major was drunk. He stopped himself and cocked his head. 'What was I saying, sir?' He took a long drink from his glass. 'Colonel, you should get drunk with me more often. We could go down in history, sir, as a damn good pair of … what shall we call ourselves … drunken sots, eh!'

'You were talking about the pride of men like Carlyle and Webley.'

'Ah, I was. Well, the truth is that it's all a confounded lie. What shall I call you? Give me a good schoolboy name. Can't keep calling you Colonel. It makes us seem like enemies. Something I can remember you by. How about … oh damn, used to be good at this once … I say, what about "Gusty" … you don't mind, d'you, eh? Hah ah hah. Listen, Gusty old boy—a good name, eh! good fun, a joke. Well, I've worked the truth of it all out, sir. The truth is, we're all one enormous army, there's no England really, there's no Oudh, no Rajputana, no Moguls, no Mahrattas. We're all just a scum of mercenaries, paid by some buggered shopkeepers, Leadenhall Street and babus, all duns, sir … they feed you the story about becoming nabobs, eh! Quick riches. Tell you that a soldier can make a fortune, sell you to a Moorish regiment. Soldiers of fortune. Hell! Gusty, listen to me.

I shouldn't have stayed with it. Tell Webby I should have done as he did, got my own army. Tell him I'm proud of him. I am. Then I'd have made a fortune too.'

Augustine felt like telling the Major the truth, that Webley had no money. He'd never seen a fortune in his life and probably never would. But then perhaps the Major knew already. He looked down at the man with his peruke askew, blithering into his wineglass. Augustine didn't have the heart. He rose to leave. Fitzroy-Morris waved his hand and Augustine didn't know whether the Major meant to dismiss him or have him stay.

'Prepare to be shot at, sir.' The Major finally got the words out. 'And goodbye.'

Augustine left with a peculiar feeling, as if he had suddenly learned something very important and then forgotten it at once. Though he had lost the thought, the feeling remained in its place, an annoying residue, a sensation, the spoor of an image. He returned to the Major's words, thinking them through one by one. Was it the nickname? Was it Webby, Fitzy, and now Gusty? Something clung to his mind, not a thought, for he would have remembered that, but a feeling, an emotion. Was it the Major's candour? Was it his hatred for Carlyle? Nothing could bring it back to him now. It had gone. The irritation faded quickly, though, when he saw Carlyle hovering over the trenches, like a bat over a grave. They ignored each other. Augustine rode slowly through the trees, listening to the familiar sounds of the camp and the forest. He heard above him the groans of the traitors, languishing in the heat, the noises of the fort, guns being shot off to clean them, shouts, the rattle and growl of cannonballs being rolled over the slate floors. The sentries at the gate of the stockade saluted him. He nodded to them and softly told them to get ready, in the Major's words, 'to be shot at'.

There was suddenly excitement within the fort. Men rushed to the battlements and stared out across the plains. In the distance, looking at first like a shadow or a dark smudge, an army was moving towards the Bijilli Gargh. It was not a large army, two thousand men at the most. Augustine knew who they were even before he looked through the telescope. It was Kirpan Singh and his Sikhs. They had crossed the Jumna. Were they coming to help the English rout Webley and his army, or were they answering Augustine's call for help? They moved silently. Sometimes the forest absorbed them. Through his spyglass, Augustine could make out the horses and riders, the dark uniforms and turbans, the lethal kirpans at their waists and the glint of their lances. They seemed to flow over the valley. As Augustine watched, he suddenly realized what had been bothering him. He remembered almost word for word what the Major had said: 'We are all mercenaries.' It had meant nothing, part of a drunken man's contradictions. But the army moving across the Dun frightened Augustine, for it had a unity. There was a force which held them together and pulled them along. They were not individuals but a wave, a monster, a disease. He remembered Kirpan Singh's words about legitimacy and the end of an age. And then it began to make sense to him. We are soldiers of fortune, without a fortune. We have prostituted ourselves to others, to an ideal, to nothing. Not to gold, but to a profitless life. There was the adventure, the killing, the vanity. But what good was that without fortune? He began to regret it all. From the height of the fort, it looked like a miniature world below him. The clouds cordoned off the distances, the breadth of the plains beyond the Siwaliks, the altitude of the Himalayas. He felt small himself. Augustine ran the telescope over the valley. That circular vision, magnified and yet remote, seemed to be all there was. He felt as if he had shut his good eye and suddenly his glass eye was looking out on the valley, as if through a tunnel or the barrel of a gun. Within the spyglass, he could make out details, the complexity of branches, a flock of green pigeons, clusters of rocks, single men cut off from the others. There was no space for anything but a momentary glimpse of a tiny detail. Here were no ideals, no history, only a collage of images flashed before his eye. In that he saw what the drunken Major had meant.

For someone without an identity, a caste, a race, a people, a history, there was no place in this new order of things. Chaos had given him freedom. Now he felt only exclusion. He hated the English, hated their unity, their closed doors. Yes, he could have enlisted as a bandsman or a farrier for the Company. But that only meant exclusion. The English had destroyed for him his only world, his only heritage, his mother. In her there was a security, a tradition. Her voice, her stories about England, her loyalty to her husband, his image, had been for Augustine a protected sphere in which he lived happily, contented. But her death threw him open to the world, exposed him. With her death, he lost all associations.

He was nothing, anonymous. His memory could form images of himself, as he wanted, but he could share them with no one. He was not part of any fraternity, not a stork, not an Arab, not a nawab, not a Sikh, not a Gurkha. He was a bandit, a soldier without any loyalties. He owed allegiance to no one. Augustine had not sat on the bed with Fitzy, Webby, and Solitary Woodenham and sworn to be true to his friend forever. None of those ties bound him.

What he lacked was that force he had recognized in Kirpan Singh's army. Was it patriotism? Was it religion? He could not say. Augustine had believed that there was some identity waiting for him. He had only to find it. In a sense, he had believed that if he supported Webley, created a legitimacy around him, he himself would become a part of that legitimacy. No longer would he be without a face to call his own. Webley would give him credentials, personal legitimacy.

However, the Major had shattered all that. He had said, 'Come along, join the club,' when there was no club. Though he spoke about school days, about their pranks, their roguish fraternity, even flattered Augustine by including him in the group, giving him a nickname as well, absorbing him directly from the present into the past, from their first meeting into his memory, he had shown Augustine that there was nothing to it. Those boyish vows, those ideals, fell apart. They were soldiers; they had regiments to call their own. And yet, as Fitzy had said, they were all mercenaries in search of their individual fortune, that false belief in the Pagoda Tree. They could shake it as hard as they wanted, but nothing would fall from the branches. In the end they were always dependent on the merchants of Leadenhall Street, of Lucknow. They lived under the patronage of men like Ashgar Hasan, the Gaekwad, the Governor General. On their own they could not survive.

Augustine had always wished that he had some place to go back to. It could have been Chittoor, but now there was nothing there. Behind him there was emptiness. He had no Arabia to run away to, no sand dunes into which he could disappear. He had no England. 'Country-born,' he thought to himself—is it any different from being 'native'? Then, with a strange feeling he realized that the only people who had some tradition to stand on, a place to return to, were what Webley called 'natives'. That derogatory term held, in fact, the object of his desires. Augustine wondered why he wasn't one of them. His father had been a Rajput. Had his mother's blood alienated him from the land? Had he cut himself free? The Major had said that the worst part was leaving. Well, he could not leave and he could not return. Augustine was caught in the middle, in limbo, as if forever on a journey between Hindustan and England. For a moment he even wondered whether there really was an England. Perhaps that, too, was a lie. These whitefaced men had bluffed their way into Hindustan with a false legitimacy.

And then he remembered Lucknow and realized that in that city there was a legitimacy, that within the chaos and squalor of emotions there had been a security which allowed the excesses, allowed palaces like Ashgar Hasan's to be built. He also realized that there had once been a legitimacy which had allowed the Bijilli Gargh to be constructed. Though Webley hid within those walls, he had no claim on their past. And here they were, Augustine and Webley, Fitzroy-Morris and Carlyle, none of them with any claim on the land, and yet fighting over it, surrounded by Sikhs on the one side, Gurkhas on the other, watching with amused detachment. Augustine laughed as he remembered the animal fights, how the animals fought desperately, violently. Those animals had been alienated from their forests. Ringed about by men, they sought to destroy themselves, each other. Their frustrations, their loneliness, turned to violence.

'Your opinion, Colonel,' said Webley. 'Are they friendly or not?'

'If we win they will be friendly. If we lose, they will follow the English in and claim a portion of the victory. But until the battle turns in one or the other direction, they will camp in the forest and wait.'

'Like jackals waiting for us to die.'

'Maybe they are just curious,' said Augustine, musing.

They were standing on the ramparts, each with a telescope to his eye, talking while they surveyed the Dun. Webley had just come up beside the Colonel.

'And how was your tête-à-tête below?' asked Webley.

'Dull and unproductive.' He had been trying to think of what to say to Webley, choosing the best words to keep him going, keep his energy at a pitch. He was ready for the next question, though now nothing seemed to matter to Augustine. Victory and defeat held no suspense for him.

'And Fitzy? How is he?'

'I think you are mistaken there. He didn't seem to know you.'

'Didn't he?' asked Webley. 'You checked his teeth?'

'Yes. They were intact, though falling out at the back of his mouth. No broken ones.'

Webley was puzzled. 'You told him that I remembered him from school.'

'He gave another school.'

'I don't believe it, someone told me he was in India.'

'He told me to say that you must be mistaken,' said Augustine.

'The bastard. I'm sure it's him. The coy bastard, does he think he's too good for me?' Webley was in flames.

'He called you a deserter. *Mister* Webley, in fact.' Augustine urged his anger on.

'Did he, indeed! That sucking bastard. We were chums together, you know. I've told you all about it, man. The sucking …'

Webley stopped and smiled.

'Did you tell him that I would knock the rest of his teeth out. Losing them in the back, is he? You should have told him he'd be sucking broth between his gums pretty soon, if that!'

'He was drunk, tight as a fig.'

'Does he think I've dishonoured myself? Did he say that, Augustine? Well, go right back down and tell him that he's the one without honour. An Indian service, for him! Heigh ho! He used to talk about his family and their fortune as if he had it tied up in his handkerchief. Why's he here, man? Where's that fortune that was supposed to buy him a colonelcy in three years?'

Webley still had the telescope to his eye. Augustine had put his down and was watching Webley with a mixture of satisfaction and sadness. There was something pathetic about the insults, the bickering. He was like a schoolboy, thought Augustine.

He felt pathetic himself. What was he driving the man towards? They were cornered. If the English fell to their guns, there would be a few months' respite and then more English. Wasn't this what Webley had told him in the beginning? And yet it wasn't the numbers, it was the hopelessness of their struggle. If they defeated this army and a dozen others, they would still be where they stood now, outlaws. Regret and anguish filled Augustine and he felt as though he should tell Webley the truth, how he had tricked him, egged him on with lies and conspiracy.

'By the way … they'd just received news this morning. Wellington defeated Napoleon's brother at Vitoria … a thorough victory.' Augustine announced it without any feeling in his voice.

Webley turned suddenly, his face beaming. 'Hurrah!' he shouted, 'Bravo!' and like a schoolboy, he threw his hat in the air.

Augustine was surprised. He had expected happiness, but not this glee. The victory seemed to have nothing to do with them. It was so distant and out of sight. By Webley's reaction, he would have thought that the victory had been their own, against the English. Instead, with the strange tangle of loyalties which was part of his character, Webley was celebrating the victory of his enemies.

It was then that Augustine saw the situation more clearly. All of the armies, the English, the French, the Gurkhas, the Sikhs, their own, the Mahratta confederacy, Mysore, Awadh, Chittoor, seemed to congregate in front of him. Their little war with the English became part of the enormous conflict which spanned continents and hemispheres. It made Augustine feel insignificant and grand at the same time. He saw the world as nothing but an enormous battleground, like one of those huge canvases depicting all the events of one battle at once. The flags, the banners, the uniforms were insignificant. There were no sides, no real loyalties, only a fluid mass of cavalry and infantry, trampling each other, fighting first with one and then another. There was no defeat or victory, only a swirling, bloody chaos, cannons firing on all quarters of the field, columns marching in and out in a crazy formation, interlacing, criss-crossing, blundering into each other. In a sense it was like a storm of men. Augustine saw Trisuldas Thakur, he saw Somdas, Webley, Jules, Fitzroy-Morris, Carlyle, Wellington, Napoleon, all at different points on the field, despatching orders, leading charges, watching each other through telescopes. It was a dizzying and terrifying vision. Augustine felt himself plunging into the turmoil, as though he were diving into a roaring torrent, from off a high cliff.

∽

The English cannons started again. Kirpan Singh had drawn his army south of the Bijilli Gargh and at the first report they stopped and began milling around. Augustine could see their scouts far ahead. They had found their camp. There they would await the outcome. Webley began giving orders furiously. He told the gunners to keep a hail of grapeshot landing on the riverbed. Sharpshooters began firing intermittently through the loopholes.

Augustine had his jacket creased by a stray bullet as he leaned over to see the traitors tied and struggling. An English cannonball landed above one and a section of the plaster was dislodged, killing the man. Fitzroy-Morris obviously had no respect for these men. This was their payment for double-crossing. They were all dead by evening, when Webley's men cut them down and took them away to be burned.

∽

Augustine had promised himself that he would not go to see her. Khasturba was doing her job well and there was no point in stirring the fire, for Webley had that dangerous gleam in his eye.

Maybe his hair will grow out with these exertions, he thought, and laughed to himself sarcastically, knowing that in the end nothing would make any difference, not even Khasturba.

But she came to him. She found him in his room, cleaning his guns carefully with oiled rags, brushes of wire, and felt. He looked up with surprise. She stood embarrassed, wearing one of the scanty outfits Webley had ordered for her. Khasturba had lost none of her loveliness, nor her innocent smile.

'How is the virgin?' asked Augustine, with a comfortable laugh. 'You should not have come here. The more he loves you, the more jealous he will become.'

'I have come to tell you something you will not believe.'

'What is it?'

'That I love him.'

Augustine laughed, but he felt a strange feeling of reservation and uncertainty at what she told him.

'I love him as I had begun to love you,' said Khasturba.

'Don't talk rubbish. Tell me if he loves you.'

'I think not yet. He is a very gentle man sometimes, when he is spent, when he falls on my shoulder exhausted and his hand touches my breasts so lightly that I cannot tell if it is the bedclothes or his fingers.'

'Who isn't gentle after making love?' said Augustine.

'No, it is not just that he is tired. It is as if all his anger has been spilled, all of his bitterness. He is like a child.'

'Does he cry?' Augustine asked eagerly.

'I will not tell you that because I love him.'

'Hah! That means he does,' said Augustine. 'How does he cry, with a whimper, or with long aching sobs?'

Khasturba said nothing.

'I think with a whimper,' Augustine went on. 'You say that he is like a child. Does he ask you if you love him? I am sure he does.' Augustine laughed. 'I cannot imagine it, Webley as a tender man.'

'You said once that you loved him,' Khasturba whispered.

'I still do.'

'No, I think you hate him, more than you hate those men camped below us, those Englishmen.' Khasturba's voice was hushed and level.

'Of course not. He is my friend, my dearest fellow,' said Augustine.

'You said that you loved me and then in as little time as it takes to kiss, you changed your mind and gave me away. Do you think I am like that button on your coat, that you can throw away to anyone, as you fancy?'

'It shows how much I loved him,' said Augustine flippantly. 'I gave him someone I love equally.'

'You do have a blind eye, which you can turn on everything. It hides those things you don't care to see. I do not think you can love anyone. You have only ambitions, for yourself, for others. You dream of becoming powerful, feared, noble. And yet in the moment of your success, when you achieve this, it will all mean nothing to you, just as your love for me meant nothing. The glory will radiate around you. The English will fall like ants in front of your guns. They will crawl forward to die at your feet. But you have no patience with success. In you, Augustine, there is something which stops you from achieving what you dream about. You will win battles and establish power. But once that is done, you will rebel against your own victory, tear your success apart. Because you cannot tolerate peace, the quiet aftermath. In you is a desire to destroy things, kill the most innocent animals, peaceable characters. You are a product of an age that has disappeared, vanished. You will destroy everything, your army, your friends, your lovers, myself, Webley, even perhaps your own self. It is an anarchy of spirit, Augustine, an unquenchable desire for death. It is a creed of destruction you follow. You were born to it. No, it is not failure which you seek, either. But something between the two, a middle ground, the moment of battle, of conflict.

'I don't guess at any of this. I know. A whore is like a scale. She has felt the weight of many different men and can judge them accordingly. You have treated me with affection, like a newly married man treats his wife, kindly, gently, with all of the consideration a bride deserves. And yet I am not a bride. I am a prostitute. For a long time I wondered why you came to me this way, with so much tenderness. You were a soldier who had driven a lance through a dozen men. How did I come to deserve such tolerance, so much love, as you called it? But then I knew what it was. There is a fool inside me with whom I am always fighting. She had fallen in love with you. But then I stopped her, convinced her that you were lying, that those words which you believed so strongly yourself were nothing more than wind against the shutters. They had no meaning. I am not angry with you, Augustine. Why should I be, when I know that you could not help it? You had no choice. You did not know how you would change. A woman realizes that. I do. We are not systematic creatures who can be taught to love and never forget. I have no faith in promises. They are dull excuses which buy only a few hours' security.

'I remember everything you said to me, not as if the words had come from you, but rather from a book of poems, in which the romance was so real and delicate, but which I could not touch and bring to life. You did not know you were lying.

'You wept, not from sorrow or happiness, but from a strange emotion which was nothing that I have ever felt before. It is as if you have no feelings, no sensitivities, instead a harsh and painful sentimentality, dead and meaningless emotions which linger on. Perhaps they were your mother's or your father's, perhaps they are

Webley's. But they mean nothing to you. When you cry it is not an impulse but a habit, something which comes from the mind and not the heart. It is your memory which sets you crying, as if some tragedy long ago had surfaced in your mind. You cry not because of pain, or the present distresses of life, but out of a need to cry. Your emotions are like my opium, they are outside you, enter you and capture you, but they are not part of you. You give yourself to them, abandon yourself to their powers. They are induced by the subtle magic of your imagination.

'Augustine … a strange name. Your mother must have liked that name. She brought it with her, like some delicate article in her boudoir. I could not pronounce it for a long time. It did not seem to fit you. I wanted to call you by a soldier's name, Mehrab Khan, or Akhtar Ali Beg, or Muhammed Latif, a name with blood spilled on it. But no, you held on to your English name with strange fondness. It made you seem a madman, no part of this world, this Lucknow.

'I lay for hours on the bed, longing for you, wishing that you would make love to me, take me as a soldier is supposed to take a woman, as if I was the last you would ever love. I waited in that room expectantly, hoping that this time you would come ravenous and full of the lust which I can recognize. With some men I do not enjoy embraces and the heaviness of their bodies, but with you I would have gladly died in your arms, crushed like a flower under a stone. If only you had given up those mad ideas of yours, that fantasy that I was innocent, that I was not a woman but a young girl. You loved my tiny breasts, the tightness of my body, but not in the way I wanted you to. Instead I was a goddess and you worshipped me. I was perfect in your eyes when all I wanted was for you to see my flaws, hate them, love me, and then go away with the dawn. But you were persistent and wouldn't let me alone. I was exhausted by your attentions, your gentleness was more painful than any violence you could have done to my body.

'I told no one about you. The other women saw how often you came and caught glimpses of your presents. But I acted as if you were no one, as if you were fifteen different men who came to me on fifteen different nights ...'

Augustine had not listened to what she said. He was more interested in Webley.

'Does he whisper endearments in your ear?' he asked.

Khasturba was furious. 'I will not tell you anything about him. He is your dearest friend, or was. You should know these things.'

'Have you forgotten our conspiracy?' asked Augustine.

'No, but I have come to tell you that it is over. I am here now because I love him, not because you stole me away from a brothel to be his mistress. And I will tell him why you gave me to him, everything you said.'

'He will hate you then,' said Augustine, his muscles tightening.

'No, he will love me and hate you,' said Khasturba.

'It will kill him to know.'

'Know what? He is no idiot. By now he has probably guessed it.'

'He will never fight the English if you tell him.'

"I will say that his Colonel, his faithful Augustine, asked me to make a milksop out of him.'

'He won't understand,' said Augustine. 'He will not believe you.'

'Of course he will. I am his lover. You are only a friend.'

Khasturba's eyes were bright, fiery with her conviction. Augustine put down the gun he was cleaning and began to move towards her. She whirled around and was across the courtyard, running to Webley's room. Augustine looked up and saw the Englishman talking to Mehboob Rashid. They stood beside one of the guns, stooped slightly behind the wall, which shuddered with each shot as it lodged itself in the Bijilli Gargh. Webley did not see her running.

Augustine was worried. If she told Webley his plan, it would destroy any chance of hitting the English. Webley would give in. He would become afraid, afraid of himself: he would hate Augustine for trying to fool him, for using him like a piece of weaponry. He was a commanding officer and he would hate Augustine for trying to trick him into fighting the English. That old fear would return, destroy the clever balance of emotions which Augustine had constructed so carefully. He would hate Khasturba, too, for conspiring with Augustine. Suddenly it all seemed so fragile. Webley was just a gaunt old man, a twig in the wind. All that Augustine had made him into had been ripped apart, torn out like stuffing from a pillow. He was like a mounted tiger, nothing but the skin, the teeth, the image of strength and frightening power. Augustine saw how dangerous things had become. He had been tampering with a delicate mechanism. It was like opening up a pocket watch, trying to fix it, and ruining it beyond repair in the process. He felt a certain guilt and shame at the thought. Khasturba's words stung him. He had said that he loved Webley, and somehow he now realized that he loved that image instead, that stuffed soldier, packed full of his own imagination. Webley was nothing without him. He would shatter.

The fury inside Augustine was insatiable. He had to strike out at something. He had to vent his emotions on someone or something. There was no release for him in thoughts, no consolation, only in action, in violence.

∽

15 September 1813: The Bijilli Gargh. Early this morning, before I had risen, a cannon fired from the fort. It was still dark, the stars still embroidering the sky. As I stepped outside my tent, I saw that Carlyle had also woken to the shots and stood with his head protruding through the flaps of his tent, rather like a curious tortoise with a canvas shell.

I inquired as to his opinion and he said he thought it must be an execution, for at that hour there could be no other explanation. We had sent spies up to the fort, but they reported nothing untoward. Webley plans to hold out to the last man was their only intelligence. Evidently there is trouble brewing in the Bijilli Gargh and I lay down with some satisfaction to await the dawn, hoping that perhaps they would all kill each other and save us the trouble.

~

Augustine had struck out blindly, hitting in his fear and frustration the first person he could find. He had forgotten entirely about Pratap Bahadur until the night before, when he was racking his mind for an escape, a way out of the dilemma. And now, in a macabre and senseless act, he had seemingly made a sacrifice to his God, whoever that was: Webley, the night, himself.

The little Gurkha was nearly dead, a wretched figure, his smooth features whittled down to nothing more than wrapping for his skull. He could hardly talk and drooled when he opened his mouth. Two of Augustine's men dragged him up the dank stairway and into the courtyard. Augustine stood with his hands behind his back, his legs apart.

On seeing the little man, a shudder of horror went through his body, not of sympathy, but of revulsion. This grovelling figure seemed so helpless, so wretched. He was already dead, for all purposes, a corpse with the nerves still twitching. He was lifted up onto the ramparts and carefully tied across the orifice of an eight-pounder which had been loaded with grape.

Augustine made no speeches. He said nothing. After Khasturba had spoken to him he had not been able to sleep. For hours he had tossed about on his cot, as if wrestling with an invisible opponent, or with himself. The dull terror in Pratap Bahadur's eyes, the half-choked yelps which came from the little Gurkha, struck Augustine and he felt not pity but anger. He ordered the fuse lit and did not even flinch when, with a gust of flames and a muffled roar, the cannon scattered the little man into the darkness.

He felt relief flood through him, like a tonic or a soothing medicine. It was as if with Pratap Bahadur's death he had killed the little man within himself, the struggling dwarf caught within his giant frame. It was the morbid relief which one feels after death, as if all the nerves had suddenly sagged. The tensions and suspense went slack, and for a moment everything died. The darkness was complete, except for the glowing pot fire beside the cannon, which lit the faces of the executioners as they untied the grisly remains.

Mehboob Rashid emerged from his room and came up beside the Colonel.

'What is this?' he asked.

'I was putting the Gurkha out of his misery.'

'Have you gone mad? You will have their whole army out of the hills as soon as they know the truth. They will surely join the British.'

And perhaps that will be a better thing than this stalemate, thought Augustine as he turned to go. The hopelessness of their situation, the stagnancy, had frustrated him. He had wanted to take some action, loosen the jam, taunt his audience. He felt like an actor in a lame performance, angry at the imbecility of those watching, angry at himself, angry with the other actors, angry at the clumsy script which had been handed to him. With dramatic ruthlessness he had shattered both the man and the situation. He had no reason for the act, no excuse. It had been an impulsive murder, no different from chasing down a rabbit or killing a lizard.

~

16 September 1813: The Bijilli Gargh. This siege is carrying on with tedious ineffectiveness. I am almost inclined to call that Colonel down for another drink, just for the sake of his company. It doesn't seem as if Webby is going to come down or invite me up, which is very dull of him, I think. He could at least have sent his regards, but not just an envoy—though the Colonel was a pleasant enough man, certainly more interesting than dear Captain Carlyle, who has gone sour on me, 'for fraternizing with the enemy'. He told me that perhaps it would be a better idea if we kept a cold eye on the fort, rather than plying them with port. Those were his words and I must admit it did not recommend him to me. We have started taking meals in our separate tents, rather than together, as was our habit. He speaks only when necessary and I out of pride have been forced to do the same. This leaves me bereft of any company, a truly dull state of affairs.

If we get out of this alive, which I am beginning to doubt, I am going to report the Captain's conduct to the Commander-in-Chief. It is certainly not becoming in an Indian officer. They may be our enemies, but certainly we can afford them the courtesies any Englishman, friend or foe, deserves.

~

Augustine was sitting outside his room, his back against the wall, a bottle of claret beside him. He was listening in the darkness to the sounds of the fort. Here and there a soft light glowed, exposing a doorway or a window frame. The voices of the soldiers were subdued and tired, the stories were not told so easily after a long day of action. Here and there a snoring broke out and then was silenced. Someone coughed. The night hung limp about him, with the smell of mildew and gunpowder. That afternoon a misting rain had started up with the cannons, clouding the fort over in fog. Through it all the thunder of the eight- and twelve-pounders rocked the slate of the courtyard. The Colonel was exhausted as well, but couldn't sleep. He had drunk some of the wine to help him fall asleep, but it had yet to take effect. Webley's voice roused him from his thoughts and he looked up quickly from where he was sitting.

He thought a moment, trying to recall what it was Webley might be talking about. Then he remembered. Khasturba had told him. He saw Webley's teeth set in a smile.

'My Colonel, I didn't thank you adequately for your gift. The full significance of its worth escaped me.'

'Which gift?'

'Why, the girl of course.'

'What did she tell you?' he asked.

'Oh, nothing important or indiscreet, I hope. But, I must say, flattering indeed. Noble. Noble!'

'What did it concern?'

'Oh, just a story, a silly girl's talk, something about you wanting her to spur me on. Rather patriotic of you, Colonel, I should say! Were you worried that I'd funk like the last time? Was that it?'

Augustine said nothing. He felt a rage building up inside him, a hopeless, desperate feeling of having been found out and a desire to revenge his embarrassment.

'Come now, Colonel, I appreciate the sentiment attached, the kindness. But I must say it was not a very good idea. Did you think that she would make any difference? Has she? I would have fought the English despite her. Have no fear. And let me say this, that I will fight them with intelligence, not with the brash emotional warfare which you yourself deployed at Deoband. I am no coward. I think my battles out beforehand.'

'In the pleasure gardens of Lucknow. You are right, she doesn't matter any more, no difference.'

'No, you mean in the girl's arms,' said Webley. 'Do you think that I would take her seriously? No, I don't fall for women like a cannonball that has reached the limit of its range. Women are like fighting the English, they take intelligence.'

'She has done you good,' said Augustine.

'Has she now? Perhaps my health has improved. The blush is back in my cheek. But imagine, Colonel, a man of your strict discipline falling for an immature hussy. She told me, you know, all about it, how you refused to sleep with her. What was that, Colonel? Love? I say, I never would have expected it of you.'

Augustine's temper was rising. He knew Webley was taunting him. He remained seated and took another drink from the bottle.

'Temperance, Colonel, that was what you taught me, eh? But you yourself went after her as if she were your first love … as if restraint and abstinence were a virtue. You know, she's a good girl, but needs more than just an old man's love. She needs to be ridden, like a good horse.

'A charming idea, my Colonel. Perhaps you would like a medal, or was it enough to give your button back? Yes, it was a sweet little plot, sir. Devotion, honour, true subordination. Well, I'll tell you I am surprised. We've fought through so much together, sir, that I couldn't believe it when she told me that you thought I'd funk … really!' Webley's anger began to pick up momentum until he finally gave Augustine a full charge of his fury.

'You, sir, should be shot for distrusting your senior officer. It is insubordination of the worst kind. Damn it, Colonel! Would you call me a coward to my face? Would you? Well … heh … you've done it, sir, and consider yourself dismissed. I'll show you who's a coward. Afraid to lie with a woman, a girl of sixteen, hardly a woman … by God!'

'Do I understand you properly as saying I am no longer in your service?'

'You do … that is correct! Indeed, begone with you. In the morning don't let me see your face!'

Augustine lifted his hand to his brow in a mock salute and turned his face away. Webley, now shaking with fury, snapped about and was gone with a clatter of boot-nails on the slate.

It had happened so abruptly that for a moment Augustine sat there, just as before, and looked above him at the mountains where the sparks of light from the Gurkha encampment could be seen along the top of the nearest ridge. His good eye seemed to dilate, and then he felt the tears in his eye, filming over his vision, so that the blinking lights became like reflections in a stream, their fluid brightness rippled by the current.

That recurring emotion caught hold of him and wrenched him to his feet. It was like the night on the deserted battlements with Webley drunk in his arms. It was like those days and nights on horseback, wandering across Rajputana, after his mother had been killed. It was like the evening he had found Webley in bed with Khasturba. Each of those times his body had been racked with the same emotion. It was like a recurring fever.

But this time the tears stopped flowing after a few minutes and the emptiness inside him suddenly filled with determination. It was as if he had thrown himself open to the night, shattered the inner world of terrors, the brooding afflictions. It was the same sort of conviction which had followed each of the other times, but now it was stronger than ever, more concentrated, and he knew exactly what he wanted. No longer would he remain beneath Webley. The army was his as much as the Englishman's. There was no reason why he shouldn't topple Webley and take his place. The men would follow him.

She was dishevelled, her hair as if windblown, though Augustine wondered if she had ever been out in the clean air. Her face had a paleness in daylight, like the moon still up after dawn. Khasturba was created for the night, for the hours of darkness. The lustre of her skin died during the day. The Colonel did not knock, but swept the curtains aside and stepped in, the nails on his boots announcing his arrival. He knew that Webley was up above with the gunners and there was no danger of his coming to the room. Khasturba flung herself around and glared at him, her eyes hard and frightened. She did not smile.

'How is the battle going?' she asked.

'You needn't worry,' said Augustine. 'There is a handsome captain in the enemy who will take you away with him if they should win. You aren't one to think of consequences, though, are you?'

'I am afraid.'

'You shouldn't be. Once you said to me that death would be the only solution to your life, a return to being a child.'

Khasturba stood up slowly and dragged herself to the heavy wooden chest inlaid with brass. She struggled with the hasp and finally pushed it open. From inside she took her pipe and the ball of resinous opium. Augustine watched her carefully; then just as she was filling the pipe, he took one step forward and grabbed it from her hands and threw it aside.

She looked at him with curiosity, like a child who has just been scolded.

'You have told him our plan,' said Augustine.

'No, I have not,' said Khasturba. 'Give me back my pipe and leave before I call for him.'

'What will he do?' asked Augustine. 'Run me through with his sword? Do you think he could? He should run you through as well, kill you for such treachery.'

'It's not treachery. You talked me into it, and he was your friend.'

'I have come to take you back,' said Augustine.

'You cannot have me.'

'I will,' said Augustine, taking hold of her roughly. She did not resist but looked at him, frightened, shivering.

Today she looked like a beggar girl off the street. Augustine could feel nothing for her, not even a faint arousal after weeks without a woman. He stared at her helplessly, she at him. In her eyes he saw her childishness. They stood there. Without the opium she was helpless, exposed to the world. The drug had protected her. Augustine had protected her, and now as he stared into her eyes he found himself unable to harm her, unable to rape her, unable to love her. He felt as impotent as Ashgar Hasan. There seemed to be nothing left of himself. He was drained of his feelings. Augustine struggled, trying to coax some emotion, whether it be love or hatred, from inside him. He felt empty. Gently he dropped her arms and left the room without a word, dejected, defeated.

Augustine knew that she was no longer his. He had given her away. He also realized that he would not be able to take the army away from Webley, either. The Englishman held them both like a powerful magnet, his strength and attraction invisible and yet undeniably there.

Augustine had known that Mehboob Rashid would desert them. He had been waiting for it to happen ever since the incident with the leopard. The Arab had begun talking too much. It was unlike him. While he kept silent, Augustine knew he was loyal, but as soon as he began to speak about Webley, express his hatreds, the Colonel was sure he would disappear.

It happened two days after Augustine was dismissed from the army. Fear drove the Arab and his depleted band out of the Bijilli Gargh. They did not make for the British camp but dodged around to the south and crossed the *sot* much lower down, even below Kirpan Singh's encampment. From there, the pickets reported seeing them riding towards the Siwaliks and disappearing into the jagged silhouette of those mountains. No one followed them. Augustine imagined the tiny group. Eight men survived out of the original thirty. With them were two women whose faces nobody had ever seen. The other women were said to have committed suicide on their husband's death. Augustine had seen them one morning carrying the bodies down the hill behind the stockade and burying them in deep graves. Among the Arabs there had been a fraternity, their exile bound them together. They kept their customs and their tongues. Augustine thought about their women. They, too, were soldier's wives, and by committing suicide they had affirmed that loyalty. His mother would have done the same, he thought, if she had had the chance.

Nothing mattered now and Augustine felt relief on hearing the news that they were gone. One coward among men can frighten a dozen heroes. The news that he had been dismissed spread quickly among the men. They looked at Augustine strangely, not sure whether to salute him or not. He only smiled, staying in his room most of the time, cleaning his guns. He could have left the fort, ridden down and joined Fitzroy-Morris, or gone away into those wide distances of Hindustan, just as the Arabs had done. But something held him there. At first he thought it was Khasturba, but after seeing her he knew she mattered little to him now.

Somehow he felt that within the fort lay his destiny. He had to remain. Webley did not speak to him after their argument, but nothing was done to harm him. He was free to roam the battlements and study their position with his telescope. In a sense he felt like Kirpan Singh and the Gurkhas. He was simply waiting and watching. It was no longer his battle. He had been freed of it. The news, the rumours still reached him, but he ignored them.

At times he felt frustration, an urge to take up a musket and fire at the trenches. He wanted to lead sorties at night, attack the British trenches. But all of that was denied him. He spent long hours cleaning his guns until they shone. He couldn't fire any of them; they just lay there, useless.

Meanwhile, Webley paced about more furiously. He ignored Khasturba. He had become a madman. Augustine watched him moving about, plotting, angry with everyone—a temperament whose mood filled the entire Bijilli Gargh with its charisma. Each man felt a part of that desperation; they were all angry and defended their positions fiercely. But it was a stagnant battle, like the smoke which hung about them. There was nothing decisive. The walls of the Bijilli Gargh refused to give in. They had supplies for another month of siege and plenty of ammunition. The frenzy inside Webley, and inside all his men, came from this stillness, the indecisive firing. Each cannon shot, each ball, seemed meaningless, as if fired into the air. Everyone was waiting, waiting for the impatience which would turn the tables of this deadlock.

He knew what was coming. He could see it in Webley's stance; in his barking voice there was a shrill abruptness. Augustine knew that Webley would betray himself. Fitzroy-Morris had only to wait, sit it out, drink his port, and relax. His classmate, school chum, would detonate himself. Though Augustine feared what would happen, he watched in silence, almost eager to see the outcome. It was like wanting something terrible to occur, so that it would be over and done with. The tension was that of a drumhead, stretched and quivering. The vibrations seemed to shake the walls of the Bijilli Gargh, though Augustine knew it was only the shock of the English cannons pounding against the fort.

14

It all happened very quickly, taking Augustine—taking everyone—by surprise. The news reached him early in the morning, waking him out of a dream. He dressed quickly and mounted the ramparts to see what preparations were being made. Below them the Company forces were silent, unsuspecting. Within the fort the soldiers moved about briskly, their boots clattering on the flagstones. Dawn was settling through the banks of clouds. Augustine sensed rain in the air. In the mountains he could see the flashes of lightning. The Gurkhas were being rained upon. They had done nothing about Pratap Bahadur's death, though word of it must surely have reached them. Across the valley the Siwaliks had a melancholy look about them, like a fringe of black lace on the hem of the lush Dun. Even in his desperation, Webley had chosen his day well. The weather was in their favour. The rain would hit the English as soon as the horses did.

Augustine heard a flapping overhead. He looked above him and there he saw the British flag flying from a bamboo pole. It gave him a strange feeling, as if the Bijilli Gargh had already been captured, for he had always fought against that flag and thought of it as a target, a symbol of the enemy. He remembered seeing this flag once before, neatly folded at the bottom of Webley's trunk, under a pile of silk shirts. He had always wondered why Webley kept it.

The horses were being led out now, the syces patting their muzzles affectionately. This was the time of parting, when the war horse left his syce for his master and entered battle. They gathered in the courtyard, over fifty horses, the sweet, rank odour spreading through the courtyard. There were Arabs and native horses, mixed bloods, English mares mated with stallions of the soil, no pedigrees, no distinctions, but lovely horses, of all colours, from a soft fawn to a jet black.

Webley's mare was led in, tall and glossy, shaking her head impetuously. The syce held her bridle and his other hand rested comfortingly on her neck. Instantly there was silence. Then from all corners of the courtyard, as if the scene had been staged, the horsemen came out to claim their mounts. It was splendid. Each man was dressed to perfection, turban tied jauntily askew. Bandoliers flashed, brass buckles gleamed. The uniforms were as varied as the soldiers themselves. Some wore cutaway jackets and high collars with embroidered facings. Others were dressed in baggy pantaloons with long kameez. Some wore ornate vests, others were stern and simple, but not the less impressive for it. Talwars swung at their thighs; lances, muskets, pistols, and all varieties of Indian weaponry adorned these men.

Augustine wished he could have been among them. He stood on the ramparts and watched with a feeling that he was witnessing a finale, the end of all his hopes and desires. And yet the thrill of it brushed aside his sadness. The details were so elaborate, the way each man displayed himself. Some smiled as if this was to be nothing more than a parade, others were solemn and spoke to no one, staring straight ahead of them, or muttered to their horses as they checked the saddles and stirrups. A few were afraid. Augustine could see it on their faces and felt sorry for them.

Webley appeared conspicuously. Every head turned as if there had been a fanfare. He wore a helmet with a pugaree of peach-coloured silk wound around it and a peacock's feather stuck in one side. Around his neck was a gold kerchief, knotted and tucked into the collar of his shirt. He wore his jacket open. It was a red jacket with black facings and gold epaulettes. The bright colours were in contrast to the grey morning. On his face was a cheery good-morning look, as if he were setting out for a few hours behind his hounds. He wore high boots and his breeches were a cream-coloured moleskin. His sword moved comfortably with his stride. A pistol was stuck in his cummerbund. He walked out proudly, stopped beside his horse, checked her carefully, gave her a kiss, and then thrust himself into the saddle.

At that moment, Augustine found his syce beside him. The thin little man looked up at him anxiously. 'You are not going with them, Huzoor?'

'No,' said Augustine shortly.

'But, Huzoor! It is to be a charge, a surprise attack.'

'I know.'

'I have saddled your horse, Huzoor. It is waiting in the stables. Shall I bring it out?'

'No,' said Augustine.

'Why not, Huzoor? … A charge.'

'I am not dressed for the occasion. I will call for my horse when I am ready.'

The syce smiled with a puzzled expression behind his gleaming teeth.

Augustine caught sight of Khasturba. She stood with two of her ladies in the west turret above the gate. Her head was covered and she stood still, like a carving. His eyes went from her to Webley and then back again. She was there to watch the battle. It was probably the first time she had ever seen fighting. The eternal virgin, he thought, and smiled.

Quickly he rushed down the steps and into his room. He snatched up his sword and topi, also a pistol which he kept loaded by his bed. As he came out of the room, the gates had opened. Webley was already through them and the men followed him down the steep hill to the stockade. Augustine climbed the ramparts again and watched as they passed through the stockade and streamed down the slope. They did not try to conceal themselves but rushed down as fast as the treacherous incline allowed, screaming curses at the top of their lungs.

The English pickets began firing, and suddenly the entire forest was alive with activity. Augustine saw heads moving about in the trenches and gunners in the sot began tamping down their cannons furiously. Four salvos from the fort covered the charge and then there was silence, for the riders were now amidst the trees and there was danger of the cover fire hitting them. The English gunners fired once and the balls and grapeshot thundered into the Bijilli Gargh. A part of the stockade was blown into the air. For a moment, Augustine feared for Khasturba's safety, but then he saw her, motionless in the turret, and decided that she was as safe there as in her rooms. Frantically the English gunners were trying to lower their cannons to meet the charge, but before they could reload, Webley's horses were among them, cutting them to pieces.

A few minutes later, Augustine caught sight of the mare. Khasturba had not seen it. She galloped madly into the sot, blood smeared in a dark stain across her side. Webley was not on her back. Augustine could almost hear the animal's screams of terror above the firing.

Instinctively he took the steps in three bounds and yelled for his syce. The horse came out at a trot, and before it had even stopped, Augustine had thrown himself into the saddle. He did not stop to think. The gates were opened and he was outside. Without bothering to wait for the gates of the stockade to open, he headed for the breach. Jumping the shattered palisades, he felt the horse skidding down the hill. They reached the bottom and entered the thick jungle. Smoke drifted in and out of the hoary trees, most of them splintered and crippled by the cannonade. He had to force his way through the lantana and other brush, all the while trying to find his men. They had scattered, and when he came to the riverbank, Augustine could make out their mounted forms dashing about within the choking smoke. Dead sepoys lay heaped on their cannons. They had fallen back to the second line of trenches and it was there that the volleys, one after the other, cut ruthlessly into the horsemen, most of whom had abandoned their muskets and were using only their swords and lances. The rain had begun to fall and the ground was slippery. The dry sot had a muddy trickle of water running through it.

Augustine could not find Webley. He knew that he must be somewhere, either on another horse or dead, wounded, dying. Fitzroy-Morris and Carlyle were visible in the trenches, directing the fire in hoarse screams. Augustine could see that Webley's men had no chance. The initial surprise had done its damage, but the English had rallied and now they were closing the gap.

Augustine felt somebody leap into the saddle behind him. The Colonel half-turned, his pistol cocked. There was Webley, smiling. It was like an apparition. He was not wounded, but there was dirt on one side of his face from where he had fallen off his horse.

'Turn back,' said Augustine. 'If we fight on we'll all be killed. Turn them back!'

Webley looked at Augustine with astonishment, as though he understood nothing. There was a wildness in his face, a look between terror and glee. Those brilliant eyes burned like coals under a bellows. The bloodless face didn't seem even to recognize Augustine.

Webley's pistol appeared in his left hand. He thrust it into Augustine's ribs.

'Go on,' said the Englishman in a hoarse whisper. 'Go on. Charge!'

Augustine spurred his horse forward. They were at the rim of the sot and the horse scrambled down into the riverbed. Here the fighting was thickest. Augustine used his sword, while Webley shouted encouragement to his men from behind. There was no direction to the battle now. It was a jumble of men and horses. The rocks and mud were slippery with the rain, which added to the confusion. Most of the English were on foot. They hacked at the horses with their swords. All discipline had vanished except for the lines of sepoys crouched behind the embrasures, firing with mechanical regularity into the dense mass of horsemen.

Augustine saw Carlyle standing to one side, ordering the fire. He whirled his horse around and charged the embrasure. The packed mud was slick but his horse leapt cleanly over the barrier. Carlyle saw them coming and fired. The ball spat past Augustine's ear. He ducked low in his saddle as they bore down on Carlyle. Augustine used his sword. The Captain had turned frantically to escape, but Augustine was already on top of him, and with one easy blow he cut him down. Carlyle went under the hooves of Augustine's horse. The Colonel looked back to see him spread out on the ground, dead. But in that same instant he realized that Webley was no longer behind him. He wondered if he had fallen off or whether he had been shot. Perhaps Carlyle's bullet had killed him. Augustine turned his horse around, but beyond the embrasure the men had closed in like a tide and he could not see the corpses for the living men. He looked for the red coat, but the confusion blurred his vision. The rain was falling thickly now.

He shouted as hard and loud as he could. Only a few men heard him and turned. Others kept on fighting. He screamed and ordered them all back into the fort. Some hesitated. A few more of them were killed, but gradually they turned away and galloped back into the trees and finally up the slope. At an order from their officers, the English sepoys in the trenches came out from cover with a scream, not human, more like the cackle of a hyena. Augustine was the last man inside the stockade. He waited there until the Company sepoys came streaming up the hill and then ordered the gate barred. He had placed twelve men with muskets at the breach. They held off the attack until the cannons inside the Bijilli Gargh could be lowered. Shooting almost vertically, the gunners rained grape- and chain-shot on the Company troops until they finally retired.

Only in that silence, the hush which followed the bellowing of the cannons, could Augustine assess his losses: Of the two hundred horsemen that had ridden down, only half remained. Augustine felt a chill run through him as he realized these would not have returned had he not given the order. Like Webley they would have died below. And he didn't doubt that a few of them wished they had been killed, rather than survive their commander.

Augustine went to tell Khasturba, but she had her ladies send him away. She knew already.

Now that he was in command, Augustine had no heart to continue the battle. He wished he had left before, when Webley had dismissed him. He should have ridden away then. But now a numbness took hold of his mind and body, subdued his thoughts. His hands shook, his eyes blurred with tears. He felt nothing. It was as if he had lost quantities of blood, though he had no wounds. His head went muzzy and he returned to his room to lie down. It was not sadness which overcame him but exhaustion. He felt nothing but a weary sensation in his legs, as if he wouldn't be able to stand. All of the tensions, the anguish of those earlier months seemed to descend on him now. He slept soundly, though it had only been three hours since he had waked that morning.

∽

28 September 1813: The Bijilli Gargh. A bloody morning of fighting today, the most casualties we've suffered yet, including Captain Carlyle, who fell under the country-born Colonel's sword—a fitting death. They came down on us just at the first light, like a horde of Moorish banshees, making the most unholy noises. I awoke just in time to pull the men back into the trenches behind our embrasures. In the process we lost a good many fine sepoys, never to be replaced by the likes of them.

But the enemy lost their Commander-in-Chief. He died brilliantly, proving that even in death there is glory for the brave—a maxim of war my father used to use. Only today did I realize the significance of those words. He rode down on us like a charging boar and it was a lucky bullet that stopped him.

Even dead, Webley looked the same as I remember him, older, but still as gaunt, as if between the skin and bones there was no flesh, just enough to hold him together. His lips were white and set in a grin, his eyes staring straight into the sun without a squint. I had him covered quickly, for I prefer to remember a man as he was alive, not as a corpse. I felt no sympathy. It had been a long time. But perhaps in my heart there was a little sadness, that it had to be myself who stopped his life short, a life which in my heart I knew that I admired.

But there is a curious feeling in me which I am embarrassed even to note down. It is a feeling which no honest man can deny and yet which is hardly ever expressed for fear of sounding inhuman, morbid somehow.

It is the same feeling I get when I land a fine trout or shoot a tiger. It is as if the contest was suddenly resolved. War is nothing more than the killing. There is no regret in it. Carnage is not something I enjoy, but the death of an individual man, amidst all that slaughter, to me is as glorious a thing as any man can know. That one death should eclipse all others, that one man's valour was so enormous that the lives of others mean nothing in comparison to his—that is certainly something. I do not feel as if I have achieved something with his death, surpassed a record, but in me there is a peculiar fulfilment, albeit a sadness, but also a reaffirmation of my life as a soldier…

The events following Webley's death were unexpected, macabre twists of fate. Augustine sat immobile. He wandered about the fort helplessly. When his men came to him with requests for orders, he looked at them blankly and muttered under his breath, telling them to do as they thought fit. The afternoon after the charge, a lone rider came up the trail with a corpse slung across his saddle. The gates opened for him. He came to the centre of the courtyard, gave the dead man a shove with his knee, and let him collapse to the ground. Without a word, he turned and rode back down to the British lines.

The place where bodies were burned was about a mile up the sot from where the English were camped, just inside the mountains. Augustine told his men to cremate Webley as soon as possible. The stacks of charred logs were piled all about the riverbed waiting for the occasional flow of water to wash them away. Augustine watched silently from his horse as the men stacked the pyre high with wood collected from the forest. The body was laid on top and there was a reverential silence. Augustine tilted his head and waved one of the men forward. He carried a flaming torch with which he lit the bonfire. It burned slowly at first but then gained momentum, until they all moved back out of the searing heat.

When the fire was at its zenith, Augustine caught sight of Khasturba out of the corner of his eye. She was dressed as she had been that morning, her head covered. Two of the men led her towards the fire.

Horror gripped Augustine as he realized what was happening. He caught a glimpse of her eyes, dull and opiated. But he could not move. He sat transfixed in his saddle, as impotent as the last time he had spoken to her. All heads turned and watched the procession. It was as if the crowd demanded this of her. Khasturba's feet stumbled and Augustine guessed she had smoked several pipefuls of opium. His lips went dry. He could not shake himself out of his immobility. For a moment he almost stopped her—the cry was on his tongue—but then, with a sob, he broke down and wept. Finally the two men let go of her and stepped aside. A low wail came from the back of the crowd. It was her ladies crying. The solemn faces of the soldiers did not flinch. The firelight on that sullen evening lit all their expressions with an eerie brightness. They had all come, the survivors, for the final farewell to the man who had brought them so far. A leaden twilight had crept over the mountains, giving the scene a ghostly atmosphere. Tears blurred Augustine's vision. He felt a barbarity inside him. It was horrible and yet it was glorious. His mother would have immolated herself this way if she had not died first. Augustine saw Khasturba step forward, walking into the glare of the fire. Her face seemed to glisten. She made no sound. He could see her dull, sightless eyes staring as if already dead. As if she could feel none of the heat, she walked straight into the fire, like a goddess, unafraid. Her skirts singed and broke into flames. She hurried, scampered almost into the fire, throwing herself as if into Webley's arms.

Khasturba gave herself to the fire as she had given herself to so many men, with abandonment, as if nothing mattered. Augustine rode away. He tasted a sourness in his mouth. He felt as if he had just witnessed an adultery, nothing more. It sickened him. He wondered for a moment if she had gained her innocence now, whether those flames had purged her. The fire had taken her violently, as he had once wanted to do. Then he realized that Webley had done for her what he himself had been unable to achieve. Webley had died a soldier and she a soldier's wife.

Augustine felt something close to elation. The deaths of Webley and Khasturba had been, in a sense, what he was waiting for. He felt a morbid wave of relief cover him and he could almost have laughed. Had he wanted them to die? Perhaps. There was that loneliness again, the feeling of abandonment, and it was strangely comforting. Augustine half-wondered if he was going mad. He felt a laugh strangling him again, but stopped it in his throat. What a glorious ending! They had died like the king and queen he had imagined them to be. They were his creations, a part of his madness, products of his lunatic vanity. He had primed them, taught them, loved them, and now he had destroyed them. Their pettiness, their human failings seemed to fade. They were nothing to Augustine but symbols, puppets, such clumsy things, which only his imagination could have animated.

~

The futile bombardment continued, starting up the next morning and carrying on for most of the day. To add to the melancholy of the events, heavy clouds seemed to gather more thickly. Rain fell sporadically but not with any force. The next afternoon Augustine dragged himself out of his stupor to have a look at the British camp. He felt trapped now, by the responsibility of his command, the disadvantages of their position, and the fates of his friend and of his lover.

A silence filled the valley as Augustine stood there locked in his own thoughts, unable to reason, to calculate their next move. The firing had stopped, and for a moment he wondered if the Company troops were planning to attack.

Then he heard a familiar sound, though he didn't recognize it at first: a low, humming sound. The sky grew darker. The humming grew louder and he realized it was outside himself. A shadow fell over the mountains. The noise was coming from that direction. Was it the Gurkhas? But their tents stood out clearly on the high ridge above the fort. Kirpan Singh's camp was also visible. Neither army showed any hostility. He was puzzled for a moment, before the truth struck him.

He didn't want it to happen. It was too absurd, too horrible a thing. The wave fanned out into the broad *sot* as it left the mountains, a grey mass of sludge and water. There was a crushing sound, like the undertow of a wave, the grating of stones. He stood there stunned, for the second time in two days, unable to do anything as the relentless wave came crashing down on the Company lines. The flash flood was over the trenches and cannons before the men could escape. Augustine heard shrill, terrified screams. Then, as if the battle had been wiped out of existence, Augustine saw only the broad current sweeping relentlessly by, carrying Webley's and Khasturba's ashes with it, tossing the gun carriages about as if they were toys, drowning the sepoys of the East India Company army in its sudden fury. The flood had no respect for legitimacy. It roared on and on, and the first drops of rain followed it out of the mountains, heavy, like soft fruit dropping from a tree, spattering on the flagstones.

∽

He rode alone, his horse was anxious and jittery. In the forest he found one or two of the sepoys wandering about aimlessly. No one challenged him. They had the glazed look of survivors in their eyes. The catastrophe had marooned them. The flood had destroyed more in one instant than two weeks of fighting had been able to inflict.

Augustine left the trees and entered the grassy plain where they had hunted that day, three months before. So much had passed between. But the flood had wiped all of it away. His memory was blank and he rode into the plain with only a vague sense of returning somewhere he had been before. And yet it was not the place or the memories which he recalled but the emptiness in his chest, the same feeling he had suffered when his mother was killed. A strange wanderlust took hold of him and he felt himself pulled inexorably forward, towards nothing, into the broad distances ahead.

A shout from behind made Augustine turn around. A horseman galloped after him through the high grass. He hoped it wasn't one of his men, for he no longer wanted an army or followers. He wanted to ride alone.

Fitzroy-Morris brought his horse up in front of Augustine. He was flushed and breathing hard.

He looked as if he was going to say something, then collapsed into silence. They turned together and rode on towards the Siwaliks.

A lone kestrel, its feathers silver in the soft light which followed the rainstorm, rose out of nowhere and hung above them, thirty yards to their right. It seemed to be scanning the ground for prey, salamanders or rats. Augustine drew his pistol from his cummerbund, raised it in line with the kestrel, and fired. The tiny hawk spun about in the air, its silver feathers scattering, and then plummeted to earth, dead when it landed.

'Bravo!' said Fitzroy-Morris. 'Bravo!'